Christmas Carols and a Cornish Cream Tea

Cressy grew up in South-East London surrounded by books and with a cat named after Lawrence of Arabia. She studied English at the University of East Anglia and now lives in Norwich with her husband David. *Christmas Carols and a Cornish Cream Tea* is her tenth novel and her books have sold over half a million copies worldwide. When she isn't writing, Cressy spends her spare time reading, returning to London, or exploring the beautiful Norfolk coastline.

If you'd like to find out more about Cressy, visit her on her social media channels. She'd love to hear from you!

Also by Cressida McLaughlin

Christmas Carols and a Cornish Cream Tea

Cressida McLaughlin

HarperCollins*Publishers*

HarperCollins*Publishers*
1 London Bridge Street
London SE1 9GF

www.harpercollins.co.uk

HarperCollins*Publishers*
1st Floor, Watermarque Building, Ringsend Road
Dublin 4, Ireland

Published by HarperCollins*Publishers* 2021

2

ISBN: 978-0-00-850363-5

Typeset in Birka by Palimpsest Book Production Ltd, Falkirk, Stirlingshire

Printed and Bound in the UK using 100% Renewable Electricity at CPI Group (UK) Ltd

MIX
Paper from
responsible sources
FSC www.fsc.org **FSC C007454**

This book is produced from independently certified FSC™ paper
to ensure responsible forest management.

For more information visit:
www.harpercollins.co.uk/green

To Mum and Dad,
who always made our Christmases special

Prologue

Ten Years Ago

Three days ago, Meredith Verren's world had changed completely. Since then she had been flailing, treading water in a too-choppy sea. Now, for the first time since that moment, she felt a sense of calm. Only here, where the sky was uninterrupted and the clouds raced overhead, where nothing stayed the same, even for a second, could she begin to process it.

She scrambled down the steps cut into the rock, tufts of grass and scatterings of sand under her thin soles, the December wind stinging her face. Below her the tide was out, the patch of sand shaped like a crude pocket, a curve nestling into the cliff, the white foam of the sea edge a jagged line topping it. Even now, with the sun hidden behind layers of grey, the water hadn't entirely lost its blue depths. There was something so different about Cornish sea, something almost fantastical. It was never flat or colourless.

Meredith jogged onto the beach, the downwards momentum spurring her on. She shut her eyes and breathed

1

in the sharp, salty tang. Spray peppered her face and the cold thrummed through her body, waking her up. She had been tense for the last three days, her body tight, limbs constricted, as if she was bracing herself for something horrible. But it had already happened, and now she was here, untethered and disbelieving.

She strode purposefully forward, controlling what she could when so much had been taken out of her hands. There was a large, flat rock at the edge of the cove: a cove so small, so secluded, that she and her brother Tommy felt it belonged to them. Of course this wasn't true. There were stairs, after all, and a shabby patch of gravel at the top of the cliff, a shaky road – somewhere between a country lane and a farm track – leading to it. People knew about it, but she hardly ever saw anyone else here. They had named it Charmed Cove, the title feeding into the sense of magic they felt when they were here.

The rock was big enough for two bums to sit comfortably, a pleasing ledge at just the right position for Meredith to rest her feet on, as if nature had created the perfect lookout spot. Here she could see to the horizon, today a clear slash of a line, seagulls wheeling overhead but nobody else in sight.

If she twisted to her left, towards the beach and the stairs, the shelter of the cliff with its grass hat, she could just make out the white house. It was nestled between two slopes, as if it was falling between giant sofa cushions, but it wasn't small. An attractive cottage with large windows, a slate-grey roof and a fence marking off some of the endless green around it as a garden.

From the first time she had been to the cove, Meredith

had envied whoever lived in the house. It was a fair way from the family farm at the edge of Bodmin Moor, but worth every moment of the journey – even on her own, her driving licence only months old and her hands shaky on the wheel of her brother's beaten-up Fiesta. Did the owners think Charmed Cove was theirs? Had they noticed her, all the way down here, and felt a spark of annoyance? She had never seen a track leading from the house to the beach, but she supposed it must be possible to make your way down. The cliff was sloped rather than sheer, the grass at that point giving the impression of softness.

She wondered what kind of Christmas they'd had; whether they were still in a contented stupor the day after Boxing Day, surrounded by presents and open boxes of chocolates, the kitchen still faintly smelling of roast potatoes. Meredith should have had all those things too, but instead, she was here, alone. She didn't want to think about the scene at the Verren house right now. She rubbed her hand against her chest. She felt an emptiness there and wondered if it was possible for her heart to be hollowed out; sucked dry of warmth and the love that beat inside it.

She turned her gaze to the sea, her palms flat on the rock behind her, and inhaled the chilled air. She slid her arms back, raising her face to the sky, and splayed her fingers wide. Her little finger grazed something with sharp edges.

Meredith twisted round to see what it was. A piece of slate had been left on her sitting rock – not unusual on this beach, where rocks and boulders, slates and stones of all sizes, scattered the sand, creating their own landscape. Except this one stood out against the muted December shades, because someone had painted on it.

It was a seascape: sand and water and sky, just three basic elements. And yet, despite the small canvas, the miniature frame they'd had to work within, it made her breath catch. She could see perfectly the kind of day it depicted; far from the cold winter months, a time when the sun sparkled on the waves. She could almost feel the warmth of the currents below, could imagine the softness of the sand beneath her bare feet. It was stunning, clearly painted by someone who could shut their eyes, conjure up a scene and then recreate it with well-placed colour and a few simple strokes.

She looked in the corner of the slate for some kind of signature, but she couldn't see anything. She glanced around her, searching for other signs that she wasn't – or hadn't been – the only one in the cove. There was nothing. She was alone apart from the seagulls.

Except that she wasn't, because someone had left this here, on her rock, for her to find. They may not know she existed; they may have dropped this or left it as an offering to the sea, intended to stay in Charmed Cove forever. But on this cold, grey morning, when she should have been full of Christmas cheer but wondered if she'd ever feel it again, the painting was the one thing that had made her smile.

She put it in her coat pocket as she slipped off the rock and walked closer to the water. She felt only a second's guilt about taking it. Right now, she needed all the comfort she could get.

Chapter One

It was the first of November, and Meredith's neighbour had her Christmas decorations up. Honestly. What about showing some respect and waiting until after Remembrance Day had passed? Or at least until Fireworks Night had gone with a bang? Why did these Hallmark days have to come tumbling on top of each other, with no breathing space in-between?

Meredith's narrow terrace was devoid of festive adornments, and even the thought of getting hold of a tree, somehow hauling it from the shop to her house, and then decorating it, made her feel weary. It was just before seven in the morning, and the neat street in the harbour town of Port Karadow where she and her neighbour Bernie lived was still shrouded in darkness, just a faint line of gold sky showing in the east.

The air was sharp and dry, Meredith's lips tingling the moment she stepped outside. She hovered at her front door for a second, then went back inside and peered into the living room. Smudge, her British blue shorthair, a rescue cat she had chosen after the owner had decided to move to Spain and leave him behind, was curled up on his favourite cushion, and Crumble, her beagle puppy, four months old, with the cutest snub nose and full of energy, gazed at her with big dark eyes from his bed in the corner.

'I won't be long,' she told him. She wished she could take him with her, but he was still young, and she didn't trust him to stay put on the beach while she swam. Crumble whimpered softly, and Meredith tiptoed over to him. She stroked his silky ears and kissed his head, then quietly shut the door and stepped back outside.

She heard Bernie's door open, and resisted the urge to hurry to her car. She turned and put on her brightest smile as she tied her brown curls into a messy bun.

'Bernie, hi,' she said.

Bernie, who Meredith guessed was in her fifties, had her dark hair cropped close to her head and hardly ever met Meredith's eye, grunted noncommittally and stared at her doorstep.

Meredith tried again. 'I see you've got your decorations up already!' She pointed to the overly cheerful red and gold garland looped in the window, the fir tree with spiky green needles squished up against the glass, overladen with brash baubles in the same colours. She shouldn't have been surprised they were already up, an eyesore in the window next to her calm little house. She had moved to Port Karadow in November last year, and Bernie's decorations were one of the first things she'd seen. It hadn't been an auspicious start, though things had got much better since then, even if her relationship with her neighbour had yet to mellow. 'You'll be rivalling the supermarkets at this rate,' she added pointedly.

Bernie glanced up. 'Tesco's had Advent calendars in September. My milk isn't here. Have you seen it?'

Meredith hid her exasperation. What Bernie meant was: *Have you stolen my milk?* And of course she hadn't. It was bad enough that her neighbour already treated her like a pariah, without her giving her any actual, legitimate reasons to be mad with her. 'I haven't, I'm afraid,' she said. 'I haven't even heard the milkman come past.' She thought the electric float sounded like a moaning zombie. Before she'd moved to Port Karadow, she hadn't realized milkmen still used them. 'Maybe he's running late?'

Bernie was giving her doorstep a thorough search, as if two pints of semi-skimmed could somehow be slipped under the doormat. Or maybe she just wanted to avoid meeting Meredith's gaze, as usual.

Meredith sighed. 'I'd better be off, then. Nice to see you.' She walked to her car.

'Off swimming again?' Bernie called. 'Pretty cold, I expect.'

Meredith turned back, surprised. Had she ever spoken to Bernie long enough to tell her what she did most mornings? She thought of all the times she'd prattled on, trying to make small talk, and assumed Bernie wasn't listening. The possibility that she had been was both heart-warming and a little disconcerting. 'I've got my wetsuit,' she said, but by the time she'd finished the sentence, Bernie was back inside, leaving her talking to her red front door.

Meredith glared at her neighbour's window display, then got into her car. As she pulled away from the kerb, she decided Bernie's early decorations wouldn't be so galling if she had the sparkly disposition to match, but since Meredith had moved to Port Karadow, she had behaved as if Meredith's mere presence were an insult. She had gone over their first few encounters. Had she said something to upset her neighbour? It had been such a busy time: she had been settling into her house, unpacking, and getting ready for her new job, and her memories were vague.

She loosened her fingers on the wheel and focused on the journey to Charmed Cove. It was her favourite place in the world, and now she only lived a ten-minute drive away. Her early morning swim had become a necessity, the wetsuit shielding her from the worst of the cold in the autumn and winter months, and she couldn't get enough of it: being surrounded by the sea and sky, feeling exhilarated and calm all at once.

Over the years she had returned to the cove as often as she could. Her visits had been sporadic when she'd been away at university, but her move here, following her job change from running the shop on the Lagowan estate, to Cornish Keepsakes in Port Karadow, meant her beach swims had become daily instead of weekly. She didn't think it was a coincidence that she'd felt more settled in the last year than she had done in a long time.

She parked in the gravel car park at the top of the cliff and, taking her towel and change of clothes, and with a hoody and trainers on over her wetsuit, made her way down the chaotic steps. Just enough of the sun had emerged for her to be able to see, though the sand and sea were still shrouded in a pre-dawn cloak of purple, and the chill in the air made her shiver. She skipped easily down the steps: she had slender limbs and a compact, five foot five frame, her arms and legs stronger since she'd upped her swimming. She put her things in a pile and took off her shoes and jumper, enjoying the press of the cold sand against her soles.

Charmed Cove was the same as ever, its rock formations and tideline more familiar to her than the rooms in her own home. Her gaze skittered to the large, flat rock, on the lookout for telltale, bright colours. Today it was empty, but she had expected that: it was far too soon for another painting to have appeared. They were treasures, few and far between, and she was lucky to have the ones she did.

Meredith walked to the water, her feet burning then numbing as the icy waves lapped over them. She kept going. Hesitating, she had learned, only made it worse. Soon she was swimming her usual path, over to the left side of the cove, before turning and retracing her journey to the right. It was sheltered enough that the swell was never too big, the riptides never alarming or unexpected. For Meredith, the cove really was charmed. It gave her everything she needed, the only surprises the beautiful artworks.

She had five now. Five miniature paintings on pieces of slate: the first on that horrible day ten years ago. There had been one roughly every two years, though the gaps hadn't been evenly spaced, and she hadn't found any pattern to them. They had all been left on her sitting rock, and they were all expertly done, conveying a scene or a mood with a few colours and the briefest of brushstrokes.

She had two seascapes, one rural landscape, the sun through a forest of trees and the one she had found three days ago. It appeared to be Charmed Cove viewed from the sea, looking back at the sand and the cliffs, the wash of cool blue sky putting her in mind of a clear winter's day.

Meredith had wrestled with her conscience, but had still taken every one. They were too good to be left to the mercy of the waves or the rough, salt-thickened winds. Maybe there had been more paintings, and other people had taken them? She didn't like to think of her collection being incomplete; of there being some out there that she hadn't seen or run her fingers over.

She concentrated on her strokes, on the light changing on her face as the sun rose slowly, on the shifting currents; icy cold around her legs, slightly warmer further up, as if the sea had arms and was wrapping them around her. She focused on her rhythm and her breathing. It was the one time when alone didn't feel like lonely, and she had the nugget of reassurance that her best friend Anisha knew where she was.

Meredith would always text when she reached the car park, and Anisha would send back a random emoji – today the broccoli floret – to show she had got the message. Of course, if Meredith got into trouble in the water, there would be no time for anyone to reach the cove and save her. But she was a strong, confident swimmer, and she never felt any fear here.

She finished her usual route and swam towards the beach but, as she was about to put her feet down, she saw that she wasn't alone in the cove. A man was standing on the sand, staring out at the water. Meredith was at the north end, close to her rock, and he wasn't looking at her. She slowed her pace and slunk towards the beach on her stomach. He seemed captivated by the view, and it gave her time to look at him.

10

He was around her age – late twenties or early thirties – and his hair was pure, golden blond. It was cut fairly short, and had curls running through it. The early morning light cast him in relief, his stillness adding to the effect that he wasn't quite real, but instead something carved or conjured. His face was the kind of handsome that put Meredith in mind of well-bred families who owned secluded Cornish mansions: high cheekbones, a proud nose. He was wearing dark trousers, chunky boots, and a fern green quilted jacket with the collar turned up. His brows were slightly lowered, making him seem stern and inscrutable, and a ripple of curiosity washed through her.

She couldn't keep slinking forward unless she wanted to look like a seal, so she pushed herself to her feet, choosing to walk out of the water the way she had walked in: with purpose. The movement must have broken through his daze, because he turned his gaze on her and his face changed, the sharp lines softening.

'I wasn't expecting to find a mermaid on the beach this morning.' His voice was deeper than she had imagined, the words perfectly enunciated.

'And I wasn't expecting a Michelangelo,' she replied, then immediately felt stupid. She had just meant a sculpture, but the most famous Michelangelo was *David*, with all his ludicrously defined abs.

Something gleamed in the man's eyes as she walked closer. He was standing close to her heap of belongings: he must have seen them. Had he been aware of her the whole time? She wished she'd had a better response, but a mermaid, really? The only one she could picture was Ariel, from *The Little Mermaid*, and Meredith's own mid-brown hair, hazel eyes and freckles were a far cry from the Disney character's red tresses and alabaster skin.

'You were very still,' she clarified, bending down to retrieve her towel. A thick strand of her hair had come out of her bun and she could feel it, like a tendril of seaweed, against the side of her face. 'What were you looking at?'

He gestured ahead. 'The water.'

She waited for more, but it didn't come. She wrapped the towel around her and shrugged. Now she was closer, she could see that his eyes were blue. He looked polished and poised, and she decided that he must be a rich tourist or a holiday-homer. But he was also summer on this cold winter's day: his cheeks were faintly tanned; he belonged on golden sand in long shorts with a surfboard, not in a jacket buttoned up against the wind.

'What did you find in the water?' she asked.

'You, among other things.'

She pulled her towel tighter. 'You didn't *find* me, because I wasn't lost. And as you can see, I'm clearly not a mermaid, because I have a perfectly functional pair of legs.'

His grin was sudden and unexpected, and showed off white, even teeth. 'And I'm certain I'm wearing too many clothes to be mistaken for a Michelangelo, though some people have referred to me as a masterpiece in the past.' He paused. 'Or was it a piece of work? I can't really remember.' He shrugged lazily, and Meredith couldn't help laughing.

All of a sudden, the tension was gone, and he wasn't stilted or unnerving. He was funny, trying a bit too hard perhaps, and she liked how his smile widened when she laughed at his stupid joke.

'I'm Finn,' he said, holding out his hand.

After a beat, Meredith clasped it. She felt guilty for the chill of her fingers against his warm ones.

'Meredith,' she replied.

'Meredith the mermaid.'

'Don't you dare!' She took back her hand. He was a few inches taller than her, and he was wearing sturdy boots to her bare feet. 'I need to get dressed and go to work.' Her words trailed off as she wondered how she would change with him there. She didn't usually have to hide from anyone.

'Do you swim here often?'

She narrowed her eyes at his twist on the corny chat-up line.

'Oh come on,' he added. 'It wasn't *that* obvious. I changed one word, at least. Besides, I'm just curious, not hitting on you.'

'I didn't say a thing.' She held her hands up, her lips smiling without her permission. 'And yes, I do *swim* here often. Every morning.'

He raised a blond eyebrow. 'Every morning? Even when it's raining? *Snowing?*'

She nodded. 'And sometimes without a wetsuit.'

The second eyebrow joined the first. 'You swim here *naked?*'

'No, I—' She stopped when his grin widened. She folded her arms. 'I leave swimming naked to the foolhardy. Or plain fools. What about you? I've not seen you here before.'

'No, I don't make it here very often. Or . . . not as often as I would like.'

'But you know the cove.' She couldn't help the defensiveness that had crept into her voice.

He looked faintly amused. 'I do. A little bit.'

'But you don't live round here,' Meredith went on, because in the face of his unenlightening answers she wanted to fill in the gaps. 'Are you on holiday?'

He shrugged. 'Sort of.' His gaze drifted back to the water, and Meredith lost her patience.

'I have to get on.' She picked up her clothes and shoved her wet, sandy feet into her trainers. She would have to get changed in the car, or put her towel on the seat and wait until she got home. 'It was nice to meet you, Finn.'

'You too, Meredith.' He turned towards her, shoving his hands in his trouser pockets. 'Merry? Red?'

'What?' She put her rucksack on her shoulder, the strap sticking as her wetsuit began to dry.

'What do you shorten it to? Are you Merry, or Red?'

'I'm Meredith.'

'Always?'

'Why is that so hard to believe?' God, he was infuriating. Summer sunshine that blazed in through the window, catching you right in the eye so you couldn't bloody ignore it.

'It's a name with a couple of good options, that's all. Don't you think Meredith is a little . . . stuffy?'

Her mouth fell open. Instead of looking contrite, he smiled.

'What's your name short for?' she shot back. He'd reduced her to engaging in playground tit-for-tat. She needed to leave.

'Finnegan,' he admitted. 'As you can see, it's much better shortened.' He wrinkled his nose in distaste.

'Next time I'll be sure to call you Finnegan.' She spun on her heel, which was quite difficult in the sand.

'There's going to be a next time?' he called after her.

'Depends if you come back to the cove,' she shouted, not

bothering to turn around. She reached the steps quickly, then made herself take them as carefully as usual. She fancied she could feel his gaze on her as she climbed, her towel too small and her wetsuit too skintight.

At the top of the cliff, she allowed herself to look back. Finn was sitting on her rock, his legs drawn up in front of him, his elbows resting on his knees. His eyes were trained on the water again, as if she'd never been there.

Her irritation flared. The cove was her sanctuary, where she could swim and think and be alone. How would she get peace if he came back again, watching her or asking penetrating questions? And he'd held her up, so now she was going to be late for work unless she put her foot down. Adrian, her boss at Cornish Keepsakes, had something important to discuss with her this morning. She needed to be there on time, bright-eyed and enthusiastic.

She reassured herself that Finn wasn't there very often; he'd told her that himself. He was on holiday – probably cosied up in some overpriced cottage with his posh girl-friend – and had stumbled on Charmed Cove on the brisk, early morning walk he'd told himself he should take because that was what you did on Cornish holidays.

Satisfied with her story, and the thought that tomorrow things would be back to normal and she'd have the cove to herself again, she drove towards the main road, leaving Finnegan and his sculpted features firmly in her rear-view mirror.

Chapter Two

Cornish Keepsakes was up a steep, pedestrianized road in the heart of Port Karadow, next to a thriving coffee shop called Sea Brew, where Meredith bought too many lattes, and an empty building that had once been an independent bookshop, but had closed down just before she had moved to the town. She made it to work on time, her beagle puppy trotting alongside her in his red harness, sniffing everything they passed.

She settled at her desk in the office behind the shop, where they sold a variety of gifts with a decidedly Cornish theme: candles smelling of sea salt or lavender; sea-glass jewellery; hammered silver trinkets by local artists, and their trademark, the Cornish hampers that could be tailored for a particular occasion or recipient. Most of them were food-and-drink based, with added extras including elegant corkscrews and Cornish-themed coasters.

Meredith picked up the teal Biro that had appeared mysteriously on her desk a few days ago. It had a crude plastic mermaid on the top surrounded by blue-green fluff, and it inevitably took her thoughts back to Finn, and those first words he'd said at the cove. Crumble, already learning which behaviours would result in luxurious strokes and puppy treats, settled into the dog bed behind her chair, tugging at the tartan blanket that lined it.

'Alright, Mer,' Enzo said, slinking out of the kitchen. 'Adrian wants to talk to you.'

'I'll go through in a moment,' she replied, and Enzo nodded distractedly, as if his mind was already elsewhere. He was seventeen, on a gap year before heading to Northumberland University, and had chosen to spend that year working at Cornish Keepsakes. Meredith could name a hundred other jobs that would allow him to save a good chunk of money or have a life-altering experience before he continued on his chosen path, but she'd never pressed the issue: it was his choice, after all. He was a lanky six foot two, had dyed black hair and seemed permanently chilled out, regardless of how tiresome Adrian was being or how complicated the orders got.

Meredith had hoped that, being ten years younger than her, he would add a dynamism that would help her bring the business into the present, but while Enzo had many good qualities, dynamism wasn't one of them. He also called her Mer, which she found faintly annoying. It certainly wasn't a variation of her name that she wanted to pass on to Finn – not that she would ever see him again, she reminded herself.

'Ah, Meredith!' Adrian always had his volume turned up, and today he was even louder than usual. 'Good swim?'

'Lovely thanks,' she called.

He emerged from his office doing the strangest walk Meredith had ever seen, a mix between Frankenstein's monster and a penguin. He always wore a suit paired with a ridiculous tie, and today's was red with oranges on it, some whole and some sliced in half to reveal the segments inside. His dark hair was receding at the temples, even though he was only mid-forties.

He had a slightly old-fashioned air about him, which was probably a contributing factor in Cornish Keepsakes being behind the times. It was the main reason Meredith had wanted the job: it was a project she could sink her teeth into. Cornish-themed gifts would always be popular, but Adrian's company would never grow if the only people who knew about it walked past the tiny shop, or were already aware of it and phoned their orders in. Port Karadow was a popular tourist trap, but it was still a miracle it had survived this long.

In the year that Meredith had been here, she'd written a business plan and was slowly working her way through it, looking at every stage, from product lines and logistics, to the way they reached and sold to customers. Since the summer tourist rush had died down, she had commissioned a new website which included an online shop feature, and set up a distribution site in a business park a couple of miles away, with a small team of staff due to start in the new year. They just had to get through Christmas hamper season – *get through* being the operative words, for Meredith at least – and then, she saw good, expansive things coming Cornish Keepsakes' way.

'Are you OK?' she asked Adrian as he lurched out of his office towards her.

'Small issue, no real problem.'

Meredith winced. 'Whatever it is, it looks painful.'

He stood in front of her desk, his torso angled slightly to the side.

Meredith jumped up. 'Have my seat.'

He waved her away. 'It's actually less painful if I stand.'

'What did you do?' she asked, settling back into her chair.

'Golf course injury.' Adrian gave her a rueful smile.

'He jarred his back trying to get his ball over the pyramid at crazy golf,' Enzo called.

Adrian's cheeks pinked, clashing with his tie.

'Hole sixteen is very challenging,' he said sheepishly, and then asked Enzo, 'How did you know?' The closest crazy golf course was a couple of miles out of town.

Enzo shrugged. 'My mate saw you. Said you were screaming blue murder and Tillie was acting like you'd been shot.'

Adrian's chest deflated. 'It was very painful – it still is. But enough of that. I wanted to talk to you about the hampers, Meredith.'

'Of course.'

They were almost ready. She had ordered new lines of stock to elevate the different offers: hampers for her, for him, for couples, for savoury lovers. One called Fizz and Sparkle, and their most popular – the Cornish Cream Tea hamper.

'I think I've already mentioned that we have certain . . . ah . . . VIPs in Port Karadow?' Adrian smoothed a hand down his tie, and Meredith felt a familiar mix of fondness and annoyance.

Adrian Flockhart, along with his wife Tillie, considered themselves Port Karadow socialites. There were some expensive, secluded mansions on the outskirts of the town, the kind of places where high-flying London executives had holiday homes or celebrities came to retire, and Adrian saw himself as part of that crowd with his Cornish-centric business. He was a kind man and a generous boss, but he viewed everyone in hierarchical terms: how important or useful they were; how popular or wealthy.

He had a list of local VIPs that he dropped into conversation whenever he could: *Tillie and I went for dinner at Cecily Talbot's place last night – wonderful lobster.* Or: *Did you see the Keegans have sponsored next month's Fish Festival? Such generosity when they've had all that bad press.* Meredith didn't know much about these people, except that they were on his Special List. A list that was now, apparently, important in relation to Christmas hampers.

'You have mentioned them,' she said, keeping her expression neutral. Behind her, Crumble growled softly at his blanket.

'Good, good. I don't know if I also mentioned that, this year, I am planning on giving these fair humans a hamper.' He rubbed his hands together, the movement jerky.

'I don't think you did,' Meredith said. 'But I can make up some special hampers if you let me know how many and who they're going to. Email me a list, and I'll get working on it straight away.'

It didn't surprise her that this was one of Adrian's ideas. Apart from treating the online world as if it was an exotic holiday destination he wasn't quite comfortable visiting, he was all about bolstering his reputation within his group of privileged friends. But, regardless of who they were going to, there was something incredibly satisfying about creating

20

a personalized box of treats for someone; finding the ideal gifts to suit their interests and personalities. The only issue this time was that they would have to have a Christmas theme, and Meredith had already had enough of Christmas. She pictured Bernie's festive window and her spirits sank, like a lift juddering to the floor below.

'Good-oh,' Adrian said. 'And of course we'll want the personal touch,' he added, as if he'd been reading her mind. 'Something that I, very unfortunately, will be unable to contribute this time round.'

'What do you mean?' she asked.

'I'd like you to deliver them,' he explained. 'Along with promoting this year's hampers as much as possible before the website is . . . switched on, I thought you could deliver these particular hampers yourself.'

Meredith's mouth dried out. 'Me? Why me?'

'Because my back injury means I'm unable to drive, and while Tillie is being incredibly accommodating, I can't ask her to do this as well as everything else. Not to mention, Meredith, that you are our shining light.' She thought she heard Enzo snort softly through the open door between the office and the shop. 'After a year of so many changes, all the wonderful things you've already achieved, it would be the cherry on top – the holly on the Christmas pud – if you delivered them. Wouldn't you like that?' He frowned, as if he couldn't imagine anyone wanting to turn down such an opportunity.

Meredith hesitated. She didn't want to reveal her lack of Christmas joy to Adrian when she worked in a business that couldn't be more tailor-made for the season if it covered itself in tinsel. She was a huge fan of well-thought-out,

21

curated gifts, and Cornish Keepsakes was, at its heart, a warm, friendly business that offered those.

Her problem with Christmas was that there was so much of it. So many gifts and trinkets, sparkles and embellishments, that the meaning, the thoughtfulness, got lost amongst the sheer excess of it all. It was a celebration that Meredith thought had lost its soul, and over the years her dislike had turned into a genuine aversion.

Still, it was just a couple of months, and the beacon of the new online shop loomed large, a triumph that definitely had meaning, and one she could celebrate in the new year. Two more months, and Christmas would be behind her.

Some of her thoughts must have shown on her face, because Adrian hurried to reassure her. 'There are only a few VIPs, but they are incredibly influential in this town, and if we deliver the hampers in November, it should bolster our sales with local customers. Cecily Talbot has a very large following, I'm told, on the Instagram. And I thought I might organize a photo shoot with the paper, once you have the schedule in place.'

Meredith wasn't sure the local paper's reach was that wide any more. Certainly not as wide as 'the Instagram', anyway. She made a mental note to look up Cecily Talbot. Did she really need to deliver the hampers herself? To exude all the Christmassy cheer she did not actually feel? She closed her eyes, imagining herself on the doorstep of a honey-coloured mansion, a luxury hamper at her feet as she asked Mrs Keegan whether she was having goose or partridge for Christmas lunch. It was a straightforward ask, really. She'd worked many a Christmas at the farm shop in her previous role and hadn't had any complaints, though the effort of staying upbeat had worn her down.

She had thought this job, with all the changes she had made over the last months, would be a move to behind the scenes. She could hide her true feelings about Christmas behind social media posts and an email newsletter campaign, teasers for the new website. The digital age meant you didn't have to put yourself out there personally if you weren't the brand. Except, it was clear the opposite was still true for Adrian, and while Meredith was still finalizing the Cornish Keepsakes digital revolution, she didn't really have a counter-argument.

'That all sounds wonderful, Adrian,' she heard herself say. 'If you could email me a list of the VIPs and their addresses, and anything you think I need to know that will help me tailor their hampers, I'll start bringing it together.'

Adrian's smile split his face, and he tapped a rhythm on the edge of her desk. 'Of course! I will send those details through forthwith. This is an excellent project, and I'm glad you can see its merit.'

He turned and lurched away, then twisted back round as if he meant to say something else, but his face contorted into a look of pure agony.

'Are you—?' Meredith rose from her chair.

'Fine, fine.' He waved her concern away. 'I keep forgetting I have this.' He tapped his lower back gingerly, then continued his slow totter back to his office.

Enzo poked his head through the shop doorway. 'Adrian's got you as his personal Santa now, has he?'

Meredith rested her elbows on her desk. 'Should he even be here? He looks in so much pain. And if he can't sit down for long periods . . .' She shook her head.

23

'You know Adrian. He can't let go of things, not even when he's slipped a disc, or whatever it is.'

Meredith winced sympathetically, then thought of her new task. 'I have to deliver the hampers though.' She screwed her face up. 'Fancy being a reindeer, Enzo?'

He gave her a laconic shrug and returned to the shop to wait for the smattering of tourists who were brave enough to come to Cornwall at this time of year. Already this day had been far too Christmassy for Meredith's liking, and it was still only the first of November.

The following afternoon the sky was overcast, different greys layering themselves one over the other like filo pastry, the lowest black and threatening. Meredith got home with Crumble and fed him and Smudge who, from the looks of things, had spent most of his day curled up on the sofa.

Once she had changed into jeans and a warm green sweater, and made herself a quick dinner of pasta, cherry tomatoes and pesto, night had fallen over Port Karadow, and the wind was rattling the windows in their frames. It was the kind of night to snuggle up under a blanket, pull out a favourite crime thriller or scroll to a juicy box set, but she couldn't tonight, because on Tuesdays Meredith went to choir.

The Port Karadow choir was the only part of Christmas she didn't shy away from, because she loved singing even more than she hated the festive season.

She had been welcomed into the choir with open arms, and had been an enthusiastic member of their spring and summer programmes, the concerts taking place in Port Karadow's town hall. Now they were rehearsing for their

Christmas concert, and she was content to stand on the back row, sing 'O Holy Night' and 'We Wish You a Merry Christmas', and hope that the passion of the other members would hide her lack of it.

She put on her sky-blue winter coat, as warm as a duvet and almost as thick, with a fake-fur trim round the hood, and her white bobble hat covered with sequins, picked up her handbag and, giving Smudge and Crumble a kiss each, left the house. As she closed her front door behind her, she heard her neighbour's open.

'Meredith,' Bernie said, her voice sterner than usual. 'There's dog poo on the path outside my gate.' She pointed to the pavement just beyond their stamp-sized front gardens.

'I'm sorry to hear that,' Meredith replied. Had Bernie been waiting for her to come outside?

'What are you going to do about it?'

Beyond her neighbour's head, Meredith could see her decorations glinting in the window. 'It's not Crumble's,' she said. 'I would never leave his mess lying around.' To demonstrate how committed she was, she pulled a poo bag out of her pocket. By now she probably had at least one in every coat, bag and cardigan she owned. It was the one thing you didn't want to be caught without.

'Even so,' Bernie said.

Meredith waited for more, but her neighbour just glared at her. 'You're not holding me accountable for all dog-walkers, are you?' Her voice was weaker than she would have liked.

'Why not?'

'Because I'm not—' she started, then realized it was a

lost cause. 'I'm sorry about the dog poo. It wasn't me, I promise, but I'll clear it up for you, if you like?'

She waited for the gratitude. Bernie simply nodded and went back inside.

Meredith groaned and went to find the cause of the fuss. She hated dog-walkers who didn't clear up after their pets: this wasn't her fault. But, she reasoned, as she crouched, put the bag over her hand like a glove and picked up the offending clump, if she didn't do it, Bernie would only wait until she got back from choir to accost her.

By the time she had gone back home to wash her hands, said goodbye to Smudge and Crumble again, and left the house for a second time, she was running late and the wind was getting up. It was a brisk fifteen-minute walk to the town hall, and although it would have been quicker to drive, there was never anywhere to park and she would have lost all the time she'd gained looking for a space. She pulled her hat down lower and set off.

She had to walk through the centre of town to get to the hall, and she heard the familiar, muted hubbub of early evening drinkers inside the Sea Shanty as she approached. She glanced at her watch; she had three minutes before practice started. She looked up and—

'Whoa, steady there!' Firm hands grabbed her upper arms and she found her eyes level with someone's throat, a blue woollen scarf wrapped around it, her senses assaulted with a delicious, masculine cologne. She smelled black tea and honey, notes of vanilla. Working in the gift business had given her a good knowledge of luxury smells, and this one was particularly enticing. 'Meredith?'

She raised her gaze and found the blue eyes and striking

features of the man she had met on the beach the day before. 'Finn,' she said, the shock of her abrupt halt jolting through her.

'If you're in that much of a hurry for a drink, I can carve a path to the bar for you.' He smiled at her.

'I'm not going to the pub.'

'OK.' He released his hands and put them in his pockets.

'Thank you, though,' she said. She was slightly breathless, and knew that her fast pace and the wind chill would have turned her cheeks rosy.

'What for?' Finn asked.

'Offering to get me to the front of the queue. If I had wanted a drink, I mean.' She winced. She was hurrying to get to choir, and wasn't in the frame of mind for spontaneous repartee. Finn's amused expression suggested he'd realized that.

'You're very welcome,' he said. 'Sure I can't tempt you? They've put on a fresh pot of mulled cider.'

Meredith scowled. Even the pub was taking its Christmas cues from the supermarkets. 'I need to go. I'm going to be late.'

'Late for what?' Finn asked as he stepped back, his boots against the pavement echoing in the night air.

She thought of telling him she was going to choir, then realized he would have more questions if she did. He seemed to have a lot of questions for her, and right now she didn't have time. 'Thank you,' she repeated pointlessly, and hurried past him.

'You can't White Rabbit me forever!' he called after her.

She laughed and waved her arm in the air in goodbye.

'Merry, or Red?' he shouted again, and she knew some

27

of the locals would be paying attention, muttering about rowdy incomers spoiling their night in the pub. Meredith picked up her pace, and then, as she reached the arched doorway of the pretty town hall, its outdoor lights glowing in welcome, she touched a hand to the white bobble on her hat. She didn't know why – she wasn't particularly a fan of *Alice in Wonderland* – but she quite liked being called a White Rabbit. It had sounded playful and inventive, coming from Finn's lips. And with that disconcerting thought, she pushed open the door and went to meet her friends.

Chapter Three

The hall was warm and slightly dusty, with strip lighting and posters from projects at the local primary school on the walls. It was a friendly space, and as Meredith took off her coat and hat she waved at the choir members who were already there, including Patrick, their baritone and a proud butcher in town, and Emma, their organizer and conductor. In her late fifties, she'd retired early from her job as an art teacher, and sometimes treated them with the firm hand she must once have needed to corral rowdy fifteen-year-olds. Meredith thought of her as a surrogate granny – both of hers had died when she was much younger – but she would never tell Emma, because Emma was nowhere near old enough to be Meredith's grandma.

'Hello, pet,' Emma called over now. 'Rough night out there!'

'It's a bit windy,' Meredith agreed, her smile widening when her best friend, Anisha – who was the reason she was a member of the choir in the first place – hurried over to her.

'Meredith!' She pulled her into a hug, her slender arms deceptively strong. 'I thought for a second you weren't coming!' She stepped away, and Meredith noticed her dark eyes were bright with something; some news she was desperate to share. Sure enough, she said, 'I need to talk to you in the break.'

'Chop chop!' Emma clapped her hands and herded them towards the rest of the pack. 'We have a lot to learn, and not much time to learn it. I want our Christmas concert this year to be unparalleled in Cornwall. We have a medley to perfect, and I am determined to have "Carol of the Bells" as the centrepiece: St Austell can't steal it from us.'

'Not sure you can steal a song performance,' Dennis said from the back row.

'Are we doing "The Most Wonderful Time of the Year"?' Meredith asked quickly, in an attempt to head off the inevitable bickering.

Anisha gave her a curious look. 'Most wonderful? Is that what you think about Christmas now?'

Meredith rolled her eyes and tried to communicate what she was doing without speaking, but Emma was frowning at them, and it was time to get down to business. Despite the sometimes stern countenance of their leader, and the current less than ideal musical selection, Meredith felt a tingle of excitement. She felt happiest when she was singing; she could forget everything except the words and the music, the effort and technique needed to create a beautiful sound. She grinned at Anisha, and her friend returned it before facing the front, her long black hair, tied in a high ponytail, flicking over her shoulder.

They had met five years ago, when Meredith was working on the Lagowan estate; Anisha had just married her university boyfriend, Nick, and they'd settled in Port Karadow. She'd come in asking for help with candles and cushions, which was just the sort of thing the upmarket shop at Lagowan excelled at. They'd struck up a rapport – Anisha had a self-deprecating sense of humour, aware that her organizing sometimes looked obsessive – and stayed in touch after her second visit to restock her reed diffusers.

Now Nick and Anisha had Jasmine, who had recently turned five, and Ravi, who was a pudgy, good-natured three-year-old, and a beautifully furnished house in town. Meredith loved her friend, adored her kids and husband, and another bonus of taking the job at Cornish Keepsakes was that her drive to their place was now five minutes instead of forty.

Emma flung them straight into the Christmas medley, which seemed an impossible mix of 'Merry Christmas Everyone', 'We Wish You a Merry Christmas' and 'Fairytale of New York'. They all struggled through it, while Emma huffed and corrected and, eventually, threw her hands up in delight when they got to the end without sounding like they were working on an experimental jazz piece.

'Exactly this,' Emma said, nodding. 'Well, not exactly, because it's very rough around the edges. But the form's there, we just need to work on the harmony, and the tempo, and getting those crossovers really snappy.' She clicked her fingers rhythmically. 'Right, take five minutes, my little

Roxie Harts and Billy Flynns, then we'll move on to the slower numbers.'

They gratefully disbanded, and Anisha led Meredith to the corner of the hall, where they could talk uninterrupted.

'You're not really flinging yourself into full-on Christmas mode, are you?' Anisha asked, unscrewing her bottle of water. 'I know you love the singing, but the rest hasn't changed, has it? You're not going to dress up as Mrs Christmas and petition to bring the pantomime back?'

Meredith shook her head. 'Nope. I was trying to head off a sparring match between Emma and Dennis. Nothing else has changed.' Except for her new work project – being the Christmas fairy for Adrian's VIPs. She didn't want to think about that now.

'I didn't think so,' Anisha said carefully, then gave her a warm smile. 'You know I'd love you to come to ours this year. It will be full-on Christmas – as big as Diwali – but it's mostly about the kids, so you shouldn't feel too over-whelmed. I just don't want you to be on your own.'

'Are you ready for Thursday?' Meredith asked, eager to change the subject. Diwali started at the end of the week, and Anisha would be going all in, because she always did. Meredith hadn't known her friend to ever do things – cele-brating, especially – in half measures.

'The house is polished from attic to under-stairs cupboard,' Anisha said, 'and I've got tomorrow off to sort out the lanterns and make *mithai*. Jasmine wants all our lanterns to be pink, so I'm trying to teach her about compromise. But that's not what we were talking about. If you don't want to come to ours, are you going to see Tommy?'

'He'll probably drive over from Somerset in the next couple of weeks.'

'But not on Christmas Day?' Anisha pushed. 'He and Sarah are so close. It's not like they're as far away as Leeds, is it?'

Meredith winced. 'Your mum and dad aren't coming down?'

Anisha had just come back from a few days visiting them. 'I would be made up if they did,' she said, 'but it's not going to happen. We've got the room, but Mum's arthritis is getting worse. Mornings and evenings, she was so stiff that even standing up was an issue. The journey, sitting in a car for so long, would be a huge effort for just a few days here. And taking Jasmine and Ravi up there – all that way and with all their stuff . . .' She shook her head. 'There's no easy option.'

'I'm sorry,' Meredith said quietly. 'I know how much you want to have everyone here.' She felt bad that Anisha wanted the big family celebration, that her parents were keen to see their grandchildren even if Christmas itself wasn't important to them, but circumstances made it too hard. Whereas, with her . . . 'I'm sure Tommy and Sarah will want to snuggle up together, just the two of them,' she tried, squeezing her water bottle until the plastic cracked.

Anisha sighed. 'I'm going to say something now, OK?'

'Is it the same thing you say every year?' She gave her friend a quick smile.

Anisha ignored her. 'I know Christmas is your least favourite thing, and that you'd rather swim from here to Jersey without your wetsuit on than drape yourself in tinsel and act like you're enjoying it, but Tommy would love to celebrate with you, even if it was something small – a lunch, maybe. And Nick and I would, too. I hate the thought of you being home alone, without even a tree. Can't you just get a tiny tree?' She held a hand up when Meredith opened her mouth to protest. 'Smudge would probably pull the decorations off it, but that's the point. And you have a puppy now: that's a big responsibility. You can't expect your puppy to miss out on Christmas, can you?'

Meredith bristled, then saw her friend's mischievous smile. 'I'm singing this ridiculous Christmas medley in the concert, aren't I?' She'd lowered her voice because Emma had hearing like a large-eared bat.

'You love singing,' Anisha whispered back. 'And the bits between the singing, like when you're walking to your position or flicking through the music to get to the right place, your glare could melt snow. Christmas is about coming together; putting your differences aside.'

'So I'm meant to embrace things I hate, just so other people can feel less awkward about me not being a ray of sunshine?'

'You're so stubborn, you know that? And deliberately obtuse, I might add. I only think . . .' Anisha chewed her lip. 'I think if you opened yourself up to it, if you didn't automatically hunch your shoulders against everything festive, if you let in a few of the fun, *happy* things, you might find that it isn't as bad as you think, that they don't all have negative associations.' She nudged her shoulder.

'Maybe,' Meredith muttered, but her friend's familiar words hadn't sparked any kind of epiphany. Everyone's likes and dislikes were different, and she didn't consciously parade her Scrooge-like nature in front of other people. She ignored the burning behind her eyes, the sensation of

34

feeling hot and cold at the same time. Now was not the time to do a deep dive into her emotions. This was a rehearsal, not a sharing session. 'We should get back to it,' she said, as the others assembled on the small stage. She stood and pulled Anisha to her feet. 'I'll think about what you've said.'

'Good.' Anisha's voice was bright, determined. 'And if you want to come round and help me paint pink and blue stars on lanterns tomorrow evening, you're very welcome.'

It was as they were putting on their coats, the melody of 'Silent Night' on a loop inside Meredith's head, when she remembered Anisha's first words to her that evening. 'I'm sure there's something else you meant to tell me,' she said. 'You're excited about something and I want to know what it is.'

It only took a second for her to spill the beans. 'Andy's put me in charge of the Port Karadow light display this year.' She bounced on her toes.

'Seriously?' Meredith squeaked. 'Anisha, that's wonderful!' Her friend worked for Cornwall Council, in the planning department at the Bodmin office, and had been angling for more creative projects ever since she'd been there.

'Josie, who left at the end of last week, was supposed to have started work on it months ago, but when she did her handover . . .' Anisha shrugged. 'Seems she gave up on her job a while back, and she's seriously dropped the ball. Andy's given it to me, because he knows I can get it done.'

'Because you are organizer extraordinaire,' Meredith said. 'Have you got ideas? What do you think you'll do?'

'I have so many ideas,' Anisha gushed. 'He only told me it

was mine yesterday, but I need to get a move on. Light switch-on is usually the last week of November, but that leaves sod-all time. We'll see.' She shrugged, but she was grinning.

'I'm so glad you've got something to get your teeth into,' Meredith said as they walked to the door.

'If this goes well, then who knows what I'll get to work on next? Hopefully, in a few years' time, this place is going to be mine: verges left uncut to encourage wildflowers; potholes dealt with in twenty-four hours; more signs in Cornish and English, to keep locals and visitors happy; some serious upgrades to the harbourside. You can create a lot of harmony with some strategic, innovative planning, and Port Karadow could do with a boost.'

'It could,' Meredith agreed, thinking of the empty shop-fronts on Main Street, the way owners of the existing businesses sometimes stood in their doorways, as if their presence could entice customers inside. 'All boosts are very welcome, even the twinkly ones.' She hugged her friend on the steps.

'I can give you a rundown tomorrow night.' They said their goodbyes, and Anisha went to get the fish and chips she took home for Nick on Tuesdays.

Meredith turned in the direction of home, walking against wind that blew directly into her face, pulling her hat down lower, and her fur collar up.

Anisha was in charge of the town's seasonal lights display. She wanted her best friend to succeed, but did it have to be with a festive project?

It was the second of November, but Christmas was already closing in on her from every direction, reminding her that there was no escape. Should she be more open

36

to it? The thought flickered, bright with possibility for a second, but then she imagined spending Christmas Day with her brother and his girlfriend: eating too much food, opening pointless gifts that would soon be discarded, faking cheerfulness until she could leave. She shuddered at the thought. Nope. At the moment, a strange rendition of 'Merry Christmas Everyone', 'We Wish You a Merry Christmas' and 'Fairytale of New York' was as far as she could go.

Meredith pulled her car into the loading bay at the top of Main Street, the creatively named road on which Cornish Keepsakes was situated. It was pedestrianized, so this was the closest she could get. In her boot she had a box of squat, bulbous Kilner jars that she'd painted with gold and silver stars and was planning to fill with chocolate coins for the VIP hampers.

She had got the idea when she was helping Anisha, Jasmine and Ravi paint their Diwali lanterns. Adrian wanted the personal touch, and what could be better than a couple of homemade gifts alongside the usual Cornish Keepsakes offerings? She had never had the money to buy school friends anything growing up, and the presents she'd shared with her family had leaned towards the crafted and thoughtful rather than the extravagant.

She slid her fingers under the heavy box of jars, bent her legs and tried to ease it out. It got caught on something and, as she tried to detangle the cardboard corner from whatever it was, she could feel the weight shifting, threatening to send the box and its contents onto the road, probably with her underneath it.

'Shit, shitty shit shit,' she muttered, as she tried to push the box back into the boot. 'Fucking stupid shitty jars.'

'Hello, stranger,' said a voice behind her, and before she could reply she got a waft of familiar aftershave, and arms reached over hers to take the box. She looked sideways and found her face inches from Finn's. He stood up and stepped back, holding the box against his chest as if it weighed nothing.

'Thank you,' she said, dusting down her trousers. Was he *following* her? 'That was very kind.'

'Did they offend you that badly?'

She went to take the box from him, but he moved it out of her grasp.

'What? Who did – what?'

'The fucking stupid shitty jars,' he clarified. 'They've wounded you deeply, I can see that. Do you need me to take them outside and show them what I'm made of?'

Meredith bit her lip. 'You think you can take them?'

'Absolutely. As long as it's one at a time.' He glanced down. 'A full assault and I might be in trouble. They've got quite a girth.'

Meredith snorted, and Finn's smile widened. 'You're all right,' she said. 'Though I would have loved a ringside seat to that particular spectacle, they haven't properly offended me. They were just being awkward.'

'Want me to take them anywhere for you?'

Meredith glanced down the hill. The Cornish Keepsakes office wasn't that far away, but she didn't want to leave Crumble in the car, even while she dropped them off. As if reading her thoughts, he barked from the back seat, and Finn's gaze shot to the window.

'Who's this?' he asked, his tone gently curious.

'That's Crumble. And if you could carry the box while I get him? Thank you.'

'No problem.' Finn stepped back while she extricated her dog and locked the car.

'Just down here.' She kept pace with Finn while they walked, a sudden awkwardness drying up her words. Why was he here? Three separate locations, and he'd been exactly where she was.

'What are the jars for?' he asked, breaking the silence.

'Christmas hampers. I painted them last night.'

He looked into the box. 'You're giving all your friends and family hampers for Christmas? That's very generous.'

'No,' she sighed. 'My boss is giving hampers to his closest and most influential friends.'

Finn laughed and glanced at the Cornish Keepsakes shopfront as they came to a stop. It had a swirly, slightly faded nameplate above the window. The background was burgundy, the lettering cream picked out with sky-blue highlights. It was another thing Meredith thought was outdated: giving the shop a refresh was in her business plan.

'From this place?' Finn asked, as if he couldn't quite believe it.

'Home sweet home,' Meredith said, reaching for the box. 'Thank you again. I think Crumble and I can manage from here.'

Finn shook his head. 'I'll bring it in for you.'

'It's pretty Christmassy in there already,' she warned.

'What's wrong with that?'

Meredith wrinkled her nose. She didn't want to get into the whole Christmas thing with him: he would have at

39

least a hundred questions about her bah-humbug attitude. Always with the questions, this blond man who kept talking to her.

'You don't like Christmas?' he asked, as if to prove her point. 'And yet.' He paused for a long moment. 'You work for a gift business.'

'It's complicated, OK?' She reached for the box again, expecting him to pull back, but this time he didn't, and her hands landed on his.

He met her gaze, the amusement in his eyes extinguished. 'I have time for complicated,' he said softly.

'I don't.' She gave him a bright smile. 'My boss has hurt his back, so I haven't just got to put together these hampers, I've got to deliver them to the great and good of Port Karadow as well, and I have to be supremely festive while I'm doing it. If I . . .' she shook her head. 'I need to make a start.'

'Who are you delivering them to?' Finn asked.

Meredith still had her hands over his. His skin was warm, and she could see golden stubble glinting along his jawline. It did something funny to her insides; his woollen scarf, his gentle, deep voice and then that hint of roughness. She let go of the box – and his hands.

'Does your nosiness know no bounds?' she asked with a forced laugh.

'Curiosity,' Finn corrected, and this time when she tried to take the box, he let her, ensuring she held it firmly before he released his grip. 'We keep bumping into each other, and I can't help being interested. You painted the stars with acrylic?'

'Is that particular medium frowned upon?' She huffed, then softened. 'Port Karadow is a small place. It's not that

40

surprising we've seen each other more than once. I bet if you thought about it, you'd realize there were other people you'd spotted several times. I really appreciate your help with this, but I need to go now.' She turned away from him.

'Are you going all White Rabbit on me again?' He had crouched down and was running his hands over Crumble's silky ears. His fingers were long and slender, the nails short and neat. Her dog pawed at him, clearly in canine ecstasy.

'I'm not late this time,' she said. 'Just busy.'

'Ah.' Finn looked up, his blue eyes meeting hers with such intensity that Meredith almost dropped her box. But she held on, and so did Finn's gaze. 'Understood,' he said softly. He stood up, and Crumble whimpered.

'Nice seeing you, Finn,' she said.

'You too, Meredith. Stay Christmassy.'

'You can mock,' she said, stepping closer to him so that nobody would overhear, her arms beginning to ache, 'but you're not the one having to traipse around town like Santa Claus when it's not even December!'

Finn responded to her quiet outrage with a grin. 'No, I suppose not. Stay Scroogy, then.' Before she had a chance to respond, he turned and walked away, his hands back in his pockets.

Honestly, Meredith thought, as she went inside with her dog and her starry jars, it wasn't just Christmas that didn't want to leave her alone; she had her very own, inquisitive shadow. She wondered if she should set up a Wikipedia page for herself, and then, the next time she bumped into him, give him the link to save them both some time.

'Ah. Meredith,' Adrian said, standing in the doorway of his office, his hand pressed against the small of his back, today's tie designed to make it look like a colourful, bug-eyed fish was swimming towards his belt buckle. 'How are you getting on with those Christmas hampers?'

Meredith took a deep breath. It seemed that – even though Finn had gone – she hadn't escaped the barrage of questions quite yet.

Chapter Four

The sun was shining when Meredith made her way to Charmed Cove on Saturday morning. The November wind was unrelenting, kicking up foamy edges on the waves as she walked down the steps, her wetsuit already on. She needed this respite; being able to swim for longer than her weekday mornings allowed her.

Everything about this week, from Adrian giving her the hamper delivery job, to Anisha's sadness at not seeing her parents over Christmas, to her meetings with Finn, had left her feeling unsettled. She had resolved to do her job, keep her head down, then emerge from the excess of Christmas into a calm, clear new year. Right now, it didn't seem like it was going to be that straightforward.

The sand cushioned her feet, and when she slipped her trainers off, the water welcomed her, too. It was ice-cold, stealing her breath for several long moments before she was able to settle into her strokes. And yet, even now, when the day stretched ahead of her, blissfully empty until she was due to see Anisha and Nick this evening, invited to be part of their Diwali celebrations, she couldn't fully relax. She kept glancing towards the beach, her thoughts trickling in: *he might be here; if he is, he'll have more questions; how bright would his hair and eyes look in sunshine?*

By the time she'd got out of the water and wrapped herself in her towel, she realized she was disappointed that she had the cove to herself. Seagulls soared overhead, and she could see the shadowy bulk of a tanker breaking up the horizon line. The white house was nestled in its clifftop nook, its sea-facing windows blank squares with no indication of who was inside.

She shouldn't want to see Finn again. He'd been helpful, but equally infuriating. She knew nothing about him, except that, if he was here on holiday, then he'd been in Cornwall almost a week. He might be travelling home today. Not that she cared. Wrapping her towel tightly around her, she made her way up the steps, back to her car.

On Saturday night, Anisha was full to bursting with ideas for the Port Karadow Christmas lights, and Meredith had resolved to be the perfect sounding board. She knew how much the project meant to her friend, and having Anisha in charge could only benefit the small town. Nick and Anisha's house was decorated for Diwali, the lanterns Meredith had helped paint were crowded on surfaces and windowsills, turning the cosy space into a glowing, flickering haven; welcoming and full of warmth. Music played softly in the background, and the smells of homemade food competed with the lights to get Meredith's attention.

'We need some kind of floating platform in the harbour,' Anisha said, handing glasses of lemonade to Meredith and

Nick. 'And I want a treasure trail too, with the lights telling a story, leading everyone on a path through town. If I put the effort in, we could rival Mousehole this year.'

'You do realise it's the sixth of November,' Nick said gently. He was smiling, used to his wife's enthusiasm once she got her teeth into something.

'Yep,' Meredith added with a grin. 'Far too early to be thinking about this stuff.'

Anisha looked at her, aghast. 'I'm three months *behind*! But that doesn't mean it can't be done, I just need to focus. I'm thinking elves, Santas, stars, gifts, candy canes. I've drawn up a list of suppliers we've used in the past, as well as looking further afield.' She turned her iPad towards them.

Sitting at the large island in the kitchen, Nick and Meredith submitted to what amounted to Anisha's pitch for the Christmas lights project, even though it was already hers, and she hadn't had to do a pitch in the first place.

'It sounds wonderful,' Meredith said, which was true, if you liked that sort of thing.

'Very thorough,' Nick added. 'And I have no doubt you can pull it off, because you are the most impressive person I know.' He held his arms open, and Anisha walked into them to collect a hug. Nick had a kind face, mid-brown hair that stuck straight up from his high forehead whether he wanted it to or not, and lots of smile lines. Meredith had liked him immediately, and that had only grown the more she got to know him.

Anisha looked down at him. 'What do you want?'

'Nothing,' he said. 'Except for you to stop talking about work and come and sit down. Project Port Karadow can resume on Monday morning. Right now, we have guests.'

Anisha sat on a stool and pushed a plate of homemade onion bhaji and *aloo bonda* towards them. 'It's just Meredith. She doesn't really count.'

Meredith laughed.

Nick took a bhaji and shook his head. 'When I said impressive, what I meant was . . .'

'We all know what you meant.' Anisha smiled at him. 'Meredith, tell me about this swimming challenge you're thinking of doing.'

Meredith shifted on her stool. She didn't know why she'd mentioned this to Anisha; it wasn't even a fully formed plan, just a vague idea she'd been mulling over. 'I want to swim to the next beach along from Ch . . . the cove I swim at.'

'It's around rocks, isn't it?' A line had appeared between Anisha's brows.

'I'm a strong swimmer, and I've looked into it. It should only take about twenty minutes with the right conditions.'

'With a boat to accompany you,' Nick said, 'like they do on Channel crossings?'

Meredith laughed. 'It's not quite that epic a swim. It would be a waste to get a boat-support crew for twenty minutes.'

'But how would we know you were safe?'

'You could wait for me on the beach.'

'So it would be a case of being glad when you showed up, and worried if you didn't? It doesn't seem entirely problem-free.' Nick folded his arms.

'You know,' Meredith said gently, 'I could just do it. One morning, on my own, if I wanted to. Nobody would know.'

Anisha huffed. 'That is *exactly* the problem. Nobody would have a clue what you were doing, and if something went wrong, that would be it. Can't you get someone to go with you? Some swimming . . . champion, or something?'

'Do you mean a man?' Meredith couldn't help being put out: she knew her own capabilities.

Anisha shrugged. 'Feminism aside, men *are* the stronger of the species, if you pick the right one.'

'Which wouldn't be me,' Nick added. 'But Nish has a point. There's no pride lost in making sure you're safe.'

'I'm not a member of any wild swimming clubs,' Meredith said. The whole point was that she liked being on her own, with no expectations on her to fit in with anyone else.

'So investigate one,' Anisha replied, taking a sip of her drink. 'Not because you can't do it on your own, but because the water is unpredictable and this seems risky. Humour me.'

Meredith rolled her eyes, even though she was grateful for her friends' concern. Aside from Anisha and Nick, she didn't have anyone she could call on at a moment's notice. There was Adrian and Enzo at work, but she didn't know them well enough to socialize with them, and was never sure about crossing friendship lines with a boss. Emma, Dennis, Patrick and the others at the choir were always up for a drink to celebrate a successful concert, but then went their separate ways.

She got on with Tommy, but with him and Sarah in Somerset, their relationship mostly consisted of WhatsApp messages and phone calls. She had yet to tell him about her idea of swimming along the stretch of cliff that separated Charmed Cove from the next beach to the north, but thought he would have the same reaction as Anisha and Nick. Maybe it *was* something she shouldn't be doing solo?

She might have a strong desire to hibernate until Christmas was over, but she didn't want to do it in a cave along Cornwall's coastline because she'd got herself trapped and nobody knew where she was.

After Saturday with her friends, and a Sunday where she had taken Crumble for a long training walk that was in equal parts frustrating and adorable, Meredith's batteries were fully recharged by Monday. Even the thought of assembling VIP Christmas hampers didn't make her leaden with dread. She'd sourced sweets and chocolates to go in her star jars, and was mid-email discussion with a local pottery company about the possibility of ordering Christmas-themed mugs.

Cornish Keepsakes already sold a Christmas tea flavoured with cinnamon and nutmeg. It was a staple of their Cornish Cream Tea Christmas hamper, and Meredith wanted to up the wow factor by offering an option with mugs and, for the high-end hamper, a matching teapot. Tea – especially when it had *Cornish* and *Cream* tacked on the front – was something she could get behind.

'Morning, Enzo, morning, Adrian!' she said as she settled Crumble, who seemed suspiciously less well behaved since their training walk, in his bed.

'Morning, Mer,' Enzo called from the kitchen. She heard him swear as the Nespresso machine made a noise like it was being strangled, and decided she would go to Sea Brew for a latte later.

'Good morning, Meredith,' Adrian called from his office. He sounded his usual jaunty self, even though his back must still be giving him trouble.

'Morning, Meredith,' came a third greeting, and she looked up to find Tillie ambling out of her husband's office. Tillie was a few years younger than Adrian, and wore clothes in pastel colours – pink jeans and lemon-yellow cashmere jumpers – and curled her long, highlighted hair into beach waves every day, as if her life was one long red carpet. She had warm hazel eyes and her friendliness seemed genuine, and so even though she didn't know her at all well, Meredith liked her a lot.

'Hi, Tillie.' Meredith switched on her ancient PC, hoping that after Christmas she could nudge Adrian towards the technology upgrade section of her business plan. 'How are you?'

'Great thanks,' she said, leaning on Meredith's desk, clutching a cup of coffee. 'What about you?' Her eyes tracked over the items Meredith had laid out; the empty hampers, and the goodies waiting to be placed inside.

'Good – busy of course,' Meredith replied. 'It's a frantic time of year. How's Cosy Cornish going?' Cosy Cornish was the blog Tillie wrote, showcasing her lifestyle living in one of Cornwall's quaintest towns, in a home that was beautifully appointed and therefore an Instagram dream. Meredith hadn't been to Adrian and Tillie's house, but she had nosed at all the pictures Tillie posted. For someone with such an online-centric wife, Adrian's tech ignorance was even more baffling.

'Gearing up for something festive and fabulous,' Tillie said, her eyes widening in delighted anticipation. 'I might need a hamper for some of my posts, if that's OK?'

'Of course. Having you highlight them is bound to increase sales. We could even work on the caption together, if you're happy to? Share the post across all our social media channels at the same time, so we could make a bigger impact?' She looked at Tillie hopefully, watching as a slow, catlike smile spread across the other woman's face.

'I'd love that! Shall we have a powwow sometime in Sea Brew? Always good to get out of the office, isn't it?' Her hazel eyes flashed, and Meredith wondered what kind of office Tillie had worked in. She felt herself warming to her boss's wife even more, despite her use of the word powwow.

'Excellent idea. How about . . .'

She clicked on her mouse to wake her screen, about to open her calendar, when Enzo's raised voice distracted her. 'Excuse me,' he said, 'you can't go back there! The shop finishes here. It's private beyond that.'

'Enzo, is it?' The reply surprised Meredith, because it suggested Enzo was actually wearing his name badge, and also because the voice was familiar.

Tillie spun round, revealing Finn standing just beyond the office doorway.

'Right,' Enzo mumbled.

'I'm sorry to be so forthright,' Finn continued, 'but I need to talk to Meredith about something. I wasn't aware the rules about the office were so strict, but you're quite right. Security's very important, especially these days.'

Enzo's surly expression dissolved into a smile, apparently pleased with Finn's hammed-up compliment. 'You know Mer?'

'*Mer?*' Finn shot her a look, and she knew he was going to store the abbreviation away for future use. 'Yes, I do.'

'Oh.' Enzo shrugged. 'Go on, then.'

'Thank you, Enzo.' Finn grinned at him and walked into

the office. Meredith noticed Tillie stand up straighter, and honestly, she couldn't blame her.

Finn was wearing his quilted jacket over jeans and boots, his blond curls had been mussed by the wind, and his cheeks were flushed, his eyes bright. He was a picture of handsome invigoration, and Meredith wasn't entirely unaffected by the way he filled the cluttered space.

'Hello,' Tillie said brightly. 'I'm Tillie. Joint owner of Cornish Keepsakes.' She held out her hand and Finn shook it.

'Hi, Tillie,' he said easily. 'Great to meet you.'

'Have we met before?' Her smile must have been making her cheeks ache.

'I don't think so,' Finn said. 'I couldn't say for certain, but I think I would have remembered you.'

Meredith resisted an eye-roll. Tillie giggled, which brought Adrian lurching out of his office, and Finn introduced himself to her boss with the same confidence, as if he was the company's sole investor.

'You know, you *do* look a little familiar,' Adrian said jovially, once introductions had been made.

Finn went very still for a second, as if someone had pressed a pause button. It was the first time Meredith had seen him looking remotely unsure of himself, but then he laughed, breaking the spell, and she wondered if she'd imagined it. 'I've bumped into Meredith several times over the last few days,' he explained, 'and she pointed out what a small town this is. We've probably passed each other without realizing.'

'Of course,' Adrian said. 'What can we do for you? Would you like a coffee?'

Finn glanced at Meredith, and she got the sense he was weighing something up. 'That would be great, thank you. I was going to ask if I could steal Meredith away to the café, but actually we could discuss it here.'

'Discuss what?' Meredith said sharply.

'Good, good,' Adrian murmured, ignoring her. 'Come and see which pod you'd like.'

'Honestly,' Finn said. 'I can get it. I was sorry to hear about your injury.'

Adrian waved his concern away. 'It's good for me to keep moving. Come on.'

He led Finn into the kitchen, and Tillie leaned close to Meredith, her breath smelling of strawberries. 'Who is he?' she whispered. 'How do you know him?'

Meredith shrugged. 'I don't, really. I've bumped into him a couple of times.'

'And?'

'He likes to know things,' was all she could think of to add. 'He *might* be stalking me.' Why had she said that? She waited for Tillie's alarm, but instead she squealed, as if this was the most incredible thing that could have happened.

Meredith didn't know what to say to that, so she opened programs on her computer until Finn followed Adrian back into the office. He perched on the corner of the spare desk, the one Enzo sometimes used when he wasn't in the shop, but which still had a thin layer of dust on it. Finn blew on his coffee, cradling the mug in both hands.

'I'd like to offer my services,' he said.

'Really?' Adrian's eyebrows shot up. 'And what is it, exactly, that you do?'

'It's not what I do,' Finn said quickly. 'Not regularly, anyway. It's just that I'm in Cornwall for a few weeks, and Meredith told me about your predicament. You being unable to deliver the hampers, suggesting that Meredith could do it. Except, I couldn't help noticing, she has a tiny car.'

'My car is perfectly adequate,' Meredith said haughtily, like someone out of *Downton Abbey*. What was wrong with her?

'It's OK for carting around a tin of peas,' Finn countered, 'not a whole tranche of Christmas hampers with very important recipients.'

Adrian rubbed his chin. 'It's a C1, isn't it? That little pocket Citroën?'

'I've never had a problem with it,' Meredith said. But then she wasn't a man, so she wasn't in the habit of equating her car with anything more personal. She didn't say that, though.

'All I'm suggesting,' Finn went on, 'is that I could help Meredith with the deliveries. The other day I saw that she was struggling with the prospect of . . .' She caught his eye and gave a pleading sort of wince, hoping Tillie and Adrian didn't pick up on it. She hadn't advertised her lack of Christmas cheer to her colleagues, and was planning on keeping them in the dark about it, in case it lost her some of the free rein she'd been given.

'. . . with the prospect of fitting all those hampers in her boot,' Finn went on, smoothly covering his error.

Meredith's shoulders sagged in relief.

'And you think you have a solution?' Adrian sounded interested rather than suspicious, and Meredith couldn't help but marvel at how Finn, a total stranger to him until a few minutes ago, had put himself in charge of the situation. 'Are you angling for a job?'

'I have an SUV, which equates to a solution.' He smiled benignly, ignoring Adrian's question about jobs, and Meredith wished she'd said the thing about cars being penis extensions.

'I don't need any help,' she said instead. 'I am fully prepared for this project, Adrian, and if I'd had any concerns I would have come to you before now.' *Was* Finn after her job? Panic thrummed a rhythm in her ribcage.

Adrian gave her a puzzled frown, then turned his attention to Finn. 'What would you want in return for your help?'

'Nothing,' Finn said. 'As I mentioned, I'm here for a few weeks, and I'm at a fairly loose end. I like to be useful where I can, and this seemed like something I could help with.'

'Oh?' Adrian was definitely interested, despite how out of the blue the offer was. His VIP radar must be going off at Finn's confident bearing, his obviously expensive clothes.

Meredith's panic intensified. He was just the type of person to charm his way into a job rather than suffer through anything as mundane as an interview, and if he proved himself to have the Christmas enthusiasm that Adrian was so insistent on, as well as a huge car, then she wouldn't stand a chance. But her alarm was also tinged with disappointment. She had enjoyed their encounters – even his questions – as much as she'd been pretending to be infuriated. She thought he was genuinely interested in her, but if he wanted a job, then perhaps she was simply a means to an end.

Finn didn't reply to Adrian's probing 'Oh?' He just shrugged and smiled.

'It does seem like an excellent solution,' her boss said, after a moment.

'A solution to a problem that, until five minutes ago, didn't exist,' Meredith countered.

'You don't want his help?' Tillie was incredulous.

'If there's no other agenda,' Adrian said, sternness creeping into his voice, 'then it would seem somewhat churlish to turn him down.'

Meredith stared at Finn. He was sitting calmly on the edge of the desk, clutching his mug and looking for all the world like a well-meaning angel, but she could see the glint of triumph in his eyes. *Who was he?* How had he learned these bewitching skills and, more importantly, what did he want with her and her hamper deliveries? Was he going to tag along, steal all her thunder and then worm his way into Cornish Keepsakes?

'What do you say, Meredith?' Finn asked. 'Fancy a team-mate?'

There was a loaded pause, and then Enzo appeared in the doorway, clearly having heard everything. 'Looks like you might have found yourself a reindeer after all,' he said.

Chapter Five

Meredith still felt shell-shocked by Finn's ambush when she drove to Anisha's house on Thursday evening. How had this man who she didn't know, had never met bar a few short, random encounters, jostled his way into her life, her *business*? She replayed the way he'd smoothly got her colleagues on side, and then, when it was all but a done deal – in Adrian and Finn's minds, anyway – sauntered out with a smile that had bordered on smug.

Except, she thought, as she navigated the roads around the edge of Port Karadow, dark already at twenty past five, there had been a flicker of something else in his eyes. She hoped it was guilt. She had already resolved to turn him away when he returned to the office tomorrow. Her car was fine for ferrying Christmas hampers around. Trust the men to think that a huge, gas-guzzling vehicle was needed for *everything*. If she dismissed him before he had a chance to get properly involved, then he couldn't convince Adrian to give him a job.

By the time she arrived at Anisha's – a double-fronted, detached house with the bare, sturdy branches of a wisteria above the teal front door, the brick façade and polished windowsills comfortingly familiar – she was riled up. It was a beautiful home with old, aristocratic bones that Anisha's eye for detail had turned into the perfect blend of sumptuous and child friendly. Jasmine and Ravi bounced all over it, as they had every right to, and Meredith felt like she was being enveloped in a hug every time she visited.

Nick had inherited the house from his parents, who'd had it in their family for three generations. His mum had died when he was in his twenties, and his dad had decided to move in with his brother, on the other side of Cornwall, rather than continue with the upkeep. Meredith remembered having tears in her eyes as Anisha had told her about the discussion Nick had had with his father: 'Your turn now, Son. You're the one with a family to look after.'

'Enough,' Meredith murmured to herself, turning off the engine and getting out.

'Great, you're here,' Anisha said when she opened the door. 'There's tea brewing and a plate of cookies. Jasmine was in full control, which she would tell you herself if she wasn't already having her bath.' She pointed towards the ceiling, where excited squeals rained down on cue. 'So I can't be held responsible for the taste.'

Meredith took up her usual place at the kitchen island. Her friend's nervous energy seemed to fill the room. 'Thanks. You OK, Nish?'

Anisha sat opposite her and jiggled the teapot absentmindedly. Anisha liked her tea, whatever flavour it was, strong enough to chew. 'I'm good! Mostly, anyway. Except that I'm realizing Andy and I have very different ideas about the lights.'

'In what way?'

'In that he thinks a few well-placed strings of coloured bulbs and an impressive tree are going to be enough.' She huffed. Her dark hair was loose around her face, making her look softer, but the fire in her eyes was unmistakable.

'And you don't think it is?' Meredith asked, even though she already knew the answer.

'It could be magical,' Anisha said, stabbing a finger into the granite counter top. 'These days, lights are bloody everywhere. You can't go to the corner shop without tripping over trails of twinkly LEDs. We put some up, chuck a few garlands around a fir tree, and people won't bat an eyelid.'

'Simple trees can be beautiful,' Meredith said, picturing the tree they'd had when she was small, adorned with decorations made by her and Tommy at school, and an ancient set of lights her mum had had for decades. It had been a ritual; her and Dad getting the lights reverently out of their box and, even before they'd been draped over the tree, plugging them in to check they were working. If they weren't, it was because one of the bulbs was loose or faulty, and they'd spend the next half an hour going along the string, twisting gently, Meredith always wanting to be the one to turn the bulb that brought the soft rainbow glow back.

These days everything was LED, and though she was sure she'd rescued their original lights and buried them somewhere in a box of items labelled 'Not To Be Looked At' in her spare bedroom, she didn't think she'd be able to get any more bulbs if one was broken.

'Simple trees *can* be beautiful,' Anisha agreed, bringing her back to the present, 'and I'm not ruling out an elegant centrepiece. But it can't be a centrepiece if there's nothing surrounding it. Besides, it's not just about that.'

'It isn't?' Meredith dragged the plate of cookies towards her. Anisha said Jasmine had had full control, but Jasmine was five. These cookies would be delicious, unlike the few attempts Meredith had made on rainy Sunday afternoons, with grand ideas about taking a plate of warm, crumbling biscuits to Bernie's house and breaking down the walls between them.

Meredith's baking skills left a lot to be desired. The last batch of cookies she had tried had failed spectacularly – something about the mixture being too wet, she thought – and she had ended up with a tray of thin, inedible splodges. If she had taken one next door, Bernie would have assumed she was poisoning her, and Meredith wouldn't have blamed her.

'You know what I was saying at choir?' Anisha went on while Meredith bit into a dreamy chocolate-chip cookie. 'The lights could be part of something bigger, something that could help Port Karadow instead of just decorating it. We need to bring more visitors here over the winter, encourage locals to use the shops on Main Street. The lights could help, because if we make them an *event*, then people will go out of their way to see them. You know I mentioned this treasure hunt idea—'

'It's all she can think about,' Nick finished, coming up behind Meredith and putting his hands on her shoulders. 'Hi, Meredith. If you're thinking about talking her down, I can assure you it's a lost cause.'

Anisha sighed. 'Andy knows what I'm like. Why did he put me in charge of this if he's only going to rein me in?'

'I don't think he's trying to do that,' Nick said. 'He's just being realistic about how time-critical it is.'

'I've already spoken to suppliers,' Anisha replied. 'If I get my order in by Tuesday, then I can have most of what I want by the beginning of December, which is better than not having it at all.'

Meredith sat up straighter. 'Wow, Anisha. Seriously? So you've done it, then. What are you worried about?'

Nick laughed. It was full of affection, and though Anisha shot him a look, Meredith could see her friend's lips twitching into a smile. 'Don't you dare, Nick.'

He got another mug and poured aromatic tea into all three. The steam, scented with jasmine and rose, drifted towards the ceiling. 'When Nish says *most* of what she wants, the other stuff is the complicated part. Some sort of frosting—'

'They're called net lights and tree wraps,' Anisha cut in.

'—to go basically everywhere,' Nick went on, as if she hadn't spoken. 'She also hasn't mentioned the premium this lights company is charging to get her the other stuff for the beginning of December. It's a premium Andy isn't going to stand for, because he works for the council, and they never have money for frivolous things like Christmas lights.'

Anisha squared her shoulders. 'I think you, Andy, *everyone* is underestimating the positive effect this could have on the town. I'm not just talking about improving everyone's mood, but the boost to the economy if our display is impressive enough. We can create a Christmas wonderland if we accept that this is important, and not a bit of frivolity: if we

60

commit to helping this town get back on track. We need to show people that instead of going online or to the bigger towns like Truro, they can get unique, independent gifts and services here, from businesses that will treat them like individuals.' She lifted her chin, and Meredith thought Andy had probably also been on the receiving end of this impassioned speech.

'I think,' Meredith said, pointing what was left of her cookie in Anisha's direction, 'that you're being pretty ambitious with the timescale you've got, but that everything you're saying is right. Part of the reason I'm adding an online shop for Cornish Keepsakes is that it's not going to survive much longer with just the local custom, but Adrian's intent on boosting our image in Port Karadow, and I think the two will help each other.'

'Exactly,' Anisha said. 'And there are places like Sea Brew that can't sell further afield. Restaurants and cafés rely on local trade, and if everyone stays inside their houses, buying expensive coffee machines and cookery books online, the next time they *do* get outside, the shops will all be gone and Main Street will be a deserted ghost road. Then people will start moving away and the town will die, and—'

'This is called catastrophizing,' Nick said. 'The survival of this town isn't your responsibility.'

'No,' Anisha said. 'But I'm in a position where I can make a difference. These don't have to be *just* lights.'

'And if anyone can make a difference, then it's you,' Meredith pointed out. She felt much more comfortable discussing the regeneration of the town she already loved, than LED snowflakes. 'Andy may put up a pretence of reining you in, but I think he'll say yes to most of your suggestions. I'm sure he has an inkling that your thinking is bigger than Christmas, anyway.'

Anisha sat back, a smile on her face. 'You're right.'

Nick groaned. 'Don't encourage her.'

'You know it's a good cause, Nick,' Meredith said. 'What would you do if you couldn't get that ham you like from the deli? If you couldn't say hello to friends when you walked to the harbour, because they'd all shut up shop and moved away?'

'I'm not disagreeing with you,' Nick protested. 'It's only that . . .' He frowned, rubbing a hand over his face. 'I'm not disagreeing with you,' he repeated, shrugging.

Meredith was surprised by how tired he looked. Anisha's husband spent his days taking tourists around one of the mines that dotted the wild, southern coastline of Cornwall, no longer working other than to teach visitors and locals about its rich history. The tours had been much more popular since *Poldark* had hit TV screens and, more recently, the historical drama *Estelle* had also touched on the mining legacy. He was permanently good-natured, always laid-back – except, it seemed, tonight. Was Anisha's determination really wearing him down?

'Anyway,' Anisha said, slapping her palms on the table. 'Enough of this. What's new with you? How's Adrian's Port Karadow domination coming along? Do you actually have to lick some arses when you deliver these hampers?'

'Fuck's sake, Nish,' Nick muttered, giving a pained laugh.

Meredith shuddered at the idea of adopting her boss's sycophantic ways when she went round with her sumptuous gifts. Although, she thought ruefully, Finn wouldn't bat an eyelid at being asked to butter up the great and good of the town. He and Adrian were a match made in heaven.

'That bad, huh?' Anisha pushed the cookies towards her and gave her a sympathetic smile.

'I've been ambushed,' Meredith said, then instantly regretted blurting it out. For some reason, she had wanted to keep Finn to herself. Was that partly why she'd been so annoyed at him swanning into the Cornish Keepsakes office and introducing himself to everyone?

'What do you mean? Ambushed by who?' Anisha asked.

Meredith took another cookie.

'Is this something I need to be worried about?' Nick added, and Meredith gave him a grateful smile. She found Nick's protectiveness endearing; it was as if he was taking on the big-brother role that Tommy was too far away to fulfil.

'Not worried,' Meredith said. 'Irritated. I mean, I am. There's no reason you should be.'

'Explain,' Anisha said.

'Right.' Meredith took a deep breath. 'There's this guy—'

'Oh my god, *what?*'

Of course, that had been the wrong thing to open with.

'Do I need to go and . . . uh . . .' Nick pointed to the doorway.

'For a member of the male species, you seem to be particularly allergic to any conversation relating to them,' Anisha said. 'Is that because you consider yourself the only one worthy of the title?'

Nick let out a weary sigh. 'Such disdain,' he muttered. 'Carry on, Meredith. We'll try to act like adults as you tell us about your ambushing male.'

Meredith laughed, her friends making her feel instantly better.

'Can I just check, though,' Anisha said, 'this is the first guy since Taylor, right?'

Meredith shook her head. 'Definitely not.'

'You mean there's been someone else and you haven't told me?'

'No,' Meredith replied, matching her friend's forcefulness. 'This isn't a *guy* guy, just a guy—'

'Oh right,' Nick cut in. 'That makes perfect sense.'

Meredith shot him a look. 'I'm going to start again. I have encountered a male human person in town over the last few days. One I've had very brief, inconsequential conversations with.' She paused, waiting for questions or comments, but her friends seemed to have got the message. 'And then, on Tuesday, he turned up at Cornish Keepsakes, and offered to help me with hamper deliveries. He convinced Adrian that his SUV would be better than my C1 for delivering them—'

'It probably would, to be fair,' Nick said.

'It's utter bollocks,' Meredith replied. 'I have a perfectly good car. I was sorting out this project on my own. He doesn't know me, and I don't want his help or advice about my logistical choices.'

'Why is he offering to help you?' Anisha asked. 'And also, does this human have a name?'

'Finn,' Meredith supplied. 'And I have no idea, unless he's after my job. But if that's the case, this is a weird way to go about it. I met him at the cove after a swim, we exchanged pleasantries, then I saw him again on the way to choir, and outside the shop. And *then*, because I was stupid enough to mention the deliveries, he decided I was a damsel in distress.'

'So he fancies you,' Anisha said, as if the case was closed.

'He doesn't know me; I don't know him. He said he was in town for a bit and that my hamper deliveries were something he thought he could help with. It's so strange that he's offered.'

'Maybe he's a spy,' Nick suggested.

'Not a very good one if he's picked Adrian as his fount of knowledge,' Anisha countered.

'I don't know,' Meredith said. 'Adrian may not have the influence he thinks he does, but he's very diligent with his research. Also, he would no way suspect Finn of being a spy, so . . . wait! What are you two doing to me? Finn is not a spy! Perhaps he's moving here and wants to get a feel for the town?'

'By helping a random, if very attractive, woman deliver Christmas hampers?' Anisha's tone was sceptical.

'Maybe he has a Santa Claus complex?' Nick suggested. 'I read about it – it's actually a thing. It's called Santaphilia.'

Anisha wrinkled her nose. 'I don't think that's about wanting to *be* Santa. I think that's about wanting to *do* Santa.'

'OK, guys, enough!' Meredith held her hands up. 'This isn't doing any good. Finn isn't a problem to be solved, anyway. He's meeting me at the shop tomorrow to plan out dates and routes – agreed by Adrian, I might add – and I'm going to send him on his merry way. It would be just my luck if I attracted some guy who has a Father Christmas fetish. Talk about the irony.' She shook her head. 'Let's change the subject.'

Anisha's neat brows were drawn together. 'I'm not sure I like the idea of you being hit on by this man.'

'He's not hitting on me, and also, what, you'd prefer it if I was never hit on again? Never interacted with another man and ended up a lonely old spinster with Smudge and Crumble' – at the sound of his name, the beagle puppy raised his head from where he'd been snoozing on the rug – 'and nobody else to love me?'

'It's the way he's gone about things. Why has he offered to help you?'

'I'll ask him tomorrow before I tell him to sod off,' Meredith said. 'I'll even text you the answer.'

'Right. Fine. Good.' Anisha nodded.

'And if you ever need a bit of muscle . . .' Nick added.

'I'll advertise on Facebook,' Meredith finished with a sweet smile.

'Ha-ha.' Nick stood up. 'On that note, I'm going to go and lick my wounds in front of my documentary about *HMS Victory*.'

Meredith and Anisha waited until he'd left the kitchen to exchange grins.

'Have you found a love of Christmas hidden at the bottom of one of your hampers?' Anisha asked. Her words were casual, but her gaze said more; there was determination, but also compassion, as there always was.

'Nope,' Meredith replied, hoping to close the subject down. She thought of the way Finn had accurately interpreted her look on Tuesday; that she didn't want to communicate her lack of Christmas joy to Adrian. She'd been in his company for such a short time, and yet he seemed to already understand her. 'Anyway.' She shook her head, trying to clear her thoughts. 'What about you? You're happy with a Christmas just the four of you?'

Anisha sat up straighter. 'We're going to see Nick's dad and uncle, so that'll be fun.'

Meredith nodded. 'There's really no chance of your mum and dad coming to stay?'

'I'd love them to, but it's such a big thing for them now. They'd have to come for a fortnight to make the journey worthwhile and, although I would love that, I'd still have to work, and Nick would spend his days off bowing to their every whim. And they have a lot of whims, believe me.' She chuckled, affection warming her voice.

'Nick wouldn't mind, though, would he?'

'Oh no,' Anisha said, 'he'd be as charming and accommodating as always – on the surface at least. But it's a lot to ask. The last time Mum and Dad stayed, a couple of years ago, it was only for three nights, and I thought Nick might ask for a divorce once they'd gone home. It was as if my parents were pulling the thread of our marriage between them, testing it to its limits.'

Meredith rubbed her forehead. 'They could stay in a hotel?'

'For two weeks, near Christmas?' Anisha shook her head. 'They'd want to go somewhere like that Crystal Waters place in Porthgolow, and nobody has that kind of money lying about, except your Port Karadow VIPs. It's good having breaks, anyway. It means it's more of a treat when you see them next time.' Her smile was almost convincing, but Meredith knew Anisha would love nothing more than to have her entire family at her house for Christmas. 'Anyway, I want to know more about this Finn guy. What does he look like?'

Meredith pictured his blond curls and the blue eyes that gleamed with humour and curiosity. He seemed to want to know everything about her, and there was something attractive about that; he hadn't already made up his mind about her, and he also wasn't intent on talking solely about himself whenever they met. In fact, she still knew almost nothing about him.

'Meredith?' Anisha prompted. 'Your eyes have gone all misty.'

'Misty eyes isn't a real thing.'

'So he's not attractive?'

'He is almost sinfully attractive,' Meredith admitted. 'The first thing I said to him was that he was like a Michelangelo. Ugh.' She pressed her palms against her cheeks. 'I'm burning up just thinking about it.'

Anisha laughed. 'This is so much more exciting than I thought!'

'I didn't want Nick to go all caveman on me,' Meredith explained. 'Anyway, I still have no idea why he's paying me attention. I'll find out tomorrow, I guess.'

'Can you take a photo for me?' she asked. 'You can't send Mr Almost Sinfully Attractive off into the sunset without letting me see what you're turning down.'

'Oh sure,' Meredith said, feeling Crumble's damp nose nuzzling her ankle. She got off her stool, lifted him and then climbed back up, settling the dog on her knee. 'It's going to be so easy for me to take a clandestine photograph while simultaneously telling him to get out of my life.'

Unsurprisingly, Anisha wasn't deterred. 'You'll manage it. Or else you'll just have to find out where he's staying, so I can orchestrate my own accidental meeting with him.'

'He's basically everywhere,' Meredith said, pushing the plate of cookies away from her dog's inquisitive nose. 'No, Crumble, you can't have chocolate: ever ever ever.'

Anisha gave the dog a sympathetic look. 'I'll make some doggie cookies next time; there's a recipe in the back of one of my books.' She clapped her hands together. 'You have to tell me everything, OK? This is exciting.'

Meredith frowned. 'It all seems fairly surreal to me. But,' she sighed, thinking of the way Finn had inveigled his way into the hearts of the Cornish Keepsakes crew in less time than it would take her to make them a round of coffees, 'I'm not sure getting rid of him is going to be as easy as I'm hoping it will be.'

Anisha folded her arms on the counter and rested her chin on top of them, her gaze serious. 'Don't let him bully you,' she said. 'If you don't want him to be involved, sinfully handsome or not, then tell him. He has to respect your wishes.'

Meredith nodded. He was a jammy bastard, but she had the sense that he was kind, too; that he wouldn't push it if she really didn't want him to. 'I think he'll listen to me.'

'But? I sense a "but" coming.'

Meredith looked at her puppy, who was trying to get her attention by nudging his nose into her chin. 'Adrian already loves him, and I get the feeling that if I send him away, my boss will find some way of keeping him around.'

Anisha raised her eyebrows. 'He was that much of a charmer?'

Meredith thought back to the ambush and the way Adrian, Tillie and even Enzo had basically fallen at Finn's feet. 'He'd give Crumble a run for his money, let's put it that way.'

As if in agreement, Crumble let out one of his tiny but determined barks, and Meredith's heart melted a little bit, unable to resist her puppy for even a second. She realized, then, that her comparison – which must have come from a place of truth, even if it was somewhere deep inside her – had been a dangerous one, and that she might actually be in a little bit of trouble with the mystery man who had walked into her life.

Chapter Six

The next day, Meredith woke before dawn to the sounds of Smudge giving his breakfast yowl, and the gentle tick-tick-tick of the heating. She hadn't slept well, replaying her conversation with Anisha over and over, and her sweaty feet were tangled in the sheets. She had been so sure with her friend about how the conversation with Finn would go today: it was always easier to be certain with someone who knew you inside out, who had seen you at your lowest, and your most ridiculous.

The glow from the streetlight outside painted her bedroom in a yellowish hue, and the door was ajar, which had allowed Smudge to come in and paw at her shins, something she was used to but which never got any less painful. Meredith scooted forward, lifting her cat and cradling him against her chest. Crumble would be waiting for them in his crate downstairs, and she imagined the puppy furiously indignant that he didn't have the run of the house like his feline friend.

She had been meaning to fix the bedroom latch for ages, one of the small jobs that would make her home cosier, but wasn't big enough to seem urgent. But these early morning wake-ups, especially in December when it was so cold and dark, were jarring. And she needed to be fully functioning today, because she was going into battle with Finn.

She showered and dressed in a navy woollen jumper and jeans, pulling her slipper socks on over the top. Thanks to her pets' need for food, she had a couple of hours before she had to leave, and although she knew a swim would have calmed her thoughts, there was something else that, this morning, felt more important than her regular trip to the cove. She'd found a simple gingerbread recipe online, and had been imagining turning up at Cornish Keepsakes, wowing Enzo, Adrian and Tillie – because she would be there, Meredith was sure, if Finn was coming back – with her culinary creations, then telling her would-be knight in shining armour that his services had never been required.

She set to work in her snug kitchen, cluttered with para-phernalia that went back to her days working at her first farm shop, during her GCSE and A-level years. She had a jar shaped like a sheep, its lid the sheep's head complete with smiling face, for her tea bags; a rosette from York University pinned to the magnetic whiteboard on which she had intended to write her to-do list every day, but that currently only said *Register with the local doctor*, something she'd done a year ago, and *Paint hallway*, which she still hadn't got round to.

There were tartan curtains at the window looking out onto the small square of patio that passed for her back garden, and on a shelf above the kettle was the teapot, cup and saucer set she'd been given as a leaving present by the

Lagowan estate staff, a Cornish seascape design in soft blues and yellows.

Tommy had once pointed out that the reason she was so good at marketing gifts was because she was a sucker for them herself. He'd referred to them as pointless trinkets, and she'd given up trying to change his mind. She loved her space to be colourfully chaotic: not messy, but with things reflecting her personality scattered around her. The paintings from Charmed Cove had pride of place on the mantel above the living-room fireplace, each one displayed in a stand she'd bought specially, the slate pieces angled to show off the artworks to whoever stepped through the door.

'Right then, guys,' she said to her furry audience, 'let's see about this gingerbread, shall we?' She pictured herself as an elegant chef on a cookery programme, more modern than Delia Smith but just as accomplished, with graceful movements and an unfaltering smile. As things started to go wrong, the vision began to disintegrate.

First, she burned the syrup and butter mix in the microwave, then the dough didn't seem the right consistency, sticking to her hands and the counter top and refusing, even when she sprinkled copious amounts of flour on it, to hold together. When the doorbell rang, she was irate and hot-cheeked, her hands resembling those of a swamp monster.

'Hang on!' she called, running her fingers under the tap, watching a good portion of gingerbread glue go down the sink. She took so long, she expected the bell to go again, the postman or whoever it was running out of patience, but instead there was silence.

Meredith dried her hands and hurried to the door. 'Hello, sorry about—' her words left her in a breath.

'Hi, Meredith,' Finn said gently. 'How are you?'

Meredith could only stare back. What was he doing here? He had the collar of his quilted jacket turned up, his cheeks pink from the cold. The sun was slowly rising in a golden, watery curtain behind him, making his curls gleam. *Sinfully attractive*, said the voice in her head, and she added *sinfully annoying* to balance things out. His expression was contrite, tentative, as if he'd already decided this impromptu visit was a bad idea.

'Good thanks,' she managed. 'But . . . what are you doing here? How did you know where I lived? Adrian didn't tell you, did he? This is getting a bit—'

'I'm sorry,' Finn cut in quickly. 'I didn't know if . . .'

'Sorry for stalking me?' At least this made things easier. She was definitely going to tell him to piss off now.

He took his hands out of his pockets and shoved them under opposite armpits. He looked instantly softer, less cocky. 'You mentioned which road you lived on when you and Adrian were discussing logistics for the deliveries the other day.'

Meredith's annoyance faded slightly, because that was true. Still.

'I know which car's yours from the jars incident,' Finn went on, 'and I . . .' He exhaled, glanced away from her, then back. 'I'm sorry. This was a mistake. I just thought—'

'Thought what?' Meredith narrowed her eyes. '*I* thought I was meeting you at Cornish Keepsakes.'

He ran a hand over the back of his neck, his gaze dropping to the floor. 'I thought it would be easier to have this conversation away from your office.'

'What conversation?'

He looked up at her. 'The one where you tell me you absolutely, on no account, want my help delivering your hampers, and I convince you that you do. Except I haven't gone about this the right way, I can see that.'

Meredith gritted her teeth.

'If you wanted, we could go for a walk?' Finn said. 'Or I could . . . maybe we should meet at the coffee shop on Main Street later. Sea Brew, is it?'

Meredith chewed her lip. Her gingerbread dough needed to go in the oven. It was cold outside. Even in Sea Brew there would be eager ears waiting to home in on their conversation, because it was a small town and nothing was ever private.

Meredith let out a small sigh. 'You'd better come in.'

'Are you sure?' Finn didn't move.

She stepped back, resisting the urge to take hold of his collar and drag him inside after her. 'I don't want my neighbour to overhear us.'

Finn paused for a couple more seconds, then stepped over the threshold. 'Don't you get on?' he asked as he moved from her minute hallway, where she could feel his body heat, into her living room, and then stopped. She watched as he took in the details: the biscuit-coloured throw covering her tatty sofa; the armchair under the window; the slate paintings on the mantelpiece below the mirror. His attention lingered there, and she wondered if he was checking out his reflection. She left him to his vanity and went back into the kitchen.

'My neighbour isn't my biggest fan,' Meredith admitted, returning to the ectoplasm that was her gingerbread dough.

'Why's that?' Finn asked, coming to lean against the door frame. Smudge and Crumble looked up at him as if he was a bestower of great pet treats, and he crouched to give them attention.

'I have no clue,' Meredith said.

'You haven't shoved cut grass through her letterbox or played AC/DC at two in the morning?'

'Not *that* often,' Meredith said. Finn was busy petting her traitorous cat and dog, so she flattened the gingerbread into an approximation of rolled-out dough, and used her scone cutter to cut circular shapes. She transferred them from the counter to the baking tray, then opened the oven door and shoved the tray in.

He looked up. 'What are you making?'

'Poisoned cookies.'

He narrowed his eyes.

'Look, can we just get on with this? This rejection battle . . . thing. I don't understand why you want to help me, or Cornish Keepsakes. What's in it for you?'

Finn rested his hand on the door jamb and pulled himself up. 'You don't like Christmas.'

'I know that.' She folded her arms.

He sighed, frustration flickering over his features.

'Would you like a tea or coffee?' she asked. Why was she relenting?

His scowl disappeared. 'Coffee, please. Milk, no sugar.'

She nodded and set to work, and Finn went back into the living room and looked out of the window. Meredith could see that the street was still sleepy, the sunlight only just starting to pick out details, because it was still early. Before-work early.

She brought two coffees into the room and, handing one to him, sat on the sofa. He took the chair opposite.

'I don't accept my dislike of Christmas as a good reason for wanting to help me,' she said. 'Did you need an "in" with Adrian for some reason? Is this your way of hustling to get some work?'

Finn shook his head. 'I didn't know about Adrian or Cornish Keepsakes until I bumped into you outside the shop, then came in to speak to you. I hadn't intended to rope your boss into it, you know. I was just planning on asking if you wanted some help. Now it seems like some sort of conspiracy against you, which I promise it's not. It comes down to boot size, and the fact that I can provide the Christmas enthusiasm you don't have.'

'I won't lose my job if I'm lacking Christmas spirit.'

'But don't you take pride in what you do?'

'Yes,' Meredith said, putting her mug on the floor. 'Me. I do. I don't know you, Finn. We've simply been in the same place a few times, and now it seems like . . .' What did it seem like? 'It's strange, that's all.'

'You don't have people help you out all the time? Isn't it that sort of community?'

'Port Karadow is a great community,' she confirmed. 'But usually it's neighbours or people you know from the pub quiz, or . . . not strangers you meet on the beach.'

'OK, so I've been a bit heavy-handed. I haven't been here for a while, and when I do come, it's usually only for a few days.'

'Where are you staying?' Meredith asked, taking the opportunity to find out something about him.

'With my aunt,' Finn said. 'And I promise, I have no other motive. I thought I could help you out, but I got it wrong. Please don't call the police or get Adrian to beat me up.'

The thought of Adrian trying to punch anyone was too funny; she pictured the scene in Bridget Jones where Daniel Cleaver and Mark Darcy clawed at each other like angry toddlers, and laughed.

'Your boss doesn't go to underground boxing clubs in his spare time?' Finn asked, and Meredith's laugh became slightly hysterical. 'I thought he might have picked up his injury there.'

'The underground boxing world of Port Karadow?' she managed, gasping for air.

'You never know.'

'I won't be able to look at him the same way again.'

'He seems very fond of you,' Finn said, after a beat.

Meredith inhaled, slowing her breaths as her laughter faded, then picked up her mug and looked at him over the rim. 'Adrian's fond of everyone,' she said. 'I don't think I've ever seen him angry or upset. In fact, I think that's made me see him as a weak person. He's always upbeat, so I've thought of him as ineffectual, but he isn't. He's running a gift business, and it may not be fully up to date, but he's passionate about it.' She rubbed her forehead, expecting Finn to be amused at her reflective rant, the conclusion that she hadn't been giving her boss enough credit, but he was watching her intently. Behind him, the sun was rising and strengthening, the sparkle of last night's heavy frost on the roofs opposite almost too bright for her eyes.

'Is he holding a candle for you?' Finn asked, his voice notably casual.

Laughter threatened Meredith again. 'You know Tillie, the other woman you met?'

'The one with all the . . .' He spiralled a hand beside his head.

'Beach waves? Yes. She's Adrian's wife.'

'Oh!' He looked genuinely surprised. 'Oh, right. So you and Adrian aren't—'

'We're most definitely not. Look, Finn,' she said, sitting up straighter, 'all this attention is very flattering, but why are you really here?'

'Because I want to help you.'

'Aren't you on holiday? Do you have that much of a work ethic that you have to find some project to take over when you're not doing your own job? What do you do, anyway? You've come here, asked all these questions, and I know nothing about you.'

Finn rested his mug on his knee. 'I work in front of house. In London.'

'Ah. Hence the schmoozing.'

'What?'

'Please continue.' Meredith rolled her hand.

He sighed. 'I'm taking a break. A holiday of sorts. My aunt has a house down here, so I'm staying with her. I met you, you looked supremely inconvenienced at having to deliver Christmas hampers, and I realized I have both the transport and the festive zeal to make your life easier.'

He smiled, but Meredith kept quiet, and his shoulders dropped in defeat.

'I'm at a bit of a loose end,' he admitted. 'Lacking some . . . inspiration. What you've got to do seemed like fun, and I've enjoyed our conversations.'

'We don't know each other.'

'But we could, if I delivered the hampers with you.'

She huffed. 'I can be professional by myself.'

'I don't doubt that,' Finn said. 'This isn't because I think you'll do a bad job. As you've pointed out, it's none of my business and I'm aware that I'm sticking my nose in, but that's never stopped me before.' His words trailed off, and when he laughed, it wasn't his easy laughter of before. 'You're right: this is weird. I don't know what I was thinking.' He rubbed a hand over his face, then put his mug on the floor between Smudge and Crumble, who had gathered at his feet like shepherds round the manger. He stood up. 'I should go.'

Meredith stood too, panic flapping unexpected wings in her chest. He was just going to leave? 'But you don't—'

'Thanks for the coffee. I'm really sorry about all this – about thinking I could come here and interfere. I get carried away sometimes. Please forgive me?' He walked to the door, not waiting for an answer. His shoulders were tense, his body shimmering with frustration. She didn't think it was directed at her.

'How big is your boot?' Meredith blurted. The silence that followed stretched out like elastic. She could sense her pets judging her. She was embarrassed. Had he used reverse-psychology tactics against her?

He turned slowly, and looked at her with genuine surprise. 'Size nine and a half,' he said. 'And that half is very important.'

She groaned. 'Finn!'

He smiled, and she almost growled in response. Had there ever been a more infuriating man on the planet?

'It's a big Audi,' he went on. 'Big enough for several hampers, at least. And there's the back seat, too. We could make short work of your deliveries, so you didn't have to prolong the agony. You're really considering it?'

'I would be mad to consider it.'

'But you are?'

'You know in your front-of-house job,' she said, 'do you persuade people to part with thousands of pounds of their hard-earned money?'

'Yes.' He looked completely serious.

'God. What kind of restaurant do you work in?'

'When did I say anything about a restaurant?'

She was about to reply when her oven timer went off.

'Ah,' Finn said. 'The poisoned cookies are ready.'

Meredith was grateful she could escape to the kitchen for a moment's breathing space. She opened the oven, a cloud of heat wafting out along with a smell that, while not as gingery as she had hoped, was by no means unpleasant. She got her oven mitt and pulled out the tray, only to discover that her carefully cut-out shapes had melded back into one uneven, very thin biscuit.

'What *is* that?'

Meredith jumped. She hadn't heard Finn follow her.

'Gingerbread.'

'Can I try it?'

'Of course.' It had to taste better than it looked. 'Give it a couple of minutes to cool down, and I'll . . . uhm . . . break off a piece for you.'

They went back into the front room. Crumble had pulled the throw off the armchair and it was draped over him like a shroud. Finn crouched and released the puppy, then glanced at Meredith and, when she nodded, picked him up. He sat down again, with Crumble on his lap.

'Your home is beautiful,' he said. 'I bet once you light the fire in here you could stay in this room for days, with the gentle patter of rain outside, shadows dancing on the walls.'

Meredith felt his compliment in the centre of her chest. She had made it her mission to carve out her own, comforting space in the world. She couldn't help look at Anisha's elegant home with slightly green eyes, and had never considered her little terraced house would be admired by anyone but her. 'Thank you,' she said. 'It is a bit of a hideaway. Not that I hide away from anyone, but—'

'It's important to have a space of your own,' he finished for her.

'Exactly. What about you? Bachelor pad in London, or am I being too obvious?'

'No,' Finn said, a little wearily. 'You're exactly right.'

'Not that I know you're a bachelor or anything,' she rushed out. 'It's just that, whenever I've seen you, you've been on your own and I—'

'It's fine,' Finn said. 'Honestly. I am exactly what you perceive me to be.' He rubbed his forehead, his glittering charm subdued, and Meredith realized she was finally seeing some of his layers, the reality beneath the swagger. It made her want to reach out to him, to peel back more, even if what she found wasn't pretty.

'I think the cookies should be ready by now.' She hurried into the kitchen, but couldn't help glancing back, watching as Finn bent his head and pressed his nose into Crumble's soft fur. Unaccountably pleased by the scene, she broke off two bits of gingerbread, took out two Cornishware plates – part of a set Anisha and Nick had given her as a house-warming present – and took them back to the living room.

'There you go.' She handed him one and sat back down.

'Thank you.' He held the plate above Crumble's head. 'If you're really happy to let me help you—'

'I am,' she cut in, surprising herself with her conviction.

He nodded. 'Then you should tell me your game plan. Just let me know when and where I need to be, and I'll fit in with you.'

'You really don't have anything taking up your time?'

'Nothing that's set in stone.' He lifted the gingerbread to his lips and bit down, and Meredith mirrored him, her heart sinking as she chewed. Finn worked front of house in a restaurant. Or at least, she *thought* he did. Would he be polite, because he was a guest in her house, or—?

'You know . . .' he said, examining what was left of his biscuit before putting it back on the plate.

'Yes?' Meredith said quietly.

'I think, if we're going to be spending time together, we need to be honest with each other.'

She nodded. 'I'd expect nothing less.'

'Good. Because these are pretty horrible. Did you use a recipe?'

'I did, but I . . .' She laughed. 'They are, aren't they? One day, though. One day, I will get it right.'

'Baking's not for everyone.'

'I'm not giving up yet.' She was surprisingly un-offended by his – very accurate – opinion of her gingerbread splat.

'I should let you get to work,' he said. 'Come on, buddy.' He put his plate on the floor and lifted Crumble off his lap, ensuring the dog couldn't make a beeline for the discarded cookie.

Meredith scooped the plates and mugs up and deposited them on the kitchen counter.

'Thanks for coming,' she said. 'And for convincing me.'

He stopped in the doorway, leaning against the frame. 'Thank you for letting me.'

Neither of them spoke for a moment, and it was as if the space between them was alive with fireflies, glittering and glowing as their eyes met. This was the most bizarre thing that had happened to her, and yet she was letting it happen. She couldn't resist Finn's pull. She had caught a glimpse of the man beneath the sparkling persona, and there was still so much she didn't know about him; so many questions he'd sidestepped.

'Red,' he said.

'What?' She blinked.

'You have strands of it in your hair.' He lifted a hand, but didn't touch her. 'Cardinal red.'

'I do?' She put her hands to where her brown waves fell, slightly chaotically, around her face. She hadn't styled her hair that morning.

'I should go, Red,' Finn said. 'But we'll be in touch? Oh.' He took his phone out of his pocket and handed it to her. He'd unlocked it, and she could see the photo on his home screen: golden sand and dark water lit by the most incredible, fiery sunset. 'Add your number.' She did, then handed it back to him. He called it, and she heard her phone ring from the kitchen.

He walked to the front door and opened it, and Meredith checked that her pets weren't about to dash out into the road, before turning back to him.

'I'll fit in with your plans,' he said again. 'Just call me.

I'll be like your chauffeur, but with added Christmassy benefits.'

'OK. That sounds good. Thank you.' She wrapped her arms around herself against the cold bite of the morning.

'You might not thank me when I turn up in a sleigh drawn by six reindeer.'

'You wouldn't!'

Finn grinned, his swagger back in place, like he'd switched on a particularly bright lamp. 'You'll have to wait and see.'

'I am on tenterhooks,' she said dryly, and Finn laughed.

'OK then, I'm off to find some breakfast. Turns out I have a sudden hankering for gingerbread.' He gave her what could only be described as a wicked grin, then turned and strolled down the path. Meredith heard the jingly Christmas bell that was attached to Bernie's front door, and slid backwards a fraction as her neighbour stepped outside.

'Hello,' Finn said brightly.

'Good morning!' Bernie replied in a warm voice Meredith had never heard before. 'Lovely day for it!'

'Isn't it?' Finn said. 'I'm going to make the most of it. I love your decorations, by the way. Very classic.'

'Thank you,' Bernie gushed. 'I do put some effort into Christmas.'

'It shows,' Finn said. 'They've already brightened up my day.'

Bernie actually giggled, and Meredith stayed in her doorway while she heard the clink of glass which meant her neighbour was picking up her full milk bottles and putting down her empties.

'Bye then,' Bernie called to Finn.

'Goodbye,' he said in his deep, smooth voice and, the

85

moment Meredith heard Bernie's door close, he turned to her and winked. 'Bye, Red,' he said, much more quietly, then he walked away.

Meredith shoved the door closed and leaned against the wall. The clock on her mantel piece, next to her slate paintings, told her she had half an hour until she needed to be at work. She could picture Adrian's face when she told him that Finn would be helping with her deliveries. Then she pictured Anisha's, when she explained just how effectively she had told Finn to piss off. Honestly, she thought, as she went to throw her failed gingerbread in the food bin, if he turned up in an actual sleigh – and at this point, she wouldn't put it past him – she wouldn't be held responsible for her actions.

Chapter Seven

'That is just it!' Emma clapped loudly, the most animated Meredith had ever seen her. 'Perfect. Perfect! If you can do it like that at the Christmas concert, we'll almost be in Fisherman's Friends territory.'

Anisha snorted. She was convinced that Emma had a huge chip on her shoulder about the fishermen who had achieved musical success with their sea shanties. Emma wanted her choir to be recognized in the same way, despite the fact that they weren't Cornish fisherman and didn't often sing sea shanties, which were the two ingredients that had led to the Fisherman's Friends album and a film being made of their story.

'Meredith?' Emma added, homing in on her.

'Yes?' she replied meekly.

'You're really finding your voice. It sounds wonderful.'

'Thank you,' she replied. 'That's very kind. I haven't really—'

'How about a solo?' Emma cut in.

Meredith looked at Anisha, as if her friend could help her somehow. 'A . . . a solo? Do you mean in the new year? With the new programme?' They'd started rehearsing for this concert, so she couldn't mean this one. Her pulse slowed a fraction.

Emma laughed. 'Of course not! We need to shine a light on you now. I'm thinking one of the carols. Perhaps "Carol of the Bells"? In fact – yes! That would be ideal. You could start us off, let your voice ring out, and the others could join you after the first verse.'

'"Carol of the Bells"?' It was one of the most beautiful, but also the most challenging to sing. And it was *so* Christmassy. She was determined to stay in the background for this concert. 'I honestly don't think I'm the right person.'

'You're more than up to it,' Emma said warmly. 'And a solo would bring some extra sparkle to an already magnificent carol. I can just imagine it: the audience in awe, the Christmas lights twinkling, a crisp nip in the air and the smell of roasting hazelnuts.' She shuddered happily, whereas Meredith could feel her hands trembling in horror. 'Have a think,' Emma said, back to business, 'but I need to know by next week. Right, five-minute break to wet your whistles, then we'll move onto "We Wish You a Merry Christmas".' The small group dispersed, Meredith and Anisha moving to their usual corner.

'You would be great, you know,' Anisha said, once they'd settled on the low, dusty bench that reminded Meredith of school PE lessons. 'At the solo.'

'That carol is a fiend.'

'It is, and you can slay it.' She held her fist out, and Meredith bumped it with her own, even though she felt far from triumphant. 'It's almost like a round, anyway,' Anisha added. 'We'll all be joining in after a few bars. You have to say yes.'

'I have to?'

Anisha nodded. She had her hair pulled back, which always made her eyes look huge, and a dusting of shimmer on her cheeks. 'To make up for letting Finn walk all over you.'

Meredith scoffed. 'He didn't walk all over me. I decided to take him up on his offer of help.'

Anisha rolled her eyes.

'It's an act of kindness,' Meredith said. 'A genuine one, I'm pretty sure.'

'You really don't think he has another motive for helping you?'

Meredith had thought about little else. Right now, she thought about how she'd settled in her cosy living room as the rain poured down on Sunday afternoon, the weather perfectly creating Finn's fantasy, and been proud all over again that he had said it was a comfortable space. She thought of how, during her swim on Saturday morning, she'd kept swivelling in the direction of the shore, hoping to see him there, and been put off her stride. She thought of the messages they'd exchanged since they'd swapped numbers, his arriving first:

It's an Audi Q8. Finn.

Good to know. Better than a sleigh, at least. M.

I could be bluffing.

89

> If you turn up with reindeer the deal is off. And I'll call the RSPCA.

> Think there's a guy in a red suit who's more deserving of their attention. Forcing them to canter all over the world? (Do reindeer canter?) Making them wait on rooftops in the cold? The long shifts? Shocking! That guy really needs looking at.

> Have you heard of Santaphilia, Finn?

> I'm not talking to you anymore.

He'd sent another one a minute later.

> But please let me know when we're delivering the first hampers, Red.

It had been easy and fun, bantering with him via WhatsApp, no need to look into his blue eyes or feel the force of his presence. And so what if she'd been imagining him sitting with her on the sofa, the fire crackling and the downpour relentless beyond the glass? It was his fault, anyway. She always took compliments too much to heart.

'Earth to Meredith?' Anisha snapped her fingers in front of her face.

Meredith shook herself. 'How is project Save Port Karadow coming along?'

Anisha smiled. 'Better. Andy's on board with the treasure hunt idea – I'm going to have some of the stops close to our independent businesses, to increase footfall – and he's even OK with paying a bit more to get the lights earlier, but timing's still an issue. We should have the switch-on in the first week of December, and even that's a bit later than everyone's used to, but I don't know if it's possible.'

'Everyone will understand if it's later,' Meredith said. 'Just dial the festive factor up to the max, let the town know it's going to be incredible. You can start trailing it now.'

Anisha's eyes widened. 'You're right! I can get social media organized, tease what's coming. They don't need to know it's shrouded in secrecy because nothing's finalized.' She squeezed Meredith's arm, her expression brimming with compassion. 'I do appreciate your help with this. I know it's not easy for you.'

Meredith shrugged, her cheeks heating under her friend's scrutiny. 'If I wanted to avoid the whole thing, I could have booked a month-long holiday somewhere they don't do Christmas. Actually, why *didn't* I do that?'

'Because you're putting down roots. You and Crumble and Smudge, your role at Cornish Keepsakes.'

'And once Christmas is done with, we've got the launch of the new website, the online shop. I'm plugging that as hard as possible, and actually, the Christmas hampers – the ordinary ones that we're selling to non-VIPs – are very popular.'

'It makes sense.' Anisha nodded. 'People are moving away from individual gifts: they want to share time and food with their friends and family instead. A hamper – whether it's gin or Cornish cream tea themed – is perfect for that. Adrian's a smart guy, for all his bumbling and "jolly goods".'

'I was thinking that the other day. He's smarter than he wants us to believe.'

'Technophobe doesn't equal idiot.'

'And Tillie's going to let me do some promo with her,' Meredith said. 'A collaboration between the hampers and her blog.'

'That's great! You're on top of everything you need to be on top of.'

'And now I have someone who's going to be Christmassy on my behalf,' Meredith added. 'Seeing as he's so bloody insistent about it, I'm going to make Finn work his magic with our VIPs while I stand in the background, or stay in the car. You should have seen him with Bernie. He was something else!' She shook her head, remembering the wink he'd given her before he'd sauntered off down the hill.

'It's not a great example though, is it? If Bernie's heterosexual – and you know nothing to the contrary, do you?'

'Nope. I know nothing about her.'

'So Mr Sinfully Attractive, charm seeping out of his pores, blue-eyed Greek god-man, is obviously going to elicit a response from her.'

'I'm so nice, though. Always. I have tried really hard with her.'

'Maybe you need Finn to break the ice between you?'

'He would never let me live it down.'

'You're talking about him as if he's a friend.'

'We might almost be there with that,' Meredith said, thinking about their messages. 'He had coffee at mine; he was honest about my hideous gingerbread and I didn't mind at all. When we deliver the first hampers on Friday, I'm bound to find out more about him. If he drives me somewhere secluded and gets a shovel out of the boot, then I'll know he was after my job all along.'

'I really hope he isn't, for your sake.'

'Because you would miss me if I was buried in an anonymous shallow grave?'

'Because I think you'd be upset if he turned out to be not such a good guy.'

'I wouldn't be really.'

'I think you would.'

'Shush.'

'Right!' Emma called them back, and Meredith pressed her hand against her stomach. She wasn't sure if it was the prospect of doing a solo in the upcoming concert – was she really going to say yes? – or the thought of Finn using her, that was making her insides churn like an unbalanced washing machine.

She didn't take the most direct route home after choir practice, even though the sun was long gone and the clouds obliterated any possibility of stars or moonlight. Damp pavements shimmered under streetlights after the earlier rain, and Meredith's breath clouded in the air like mist.

She walked down to the harbour, where the water was inky and still, the boats ghostly shapes, the horizon impossible to pick out. But the sound was comforting. It was, she had decided long ago, one of the best things about the sea. Its noise was unrelenting, whether a gentle lapping or a forceful roar. It kept going, and it reminded her that, whatever she faced, she could keep going, too.

Right now, despite the overly Christmassy turn her life was taking – and it was still only the middle of November – she felt a twist of excitement. The two things that had, only an hour ago, felt like stumbling blocks in her happiness:

the challenge of a solo in the Christmas concert, and that on Friday she would spend real, uninterrupted time with Finn, now felt full of possibility. She could do the solo, if she forgot about it being festive and simply focused on the singing and, regardless of what she discovered about him, Finn wanted to spend time with her. He'd noticed her, and his attention had held. Whatever else happened, that was something she could take confidence from.

Her phone buzzed in her handbag and she took it out, already knowing it would be from him.

I had some gingerbread earlier. It made me miss yours.

She was grinning as she replied.

Shut up. It did not.

OK, it didn't. I was just using that as an opener. What you up to? Fx.

On my way back from choir.

She hit send before she questioned whether she wanted him to know that about her.

Church choir? Do you wear a long white gown? Those things can look surprisingly kinky in the right circumstances.

She laughed out loud, but pretended to be furious.

NOT church choir! Community choir. I'm wearing jeans, and they want me to do a solo.

She added a horrified face.

I assume this means you're brilliant, which doesn't surprise me. A singing mermaid. Who'd have thought?

She imagined him raising one of his expressive eyebrows, and her cheeks warmed. She typed:

What are you up to?

Booking the sleigh and reindeer for Friday. I figure if we go with three, that's not too bad for animal welfare. After all, what would reindeer do if they didn't have Christmas outings to go on?

Meredith sighed, her thumbs hovering over the screen. She had revealed something important about herself – her singing, her fear of the solo – and once again he'd deflected her questions with a joke. He wanted to keep himself at arm's length, while finding out everything about her. So far, she had let it happen, but on Friday, that would all change.

Still, she replied. She discovered that, even if part of her thought she should, she couldn't leave him hanging:

Three reindeer is overkill and you know it. What about a donkey instead?

She stood at the edge of the harbour, drinking in the dark

Cornish landscape, the waft of fish and chips and the constant, calming lapping of the waves, until her fingers had gone numb and her stomach gave up turning somersaults and demanded some fish and chips of its own.

Chapter Eight

Tommy had chosen the pub for their catch-up. It was the one he'd first got drunk in, the one he'd spent time in while he was moving incautiously from a child to an adult, and even though the ownership had changed and it was more like a fancy gastro-pub now, there were still signs that the Jolly Pirate was an old-school drinking establishment at heart.

There was the stained-glass window above the pool table that had been kept when the place had been refurbished; the chalkboard menu, the specials added to it daily in a swirling font, which had a few beer mats tacked to the corners, advertising local ales that had disappeared from the pumps years ago; and even though the floorboards looked recently polished, they creaked in a way that spoke of old age and countless pairs of feet.

'Meredith Verren,' said a familiar voice, 'if it isn't you, after all this time.'

Meredith rolled her eyes and accepted a hug from her

older brother. He squeezed her tightly, then stepped back and ruffled her hair, which made it fuzz unhelpfully. Then he got on his knees and scooped Crumble into his arms, sending the dog into a frenzy as he lavished him with affection.

Thomas – Tommy to his friends and family – walked a fine line between playing the superior big brother and acting like an idiot. He was taller than Meredith, with an easy, open face and hazel eyes, thick, expressive brows and brown hair that was a couple of shades darker than hers. He lived with his girlfriend Sarah in Somerset, only twenty minutes from where their mum had settled.

'What do you want to drink?' Meredith asked, and he pointed to where his pint was a third gone.

'This is my only one. Alcohol-wise, anyway. I'm good. Let me get you one.'

She asked for a red wine and sat on the fabric-covered bench, removing her coat and scarf, fussing with the scarf until he returned.

'Thank you,' she said. 'Cheers!' They clinked glasses. 'How are you? How's Sarah?'

Tommy gave her his lopsided grin. 'We're good. Great, in fact. Just finished having that work done on the house that I told you about. Sarah's spent the last year acting like an interior designer, but the place looks pretty good, and it's made her happy.'

'She's nesting,' Meredith said.

Tommy rested his arms along the back of the bench. 'She can do that.'

Meredith sat up straighter, watching her brother for signs of unease. He held her gaze, unwavering. 'You're really happy to—'

'For God's sake, Meredith! We've been together for five years. We've bought a house. It's all going really well.'

'How well?'

He smiled again, but this time it was a little nervous. 'I'm going to ask her to marry me on New Year's Eve.'

Meredith waited a beat, while the emotions – happiness, pride and envy flooded into her. 'Tommy! Oh my god! That is – I can't . . . come here.' She wrapped her arms around him, squeezing tightly, then they clinked glasses again. 'That's wonderful news. I'm so happy for you! Sarah's lovely, and she's perfect for you. She—'

'Keeps me in check. Yeah, I know.'

Meredith laughed. 'I wasn't going to say that. You complement each other. You'll be so happy.' She slapped her hands on her knees. 'What's your proposal plan?'

He took a sip of beer. 'We're going to a party: just a small one at a local barn, but they're having a firework display and a band. I was thinking, as the countdown to midnight starts, I could kiss her and then drop onto one knee.' He was staring at the quiz machine, though she knew he wasn't seeing it, instead picturing the moment he asked the woman he loved to marry him.

Meredith's throat closed with emotion. Her brother was happy. He'd always found things easier than her, especially the most challenging times, and this was one more example of how much further ahead he was.

'It sounds perfect,' she said. 'Have you told Mum yet? How is she?'

Tommy sat back with a sigh. 'She's good, I think. And I haven't told her yet. I thought I'd wait until after, when we could present it as a done deal.'

'In case, for any reason . . .'

He nodded. 'I don't want to get her hopes up, and then for Sarah to say no, or something.'

'She won't say no.' Meredith batted his arm. 'But I do get it.'

She looked at her brother, at the apprehension and excitement warring in his expression, and was flooded with love for him. She knew that, regardless of how much changed, how often life threw things at her that she wasn't expecting, she could always rely on him. He never made her feel like she owed him anything, and she was grateful for that.

The pub's sound system kicked up a notch and turned Christmassy, Bruce Springsteen singing about Santa coming to town, and Meredith went to the bar and got another wine for herself, and an alcohol-free beer for Tommy. She always offered him her tiny spare room when he came to visit, but he preferred to go home, saying he liked the quiet of driving at night on roads that were usually clear.

'Here you go,' she said, putting the Ghost Ship down.

'Ta. Now, tell me all about your job, and your swimming, and about training this guy.' He pointed at Crumble, who was asleep on the bench between them.

Meredith told him about Adrian, about his back injury and his strange walk, and his foibles about the VIP hampers, making Tommy laugh, and then about her marketing ideas, her 'Start Christmas Early' campaign, which she had thought of because she would rather leave it as late as possible, but knew that, for a lot of people, the opposite was true. She told him about her plan to swim to the next cove, at which point he said that she wasn't to even *think* of doing anything without talking to him, because he wanted to be there to see her do it.

At this, Meredith choked up, and had to excuse herself to go to the bathroom.

When she returned, Crumble had moved onto Tommy's lap, the two of them looking relaxed and content. The pub music moved onto Slade, a few punters sang along, and the door opened and shut, bringing in a chill blast of wind and the sound of tinkling bells. Meredith turned and saw three friends wearing Santa hats, one of them in an elf costume. The women laughed and waved at everyone before going to the bar.

'You're right about Christmas starting early,' Tommy said.

'Or they've all seen my campaign, and I've started a new trend.'

'Impressive. Especially considering that this is one instance where starting early doesn't mean you'll get it over with sooner; it'll just prolong the torment.'

She shrugged. 'I'm powering through. Staying focused and professional. The customers will get the most festive gifts and service from me: they won't know I'm a total Grinch.' She thought of Finn, how he'd promised to bring the Christmas cheer to the hamper deliveries.

Tommy stared into his drink, and she wondered if she'd been too snappy. But then he said, 'And do you, uhm . . .' He cleared his throat. 'Do you have anyone to help you train this guy?' He pointed at Crumble.

Meredith was caught off guard by the change of subject. 'I usually go to classes on my own,' she told him. 'Anisha's really busy with work at the moment.'

'What about someone to, uh . . . taste your terrible baking attempts?'

An image of Finn biting into her revolting gingerbread popped into her head, and she realized what her brother was trying to ask. She cringed at the speed with which her thoughts had turned to her blond, would-be saviour.

'Are you asking, Thomas Verren, if I have found myself a boyfriend?'

Tommy's cheeks turned scarlet.

'Why is that such a weird thing to ask?' She folded her arms. 'It's not like you were going to enquire how much sex I'm getting. You don't have to be so indirect.'

'Meredith!'

She sighed. 'No, there is nobody to help me train Crumble or eat my shitty cakes or hold hands with me during long walks on the beach.'

'You should go on some dates. Try online, maybe? That's what all the cool kids do these days.'

'Just by saying that, you've ruled yourself out of that category.'

'I'm settled, I don't need to be cool any more.'

'Yeah yeah, rub it in.' Meredith sipped her wine, and then, when Tommy didn't fill the quiet, she found herself adding, 'It's not that I don't want what you and Sarah, or Anisha and Nick, have, it's just that I'm working on other things. I have my house, my job – which is challenging, but mostly in all the right ways – and I don't want to overload myself with too much all at once. Crumble takes up a lot of time, and there's Smudge too. That's all the family I need right now. You know, aside from you and Mum.'

Tommy looked at her, his hands settled on her puppy's

back. 'You're sure? Maybe you'd find this time of year easier to deal with if you had someone to share it with.'

'I was with Taylor for two years and that didn't change how I felt about Christmas,' she pointed out. 'I hated spending it with his family. All that exuberance: the waste and the poor little partridge; eighteen different desserts; three-hundred-year-old sherry, or whatever it was.'

'That's because Taylor wasn't the right guy for you.'

'You know,' she said gently, 'a man isn't just for Christmas. I don't want to find someone purely so I can fill this hole you think I've got in my heart. That wouldn't be fair to them.'

Tommy raised his eyebrows. 'Melodramatic, much? That's not what I'm talking about, anyway. All I'm saying – and I know this isn't something you haven't realized, just something you might be willingly pushing to the back of your mind . . .'

Meredith held on to his weighty pause for two seconds before giving in. 'Go on, then.'

'It's really great being in love with someone,' he said. 'Being able to share stuff – good and bad – with another person. Letting them into every bit of you; bright and sunny, grey and gnarly. It's like having a cushion around you all the time. You know that whatever you have to face, or whatever mistakes you make, you're not on your own. Now – ' he held a hand up, stopping her from interrupting – 'I'm not saying you should find someone to make your life easier, or to inspire your missing Christmas joy, I'm just reminding you that being with someone is awesome in so many ways.' He drained his glass. 'There. My speech is done.'

'Good lecture,' Meredith said.

Tommy didn't reply, instead offering her another drink.

She accepted, and he deposited the beagle puppy on her lap so he could go to the bar. He returned with another alcohol-free beer and what looked like the world's largest glass of red wine, and Meredith decided, silently, that she wouldn't heed his advice, because finding love wasn't an item to be ticked off a to-do list. It had to be spontaneous; it had to just *happen*. She wasn't the type of person who looked for something meaningful by swiping right on her phone.

It didn't make her feel any better that, while her brother had been giving her his best *Twelfth Night* impression, she had been picturing Finn leaning against her kitchen door frame, sipping coffee in her armchair, standing outside another pub, not too far from here, his cheeks pink from the cold. He was helping her – that was all – and besides, he was far too outgoing for her, not in any way her type.

He would help her deliver her hampers, then his holiday would end and he'd go back to his bachelor pad and swanky London restaurant. No, Meredith wasn't looking for someone to share her life with right now, and even if she was in that place, it wouldn't be with someone like Finn.

Chapter Nine

'For you,' Finn said, when Meredith climbed into the passenger seat of the large orange Audi on Friday afternoon. It was raining outside, and they had hurried to load the hampers into the – very sizeable – boot, while Finn managed to look stylish despite wearing a pair of silver sparkly reindeer antlers. Other than that, he was in a chunky black cable-knit jumper, dark jeans and his usual heavy boots.

Meredith was settling into the comfort of the leather and the warmth blasting from the heater, wondering how to admit his car was much more suited to their task without sounding truculent, when he held out another pair of 'antlers'. These were candy canes rather than deer; gleaming pink and white stripes, hooked over at the ends, and slightly flexible so that they jiggled merrily when Finn waggled them. He kept his expression serious as she took them.

'They won't fit in here.' She pointed to where his own headgear was bending precariously against the car roof.

He swiped them off, then put both pairs in the compartment below the navigation system. 'We'll put them on when we get to destination number one. Where is it?'

'It's the Keegans' house, a little way out of town,' Meredith said, consulting the directions Adrian had given her. 'They live in a barn extension with their three children. He's some kind of ex-TV presenter, apparently. This is the fullest hamper; I thought the family would get a lot of use out of it.'

'"Start Christmas Early",' Finn said, and Meredith gave him a sharp look.

His smile was half-hearted, and she got the sense that he wasn't quite as cocky as usual, and as if, now it came to it, he was doubting the plan he'd barrelled her into.

'You've been spying on me,' she said.

'I've been doing my Cornish Keepsakes research,' he corrected. 'I'm here to help you promote the business, so I need to get the tone right.'

'Do hamper deliveries need a tone?' Meredith asked, as Finn started the car and it purred quietly to life. 'We arrive at the address, we knock on the door, hand over the hamper with a smile, leave.'

Finn laughed. 'I can see why you need me. This way?' They'd reached the end of the road and he gestured left.

'Yes,' Meredith said. 'Up here a bit, then when we get to Clotted Cream Cottage, we take the road just after it.'

'Clotted Cream Cottage?' Finn set the wipers to fast as the rain came down harder, the view ahead of them a kaleidoscope of headlights and water.

'It's a beautiful house along here,' she explained. 'My brother and I named it years ago, because it's painted cream, and we were probably in a cream-with-everything phase at the time. It has a climbing rose with fat, scarlet blooms that come out in the summer, and a red door to match. It's like something out of a picture book, but I've never seen anyone come in or out.'

'You have thoughts about it, though.'

Meredith shrugged. 'It's one of those holiday homes that's abandoned for most of the year, even though it's big enough to house a family of five. I'm envious of whoever owns it, and also a little bit cross with them. They should use it more.'

'This one?' Finn said quietly, as the pale house appeared as a ghostly shape through the rain-streaked glass. The rose bush was currently a fan of dark branches, making it more horror film than picture postcard, but some dainty gold lights strung along the windowsills could easily change that.

'This is it,' Meredith confirmed. 'Go left here, and the Keegans live about half a mile up this road. I'll tell you when to turn.'

'Great.' Finn kept driving, the quiet between them not that surprising when the rain was so loud, but she still felt a flicker of disappointment. This wasn't the Finn she was used to, the one who seemed to shimmer most of the time. But he was concentrating on driving; his lips pressed tightly together, his gaze set straight ahead. It was a shitty afternoon.

'These gates here,' she said eventually. 'You just need to—'

Finn swung expertly through them, followed the curved driveway and stopped in the wide space in front of the barn. A trail of blue lights danced around the double doors, and there was a white, fibre-optic Christmas tree in an upstairs window. Through one of the glass panes that flanked the dark wooden entrance, Meredith could see an umbrella stand and a sculpture of what looked like a Great Dane, at least life-sized, black and gleaming and standing to attention.

'It's stone I think, rather than resin,' Finn said, clearly following her gaze. 'Impressive work.'

'They're impressive people, by all accounts,' Meredith replied, 'which is why they're on Adrian's VIP list.'

They sat in the car while the rain pounded on the roof. Nobody inside the house seemed to have noticed their arrival, and around them, in the afternoon that had turned so dark it was almost night, the trees shimmied and shivered in the wind, leaves jumping in time to the heavy drops falling through the canopy.

Finn shifted so he was facing her, and when he spoke his voice was loud, as if he was shaking himself out of a daydream. 'So what's the plan? Do we have a spiel?'

Meredith shook her head. 'Get out of car, run to boot, collect hamper, run to door, knock on door, when they *open* door—'

'Are you a robot?'

'What?'

'God.' Finn ran a hand down his face. 'I knew you needed help, but you didn't tell me quite how terminal it was.'

'It is *not* terminal.'

'Run. To. Boot,' he repeated, doing a great impression of a Dalek. 'Deposit. Christmas. Thing. What. Is. Christmas?'

'Shut up.' Meredith slapped his arm, but she was laughing.

108

'Right then,' he said, his low, smooth voice startling her after the staccato words. 'Watch and learn.'

He took the candy-cane antlers and slipped them on her head. His warm fingertips brushed behind her ears, and the sensation was so nice, so surprising, that Meredith shivered. She looked up and their eyes held. Finn's lips were slightly parted, his brows lowered, and his fingers lingered for a couple of seconds that, Meredith thought, she would remember forever.

Then he took his hands back, jammed his own antlers on his head, and the spell was broken. He pushed open his door, and the sound of the rain went from rushing river to angry sea.

Together, they ran to the boot and Finn pushed a button that made it slide open agonizingly slowly. Meredith took out the hamper and, wordlessly, Finn took it from her. They hurried to the front door, the porch partly protecting them from the elements, though a cold slick of rain found its way off the roof and down Meredith's neck. She shivered, and Finn pressed the doorbell and held his finger on it.

A few seconds later the door swung inwards, and Mr Keegan, with salt-and-pepper hair and expensive, frameless glasses, a slight paunch visible in his seaweed-coloured jumper, peered out at them.

'Hello?' His gaze went to the hamper in Finn's arms.

'Good afternoon, Mr Keegan,' Finn said. 'We're Merry and Finn, here to get your festivities off to a cracking start, and to wish you a very Merry Christmas, from Adrian Flockhart and all of us at Cornish Keepsakes. We did have a carol prepared, but the weather's determined to outdo us on this occasion!' He held the hamper forward, not in a thrusting, imposing way, but just enough that Mr Keegan automatically took it from him, his expression a mix of surprise and pleasure.

'From Adrian?' he repeated, and Meredith thought her boss would dance a jig if he knew Mr Keegan thought of him in first-name terms. Or maybe they were best buddies, and she had been doing him another disservice.

'Yes,' Meredith said, when Finn didn't step in. 'That's right. He wanted to . . . to wish you a Merry Christmas.' She winced: Finn had already said that. 'And to remind you, to . . . you and your family, to . . . to Start Christmas Early!' She smiled, but it was weak. She wiggled a bit, hoping to enliven her candy canes, and Finn shot her a bemused glance. Mr Keegan was peering at her through his fogged-up glasses. His smile had slipped slightly.

'It's just a few bits and pieces to get you started,' Finn added, taking back control. 'Hand-picked especially for you and your family. If you have any queries, or want to know where you can get hold of more of what's inside, then please get in touch.' He handed over a business card, and in the pooling light from the hall, Meredith saw it was one of Adrian's. She wanted to update them, knowing that her boss wouldn't relinquish his hold on these little cardboard hellos, even if they were a bit old-fashioned. How had Finn got hold of them? He'd been palming it like a magician.

'Will do,' Mr Keegan said. 'And thank you, both of you. This is incredibly generous. I'll be sure to thank Adrian, too.'

'Excellent,' Finn said. 'Now, we'll leave you to your

afternoon. I'm sure you could do without a flood in your hallway.'

'Indeed!' Mr Keegan chortled, responding to Finn just as Bernie had. Just as everyone had.

Finn moved back and, a step behind again, Meredith followed him. Her foot sank ankle-deep into a puddle. She resisted the urge to swear as the rain hit them full pelt and her left foot went numb with cold. As Mr Keegan nodded goodbye and took himself and his hamper into his house, she thought she felt Finn squeeze her hand – just for a second – and then they were running to the orange car, climbing inside and dripping onto the leather upholstery.

She risked a glance at him. His curls had tightened and darkened, and he looked more serious, somehow. His cheekbones were prominent in the car's low lighting, his eyelashes dark and glossy as he turned to her, a water droplet running down his cheek. Her mind replayed the 'fingers behind the ear' moment, and she silently cursed it.

'How do you think that went?' he asked when they'd both caught their breath, the heater turned up to max so that the sound competed with the battering rain.

'You're behaving like some kind of Christmas coach,' she said, knowing what was coming. 'That isn't your role!' She'd spoken too sharply, and he dropped his gaze to his knees.

'Sorry.' He looked genuinely contrite.

Meredith sighed. 'You started by calling me Merry. It caught me off guard.'

'I prefer Red, but you have to admit you have a Christmas-appropriate name.'

111

'Which you knew I didn't want to use. You may as well have called us Mr and Mrs S. Claus!'

'You'd have preferred that?' he asked lightly. 'You know I could get hold of the outfits.'

'I wouldn't prefer that! But how did you . . .?' She knew the answer to her question. He was a master at this: able to block out the hideous weather, the water pelting him from all angles, and focus on the object of his attention. It was a gift.

'How did I what?'

'Never mind. I know I was hopeless. I haven't got the skills.'

'They're easy skills, talking and smiling. Holding the other person in your beam. I know you can do it, Red.'

She watched the blue lights round the Keegans' front door as they danced through their different phases. She thought of Anisha, working on her Christmas plans on this dingy Friday afternoon at the Bodmin office. 'Meredith,' she corrected him quietly. 'And how do you know I can do that, when you've just seen me demonstrate that I'm incapable of it?'

He shook his head. 'You're not. I promise you.'

'Flattery, on this occasion, will get you nowhere.'

'It's not flattery. I've seen you do it.'

'Do what?'

'Hold someone in the beam of your attention.'

She wrinkled her nose. They should leave now, in case Mr Keegan happened to notice that they were lingering outside his house. 'Who?' she asked.

He didn't reply immediately, and the heater and rain crowded into the quiet. Then Finn spoke, loud and clear but with a hesitation that Meredith picked up on even

112

though it was a single word. 'Me,' he said. It stunned her into silence until they were back on the road, and Finn was asking her, 'Where next?' as if nothing but idle chatter had passed between them.

Until that second, Meredith hadn't realized she had a beam, let alone one she'd been inadvertently shining on Finn. If that was the case, she was going to have to be a lot more self-aware in future.

Cecily Talbot's house was also beautiful, but there was nothing of ancient Cornwall in the modern stone mansion with its electronic wooden gates and fountain in the circular gravel drive. Meredith wondered how many of these millionaire pads there were, hidden in secluded pockets throughout the county. If she had to choose – if she ever had that luxury – she would have picked Clotted Cream Cottage over the two she'd visited today. There was something humble and honest about it, despite its size. She liked that it was on the edge of town; that it wasn't hidden away as if it was too important for prying eyes.

She hadn't told Finn everything: how she and Tommy had made up ghosts who lived within the walls in lieu of real people, Tommy weaving tragic stories that were plausible to the point where a much younger Meredith was both desperate to – and yet afraid to – walk past it, preparing herself for seeing a figure – shadowy or see-through – drift past the window. Port Karadow had been the closest town to their farmhouse growing up, and she had always looked forward to their family trips there, intent on hearing her brother's latest tale.

'Who's this?' Finn asked, stopping the Audi behind the

fountain. The rain had abated, leaving behind a sky banked with layers of cloud; white to grey to charcoal, promising more drama before too long.

'Cecily Talbot.'

Finn drummed his fingers on the steering wheel. 'Should I know her? You said that like I should know who she is.'

Meredith shook her head. 'No, you shouldn't know her. She's just . . .' *Intimidating*, she wanted to say, but didn't. 'She's in her forties, I think, but you wouldn't know it. She's the daughter of someone who made a lot of money doing something London-y.'

'London-y?' Finn laughed. 'So you've done your research, then?'

He was relaxing, his jaw not quite so rigid as it had been. She could see more of him now the clouds had shifted. She liked him better when he wasn't fully in shadow, but at this moment, she also didn't.

'You know,' she said, the uncomfortable feelings from their earlier, charged moment solidifying into anger, 'most chauffeurs wouldn't hold me to account about any of this. I should be on my own, getting on with it and – OK – perhaps not charming everyone into a stupor, but it would be fine and I wouldn't have this . . . this scrutiny, and I'd feel less like an idiot!' She flung open the door. 'I don't owe you anything, Finn! Her dad was in something corporate, banking or whatever, and none of that is important. I've matched all the items in the hamper to her perfectly. She's going to love it, and I doubt she'll care that I don't know exactly what her dad does, as long as she gets the candles and scones and cream, and the message from Adrian that he thinks she's worth getting a gift.'

114

Before he had a chance to respond, she got out and stomped round to the boot, found the button that opened it and yanked out the hamper. She was at Cecily's front door before Finn had left the driver's seat. Sod him, she thought. She had known that this would be a bad idea. She should have trusted her instincts.

Chapter Ten

Cecily Talbot was wearing a cashmere jumpsuit. She had long dark hair in gentle waves that stopped just above her boobs, and make-up that made her look fresh-faced, but had probably taken hours.

'Cecily,' Meredith said warmly, as Finn came to stand beside her. Cecily's gaze immediately went to him, and for a moment Meredith felt disheartened, but then she decided *no*. No, she wasn't going to give up. Finn might be annoying, he might have treated her like his protégée, but he was also right. She had been rubbish with Mr Keegan, and *she* was the one who wanted a future at Cornish Keepsakes, not him. These people were important to Adrian, and he'd trusted her. Besides, she should want to do a good job for herself, as much as anyone else.

With her candy-cane antennae wobbling in the breeze, and with Cecily transfixed by Finn, Meredith tried for festive.

'Merry Christmas!' she said.

Cecily looked at her.

'I'm Merry – Meredith – and this is Finn. We've brought this for you, from Cornish Keepsakes, with Adrian Flockhart's kindest regards.'

Cecily's eyes crinkled at the edges. 'Adrian? What a sweetie. This is for me?'

'Yes! For you.' Meredith held it out, the weight making her shoulders ache.

Cecily took it and put it on the floor behind her. There were no signs of Christmas in her blush-pink hallway, but there was a distinct fragrance that could have been the Ember-scented St. Eval candle. She'd picked Orange and Cinnamon for Cecily's hamper, but she was pleased that at least some of the gifts would be welcome, and she hadn't been spouting hopeful nonsense to Finn in the car a moment ago.

'November's a bit grim,' she improvised, 'especially right now.' She gestured to the sky. 'So we're encouraging everyone to get into the festive spirit early; brighten up these dull days with some cheer! After all, the supermarkets start in September – why can't we have some of their fun?' She smiled, and was surprised when Cecily returned it.

'You're right,' Cecily said. 'I've been glum today, and I'm sure part of it's the weather. I was going to put on a horror film, but I'm not sure I want to do that alone.' Her gaze drifted back to Finn, and Meredith felt a pang of sympathy. Was she really on her own in this big, secluded house? Regardless of its obvious grandeur, Meredith would hate that. Bernie might not be the friendliest neighbour, but at least she had the benefit of knowing there were people close by if she ever needed help.

Meredith waited for Finn to step in with his charm gun

firing, but he didn't. When she glanced at him, he was looking at her, not Cecily. He gave her a barely there nod.

'Why not put on a Christmas film instead, and tuck into some of the goodies in the hamper?' Meredith said to Cecily. 'That'll cheer you up.'

Cecily shifted her weight. 'Which one would you recommend?'

Meredith scrabbled through the bleak wasteland of Christmas films stored in her mind. '*Home Alone*? You're never too old to watch that. Or *Die Hard*, if you want something meatier. You know, I always had this argument with my da—' The memory popped, unbidden, into her head. She thought she saw Finn's gaze sharpen at her hesitation, but she must have imagined it. 'My dad,' she finished, then cleared her throat. 'He said there was no way it was a Christmas film, but of course it is. It all happens on Christmas Eve; there's the tree, and the *Ho Ho Ho* machine-gun jumper.' She had laughed uproariously at that bit, her chest puffed out with pride at being allowed to watch such a violent film a few years before her eighteenth birthday.

Cecily nodded, her attention fully on Meredith. 'Yeah, that's a great plan. My date cancelled on me, and I could do with snuggling up with a movie and some snacks. Aaah, guys!' She embraced Meredith, her scent like peaches and cream, and then Finn. Rather than step into it as she had imagined he would, he remained rigid while Cecily hugged him. 'You've made my day! I'll send Adrian a little note. And don't worry,' she added, picking up the hamper, 'I'll pop it on Instagram and tag you in it.' She winked and waved, waited until they had turned away, then Meredith heard the quiet clunk of the door closing behind them.

Finn put his arm around her shoulder as they walked back to the car. 'See!' he said, shaking her slightly, 'there's the beam I knew you had. You were masterful!'

'Masterful,' she repeated scornfully. 'No need to go overboard. But at least I didn't freeze.'

'You were good! Great. You dug deep and found the cheer. I'm proud of you, Red. She's going to spread the word, just as Adrian hoped she would. He's a canny bastard, your boss.'

'Meredith,' she protested, but she wasn't sure he'd heard her, because he just squeezed her shoulder and got into the driver's seat.

'Right. Where now?'

'We have one more visit to make today, and this one I'm actually a bit excited about.'

'Oh? Why's that then?'

'Because it's Laurie Becker!' She grinned at Finn, but he didn't return it. 'You know,' she went on, 'Laurie Becker, the actor? She was in that American soap, *Emerald Beach*, and there was a film with Helen Mirren not too long ago – they played sisters – but she's got Cornish roots, I think. She has a house here, anyway – close to Port Karadow. Needless to say, she's one of Adrian's VIPs.' She wondered if she'd be able to play it cool and not ask any star-struck questions. She hadn't exactly been suave and sophisticated with Mr Keegan.

Finn nodded, wiping non-existent dust off the steering wheel. 'We have time to fit this one in today?'

Meredith laughed. 'It's only half past three, and I've got Adrian's directions here.' She scrolled through the information he'd given her, his painstaking list of how to get to each house and which order to do them in, which Meredith was grateful for because putting postcodes in satnavs couldn't be relied on, especially not in the wilds of Cornwall where they often led you down deserted farm tracks. 'It's out towards the coast, near . . .' Her words trailed away as she read through the directions. 'Oh my god.'

'What is it?' Finn sounded alarmed.

'The white house,' she murmured. 'Of course.' From Adrian's instructions, it was clear that Laurie Becker lived in her treasured house overlooking Charmed Cove. She should have realized it would belong to someone like that.

'Are you OK?' Finn asked. 'We could always take this one another time if you need to get back.'

She shook her head and looked up from her phone. Finn's face was pale in the afternoon gloom. 'I know exactly where we're going,' she said, unable to hide her smile. For the first time, she was pleased that Adrian had given her this job.

They drove in silence apart from Meredith giving Finn directions. He seemed unusually subdued, as if he'd given her all his sparkle congratulating her about Cecily Talbot, saving none for himself.

They took the road that led to the scruffy car park above Charmed Cove, and Meredith said, 'There should be a turning here, just on the left.' It was already starting to get dark, the lights picking out the hedgerows more vividly than they had done even half an hour ago. 'Here it is.'

Finn drove down the road that was little more than a track, getting slower until Meredith could see the white paintwork of the house she had come to love. It had a wide front door painted buttercup yellow, with frosted glass panels either side, and a winter jasmine climbing up towards the roof. It was even more beautiful close up. Finn stopped the car at the edge of the driveway.

Meredith turned to him, surprised. 'I'm sure Laurie won't mind if we park properly. We're only going to be a few minutes.'

'I have to make a call,' he said.

'What?'

'I just realized I was supposed to call my friend hours ago. I should probably do that while you deliver this hamper.'

Meredith laughed nervously. 'You're sure you trust me to do it by myself?'

He put her candy-cane antlers back on her head, though there was none of the gentle finger-stroking there had been at the Keegans' house. 'This is your gig, Meredith. And I really do need to make this call.' He waggled his mobile, as if that was evidence enough.

'OK.' She was confused by his sudden change of heart, but now wasn't the time to question it. She got out, took the hamper from the boot, and walked up to the elegant front door.

She balanced the hamper on her knee and reached up to press the doorbell, hearing the sound of tyres on gravel behind her. She turned and watched, incredulous, as Finn did a neat three-point turn. Was he leaving her here? He came to a stop in the mouth of the driveway, as if preparing for a quick exit.

'Hello?'

Meredith spun round and almost dropped the hamper.

'H-hello,' she said. She recognised Laurie Becker instantly. She was in her late fifties, tall and slim and wearing a loose, peach-coloured dress and a soft grey cardigan. Her hair was

121

blonde and cut into a chin-length bob, the strands slightly frizzy. She had striking features, warm brown eyes and a film-star quality, but she didn't seem remotely put out by Meredith's appearance on her doorstep. 'I'm from Cornish Keepsakes in town! Merry . . . M-Meredith.'

'Oh! That darling gift shop? What can I do for you, Meredith?'

'I wanted to give you this.' She lifted the hamper up. 'As a present, from Adrian Flockhart. It's . . . we thought you could get into the Christmas spirit early! Cheer up these dark November days with a bit of Christmas sparkle.'

'You know,' Laurie said, 'that's an excellent idea. How clever of you all! Do you want to come in? I'm sure there are some goodies in here we could sample now.'

Meredith was torn. If Finn had been with her, she would have been tempted to say yes. Laurie looked over her shoulder at the car, her brows lowering slightly. Meredith was pleased with her reaction to the hamper, and felt a warm glow that the gift she had put together was so welcome. She realised that she would have loved to go inside, help her unpack it and tell her more about each locally-sourced item. It was an amazing opportunity – a woman she genuinely admired, in the house she had gazed at and dreamed about for years – and she had to turn it down.

'That's so kind of you,' she said, 'but these are all for you, and I have more deliveries to make.' That wasn't true, but it was a plausible excuse. 'I hope you enjoy them, and if you ever need anything from Cornish Keepsakes, if you'd like to buy some gifts for your friends, then please get in touch.' She didn't have a business card with her, so pointed to the hamper. 'Our details are on the label.'

'Wonderful,' Laurie said. 'This is very generous of you.' She gave Meredith a warm smile and squeezed her arm. 'I hope you have a lovely evening.'

'Thank you,' Meredith replied. Was that a weird thing for Laurie to have said? 'I love your house,' she blurted, which was definitely a weird thing to say. 'Sorry,' she added. 'Here.' She thrust the hamper into Laurie's arms, returned her smile and then hurried to the car. 'Drive drive drive!' she said as she climbed in, only half-joking.

'OK?' Finn asked, glancing behind him. He'd obviously finished his phone call.

'She seems incredibly lovely,' Meredith said. 'I'm sure I just made a massive fool of myself. But before that, she invited us – me – in! If you'd come with me, we could be sitting in her beautiful house right now, drinking tea and talking about Hollywood.'

Finn started the engine. 'Sorry,' he said quietly.

'Did your call go OK? Is something wrong?'

'Everything's great.' He gave her one of his winning smiles but, even in the car's gloomy interior, Meredith could see that it didn't reach his eyes. 'Are you heading back to the office now?'

She shook her head. 'Nope. We are officially done for the day.'

'Great, because I'm taking you to the pub to celebrate.'

'That wasn't part of the deal, was it?'

'No, but as you're impressing upon people, it's time to start the festivities. I won't ask you to drink mulled wine or wear your candy canes, but I am taking you for a cele- bratory, entirely non-Christmassy drink.' His smile faltered. 'Unless you have plans?'

'No plans,' Meredith said. 'But I can't leave Crumble at home all evening. He's been looked after by Daisy, the dog-sitter, today, because I forgot to ask you if I could have him in your car, but I need to go home.'

'You could have brought him,' Finn said. 'And we can go and get him now. The place I'm taking you is dog-friendly.'

Meredith chewed the inside of her cheek. She didn't have another excuse. Did she want one? 'OK then,' she said.

'Great,' he replied.

They turned onto the main road, leaving Laurie Becker's beautiful house behind, Finn drumming a beat on the steering wheel as he drove.

He slowed the car as they approached what looked like a rundown farm in the middle of nowhere. There was a thin light leaching around whatever covered the one window Meredith could see, and a few cars parked in a patch of gravel to the side of the building. As they got closer, she noticed a pub sign swinging gently in the breeze, though without its own illumination she couldn't see what it said.

'I know I did an awful job with Mr Keegan,' she murmured, 'but I don't know if I deserve a visit to your murder den.'

'Murder den?' Finn shot her a grin before pulling into a space next to a beaten-up Land Rover.

'You're not trying to claim this is a commercial establishment, are you?'

'It is!' Finn said, then sat back and narrowed his eyes, as if seeing the building from her perspective. He ran a hand through his hair, which had dried and frizzed in the artificial air from the car's heater. 'It is,' he said again. 'It's . . .

the current owner bought it after the pub failed, and I suppose he opted for something a bit left-field.'

'You don't say.' Meredith tightened her grip on Crumble, who they had picked up from home and who was now sitting quietly in her lap.

'Give it a chance, OK? If it's really awful, we'll go somewhere else.'

'You don't think it's awful, otherwise you wouldn't have brought me here.'

Finn paused with the door open. 'Sometimes I surprise myself with my strange tastes.'

'That isn't reassuring.' Meredith followed him, carrying Crumble against her chest.

Neither of them bothered with coats, instead hurrying to the door of the pub. Finn pushed it open, and Meredith was met with a soft glow and murmuring voices as she stepped inside. She could feel him behind her as her eyes widened, taking it all in. So much for no Christmas, she thought, staring at a ceiling covered in metallic snowflakes. They were the kind that were cut out of paper or card, their unique patterns created with scissor snips, and they were a variety of colours, twisting merrily in the gust of wind Meredith and Finn had brought in with them.

When she could tear her gaze away from the ceiling, she saw that the room was decorated in a simple, rustic style: white plaster walls, wooden benches and tables, a few haphazardly placed cushions the only nod to comfort. The bar was similar, wooden and unvarnished. It was like something from a country fair – rough around the edges, with an almost temporary feel. But the bar was well-stocked, it smelled of fruity ale and mulled wine, and the few customers seemed to be her age or slightly older; groups of friends or couples.

'It's like some kind of underground place,' she said. 'In Cornwall. Is it a secret? Have you bought me somewhere clandestine? What's with the snowflakes?'

Finn shrugged, but she could see that he was pleased with her reaction. 'Must be following the Cornish Keepsakes social media,' he said.

'Touché. Let me get you a drink.'

'You can find a table – I'm getting them. What are you having?'

'White wine please.'

'Not mulled?'

She gave him her sternest glare.

'Coming right up. Make yourself at home.'

He went to the bar and Meredith turned in a slow circle, then homed in on a bench to the side of a lit fireplace, the heat reaching out as she got closer, drawing her in. It was obviously a prime spot, the benches covered in velvet cushions that should have looked chintzy but somehow didn't, and she wondered if the other customers had performed some kind of circuit, sitting here until they overheated, then moving away.

The few minutes Meredith had spent getting drenched that afternoon made her want to stay here all night. Despite the car's efficient heater, the cold had worked its way into her bones. Crumble also seemed eager to be close to the flames, even though he'd been in her cosy front room all afternoon.

She took in the details of the strange place Finn had brought her to. If he didn't come here very often, then how did he know about it? As her chilled limbs unfurled, so did her curiosity. She wanted to know everything about the man who had given up his time to be Christmassy with her, tried to coax it out of her. If he felt at home here, would he open up to her?

She watched him at the bar. He had wide shoulders but a narrow waist, his cable-knit jumper hugging his frame so she could see the definition of muscle, the hint of biceps. His jeans were a shade darker up to the knee, showing he was as soggy as she was. His hair was drying out, the curls at his nape tight, the blond strands shining under the blizzard of reflective snowflakes that acted like a hundred tiny glitter balls, spinning above them. He was laughing with the barman in a way that suggested they knew each other.

Taking out her phone, Meredith checked there were no messages from Adrian or Enzo. She didn't want any distractions; she wanted this time with Finn to be uninterrupted. She started writing a message to Anisha, ensuring that she would be forced to relive the events of the afternoon with her later. A quiet voice in her head whispered that these were both concerning signs; her desire to be alone with him, and her need to talk about him with her best friend. Still, she wrote:

Finn bought me to some crazy pub in the middle of nowhere! If this is the end, just know you were my best friend and I loved you dearly. ☺ xx

'Here you go.' Finn put the drinks down and, even with the three dots of Anisha's imminent reply pulsing on the screen, Meredith put her phone away.

'You're not having mulled wine either?' She pointed at his glass of clear, fizzing liquid.

'I'm driving,' Finn said.

'Fair point.' She bumped her glass against his, then sipped her wine. It was crisp and cool and slightly tart. Finn leaned back on the bench, his fingers absent-mindedly running over a fabric cushion. 'We did a good job this afternoon,' she said into the quiet.

He nodded. 'We made some VIPs pretty happy, and it's clear Adrian's plan is going to generate some interest in the hampers. You're more about the digital side of things, though?'

Meredith pushed her damp hair off her forehead. 'I know a personal touch is important, but we can't give that to everyone, and you don't get anywhere these days without an online presence. If Adrian wants Cornish Keepsakes to stay successful, he needs to have both. We're launching the new website and online shop in January, but we'll still have the physical shop, the presence in town that's so important to him. I suppose with a restaurant, while you can promote it online and get bookings that way, you're all about the personal. And you're good at it, obviously.'

Finn let out a long exhale. 'It was drummed into me, how important relationships are. Even if it only lasts thirty seconds, you're breaking down barriers, finding the common ground that will get you whatever you're after, so you have to be fully committed.'

Meredith hid her surprise. It was such a clinical way to look at things. 'So all your charm is manufactured?' She wondered what he wanted from their relationship.

'No,' Finn said, his voice firm. 'This is all me. I just try

128

and make every interaction count, and I think of it as a two-way thing. Not just what I can get from someone, but what I want to give them, too. I took that drumming I was given, and I adapted it to suit me.' He shrugged. 'Anyway, it wouldn't work if it wasn't authentic.'

Meredith took a long swallow of wine. 'So none of it is manufactured? You're spinning me in circles.' She laughed, the nervous sound slipping into the space between them.

Finn leaned forward, his elbows on his knees. His blond stubble glinted in the soft light. 'Sorry. I don't know why I said any of that. It's just . . . my job is about making connections with people. I'm usually very good at it.' He frowned. 'I don't often spin people in circles. Or – they don't tell me I do.'

'I'm sure you spin a lot of people in circles,' Meredith muttered.

'What?'

She shook her head. 'Who was it who drummed that into you? About making connections to get what you want? Your dad?'

'No, he's more a "watch from the background" sort of guy. What about your dad and *Die Hard*? Is it a Christmas tradition that you try and make him watch it and he puts on *It's a Wonderful Life* instead?'

Meredith picked up her wine, but she didn't think she'd be able to swallow past the thickness in her throat. 'Not really. It just happened the once, but I would still argue that it's a Christmas film.'

'Does it slip past your embargo?' he asked gently.

'Embargo.' She chuckled, but it sounded false to her own ears.

'Why don't you like Christmas?' His voice was soft, as if he knew he was approaching something skittish that would run away the moment it got scared. 'What is it about sparkly snowflakes, goodwill and carols that you find so unappealing?'

'I'm doing a solo in the carol concert,' she reminded him.

'Are you nervous about it?'

'No. Yes. I love singing, but carols aren't really my thing.'

'Why doesn't that surprise me?' He grinned, but it faded quickly. 'You can't hate gifting, though. The hampers are put together by someone who has a good eye and understands luxury and desire perfectly. Are you telling me Adrian assembles them and you just flog them?'

Meredith's breath stalled at his mention of desire. She understood it right this moment, that was for sure. 'Have you seen the ties he wears?' she asked.

'There you go, then.' He held her gaze and she returned it, not saying anything else. He gave a frustrated sigh and ran a hand through his hair, the heel of his palm scrubbing at his forehead.

She was purposely holding back, and so was he, but despite that, Meredith felt drawn to him, as if invisible tendrils were reaching out between them, building a connection that she hadn't sanctioned.

'If you don't come to Cornwall very often,' she said, breaking their stalemate, 'how do you know about this place?'

'It's my aunt's favourite haunt,' he admitted. 'She likes things a little out of the ordinary. She's . . . eccentric. Most of my roadmap of Cornwall is put together from the places she's shown me. I'm passing her things – her car, this pub – off as my own.'

130

'You seem overly disappointed that you're not a trailblazer in this distant land of fair Cornwall.' She slipped into a broad Cornish accent, and Finn laughed.

'I want to give you something of me,' he said, then clenched his jaw, as if he regretted saying it out loud.

'But you are,' she replied. 'You've let me have you this afternoon; driving me around, turning on the Christmas charm. You've made the first round of hamper deliveries easier.' Even as she said it, she knew she still wasn't getting all of him.

'And the next round? You want my help with that, too?'

She nodded. 'Please. I mean, your car . . .'

'My aunt's car.'

'The schmoozing is all yours, Finn.'

'Great,' he said, not looking at her. 'Schmoozing.'

'Tell me something, then.' She hadn't meant to be so forceful, but if he was going to sit here and be annoyed with himself for being disingenuous, somehow, there was a simple way to fix that. 'Tell me something that's just you: just Finn. It can't be that difficult.'

He hesitated for a second, then closed the distance between them. 'When I first saw you, on the beach that morning, I didn't think you were a mermaid.'

Meredith laughed. 'You can try harder than that. It's not as if—'

'I did think you were a dolphin though,' he went on. 'Your wetsuit, dark and shiny, this elegant curve in the water. I don't know which bit of you I saw first, but—' he shook his head. 'It was like a shot of magic. There I was, early morning, with the light you only ever get at that time of day, and only where the sea and sky meet: the reflections, that haunting glow that dusts everything with gold; the pure air that reaches every atom of your body. Already, I was on a high from being there. And then . . .'

'A shot of magic.' She had meant to sound derisive, because this was unicorns and rainbows stuff. Except he hadn't made it sound ridiculous or sappy, he'd made it sound sincere, and her words came out hushed, as if she was buying into the moment.

He nodded. 'And then, there you were.'

'But I wasn't a dolphin – you must have been disappointed. I broke the magic.'

He gave her a wry smile. 'No, you didn't.'

Meredith sipped her wine. She didn't know what to make of him. *This* was what he wanted to give her? Not the name of the restaurant he worked in, or what he did with friends in London on his time off, or what he wanted out of life. She shook her head, frustration chasing the wine down inside her.

'What?' he asked.

'I can't get a hold of you,' she said, more honest than she'd intended. 'Who are you?'

'I'm Finn. Twenty-eight years old. Blond, blue-eyed. Hiding in Cornwall.'

'What are you hiding from?'

'Expectations,' he said. 'Responsibilities. Decisions I know I need to make. It's not very honourable behaviour.'

'And yet you're not doing anything about it,' she said. 'Making no moves to return to London.' She thought of him hightailing it back there, leaving Cornwall and her behind, and those tendrils stretched further, clawing at him.

'No, I'm enjoying the simplicity of not having to deal with it. For now, anyway. I'll have to face it eventually.'

'What happened?'

'I got sick of all the bullshit,' he said, a harshness under his usual deep tone. 'I got sick of pretending.'

'And you don't have to pretend here?'

He shook his head. 'I can be who I want to be.'

Meredith laughed. 'But somehow, I still know hardly anything about you. You might not be pretending, but you're definitely evading.' She gave him a steady stare.

His grin was easy, setting off a delicious thrum inside her. 'Good thing we've got more hampers to deliver, then.' He picked up her empty glass and went to the bar, leaving her even more intrigued, even more desperate to know about him, than she had been when she'd first sat down.

Chapter Eleven

'Here,' Anisha said, gesturing to the slipway that ran from the harbour wall into the water. 'I want some kind of lighted archway over here.'

Meredith pulled her coat tighter and peered through the early morning mist that was making the water, and the boats that bobbed on it, ghostly and atmospheric. 'Over the slipway?' Crumble looked up at her sharp tone. He was miserable, Meredith thought, his fur damp where moisture from the air had clung to him. Or maybe she was projecting. 'Is that going to be safe? Won't a temporary structure be a bit dangerous when boats need to get into, or out of, the water?'

Anisha turned in a slow circle, her lips pursed. The tension was vibrating off her: no sign of Meredith's calm, collected friend here today. 'But there has to be something here. This is one of the town's premier locations. We can't just have . . . nothing.'

Meredith squeezed her eyes closed, as if that would make

her thoughts come faster. 'You could have a Christmas tree either side?' She pointed to the harbour wall. On one side of the slipway there was a bench facing the water, a brass inscription on it that she had read a hundred times and yet couldn't remember, and on the other there was a tourist telescope you could activate with a fifty-pence piece.

'So many trees,' Anisha said disdainfully. 'This has to be different. It has to stand out, because otherwise people will just come and look at the trees, then they'll leave. You know the empty shop at the bottom of Main Street? You know who's enquired about renting it?'

'A drug lord?' Meredith suggested, because her friend was giving her a look that was both dramatic and traumatized.

'Nearly,' Anisha said. She paused before adding, 'Costa Coffee.'

'Costa?' Meredith thought of Sea Brew, just a few shops up. 'Oh no! No, they can't.'

'Exactly,' Anisha said. 'And while Andy's budget is generous, it's not gargantuan. Maisie in the ironmonger's told me her dad's retiring and she wants to take over, but it's making so little money now, she's in two minds about whether to give up her job at the school to do it. You can type anything into Amazon and get it delivered the next day.'

'But it's not the same,' Meredith protested. 'Not the same quality, not the same *try before you buy* you get with our fudge or chocolates. You can't smell the candles or feel the fabric. You can't take a screw to Amazon and say, "I need another one of these but I don't know what it's called."'

'This is my point,' Anisha said. 'Which is why we can't have a couple of Christmas trees and hope for the best. We need to entice people here from miles away, show them the independent businesses, show them that nothing is quite like coming to Port Karadow for your Christmas shopping – for your anytime shopping – and let them enjoy the harbour and the coffee and the twinkly lights as well. This is our mission, Meredith.'

'Our mission,' she whispered under her breath.

Anisha scrunched her hands into her hair. 'I've started promoting the switch-on, but we don't have a date yet, because I don't know when I'm going to get all the stuff through. It's a big tease, a *coming soon* extravaganza, so it really does need to be an extravaganza.'

'Nish.' Meredith put a hand on her friend's arm. The cold air tingled against her cheeks, but the wintery sun was slowly burning off the mist. 'It's going to be great. Of course it is.' She turned back to the water, trying to get her cogs to turn away from hampers and websites and other, less crucial things that were taking up her thoughts, and towards Anisha's problem. 'We need to get everyone involved,' she said. 'All the shop owners, the locals whose businesses depend on footfall.'

'Get them involved in the lights?' Anisha said.

Meredith shrugged. 'If they know what we're doing, they'll be behind it, then we'll get more publicity and – I don't know. It's just an idea. If they have a stake in it, they're more likely to help.'

'Right.' Her friend sounded interested rather than sceptical, but it was only the figment of a plan, and at this moment figments were pointless. Meredith cast her gaze over the harbour. 'The boats!' she blurted.

'The boats?'

'What if we provide all the boat owners with trails of

136

lights, and ask them to string them around their masts? LED lights are low risk, low maintenance. We could buy them ourselves: little cost, big impact.'

They stood shoulder to shoulder and stared at the glass-like water, the mist sliding off it like a guest that had outstayed its welcome, the reflections that emerged in its place almost flawless.

'That could work,' Anisha said. 'That would be beautiful.'

Meredith nodded. 'And you could treat the switch-on like the opposite of my Start Christmas Early campaign.'

'What – cram it all in at the last minute?'

'More: "This will be worth the wait", or . . . "See Port Karadow Christmas come to life". That way, you turn on the lights as you get them, however staggered that is, and when they're all in place – even if it's really close to the day – you have something to mark that. Something bigger, that will help boost Port Karadow in other ways.'

Anisha stared at her. 'See Port Karadow Christmas come to life?'

'Isn't there a certain satisfaction in more lights being added every so often?' Meredith said. 'Locals spotting new ones whenever they're out? You know: *that donkey wasn't there yesterday*, and: *now the village hall has snowflakes on it*. Turn it into a challenge, a slow burn, and everyone'll be waiting to see what happens next.'

A slow burn. The phrase made her think of Finn. Since their soggy hamper deliveries almost a week ago, all his half-truths and dolphin fantasies in that strange, nameless pub, Meredith had felt like there was a low, crackling flame inside her: embers that refused to go out even once the fire had died. Except she didn't feel like her fire was dying – it

137

was waiting to be stoked further. Had he done that on purpose? Left her with more questions than answers so she didn't forget about him? She was sure he had insecurities under all that glittering confidence: they'd started to poke through the shimmer. What were the expectations and responsibilities he was running from?

'Keep them guessing,' Anisha said, scattering her thoughts.

'What?'

'With the lights. That's a great idea! No wonder you're a marketing guru.'

Meredith rolled her eyes. 'Guru? Come on. Let's go and give Sea Brew some of our hard-earned pennies before work.'

As they walked through the quiet streets, the world waking up around them, Meredith thought of all that had happened in the last week. It wasn't just the progress she'd made with Christmas hamper sales – though Cecily Talbot had been true to her word and had sung the praises of Cornish Keepsakes in a tastefully shot Instagram post – and that she'd investigated some Christmas fairs that were happening in the coming weeks. There was also Finn, and the messages he'd been sending her. His first fact had arrived the night of their deliveries, long after he'd dropped her home. She was lying in bed, her head full of his blue eyes and soft laugh.

Before I go to bed, wherever I am, I go outside and breathe in the night air. It started because I was missing it, in London, stuck inside all day. It's become a habit. Fx

Meredith had smiled, breaking her rule about no phone ogling once she was under the covers.

And tonight?

Cool and damp. No stars. Still feels like a good night though.

It's a good habit.

The next day, when she was in the middle of dealing with a customer who wanted six hampers delivered to different locations across Cornwall, he'd sent another one:

My favourite band is Lifehouse. Cheesy noughties rock. 'Hanging by a Moment'. Do you know them? I'm not even ashamed.

She'd replied,

I don't.

She then went straight onto Spotify and downloaded their 'Best of' album. The lyrics, when she'd listened to them later that night, made those embers inside her crackle to life. It was his favourite band, nothing to do with her, but some of the songs described how she was already feeling, only a few Finn-encounters in. The messages kept coming:

Cucumbers are slimy, horrible things. May as well be eating slugs. Why do people bother?

I hate walking on grass, how prickly it is. But I could

walk on sand all day, especially right at the edge of
the water.

I have a tattoo on my back.

She had replied quickly to that one.

What of?

I don't know you well enough yet.

Is it something religious?

Not in the traditional sense. ☺

Questions spread out like an uncharted landscape at every
new revelation. She thought she would never get to the
end of him; never find out all there was to know. She
was enjoying the titbits, knowing his favourite spirit was
rum, and that he loved reading books set on the French
Riviera. He liked old-school glamour, the idea of things
burning brightly, fading but never disappearing completely,
always leaving something of themselves behind. His
favourite colour was cerulean blue, he told her. Not just
blue. Cerulean.

His messages were longer and deeper early in the
morning, fading to trivialities later in the day, and she
wondered how he structured his time. She imagined him
drinking rum late into the night, still awake as dawn broke,
when he told her about his love of faded glamour and his
tattoo. She got the sense he had been torn about sharing

that with her – especially since, as she walked to the coffee shop with Anisha after their lights recce by the harbour, he still hadn't told her what it was. Did he want to show her instead? The thought sent a vibration skittering the length of her body.

'OK?' Anisha asked, giving her a curious look.

'Sure,' she replied. 'It's cold, isn't it?'

'Let's warm ourselves up,' Anisha said with a smile. She pushed open the door of Sea Brew just as her phone rang. 'It's Mum,' she told Meredith. 'I should take it.'

'I'll get you a cappuccino!' She went inside and ordered their drinks from Max behind the counter, then sat at the last table by the window and rubbed her hand on the glass, peering out at the ironmonger's and sweet shop opposite, neither of which had their shutters up yet. How could they involve them in Anisha's Christmas plans?

She checked her phone, but she hadn't received a new Finn Fact, as she had started to call them. Was he still in bed? Walking at Charmed Cove? She had forgone her swim this morning to meet Anisha, only too happy to help her friend. Or at least she thought she'd been helping her, until the woman in question walked through the door and sat down, her head bowed.

'What is it?' Meredith pushed the mug garnished with froth and chocolate sprinkles towards her. 'Is your mum OK?'

Anisha looked up, her dark eyes brimming with emotion. 'Her arthritis has flared up, and she's bed-ridden. She's being stoic about it as usual, but Dad sounds stressed and I . . . I'm worrying about this place when I should be there, looking after them.'

'How could you help?'

'I could cook, keep Mum company. I hate that I'm so far away.'

Meredith raised her voice over the howl of the coffee machine. 'Your mum and dad are so proud of you, Nish. They love you, and they love Nick and Jasmine and Ravi, and that you have your own life down here. I think they'd be upset if you went scooting up there all the time.'

'None of this would be an issue if we lived closer,' Anisha said quietly.

Meredith tried to hide her surprise. Did Anisha want to move back to Leeds? She'd never hinted at it before. Nick was Cornwall born and bred; he loved his job at the mine, and everything about Port Karadow, and Meredith thought Anisha was happy here too.

'I know it's not ideal,' she said, 'but you can do other things to let them know you're thinking about them. We can send them a hamper, for starters.' She got out her phone to make a note. 'I can sort it out: I know what they like, and I'll consult you about everything. It'll be a care package, a place-holder until you can see them at the end of the year. One of the companies I use has these massage blocks, for muscle aches and de-stressing, that sort of thing. I'll talk to them about which one would be best for your mum.'

'Thank you.' Anisha's smile was watery, and Meredith wanted more than anything to take those tears away. 'And with the whole Christmas thing? You know I'm here for you; whatever you need. If we get other people involved, we could make the ending really big.'

'What do you mean?' Anisha blew on her cappuccino, eyeing Meredith over the rim.

'When the lights are all there, you'll want to show them

off. One big Ta-Da! Like . . . like a pageant. A Christmas lights pageant.'

'A Christmas lights pageant?' Anisha repeated, sounding stupefied. 'It's the twenty-fifth of November!'

Meredith nodded. 'This is how we can get the town involved; encourage the businesses. We have the Christmas carol concert on the twenty-second of December – we could do the pageant then. That gives us a whole month to talk to people, to see if they want a stall or to promote something specific, and include them in the publicity. You, me, Andy, Nick – Enzo would help, I bet. And Emma, and the other choir members.'

'Meredith,' Anisha said on a laugh. 'This is madness! Organize and put on a pageant, in a month?'

'We could have stalls, some kind of parade . . .'

'Did Finn drug you when he took you to that weird pub? You're talking about organizing a Christmas pageant. *Christmas*, Meredith. Hello!' She knocked on the table and then, when Meredith didn't reply, repeated the action lightly on her forehead. 'Have you gone actually, literally, insane?'

But Meredith was overwhelmed with the thought of it. It would bring more people to Port Karadow, it would involve the independent businesses that needed to maximize profits in the run-up to Christmas. It could be a big event in their small town, putting it more firmly on the map. There were no downsides, if you discounted all the work they would need to do in a very short amount of time, and that it would fill Meredith's life with more Christmas than she had had before; probably more than she could cope with. 'I bet Finn would pitch in too,' she said. 'He's all about

143

helping people, and Christmas. Those are his main things, from what I can gather.'

Anisha sat back in her chair. 'You mean this, don't you?'

Meredith swallowed, waited a beat, then nodded. 'I do. A Christmas pageant for Port Karadow. The foundations are there, we just need to add embellishments.'

Anisha came round to her side of the table and put her arms around her. 'I love you. You know that, right?'

'I do,' Meredith said, then cleared her throat. 'I love you right back. And this is the perfect solution. For you and the lights; for Port Karadow. We can make it more festive than anything in this town has ever been before.'

Anisha sat back down and held up her mug so they could clink. Meredith thought a large glass of wine would have been better than coffee, even though it was only eight in the morning and she would have been drinking alone because Anisha didn't drink.

She waited until her friend had left to drive to the office in Bodmin before she let the panic take over.

She walked back to the harbour and sat on the bench, looking out at the water. It was a beautiful, blue-grey shade that made her think of the newest slate painting sitting on her mantelpiece.

What had she done? She had enough to do, without throwing herself head-first into Christmas pageant planning, and Anisha had wanted reassurance, not another huge project to work on. And yet, even though she'd called Meredith insane, she'd happily agreed to it. Perhaps it was because they could both see the bigger picture; that this would help their struggling high street, would be a huge boost to the town, exactly when it was needed.

Meredith slid her phone out of her pocket and opened the lengthy thread of her messages with Finn. She'd replied to his texts, but had yet to offer up any facts of her own, convinced that he already knew a lot about her. But now, with the accumulation of all his small admissions, the tables were turned.

Her instinct was to tell him what she'd just done. She wondered whether he would be proud of her, or laugh. She couldn't forget the way he'd probed her feelings around Christmas in the pub, his frustration when she stepped around his questions. He was perceptive; he'd realized there was more to it. As she typed a message to him, she wondered if she'd taken leave of her senses, or if there was something else controlling her: something she wasn't in charge of.

My dad died on Christmas Eve ten years ago, and I haven't had a happy, or even a family, Christmas since then. That's why I struggle with it so much. x

She didn't give herself time to delete it. She hit send and sat back on the bench with Crumble beside her, his paw on her knee, and waited for Finn's reply.

Chapter Twelve

Meredith had been home from work for less than an hour when there was a knock on her front door. She was heating up some homemade tomato soup, because even though baking skills continued to elude her, she was perfectly competent at making good, home-cooked food. Of course, this made her gingerbread failures all the more frustrating.

She turned the gas down and, checking Smudge and Crumble were splayed contentedly on items of furniture, went to answer it. She pulled open the door and stared at Finn, the sky behind him purple in the descending dusk, a taste of ice in the air.

'Hi,' he said.

'I didn't think I was seeing you until next week,' she replied. 'For the photo shoot.'

'I don't need to be involved in that,' he said, not for the first time. Adrian had firmed up the plans for their promotional pictures, and Meredith had passed those plans on to Finn, who had seemed reluctant from the get-go.

'You can't help me deliver the hampers and get out of Adrian's publicity op. We're in this together now, and I could remind you that it was your choice to be involved, and also that you're the one bringing the Christmas cheer, which I'm assuming we'll need if we have to parade our hampers in front of a photographer.'

He bounced on his heels. 'Can we have this sparring match inside? It's cold.'

'Oh god of course! Sorry.' She stood back to let him in, watching as he walked into the living room, his hands clenching and loosening at his sides. 'Can I get you a drink?' she asked.

He shook his head. 'I'm so sorry, Meredith.'

She realized that he hadn't called her Red, and then something uncomfortable skittered down her spine. 'Why?' she scratched out. 'What have you done?'

His brows drew together. 'What do you . . .? Oh, no. Nothing. I'm sorry about your dad.'

Meredith leaned against the door frame. 'My message.'

Since she'd sent it that morning, she'd had all of ten minutes to worry that he hadn't replied, worry about being so candid with him, before she'd arrived at work and her to-do list had exploded. She'd had to contact the photographer for the photo-op, check they could use the locations he'd requested, confirm when and where the article would appear in the local newspaper. Not to mention her endless other tasks: stock orders, fair enquiries, writing the next email newsletter.

That morning with Anisha, her brilliant idea about the Christmas pageant, had been lost in the piles of paperwork on her desk along with her message to Finn. Now they both returned with full force.

'Fuck.' She put her head in her hands.

'Hey.' Finn's voice was soft, and she felt his fingers wrap gently around her wrists, pulling her hands away from her face. 'I'm glad you told me.' He bent his knees slightly, so he could look her in the eye. 'I am so sorry that happened to you. Some of the things I've said and done . . .' He shook his head. 'I wouldn't have done them, if I'd known. If I'd thought it was anything more than an aversion to twinkly lights.'

'Twinkly lights are OK,' she said. 'I don't hate them. And I don't . . . Christmas just doesn't conjure up happy memories for me, or this bubbling, building excitement, the way it does for a lot of people. Though I know I'm not the only one who finds it complicated.'

Finn nodded. He loosened his grip on her wrists and slid his hands down her arms, leaving a trail of burning sensation, even through her jumper. 'I'm sorry,' he said again. 'Can we sit?'

'Of course. Take off your coat, your shoes too, if you'd like to.'

He shrugged out of his jacket and Meredith went to turn off her soup, returning with two glasses of lemonade.

'Don't worry, I didn't make it.' She handed him a glass.

He gave her a wry smile. 'Sorry for turning up unannounced. Again.'

'It's what you do,' she said, shrugging. 'I'm starting to get used to it.' *To look forward to it*, she would have added, but she wasn't ready for him to hear that. 'And I've enjoyed the Finn Facts.'

'Finn Facts?' He laughed.

'You know: cucumber, Lifehouse, tattoos.' She swept her

eyes over his torso, and she might have imagined it, but she thought he shivered. 'Are you going to tell me what it is now?'

He shook his head. 'Your message this morning wasn't like a Finn Fact. It seemed . . . I wish you'd told me face to face.'

Meredith dropped her gaze. 'I know. I find it difficult to share that bit of me.'

'What happened?'

She took a deep breath. She couldn't remember the last time she'd said it out loud. 'He had a heart attack. He'd been tired and irritable for weeks, and I don't know if . . . part of me thinks I should have noticed. It was Christmas Eve; he came in from working on the farm and slumped in his chair – but that was normal. He was rubbing his shoulder, and I thought he must have injured it somehow, but then . . .' She broke off, swallowing.

Finn took her hand. 'You don't have to keep going, if this is too difficult.'

She shook her head. 'Mum called an ambulance, and we followed it to the hospital but, by the time we got there, he'd died. The doctor said there was nothing they could do.'

Finn rubbed his thumb over the inside of her wrist. 'I can't imagine how hard that was,' he said softly. 'Losing him when you were a teenager, and so close to Christmas.'

'We had to come home without him. Me, Mum and Tommy, my brother. The house was decorated, the vegetables were laid out on the side where Mum had been about to prepare them. I don't remember much about Christmas Day. I was numb, I think. Eventually, Mum sold the farm and moved to Somerset. I don't think she's ever recovered, not really. She hates Christmas even more than I do.' She laughed, but it sounded hollow.

'It makes sense that you hang it all on Christmas,' Finn said. 'All the emotion.'

'Hang it?'

'I didn't mean . . .' He rubbed his cheek. 'You find it easier to focus on the Christmas aspect, how it's a negative thing for you. You talk about that, but not about how it's connected to your dad. I get it.'

'You do?'

'Sure. Talking about loving – or not loving – something Hallmark and glittery, something everyone knows about, is much less exposing than talking about how much you miss your dad, and how unfair it is that he died. Other people can never relate exactly to your experience, or the way it affected you, so they get uncomfortable: they shift their eyes away and say how sorry they are, but they're already looking for an out. If you say you think Christmas is too extravagant and commercial – people can under- stand that, even if they don't agree with you. It moves the conversation on, and stops you having to send your thoughts back there.'

Meredith exhaled. 'My best friend, Anisha, knows. She's always said she'll talk about it with me whenever I want to, but I don't see the point. She would like me to be more into Christmas – she loves any excuse to celebrate, to be the perfect host and make things magical – but she doesn't force me to do anything I'm not happy with.' She shrugged. 'Are your mum and dad both around? Are you a close family?'

Finn's jaw tensed. 'They're both around. They have very different approaches, but they both want the same thing.' His eyes held hers. 'We work together. Sometimes that's a good thing, and then sometimes . . .'

'The expectations you're running from?' Meredith asked. 'That must be tough, if you're not just pleasing a boss, but your family, too. I can see how it would be intense.'

'It's not always easy,' Finn agreed. 'But that isn't what we're talking about. I came here to talk about you and your dad, if you want to? If you don't, then that's fine too, but I'm not going to skirt around it. I'm yours, Meredith.' His concerned expression suggested he hadn't realized how those words could be interpreted, or the effect they were having on her. Her pulse sped up, and she imagined moving closer to him, pressing a hand against his cheek, tilting her head so that their lips were on the same level . . .

'I told Anisha I'd help her organize a Christmas pageant in Port Karadow!' One day, she would teach her mouth not to run away with itself when she was nervous.

Finn stilled, his warm smile dropping a fraction. 'You agreed to help her?'

'I suggested it,' Meredith admitted. 'She's in charge of the Christmas lights in town, and we were talking about how some of the shops are struggling, and what we could do to help. One thing led to another.'

Finn sat back, his thumbs drumming a beat on his thighs. Meredith noticed he had a line of red under his thumbnail and winced. Had he hit it with a hammer? Trapped it in a door? It looked sore, the red bright and fresh. 'It sounds like a good idea,' he said carefully. 'But the timing, and that it's possibly even more Christmassy than the hampers?'

'And it's going to be on the same day as the concert. As my solo!'

'Meredith—'

'It's ridiculous. *I'm* ridiculous. I just – I panicked! This is what Christmas does to you! There's all this expectation, this stupid need to be bright and sparkly, to help people out and not have any weak moments, to say yes to everything because you know everyone's stressed and you have to be *as* stressed as them or you're not good enough and I—'

'Hey.' He moved closer, putting his hand gently over hers, where it rested on her knee. 'Hey, shush. You don't need to do anything you don't want to.'

She gasped in a breath. 'That's not true.'

'No.' He smiled. 'Maybe not. You do need to do the hampers, because it's your job. But with those, and with this pageant, you've got me to lean on. You know that, right?'

Meredith couldn't seem to get her breathing under control. 'I don't know anything about you.'

'Yes, you do. Not everything, but there's time for that.'

The promise of those words hung in the air, and with his warm palm laid over hers, her breathing slowed and her panic subsided, and with gentle questions – he was so good at asking questions – he got her to tell him about what she and Anisha had discussed, all their plans for the pageant, without her pulse skyrocketing again.

He excused himself an hour later, zipping his coat up, fussing over Smudge and Crumble before walking to the door. He opened it on the winter night and the glare of a house opposite that, now it was only a few days from December, had gone over the top with their glowing Santas and golden raindrop lights hanging from the roof.

'See you on Tuesday,' he said.

'Bring your game face for the photos.'

'I'll bring this one and see what happens.' He paused, lips parted, and then added, 'Thanks for the lemonade. And for talking to me. Don't forget what I said: I'll help you with anything you want, Christmassy or not.'

She laughed. It felt good, the final relaxation of her limbs after being so tense. 'Aren't you on holiday?'

He met her laugh with a grin. 'Goodnight, Meredith.'

He leaned in and brushed his lips against her cheek. Her skin tingled at the softness of them, and the scrape of his end-of-day stubble, and she swayed towards him, inhaling his smell. He turned his head slightly, his mouth brushing closer to hers.

He kissed the very edge of her lips, and then, running his hand down her arm, he stepped back. There was a light in his eyes that hadn't been there before, but Meredith couldn't tell if it was panic or satisfaction, hope or regret. It could have been any of them, if he was feeling anything like she was. He stepped onto the porch, said goodbye again, and then walked away. Except, she thought as she closed the door on the empty street, long after he'd disappeared from view, her only regret was that it hadn't led to more.

The weather on Tuesday was pure winter gold, the sky a blistering blue and everything gleaming, as if Port Karadow knew it was its time to be in the spotlight. The photographer, one Adrian had told Meredith he'd used many times before, turned up almost as soon as she walked through the Cornish Keepsakes door. He was a slender man in skinny jeans, a black polo neck and a leather jacket, his brown hair shaggy over his ears, his dark eyes warm.

'I'm Kenny,' he said, holding out a bony hand for her to shake.

'Meredith,' she said. 'Lovely to meet you. Have you been in Cornwall long?'

'I live in Surrey and go wherever the work is, and Cornwall's always a great backdrop. Hampers today, is it?'

'Hampers,' Meredith confirmed, gesturing to the few she'd made up the day before for this very purpose, each one wrapped with a big, glossy bow in a different colour. She left Kenny to set up his equipment and went to her desk, replying to emails until Adrian appeared with Tillie in tow.

There was a flurry of activity when Enzo arrived, and Meredith gathered up everything she thought she'd need. She, Enzo and Adrian took the hampers and led the way to the harbour.

The water was calm, the bobbing boats shimmering in the sunshine, the slashes of colour on their hulls and masts standing out against the blue. Meredith had a sudden worry that the shoot wouldn't be Christmassy enough. A beautiful shot of the Port Karadow harbour would inspire all the feelings Cornwall usually did, but none of those feelings were immediately Christmassy.

They were only a three-minute walk from Cornish Keepsakes, so she had time to rescue it. 'Start setting up. Give me five minutes!' She raced back up the harbour approach and along Main Street, unlocked the door and grabbed a box of crackers and a packet of elegant star decorations, and shoved them into a bag. She hurried back to the harbour, slowing her pace as she reached the bottom

154

of the hill, watching Enzo being directed by Kenny to move the hampers into the perfect position. Adrian and Tillie were standing on the sidelines, Tillie scrutinizing the photographer, as if willing him to look in her direction.

'This is the famed photo shoot?'

She should have been used to Finn surprising her by now, but she jumped, and he grabbed her bag before it could fall to the ground.

'What's this?' he asked. He waggled it, but didn't look inside.

'Props,' she admitted. 'I thought we needed a bit more festive sparkle for the photos. Are you proud of me?'

She waited for his witty response, but he ignored her question and said, 'I've missed you.'

'You have?' His coat was open, revealing a red woollen jumper. It conjured up images of nights in front of cosy fires, ravaging winds outside.

Pink stained his cheeks. 'I didn't mean to say that,' he admitted. 'But I was definitely thinking it.'

'Well,' she replied, 'I'm glad you did. It was nice.'

'It was?'

'It didn't creep me out, if that's what you're worried about. I think I would miss it now, if you weren't just . . .' she waved her arms. 'Here. Appearing, all the time, like some sort of magician.'

Finn grinned, the result almost overwhelming in the bright sunshine. 'That is one of the nicest things anyone's ever said to me.' He took her hand.

'Meredith?' Adrian called. 'Are you ready to add some zing and zither to this photo-op?'

'What is *zither*?' she murmured to Finn, and he gave her

155

a conspiratorial smile. 'Coming!' she called. Reluctantly, she took her hand and her bag back from Finn, and went to join the others.

When she reached the assembled group, she realized that Finn hadn't followed her. He was standing behind the telescope, checking his phone. Meredith strode over to the hampers, opened the box of crackers and the star ornaments, and made the set-up more Christmassy.

Kenny snapped a thousand photos from different angles, getting Enzo and Meredith to shift a star, or slant the crackers so their sequins glinted. It was fascinating how he was always calculating, between every quick-fire snap, and she wondered what it would be like to look at everything as an object of beauty.

Her mind drifted to the slate paintings on her mantelpiece. Who would want to paint them and then give them up, never having the satisfaction of seeing their work admired?

'Right then,' Kenny said. 'We'll get a few with the Cornish Keepsakes staff.'

Adrian pecked Tillie on the cheek and stepped forward, and Enzo handed him a hamper.

'Could we get Finn in here?' Meredith said to Adrian after they'd posed, holding their hampers – which Meredith had kept purposefully light – and with wide grins, while Kenny immortalized them in pixels.

'Finn?'

'He's delivering the hampers with me, and if this is going in the paper, doesn't it make sense? At the very least, he'll add something to the pictures, won't he?'

Adrian glanced at Tilly, then Finn, who was still head down, staring at his iPhone. 'He will indeed,' he said even-

156

tually. 'And he has been gracious enough to offer his time and his vehicle. Finn?' he called. 'Come over here and have your photo taken.'

Finn looked up. 'Oh, no, I—'

'Come on,' Adrian said, cajoling him in his jolly way. 'You can't be camera shy! Don't deny the people of Cornwall the opportunity of seeing your face with these glorious hampers.'

Finn's eyes were caught-in-the-headlights wide, and Meredith frowned. She had never seen him like this. He shot a glance at Kenny, who was watching with interest, then shoved his phone in his pocket and came to join them.

'I don't know why you need me in these,' he said, his smile lukewarm. 'I'm perfectly happy just delivering the hampers with Re . . . Meredith.'

'Nonsense.' Adrian waggled his arm, gesturing Finn closer, until he was standing between Enzo and Meredith.

'We can hold this one together,' Meredith said. 'We can pretend it's a cracker we're about to pull.'

Finn's smile warmed, but only by one degree.

'OK then, ladies and gents,' Kenny said. 'If you could move in slightly, Enzo, and Meredith and . . . Finn, is it? Hold the hamper a bit higher . . . great! Hold it like that.' He snapped away until Meredith was ready to drop the hamper, and she could feel Finn's discomfort radiating off him. When Kenny was done, he stepped away and turned to look at his camera screen.

Finn crouched, putting the hamper on the floor.

'Are you OK?' Meredith whispered.

He stood up. 'Meredith—'

'Finn, right?' It was Kenny.

157

Finn slid his eyes away from her and nodded at the photographer.

'Finn Becker,' Kenny prompted.

Meredith frowned at the familiar surname.

There was a moment's pause before Finn said, 'That's right.'

'I *thought* you looked familiar!' Kenny grinned. 'How's the formidable Imogen? How's Imo Art? Heard you've got a Vaserly exhibition on in February. You curating it? What are you doing down here?' He asked the last question on a laugh.

'What's Imo Art?' Enzo asked.

'I've heard of Vaserly,' Tillie said, her neat brows lowering in concentration. 'Imo . . .'

'Becker?' Meredith said, her thoughts whirring.

If Finn had looked like a rabbit in the headlights before, now he was two seconds from being flattened by the bumper.

'Imo Art,' Kenny said, the voice of authority. 'One of London's hottest art galleries. Imogen Becker heads it up, Walter, her husband, manages investments, but Finn runs it day to day. Or you do usually, right? How's Laurie? She still in that American soap, what was it called?' He clicked his fingers, unaware of the increasingly stupefied faces surrounding him.

Laurie. Laurie Becker. That was Finn's aunt? Meredith pressed her hand against her sternum, too stunned to speak.

'Oh my god!' Tillie squealed. 'Imo Art! That gallery, Adrian – the one we went to last year! The exhibition of huge oil nudes, you remember, with champagne and caviar and all those celebrities? Meredith,' she said, 'there was a member of One Direction there, I'm sure of it. But Adrian said he wouldn't recognize them if he trod on them—'

'You manage a gallery in London?' Enzo asked Finn, who was standing as still as the Michelangelo Meredith had accused him of being.

'Not just any gallery,' Kenny said. 'His mum's a legend in the art world, and Finn's taken over the reins with aplomb. You having a break, mate? This sort of thing is a bit rough and ready for you, surely.' He gestured towards the hampers.

'We drove to your aunt's house,' Meredith said quietly. 'We delivered a hamper there, and you said you had to make a call, and then you . . . you didn't want me to know? Why?'

Finn rubbed his forehead. 'I can explain—'

'The Becker dynasty,' Adrian said, awestruck, and Finn winced. 'Laurie's a complete treasure. She's your aunt? Finn, why on earth didn't you say?'

'It's not a dynasty,' Finn said, so quietly Meredith could hardly hear him. 'That's just the press being the press. I don't know when we went from being a family to a fucking dynasty. What does that even mean?' His hand went into his hair and tugged, and through her cloud of confusion and hurt that he hadn't told her any of these things, Meredith could see how uncomfortable he was.

'It means a succession of prominent people from the same family,' Tillie said. 'And there's your mum, Imogen, your aunt, Laurie, your dad and then you. I can see why they call you that.'

Finn turned his gaze on Meredith. 'Can I talk to you? Not right now, but soon?'

She nodded dumbly.

'Have you got all the photos you need?' he asked Kenny,

and when the photographer nodded, Finn shook his hand. Then he shook Adrian's and Enzo's, then Tillie's, and then he walked over to Meredith, while the others watched him as if he was a rare, shimmering unicorn instead of a man who ran an art gallery in London.

'You said you were front of house,' she murmured.

He sighed. 'I never said it was a restaurant, though.' And then, as if those defensive words, trying to justify all he'd held back from her, made him as angry as they did Meredith, he squeezed her shoulder quickly and turned away, walking briskly up the hill, shoving his hands into his pockets as he went.

Chapter Thirteen

When Meredith reached the beach the following morning, the unrelenting grey of the sky and sea almost gave her pause, but if she ever needed the mind-clearing numbness, the endorphin rush of her morning swim, it was today.

She stripped off her hoody and shoes and waded into the water, inhaling deeply as the cold hit her. She started swimming, and the feeling of being nearly submerged, the cliffs and sand on one side, the endless sea on the other – familiar and extraordinary at once – calmed her.

After the photo shoot they had returned to Cornish Keepsakes, and it seemed that all of them were keen to gossip about the newfound celebrity in their midst. Though, as Tillie pointed out, Finn wasn't really the celebrity of the family, but his mum and aunt certainly were and, according to Kenny, he was on the way to being one himself.

'He's been a shining light in that gallery,' the photographer said, perching on the spare desk with his hazelnut

Nespresso. 'Imogen has a reputation as an ice queen; impeccable taste, an eye for art that's got the gallery where it is today, but apparently she doesn't hesitate to let you know if you're pissing her off. People go there to be awed and terrified – sort of like when you watch a brilliant horror film,' he'd laughed. 'But she's brought artists to Imo Art that other galleries haven't been able to get near, and it's solidified their reputation.'

'And Finn's taking over from her?' Adrian asked.

'He's on the ground,' Kenny explained, 'managing the place, flattering the artists and clients, making the big sales. I don't think anything gets put on display without Imo's say-so, but she's taken on a more executive role, from what I gather, and Walter has always been behind the scenes. The gallery's called *Imo* Art, after all. It's her baby. No clue what Finn's doing in Cornwall helping you guys out.'

'No,' Meredith had murmured, 'it's taken us by surprise, too.'

According to Kenny, Laurie, Finn's aunt, couldn't be more different to her sister-in-law, and Meredith hadn't seen any diva-like behaviour when she'd given her the hamper. She'd seemed friendly and down to earth.

'They sound like an interesting family,' Adrian had said. 'The art aficionado and the actor, and then Finn, right in the middle and helping us deliver Cornish Keepsakes gifts in Port Karadow. Didn't you realize anything when you took Laurie her hamper, Meredith?'

She had shrugged. 'Finn dropped me off. He obviously didn't want me knowing their connection.'

Tillie had sighed. 'He must get so busy at the gallery; perhaps he wants a bit of time off from it all?'

It chimed with what Finn had told her, even if he had said he was running away, rather than having time off. But she had started to trust him. She thought they were getting close. Now she felt – and it was apt at that particular moment – completely at sea.

She bobbed in the water, letting the tide carry her for a few, lazy moments. Finn had asked if he could talk to her, but she hadn't heard from him since he'd walked away from the harbour the day before. Maybe this was it, and he was cutting all ties with her. She ached at the thought.

She got out of water, shivering as she stripped off her wetsuit and pulled on her clothes. She was shoving her sandy feet into her trainers when she noticed it. It was at the base of her rock, not lying on the top like the others she'd found.

Another painting.

Her heart sped up as she approached, scanning the beach to see who might have left it, even though it could have been put there hours ago. She dropped to her knees and picked it up, the slate cool against her palm. It showed a cobbled street with buildings on either side, the pinks and peaches of a sunset over the water beyond, hasty slashes depicting chairs and tables outside a café. Like the others, it was breathtaking, and she knew she had to have it. On her mantelpiece, it would be appreciated. Here, it might be hidden as wind whipped sand over it – or reclaimed by the sea. With only a flicker of guilt, she took the slate painting and put it in her bag, then left Charmed Cove, happy to have another slice of its magic with her.

* * *

When Finn still hadn't got in touch by lunchtime, and her message:

Hope you're OK. Here to talk whenever you want to x

had gone unanswered, Meredith arranged to see Anisha after work.

She pulled into her friend's driveway, the wisteria sprawled over the front of the house now woven with white, pinprick lights. It was the elegant, understated kind of decoration Meredith expected from her friend. The whole town was slowly adorning itself with festive gloss – there was even a *For Sale* sign further down Anisha's street that someone had topped with tinsel – and it took Meredith's breath away. She realized that the Christmassy transformation wasn't making her scowl quite as much as it usually did.

She took Crumble off the back seat and walked to the front step. A door slammed somewhere inside, and she heard voices, as if someone had turned the TV on with the volume up way too high. Meredith knocked, and a couple of seconds later Nick opened the door. His eyes were bright, his shoulders up round his ears. He didn't look pleased to see her.

'Meredith.' It came out as a bark.

'I . . . I arranged to see Nish, but—'

'She's in the den.' He flung a hand towards the back of the house. The den was a small room that led off the kitchen, with biscuit-coloured velvet sofas, a huge TV and bookshelves lining one wall. It was a space you could go to and forget about the world; somewhere for sharing confidences. From the way Nick was behaving, Meredith thought she wouldn't be the only one with things to get off her chest.

'Thanks, Nick,' she said, stepping inside. 'Are you OK?'

He deflated in front of her. 'Nish and I . . . well, she can tell you. Let her know I'm reading Jasmine her story, OK? She should come and say goodnight in twenty minutes.'

'Will do,' Meredith said. She took Crumble through the kitchen, and noticed three Advent calendars on the island: a *Frozen II* design, a *Peppa Pig* and a *Hotel Chocolat* couples calendar. Some of the Diwali lanterns were laid out along the windowsill with candles flickering inside, and a string of heart-shaped fairy lights were looped along Anisha's cookbook shelf. Like everything her friend did, it was tasteful and attractive, and subscribed to a general sense of celebration rather than focusing on Christmas.

'Nish!' Meredith headed towards the den. 'You in here?'

Her friend was bent over her laptop, the document on the screen headed: *Christmas Pageant.*

'I've started speaking to business owners,' Anisha said as a greeting. 'Mulled wine and sausage rolls from the Sea Shanty, Sweet Treats want to sell candyfloss and fudge, and Emma makes greeting cards, did you know that?' She looked up briefly. 'It will be too late for Christmas cards by then, but she's got a Happy New Year range she can sell. Have you ever given a Happy New Year card to anyone?'

'Nish,' Meredith said softly, sitting beside her. 'I didn't mean to make things harder for you. This is obviously a lot of extra work.'

Nish shook her head. 'It's brilliant, Meredith. Everyone I've spoken to is totally on board. Maisie said they've got mini strings of lights they can give away along with discount vouchers, and Andy thinks it's a great way of dealing with the issues around the light switch-on. You've basically saved Christmas.'

'So what's all this, then?' Meredith squeezed her friend's arm. Anisha's eyes were bright with unshed tears. 'Why was Nick so angry? Oh, you've got . . . seventeen minutes before you need to say goodnight to Jasmine.'

'Sure.' Anisha exhaled. 'We had a fight.'

'About the pageant?'

'No, not the pageant.' She pushed a plate towards Meredith. 'Cinnamon cookies. Go for it.'

'Not you, Crumble,' they said in unison when the puppy scrabbled on Meredith's lap.

'Don't you think it was a bit unfair calling him Crumble when he can't eat any of the cookies?' Anisha asked.

'He has dog cookies,' Meredith said. 'What did you and Nick fight about?'

Anisha's gaze skittered away. 'He thinks I should go home to see Mum and Dad again, that I'm spending too much time on all this.' She gestured to her laptop, and Meredith felt a stab of guilt.

'What do you think?' She drew her legs up under her. They were incredible sofas, the seats so deep you could easily sit cross-legged without your knees hanging over the edge.

'He's only saying that so I won't ask him to move to Leeds.'

Meredith didn't know how to reply, so she took a cinnamon cookie and bit into it instead. It was perfect, just the right balance of sweet and spice. She remembered her friend's comment the other day, but had thought – hoped – she was being flippant. 'You want to move back?' she said eventually.

Anisha sighed. 'I miss Mum and Dad so much, and I feel wretched when Mum's like this, and Dad's stressed, and they're soldiering on and pretending everything's fine. I know they're proud of me, they're happy I've got this great life here. And of course I don't want to give it up. But also . . .'

'Also?'

'I don't want to be a bad daughter. I don't want to have this constant ache from missing them. You never know . . .' Her words trailed off, and she looked at Meredith, a glimmer of guilt in her own eyes.

'You never know how long you have left with them,' Meredith finished.

Anisha nodded, unusually reticent. 'So that's our drama. I'm still figuring it out. But thank you for sending those hamper ideas over; they're going to love it, and I've put in a schedule of FaceTime calls over the next couple of weeks. Mum keeps telling me it's overkill, but I know she's pleased she'll see Jasmine and Ravi even in pixel form. The wonders of technology, eh?'

'You've got so much on your plate,' Meredith said, putting Crumble on the floor so he could explore. 'Maybe this pageant is a step too far?'

'Absolutely not,' Anisha said. 'You know I thrive on being busy, and it'll be so good for Port Karadow. Something everyone can get their teeth into. What do you think about having guising as part of the parade? As long as we have a rule that the masks can't be too horrible.'

Guising was a Cornish tradition where people dressed up as characters – sometimes scary, sometimes magical – and it often involved dancing. It would fit well with the lights and the singing, as long as the masks were kept firmly PG so children weren't terrified. 'It sounds wonderful,' Meredith said.

'Good.' Anisha typed something, her fingers moving quickly across the keys. 'We're getting there. It goes without saying that Cornish Keepsakes should have a stand at the pageant – if you decide you want something separate from the shop. How did Adrian's photo shoot go? Do you think it will generate some good PR?'

Meredith stole another cookie. 'Adrian's potentially going to get a bit more PR than he bargained for.'

'Oh?' Anisha's interest in her laptop disappeared. 'What happened?'

'So Finn—'

'Of course this has to do with Finn!' Anisha clasped her hands together. 'Of course it does!'

'You knew?'

'Knew what? I know nothing, except that according to you he's been mighty mysterious, and where there's mystery, a revelation is bound to follow. So what's his?'

'The photographer outed him as this . . .' She chewed her lip. 'His parents own a famous art gallery in London. Finn manages it, apparently, and his aunt is an actor who lives in Cornwall. Laurie Becker. She was in *Emerald Beach*.'

Anisha gaped.

'Nish?' Meredith prompted.

'Finn's aunt is Laurie Becker?'

'Exactly. And he hadn't told me.'

She shrugged. 'Maybe he was getting round to it . . .'

'We delivered one of Adrian's hampers to her, and he made a big show of dropping me off, saying he had an

168

important phone call to make. He turned the car around, Nish, as if his aunt might not recognise her own Audi. She knew it was him – I remember she frowned when she saw the car, but she didn't say anything either. He was hiding it from me.'

'Oh.' She crinkled her nose.

'Very *oh*. I don't know what I'm supposed to do with that; that he actively stopped me finding out, until someone else revealed his background.'

'He didn't tell you anything about who he was?'

'He told me he worked front of house in London, that he worked with his family, and that he was hiding in Cornwall; that he was running away from all the bullshit. When he said front of house, I assumed he meant a restaurant.'

'And he didn't correct you?' Anisha said. 'What about his bullshit? Why can't men just be straightforward?'

Meredith nodded. Finn's lack of honesty was jarring. But also . . . 'He didn't revel in the attention once Kenny recognized him. He acted like he'd rather be anywhere else, and then he left. He was polite to everyone, he told me he wanted to talk to me, and then he walked off.'

'Has he contacted you?'

'No. Not yet. But I'm sure he will.' Was she sure, though?

'He wanted to be anonymous here,' Anisha said. 'I know sweet FA about the art world, but if his gallery is hot stuff he's probably in the spotlight a lot. Maybe it got too much for him, and he wanted to be plain old Finn with you, rather than Finn Becker of the Becker family. Do you think he's staying with his aunt?'

'Yup. He's borrowing her car for the deliveries – or he was.'

'You think he'll stop that now?'

'I have no idea what he'll do. We're supposed to deliver more hampers on Friday, so I guess I'll find out then.'

'What is it?'

'What do you mean?'

'There's something you're not telling me,' Anisha said.

'No, there isn't. I . . .'

'Meredith,' Anisha said quietly. 'How long have I known you?'

Meredith picked at a thread on her sock. 'He's part of this big family. His aunt is a famous actor, and his parents . . . It all sounds so . . . so—'

'So different to you?' Anisha offered.

'He could be spending time with anyone. I feel like the only reason he's latched onto me is because he can – could – be anonymous with me.'

'That,' Anisha said, 'is utter rubbish. You think he's too good for you?'

'I have no idea *what* to think any more.' She laughed sadly.

She didn't want to admit to Anisha that, in Finn's charismatic, easy presence, she had begun to think that perhaps she could lean into Christmas, after all. He hadn't been cloyingly, suffocatingly sympathetic when she'd told him about her dad, but he hadn't been dismissive, either. He'd struck just the right balance, and made her feel as if it was OK to behave any way she had to in order to get through it. Perversely, *that* was making her question whether Christmas really was as bad as she'd spent ten years telling herself it was.

'Call him,' Anisha said. 'While I go and say goodnight

to Jasmine. He can be annoyed that he's been sprung, but he owes you an explanation. *He* walked into *your* life and refused to leave, not the other way round. And no way is he too good for you. If anything, you're too good for him.' She left the room, returning a moment later with a jug of ginger ale, ice clinking in the glass. 'Do it.' She patted Meredith's shoulder and left again.

Anisha was right. Finn owed her an explanation, even if he didn't want to continue with their arrangement. She scrolled to his number and hit the call button.

It rang and rang and then clicked over to voicemail. '*Hi, this is Finn Becker, I can't take your call right now, but leave me a message and I'll get back to you as soon as I can.*' It was polite and professional, but with his familiar charm embedded in the words.

The beep sounded for her to leave a message.

'Hi, Finn, it's Meredith. Just checking you're OK after yesterday, and seeing if you're still up for Friday? There are more hampers, and I just . . . I need to know if it's going to be your boot or mine. Give me a call.' She hit the end button and put her phone away. All she could do now was wait.

Anisha returned, asked her what had happened and then, although it hadn't been the purpose of Meredith's visit, their thoughts turned to the pageant. They ran through what they needed to do, who they needed to contact and by when, and Meredith felt her enthusiasm build. Anisha waxed lyrical about how amazing it would be for Port Karadow; how much the town would benefit, and she began to think her idea might not have been wholly ridiculous after all.

She left after eleven, a sleeping Crumble in her arms, and

as she imagined the guising and the stalls covered in bunting, the aroma of onions, chips and candyfloss encouraging people to indulge, and the Port Karadow choir lifting everyone's spirits with their carols, she knew they could create something special that might have a positive effect long beyond Christmas.

She was in her living room with a mug of hot chocolate, her brain still too wired for sleep, when her phone rang. Meredith felt a moment of panic – it was quarter to midnight, and she though it had to be Tommy: images of him, Sarah and Mum flashing in her mind – but then she saw Finn's name on the screen.

'Hello?' she said, wary.

'Meredith. Sorry I missed your call earlier.' Was it her imagination, or was he slurring slightly? 'Are you OK?'

'I'm a bit surprised after yesterday,' she admitted. 'Other than that, I'm good. How are you?'

'I'm so sorry,' he said, and she was sure, then, that his words were looser. 'I'm sorry you found out like that. That I hadn't told you any of it.'

Meredith sat back in her chair. 'I don't expect to know everything about you, but some of those key details would have been nice. Why didn't you tell me about Laurie when I took her the hamper? Why did you hide that from me?'

'Laurie's great, but I didn't want it – us – to be changed by it. I've been enjoying spending time with you, without any of it. Without the gallery or the pressure, or who my family is. I didn't want that to come into it. I just wanted to be me.' She heard him take a deep breath. 'Shit. Sorry, Red. I shouldn't have called you back tonight.'

'Where are you? That strange pub? You didn't drive, did you?'

'No, I'm at Laurie's. No driving of any sort has taken place. Thank you, though.'

'What for?'

'For speaking to me, despite everything. For sounding like you care.'

Meredith laughed. 'I do care,' she said, as if it was the easiest thing in the world to admit. The ache in her sternum came a second later. 'Don't drink yourself into a coma, OK? And come and deliver hampers with me on Friday. We can talk then.'

'That's probably a good idea. And I'm sorry for what happened. For all the things I should have told you, but haven't. *Hadn't*. It was my job to fill in the gaps.'

'Don't worry,' Meredith said gently. 'There are still a lot of gaps for you to fill in. Go and drink some water, then go to bed.'

'I wish you were here.'

Meredith chewed her lip. 'I think you can get yourself a glass of water, Finn, no matter how drunk you are.'

'No, I didn't mean that. I meant . . .' he hesitated, and Meredith thought of the second part of her suggestion; the one that involved bed. She was caught off guard by drunk, regretful Finn, and wondered which version of him she would get on Friday – though he'd better not be drunk, or it was game over for their deliveries. She wouldn't mind if she didn't get the charming, successful gallery manager, and got vulnerable, uncertain Finn instead.

'I'm going to go now,' she said softly. 'Look after yourself. And whatever it is you're berating yourself for, we can talk about it on Friday. You've got me to lean on. You know that, right?'

She heard his inhale, loud enough that, for a second, she thought he was crying, but when he spoke his voice was gentle; slurred but not choked. 'I'm glad I met you, and I'm still sorry. You deserve more than this.'

It seemed an odd thing to say, but he was drunk and she didn't push. 'Night, Finn. Sleep well.'

'Goodnight, Meredith.'

She sat there for a while longer, her hands around her cooling mug, wondering how she could feel so close to him – even closer than she had done yesterday – when everything she knew about him had been turned on its head.

Chapter Fourteen

Meredith hadn't expected to be nervous when Finn arrived on Friday afternoon. Since their phone call, she had oscillated between telling herself that she understood why he had kept quiet about his family, and deciding she would tell him to leave her alone. She could deliver the hampers herself: she didn't owe him anything. But by lunchtime on Friday, she hadn't called him to cancel, and her curiosity and need to see him again outweighed the hurt she felt.

'Hello.'

She glanced up from her computer to see him standing in the doorway. He looked the same as ever, which was to say stupidly handsome, and she was sure she was imagining the wariness in his eyes. Enzo had tacked a gold foil garland to the door jamb, and it hung lower than was comfortable for anyone. From where Meredith was sitting, Finn looked like he was wearing a crown.

'Finn!' Adrian got there first, and Meredith thought he

must have been practising levering himself out of his office chair – his back was a lot better, if not completely healed – in anticipation of this moment. None of them had seen him since Kenny had revealed Finn's connections.

'Adrian, hi,' Finn said.

'Good to see you again. I was worried you'd realize all this is beneath you!' He laughed nervously, gesturing to the hampers. Meredith had set the ones they were delivering aside, trying to retain some semblance of order in a world that was, increasingly, spinning out of her control.

'I never thought it was beneath me,' Finn said evenly. 'I offered to help Meredith, not the other way round.'

'Of course, of course.' Adrian nodded vigorously, his arms crossed over his chest. 'Are you here for a holiday, or scouting for some fresh artists for the gallery?'

Meredith had a flashback to Mr Keegan's house, how he'd commented on the dog statue standing guard at the door.

Finn leaned against the wall. 'I'm recharging my batteries, among other things. Working at Imo Art can get very intense.'

'And yet you couldn't resist this little project.'

Finn's gaze flicked to Meredith. 'I don't see this as a project.'

Adrian – and Meredith – waited for him to elaborate, but he was back to his brief, unrevealing answers. *Not today, buster*, she thought, and switched off her computer.

'We've got a different set of VIPs today,' she told Finn. 'Some of the villagers who go out of their way to help others. There's a community nurse, the woman who runs the food bank, an older couple who volunteer for several charities now they're retired. Not so many big driveways: you might have to be creative with your parking.'

Finn smiled. 'I can handle that. It sounds great.'

'It was Meredith's idea,' Adrian said, smoothing down his tie. Today it had yellow and pink rubber ducks on a silver background. 'She's involved in this Christmas pageant, too. Firmly focused on this little community, is our Meredith. It's very admirable.'

Meredith felt the blush all the way down her neck. 'I just thought it would be a nice thing to do,' she said. 'Christmas is supposed to be about goodwill, isn't it? And our other VIPs could easily afford a hamper themselves. Not everyone can.'

'Indeed!' Adrian nodded sagely. 'It's a sterling initiative. Off you trot, you two. Have fun!'

'I probably won't be back this afternoon,' Meredith said.

'Oh of course,' Adrian replied. 'Take all the time you need.'

By the time Meredith was sitting in the Audi, Crumble on the back seat and the hampers safely stowed in the boot, her palms were slick with sweat.

'Where to first?' Finn asked, his hands on the wheel, his gaze fixed on the windscreen.

'We're going to the south of town. I'll direct you.'

'Great, thanks.'

They drove in weighted silence through Port Karadow, glimmers of winter-hued fields visible in the distance. To their right, the sea sparkled. The weather couldn't be further from the stormy lashings of their last trip; the sun was bold and the breeze was light. Meredith could almost imagine that it was early spring, that she had blinked, and now Christmas hampers and twinkling snowflakes and all of *this* was behind her. Almost.

177

'I'm sorry I called you so late the other night,' Finn said eventually, when they were close to Marge and Benedict Hevingham's narrow street.

'You don't need to apologize for that.'

Finn's chuckle should have broken the tension, but it sounded forced. 'There are other things I should say sorry for, though.'

Meredith glanced at him, then turned back to the window. 'It would have been nice to know what you did. Not the stuff about your family, necessarily – though that weird trick you pulled with Laurie was infuriating now I know the truth – and just . . . not leaving me to think you worked in a restaurant. You've been a shady character, despite the blond, blue-eyed façade.'

'Façade?' He laughed again, but it faded quickly. 'I know I have. Coming to stay with Laurie is always an escape; more so than usual this time. I just didn't want to bring any of the London stuff into our time together. I was enjoying not talking about it.'

'Because you're hiding?'

'Because I'm hiding,' he confirmed.

'Did you set fire to some paintings or something? Chuck acid on your mum's prized canvases in a fit of pique? Take a left here, then the road we want is up on the right.'

'Sure. And no, I didn't deface any paintings. There's just a lot of pressure at the gallery, expectations from Mum and Dad, and I've been struggling over the last few months. I don't know if it's what I want to do any more. I got to a point where I'd had enough, so I told them they could get someone else to manage the winter exhibitions, and I came here.'

'Laurie doesn't mind?'

'Laurie is all for me stepping out from under their shadow. She thinks I should have done it before now.'

'So you didn't tell me about it because it's not who you want to be?'

Finn pulled over on the side of the road, beneath the twisted, leafless branches of a willow tree. Sunlight hit the gleaming orange bonnet, making Meredith squint. 'That's a bit deep,' he said.

'Isn't that what it comes down to, though? When you meet someone new, you tell them all the bits that you're proud of; you want to present the best version of yourself. And you've hardly told me anything about you.'

'I've told you lots of things,' he said, his voice hardening.

'You hate cucumbers. You like walking on sand. Not really getting down to the fundamental Finn Becker.'

Something flashed in his eyes. 'We've only spent a few hours together.'

'And you're the one who instigated it,' Meredith shot back. 'All of it. I know you're giving me your time, but that's not enough. I told you about my dad, and . . .' She took a deep breath. 'Unless there isn't anything you're proud of? Or in all the tutoring your parents gave you about building relationships, they said you should hold as much of yourself back as possible, go hard on the swagger and charm but make sure it's all surface level, because that way you stay in control?'

Finn's mouth pinched tight, but he didn't reply.

'*Fine*,' Meredith said. 'Let's go and deliver this hamper. Got the sparkly antler things?'

He reached into the compartment behind the handbrake

and held out her candy-cane headband. She bent her head, expecting him to shove it on; she had braced herself for his actions to reflect the frustration bubbling between them, but his touch was gentle and her head tingled in response.

She looked up at him. 'Thanks.'

'I don't feel like I can ask you to be Christmassy, after all this.'

'Well, luckily I'm not doing it for you, am I?' She directed him out of the lay-by and on to the Hevinghams' road. Their terrace was similar to hers, though the front gardens here were longer, the houses set further back. In front of the retired couple's house there were three larger-than-life-sized penguins, the kind that would glow when it got dark, with bulbous bellies and big cartoon eyes, their scarves and hats made out of red plastic. They were the epitome of cheerful Christmas, which just made Meredith angrier.

She climbed out of the car and retrieved the hamper from the boot without waiting for Finn. Honestly, she thought, as she stomped up the front path. The nerve of the man.

'Stay classy,' Finn muttered as he caught up with her.

'I think they're quite nice actually,' she said, which wasn't true, she was just pissed off with him for all his 'woe is me' melodrama. All he needed to do was open his mouth and tell her things. A few heartfelt facts, and she would feel so much happier about their . . . whatever this was.

'These?' Finn whispered. 'Maybe you can embrace Christmas after all, if you think the Pingu family here isn't a travesty.'

'You just *watch* me, Finn Becker. I am *full* of Christmas!'

He took a step back. 'Can't wait,' he said dryly.

'Ready to learn something?' she muttered and then, balancing the hamper on her knee, pressed the doorbell.

After what seemed like an age, the door swung open, revealing petite, grey-haired Marge Hevingham. 'Hello?' she said, her voice quavering slightly. 'Oh, Meredith dear, is that you?' She squinted, and Meredith bent slightly so they were on the same level.

'It's me, Marge,' she said brightly. 'How are you? I've come bearing Christmas gifts! From Adrian.'

'Christmas *lists*, dear? What do I need to do? Let me just write this down.' She patted the pockets of her green cardigan, as if she had a notepad and pen always to hand.

'Oh no, Marge, please don't worry,' Meredith said. 'It's a *gift*. A hamper. To say thank you for all you and Benedict do for the community. There's a candle, some sweets.' She crouched and put the hamper on the doorstep, planning to show her what was inside. 'There's even a couple of scones.'

'You're here to sing me a *song*?' Marge said. 'A Christmas one?'

'No, I—'

'That's a great idea,' Finn said cheerfully. 'You're in the choir aren't you, Meredith?'

'Oh, wonderful!' Marge clasped her hands, her face transforming. 'I love Christmas carols!'

'I don't . . .' She stood up.

'We can do it together,' Finn said. He launched into the opening lines of 'Rudolph the Red-Nosed Reindeer', his voice deep and resonant, if not exactly on key. After a second, Meredith realized she would feel like an even

181

bigger idiot if she just stood there while he warbled on. She took a deep breath and joined in. Marge's eyes widened in delight, and after a couple of lines of their duet, Finn stopped singing.

She shot him a glance. He was staring openly at her, and for the first time that afternoon he didn't look annoyed or tense, so she kept going. She heard a couple of other doors open, but didn't dare look: she felt self-conscious enough as it was. She sang all the way to the end, and then went back and sung the reprise, including a flourish as she hit, and extended, the final note.

'That was beautiful,' Marge gushed, as there was a smattering of applause from around them. 'I'm looking forward to the carol concert even more now.'

'And I hope you and Benedict will enjoy the hamper?' Meredith said, getting back to the reason they were there in the first place. 'A Christmassy treat for the two of you.'

'How wonderful,' Marge said. 'I do love a Cornish cream tea, and they don't just have to be for summer, do they?'

'Not at all,' Meredith replied. 'This one's got some of our spiced Christmas tea, and I popped in some fresh brandy butter just before we left.' She went to pick the hamper up again, but Finn got there first. 'There's also some cranberry jam in there, and cinnamon sugar.'

'Do you want to show me where you'd like it?' Finn said. He disappeared inside the house with Marge, leaving Meredith standing on the doorstep in her glittery candy canes.

'That was awesome,' said a boy of about nine or ten, who was standing in the neighbouring doorway. 'I love Rudolph.'

'He's a good reindeer, isn't he?' Meredith replied. 'And it shows you that people shouldn't be ignored or teased, even if they don't fit in with everyone else. Individuality should be celebrated.'

The boy nodded vigorously, then slid back inside his house, suddenly shy. Meredith rolled her eyes. He'd been talking about the song, not asking for a lecture on discrimination. She had to remind herself she wasn't used to all this Christmas stuff.

Finn emerged five minutes later, closing the door gently behind him. 'I made them both a cup of tea while I was there,' he said, as they walked back to the car. 'Where next?'

'I will only tell you if you promise not to make me sing next time.'

'Are you kidding?' Finn laughed, as they got back in the Audi. 'You have an incredible voice. I think Christmas songs should be mandatory at every delivery from now on.'

Meredith shook her head. 'Not a chance.'

'It would be good practice for your solo,' he said gently. '"Carol of the Bells", isn't it?'

'Yes, but—'

'But what? You only had a moment's hesitation, and you know Marge and I weren't the only ones listening.'

Meredith glanced behind her to check on Crumble, but her puppy was sleeping soundly. 'A few people on doorsteps is very different to the whole town. And it's Christmas, Finn. I didn't even want the solo. I just . . . when Emma asked, I—'

'Hey.' He put his hand over hers, though his eyes remained on the road. 'I don't . . . I have no clue what to say, except that if you think of it as singing, as something you love,

183

rather than Christmas singing, then maybe it'll be easier? If you take each thing, each day, in isolation, you might be able to see the positives, and not just the bad memories.'

'You make it sound so easy,' she whispered.

Finn let go of her hand to turn a corner. 'You could give it a go? If it doesn't work, then that's fine, too. It's not all or nothing – you don't have to embrace it one hundred per cent. You could try for five per cent, and if that's too hard, go back to four.'

Meredith stared out of the window at the roads she was coming to know so well. She had thought she needed to be fully committed, that you couldn't do Christmas in half measures, but why not? What he said made a lot of sense. It made her feel a huge wave of relief, though part of her – the part that was still annoyed with him – didn't want him to be so perceptive.

'After we've delivered the hampers, I've got something to show you,' he said. 'You could try it then.'

'Try what?'

'To see the good in Christmas. Although, personally, I think you're already at five per cent: getting Adrian to give hampers to people who are deserving. Actually, that's way more than five per cent.' He turned his high-watt smile on her, and she narrowed her eyes.

'I'm still pissed off with you, you know.'

'I know,' Finn said easily. 'I'm hoping by the end of the night that will have changed.'

'This is one of my favourite things about Christmas.'

Finn had stopped the car in front of a building Meredith didn't know, driving there after they'd delivered the last of

184

their hampers. It was a large red-brick house with bay windows on either side of the front door, a wreath embellished with pine cones and dried orange slices hanging above the brass knocker. The curtains hadn't been drawn, even though darkness had fallen, and in one window there was an old-fashioned rocking horse, its saddle empty, the room stretching away behind it. In the opposite window a Christmas tree stood tall and proud, draped in sky-blue tinsel, with baubles in a rainbow of colours, and crocheted robins hanging from the branches. Meredith couldn't see anybody inside, so she didn't feel *too* bad about staring at the festive scene. Still . . .

'One of your favourite things about Christmas is spying on people?'

Finn smiled. 'Their curtains are open.'

'So you're happy to just gawp at someone's house?'

Finn shifted in his seat. 'When I was growing up, Mum said that our decorations weren't just for us, that they should be enjoyed by everyone who walked past.'

'But your mum runs an art gallery, so she's got a skewed view of things.'

'Didn't you love walking through your neighbourhood looking at everyone else's Christmas trees when you were little?'

'We lived on a farm in the middle of nowhere,' she admitted. 'There wasn't much opportunity for that.'

'Right.' Finn sounded tense again. 'Sorry.'

'Why did you bring me here?'

'I wanted you to see the window.'

'This specific window?'

He ran his hand along the steering wheel. 'I found the

best windows around here,' he admitted. 'It was one of my favourite things to do in December, go on walks with Mum or Dad – admittedly in London – and see how other people decorated their houses. I just . . .' He turned to face her. 'I wanted to share some of my Christmas memories with you. I understand, now, why you don't like it, why it has bad associations for you, but I thought that if I—'

'Wait. You've gone round Port Karadow and found your favourite Christmassy windows, for me?'

He nodded. 'It's more than just the trees. It's everything. It's all these examples, little squares showing different ways of celebrating Christmas. There's a bungalow draped in twinkly gold lights. A caravan by the coast with a life-sized nativity scene outside. I thought that . . . I don't know; I guess I was wrong.'

'About what?' She couldn't help being touched by the effort he'd gone to.

'About wanting to show you this.'

She shook her head. 'It's a lovely idea.' She turned back to the window, watching as a man carrying a little girl in his arms walked to the tree and held her up so she could take something off it – was it a chocolate decoration? She remembered her dad bringing home snowmen and Santas, the chocolate shapes inside the same, the foil designs on the outside giving them their identities.

'But?' Finn prompted gently.

She didn't want to admit that seeing other families, happy and full of anticipation, made her think of how her own family had fallen apart, right when they should have been celebrating all together. She rubbed her sternum, trying to examine the feelings, waiting for the inevitable weight of grief. When it landed, it was a slightly different shape than she was used to.

'But it's not dissuading me from the very real prospect that you're a stalker,' she said, unwilling to be honest in that moment. 'Maybe even a serial killer. You keep sidestepping my questions, you've supposedly abandoned this important job in London, you come from a grand, ambitious family, yet you apparently want to spend all your time with me.' She hadn't realized, until she'd said it aloud, that this was still playing on her mind: the thought that he was too good for her, that he hadn't wanted to introduce her to Laurie because he knew she wouldn't be accepted. 'And now, *now*, you're telling me you've been driving round town to find the best houses to spy on, offering them up to me like some kind of gift?' She gave him an incredulous look. 'These are very worrying signs, Finn.'

His smile was weak. 'I'm not filling you with the joys of Christmas yet?'

'Do you know what the main problem with this is?'

He shook his head.

'This is someone else's perfect Christmas. It's not yours. You're always trying to deflect attention away from yourself.'

He stared at her, his face a mix of light and shadow. 'OK then,' he said eventually, and started the engine.

'OK what?'

'You want to know what I love doing at this time of year?'

She nodded. 'I do. I want to know all about you, Finnegan Becker. But *you*, not anyone else.'

'Fine. Buckle up. But no moaning when we get there. You asked for it; you're going to get it.'

Meredith felt a thrill of excitement at his authoritative tone, and at the possibility that she was finally, *finally* going to find out something real about her mystery Christmas elf.

Chapter Fifteen

Finn took a torch out of the boot of the Audi and hefted the tote bag over his shoulder. Meredith zipped her coat up, lifted Crumble out of the back seat and then bumped right into Finn when he turned in a direction she hadn't expected.

'What do we need the torch for?' she asked. 'I thought you were taking me to see Laurie.'

'Not tonight. And it's not a steady path down to the beach.'

'We're going to the beach?' Meredith glanced at Laurie's beautiful white house.

'Laurie's got some friends over,' Finn said, pausing to wait for her to catch up. 'And besides, you can't meet her properly yet.'

'Why not?'

'Because if someone is going to fill in the gaps, I want it to be me, not her.'

'So I can only meet your aunt once you've answered all my questions?'

'Exactly.'

'Looks like you're going to be doing a lot of talking then,' Meredith said.

Finn grabbed her hand as the torch revealed an uneven patch on the dusty path he was leading her down, and she let him take her to the cove she knew so well, but had never approached from this angle.

Once the sand was beneath her feet and moonlight presented the small beach to them like a magical scenescape, Finn led her over to her sitting rock and, reaching inside the bag, took out a blanket. He spread it over the flat surface, and Meredith wondered how many times he'd done this; how often their paths hadn't crossed, despite both of them loving the same small patch of Cornwall.

'Your picnic blanket, madam,' he offered with a flourish, and Meredith sat on it, putting Crumble on her lap. The puppy climbed off and sat next to her, and she picked him up again so Finn could sit down. Crumble, not remotely offended, stretched his small body out between them, warming Meredith's thigh.

'Night-time picnics on a beach in winter,' she said. 'Don't you feel the cold?'

'Are you cold?' Finn asked.

It had been one of the milder December days, the sun unusually strong, and while she couldn't admit to being toasty, she wasn't freezing.

'No, actually,' she said, as Finn placed another blanket over their laps, making sure Crumble's nose was sticking out of the end.

'I did tell you to brace yourself,' he said, handing her one of the packets of fish and chips they'd picked up on the way. As she unrolled it, he took out a bottle of mulled wine and two paper cups, and filled them before passing her one.

She took it, and they clinked. She wasn't a mulled wine fan, but not because she didn't like the taste. That − she thought as she took a sip, Finn's gaze unwavering on hers − was a metaphor for everything Christmassy in her life. Was it time to take a bigger gulp?

'So,' she said, after she'd eaten a few chips, deliciously salty and sharp with vinegar. 'This is authentic Finn Becker.'

He nodded. 'This is me.'

'You do this often?'

'At least once every time I'm in Cornwall.'

'Why?'

He shrugged. 'Because you get the beach to yourself. Because there's something otherworldly about the way moonlight works, the colours and shadows it picks out, the way landscapes are transformed, like a photo negative. Because I love fish and chips, and I'm lucky enough to get to stay in my aunt's house, which is so close to this beach.'

'You do this alone?' Her voice sounded small, though she didn't know if she was sad at the prospect of Finn being lonely, or sad that he might have shared this with someone else.

'Sometimes Laurie comes, or her partner, Fern. But usually it's just me.'

'Do you love art?' she asked. 'Or were you forced into it by your parents?'

'No, I genuinely love it. They probably woke it up inside me, but that side of my job, the enthusiasm for it, isn't

191

forced. It's just that . . . they're very overbearing when they want to be. They don't believe in initiative, which is ridiculous.' He started to pull his piece of cod apart with the wooden fork. 'We had a disagreement about an exhibition, and I didn't exactly throw a tantrum, but . . .' He stabbed at the batter, twisting it, then looked up at her. 'I knew I needed a breather. I arranged the exhibition just as they wanted, wrote the press release, got everything ready and then left my mum's assistant – who is more than capable – in charge and came down here.'

'For how long?'

'I don't know,' he said, his gaze sliding to the sea. 'I'm still deciding.'

'You might not go back?'

'I might not,' he said quietly. 'I've got a lot to think about.'

'But instead, you're helping Cornish Keepsakes deliver their Christmas hampers.'

The side of his mouth kicked up. 'I'm helping *you*, Meredith.'

'If I was doing something else – mucking out stables, collecting recycling every Tuesday morning on one of those big bin lorries, serving coffees in Sea Brew – would you still have offered your time?' Her heart was pounding, because now they were getting to the truth of it: why she and Finn were here, together, and it hadn't just been one chance encounter on this beach that had led to nothing else.

Finn shifted on the rock to face her, and Crumble pawed at his jeans, his nose getting closer to the fish and chips on his lap. Meredith moved her dog away without saying a word.

'I would have found some way of spending time with

you,' he said, then shook his head. 'I would have tried to find a way of spending time with you. As it was, I didn't exactly go about it in the smoothest way, so I don't know how I would have got on if you hadn't had something quite so easy for me to get involved in.'

Meredith was elated and shocked all at once. 'You know, there are these things called dates. Where two people who are attracted to each other spend time together, sometimes over coffee, or wine, or even food.'

He gestured at the spread on their knees, and Meredith laughed.

'You came to it in a very roundabout way,' she said softly.

'If I'd asked you on a date when you were struggling with your box of painted jars, would you have said yes?' He raised an eyebrow.

Meredith ate three chips in quick succession, trying to think of a reply.

'See,' he answered for her. 'You would have thought I was weird; brazen.'

'I *did* think you were weird and brazen,' she said, laughing. 'When you offered to help me deliver the hampers.'

Finn sighed. 'This is why it's all wrong.'

'Why *what's* all wrong?'

'How do two people who meet completely randomly, on a street corner or a beach, give each other a chance? It seems outlandish, *stalkerish*, even,' he said pointedly, 'to see a stranger, know absolutely nothing about them, and ask them out. It's why people who are together have stories about meeting at university or work, or they started out friends of friends, because those situations allow you to get to know each other in a way that seems natural.

'Think how many relationships have never happened because the attraction was between two strangers, and it feels wrong – creepy even – to admit to that instant connection and grab hold of it because you might never see the person again. Especially these days. How do you get to know someone if they don't have a Christmas hamper project you can insert yourself into?'

Meredith didn't know if he'd said the last bit for laughs. She didn't feel like laughing. 'I don't know,' she admitted. 'I don't know how you go about acting on it.'

'And in case I haven't made it abundantly clear, Meredith,' he said, his tone softening, 'I am attracted to you. I was from the moment you stepped out of the water, on this very beach, looking mildly aggrieved at my presence. Even then, I was desperate to speak to you. It's only been getting worse – or better, depending on how you look at it – since then.'

She laughed this time, her cheeks heating despite the cold night wrapping itself around them, the whisper of wind coming off the sea. 'And I called you a Michelangelo, so I didn't hide my initial reaction to you very well.'

He grinned but didn't say anything, and she wondered if he was used to getting compliments. They ate their fish and chips in silence for a few minutes, as if being so open with each other had left them speechless.

'I still can't believe that's your aunt's house,' she said eventually.

'Why not?'

'Because I have gazed at it, imagined who lived inside it, for years. When I was younger, my mum and dad's farm wasn't too far from here, and since I've moved to

Port Karadow, I come to the cove almost every day. It's been this fantasy house, watching over me whenever I swim. And now I know that, sometimes, when I gazed up at it on those early mornings, you were inside.' She shook her head.

'That doesn't seem like that much of a coincidence,' he said lightly. 'Not when we met on this beach.'

'I suppose not,' she conceded. 'Still. It shifts things a bit, for me.'

'In a bad way?'

'Not at all. It's just strange, isn't it, when things you think are out of your reach turn out to be a lot closer than you imagined?' Finn nodded, and she wondered if he knew she wasn't talking about his aunt's house; or not completely, anyway.

Once most of the fish and chips were gone and Finn had poured more mulled wine into Meredith's glass but not his own, because – he'd reassured her – he was going to drive her home after this, they moved closer on the rock, and Finn rearranged the blankets so that the three of them, Crumble included, were sheltered from the growing cold.

'I'll take you back soon,' he said, into a quiet punctuated by the gentle rhythm of waves breaking against the sand.

'If this was a summer's night, I'd be content to stay here for ever.'

'It's fairly spectacular, isn't it?'

'Spectacular might be pushing it,' she said.

'What? You don't think this view is worth the cold? My bum is completely numb, if we're going for full disclosure.'

'I was talking about the company,' she said.

Finn's eyes widened. They looked silver, rather than blue, in the moonlight. 'Oh, then spectacular is definitely accurate.'

'It is, is it?' Meredith's nerves were on high alert. She felt as if she had an electric current running right through her, even though her bum was also numb, and she could barely lift her cup because her fingers had turned to blocks of ice. 'You know, if this is one of your Christmas traditions, then maybe it isn't such a bad time of year after all.'

'Really,' he whispered, raising an eyebrow. 'Am I finally showing you the joys of the festive season?'

'Don't give yourself so much credit,' she said, smiling. 'You might be very persuasive, but I'm the only one who can change how I feel.'

They swayed closer, like magnets discovering that they attracted rather than repelled, and Finn brought his hand up to brush the nape of her neck. The sensation was dizzying.

'Can I call you Red, yet?' he murmured.

'You've been doing it without permission since we met,' she said, finding that it was difficult to admonish someone when your whole being was crying out for them to kiss you. 'I don't think anything I say will stop you now.'

'If you tell me to stop,' Finn said, his head lowering towards hers, 'then I promise I will stop.'

'Good,' she breathed. 'But, just for the record, I don't want you to stop this, right now.'

'What? The tugging?' He twisted her hair around his fingers, and she felt alive everywhere.

'Stop teasing,' she said, and pressed her lips against his. She kissed him with purpose, rewarding the anticipation that had been building inside her for a lot longer than she'd realized. His lips were firm, his skin soft. He tasted of vinegar and salt and smelled of expensive aftershave, and he was warm when the world around her was cold.

'Meredith,' he whispered when they broke apart, then he came back to her, returning her kiss, bringing her body closer to his with the hand that wasn't still tangled in her hair.

Meredith let him take charge, overjoyed that she'd got there first, fizzing with satisfaction at the way his kiss reached every part of her, delicious and decadent, honest and raw. Neither of them held back, actions seeming easier than words, and she lost herself in the feel of him, lost herself to this perfect night in a cove that she had known, from her first ever visit, was magical. She lost herself until Crumble let out a yelp, and she realized he was scrabbling between them, his claws trying to find purchase on Finn's coat.

'Oh!' She sat back and tried to catch her breath. She looked at where the quilted panels of Finn's jacket had been distorted by scratch marks. 'Sorry.' She held Crumble away from him.

Finn glanced down, then looked at Meredith. He swallowed before saying, 'I'm not.'

'Your coat, though.'

'It's just a coat. Meredith.' He rubbed his thumb along her cheek.

'Finn.' She didn't feel capable of saying much more. She'd heard of kisses taking your breath away, and there had been chemistry between her and Taylor, but this . . . she knew it would take a while for her to climb down from the high of Finn's kiss.

'I want to kiss you again,' he said. 'Soon.'

'Think a mermaid and a Michelangelo are compatible?' she joked, stroking Crumble's ears and settling him on the blanket.

'Sod mermaids and Michelangelos,' Finn said. 'I think it's fair to say we're compatible. I knew it from the moment I saw you.'

'Smugness with hindsight is not an attractive trait,' she managed, before his lips found hers again, and they engaged in the most delicious tug of war of Meredith's life. By the end of it, she was wondering if anyone in Cornwall's long history had used this wide, flat rock for the activity she was now imagining. But it was late and cold, it was December, she had to remind herself, though right now there wasn't a single part of her that felt chilled.

'More mulled wine?' Finn asked quietly.

She found her cup and held it out. 'Thank you.'

He poured. She sipped. The waves broke against the sand, and a bank of cloud muddied the velvety black of the sky, threatening to turn out the moon.

'Who was the last person you brought here for fish and chips?' she asked eventually. 'Before tonight?'

'Laurie,' he said. 'Though it was over a year ago, and she and Fern prefer their terrace. It's usually just me on the beach.' He paused for a beat, and then, 'I haven't brought any other women here, if that's what you're asking. I've been single since . . . February. And before that, there's only one girlfriend who has come to Cornwall with me, and that was when I was a teenager.'

'Who was your last girlfriend?'

He turned his gaze from the sea. 'She was called Clover.

She was PA to an artist who had an exhibition at the gallery. We had fun, but it didn't feel particularly real.'

'Was she glamorous?' It came out more sharply than Meredith had intended. She had another skittering thought that he was too good for her; that they were too different. But then that kiss – that hadn't felt like they were on different wavelengths.

Finn's gaze softened, as if he could hear the jealousy in her voice. 'She was glamorous, and ambitious. She wasn't particularly kind, and she didn't have this perfect dusting of freckles.' He trailed the pad of his thumb lightly over her cheeks. 'She used to turn up at the gallery whenever I arranged to meet her at a bar or restaurant; her focus was mostly on what exhibitions we had scheduled. I wasn't sure she was interested in me, as opposed to what I could do for her.' He reached into the paper packet, then put three chips in his mouth at once.

'Aren't your chips cold?' Her cheeks tingled where he'd touched her.

'Are you trying to tell me you don't like cold chips?' He selected another one and held it out to her. She opened her mouth and he put it slowly in. She hadn't realized cold chips could be erotic. 'What's your answer?' he asked.

'I like cold chips,' she admitted. 'So, Clover wasn't the woman for you?'

Finn shook his head. 'What about you? When was your last torrid love affair?'

Meredith laughed. 'Is that what you had with Clover?'

His mouth lifted on one side. She loved how he looked softer when he smiled off-centre, his striking features no longer like marble. 'That's what I try to tell myself, but it wasn't like that.'

'You think my last relationship was?'

'I don't know. Was it?'

'It was with a guy called Taylor. He worked on the Lagowan estate when I was in the shop there. We were together for over a year, but . . . actually, it was sort of the opposite of you and Clover. He couldn't settle with the idea that working in a gift shop was enough for me. Or maybe that was just an excuse.'

'He dumped you because he didn't think you were ambitious enough?'

'He did. It was miserable at the time, but I dusted myself off, thought about what I wanted, and then, a couple of months later, the job at Cornish Keepsakes was advertised, and I went for it. I moved here, put down a deposit on my house, got Crumble. It's all worked out for the best. Sometimes you need a shake-up.'

'That's true,' Finn said. 'You're happier?'

'Much happier,' Meredith admitted. 'I'm slowly getting everything sorted. I don't think Christmas will ever be my favourite time of year, but . . .'

'You're not hibernating, are you?' Finn said gently. 'I seem to remember that, as well as the hampers and performing a solo in the carol concert, you're helping your friend organize a huge, Christmassy event. You're putting your own feelings aside to get things done.'

'I'm trying,' she said, pressing a hand to her chest. It felt like a weight was slowly lifting, being able to talk about it with Finn. She had always believed that offering up superficial reasons for disliking Christmas would deflect probing questions, and that would make it easier for her. But it was calming, freeing, that he knew about her dad's death, how it had broken their family apart at the worst possible time.

'You're stronger than you think,' he said. 'I hope you don't mind me telling you, very occasionally, that I think you're amazing.'

'There you go with all this coaching business again,' Meredith said, hopping off the rock. She didn't want him to see how much his words affected her. 'Now we need to—'

'You need to kiss me again?' he finished, his eyes alive with hope.

Meredith laughed. 'I need to go home and check that my feet haven't been replaced with bits of Cornish slate.'

'They look OK to me,' Finn said. 'But I do get your point.'

Meredith lifted Crumble down, looping the dog's lead around her wrist while they folded up the blankets. They collected the bottle and the cups, the fish and chip wrappers, and walked across the sand to the path they had come down. Meredith had to remind herself that the beautiful white house nestled in the cliffs was no longer anonymous.

'Finn?' She brushed her hand against his. He was walking slightly ahead of her, angling the torch down to check for trip hazards.

'Yes?'

'You are going to introduce me to Laurie, aren't you?'

'Of course I am,' he said. 'Let me speak to her. I'll find out when would be a good time for you to come over.' He sounded lighter – happier than he had done when he'd met her at the office.

As Meredith got into the car, she wondered at the sensibleness of pressing the point about Laurie. They'd only just kissed, and she was already insisting that he introduce her to his family. But Finn didn't seem reluctant, so she wasn't going to worry about it. For once, Meredith was excited about the unknown stretching ahead of her.

Chapter Sixteen

When Meredith worked on the Lagowan estate, they had a six-month lead-in time for the bigger events and celebrations. Six whole months. In her infinite wisdom, she had afforded herself and her best friend less than one.

This was her main thought as she phoned her sixth food vendor of the morning, to ask them if they wanted a stand at the Port Karadow Christmas pageant. She had been met with several incredulous silences, but so far everyone had been professional, and she had got a 'yes' from four of the six, so it turned out short notice didn't equal impossible. That gave her the confidence to carry on.

They were working at Anisha's kitchen island, because it got good light in the mornings and was big enough for Anisha to spread out her map. She was filling in every location where they wanted something Christmassy to happen, and marking which were confirmed, which were provisional, and which still needed to be investigated. Meredith had laughed when she'd seen the A2 sheet with

Anisha's neat interpretation of the town on it, but she wasn't surprised.

'The stands are coming along well,' Anisha said, after Meredith told her who she'd booked. She ran her pen along the cobbled road below Main Street, where they had agreed to put most of the stalls. Andy had approved their plans, and the vendors' permits were being fast-tracked by their department. 'Everyone likes the idea of guising, and I wondered about singing a couple of songs at the harbour wall, before the concert kicks off.'

'Are we going to be able to take part in the concert if we're organizing all this?' Meredith asked.

Anisha narrowed her eyes. 'We're doing the work now, creating a foolproof plan, and Andy and a couple of my other team members can keep an eye on it all while we're singing, so we don't have to sacrifice things like choir solos.'

'I'm not trying to get out of it,' Meredith said. 'I'm actually looking forward to it a little bit.' She sat up straighter and drew a musical note in her notepad.

'He obviously passed on some of his confidence in that kiss,' Anisha said.

Meredith's cheeks reddened. 'He told me my voice was incredible. This has nothing to do with his kiss.'

'But was his kiss as incredible as your voice?' The smile came automatically, and Anisha laughed. 'Stalker Elf Boy has done a number on you.'

'Hey! He's not the one in charge. I kissed him.'

'Do you think he's walking around in a daze and skipping when nobody's looking?'

'I very much expect he is,' Meredith said haughtily, remembering the last kiss they'd shared as he'd dropped her home after their fish and chips on the beach. Finn *had* seemed somewhat dazed, but then she had been too, and not that far off inviting him inside and helping to warm him up after their nighttime picnic.

'When are you seeing him again?'

'Soon,' Meredith said, because she didn't know exactly when, but had been pleased to discover that idiotic dating protocols weren't part of his plan. He'd texted her when he got back to Laurie's, wishing her goodnight, and her phone had been hot with messages between them since then. No aloof, I-have-to-wait-three-days-before-I-reply nonsense. 'Anyway,' she said, forcing her thoughts away from him. 'Our pageant. Lights all sorted?'

'Nearly,' Anisha confirmed. 'Just got the arctic fox and the kangaroo to arrive, but they're being delivered on Wednesday.'

'An arctic fox and a kangaroo?' Meredith repeated. 'For your Christmas Creature treasure hunt, I assume?'

Nick wandered into the room and flicked on the kettle. 'She made the mistake of asking Jasmine and Ravi what animals made them think of Christmas. Ravi had his *Animals of the World* book open and pointed at the arctic fox, and Jasmine's friend Bella is going to Australia to see relatives for Christmas and has been telling her all about the wildlife there.'

'I'm amazed you found companies that have those animals in lights,' Meredith said.

'You're not the only one.' Nick laughed as he put teabags in three mugs. 'Sorted out the masked dancers yet, Nish?'

'Masked dancers?' Meredith turned wide eyes on her friend.

'For the guising,' Anisha explained. 'If there are some professional dancers, the crowd will feel more inclined to join in. I've got four floats booked so far, and we have to be strict about what we allow, because Port Karadow has narrow streets. We're over halfway there.' She pulled her to-do list towards her and ticked off several items.

Meredith looked at her own list. It had *call vendors* written on it, and she'd only got halfway through those. She needed to pull her weight. If she could stop thinking about a certain person and the way his lips fitted perfectly against hers, she'd probably be doing a better job.

As well as creating maps, Anisha loved being on the ground. She always said that you couldn't see the size of something unless you went through it from beginning to end. Which was why, on Friday that week, Anisha, Nick, Meredith, Andy and Emma, who had – perhaps foolishly – agreed to be on the Christmas pageant team, were walking in procession through the town, while Anisha measured and calculated, checked and double-checked, and added things to her notebook.

'There's enough room for five stalls along here,' she said, gesturing to the wide sweep of concrete in front of the harbour wall. 'We need to leave space for the platform, and the crowd, and for the floats to start and finish here. I think the main foody ones: burgers and the bar and maybe the fudge stand?' She looked up the steep incline that led to the top of Main Street. 'How will it look from up there? Emma, what do you think?'

'Ooh, I don't know.' Emma hurried after her, the bobble on her hat bouncing frantically.

Andy leaned on the harbourside railings, while Meredith snapped photos of the various locations. Today the view was shades of grey, the sun hiding behind low clouds. It was not one of Port Karadow's most triumphant days, but that made it easier to imagine the colour and sparkle their event would bring: a bland canvas to which they could add embellishments.

Nick stood beside her while she scrolled through her photos and tried not to calculate how long it had been since she'd last messaged Finn.

'Thank you for this,' he said.

Meredith put her phone away. 'For what? For sending your wife into a frenzy a few weeks before Christmas?'

Nick gave her a wry smile. 'She's loving it. You know that, Mer, or you wouldn't have suggested it. It's going to do wonders for the town, but you knew it was exactly what Nish needed too.'

'To stop thinking about her mum?'

'To stop overthinking,' he clarified. 'She can't stop worrying at a problem until she's solved it, and I was starting to think this one would send her over the edge. You've provided the perfect distraction, even if it means there's more work for the rest of us.' He grinned to show he didn't mind, and Meredith relaxed a fraction. But then she remembered what her friend had been hinting at, and squeezed her fingers into fists at her sides.

'Has Nish said anything to you about moving back to Leeds?'

Nick glanced at her, then turned his gaze to the water. 'It's come up a couple of times, but only when things are getting heated between us. I don't want to give up my job, or our life here, and I know Nish doesn't either. She's putting herself last, as usual.'

'And her parents can't move to Cornwall?'

Nick's jaw tightened. 'It would be a big move, admittedly. But the pace of life here, the sea air . . . how could that be bad for anyone?'

'You've suggested it to her, I'm guessing?'

'She says it will be too hard for them – which I get, because it would be a huge undertaking – but it's as if she refuses to even consider a solution if it doesn't involve her giving the most; whether that's time or effort or inconvenience. She needs to be busy, it's part of who she is, but she doesn't need to put herself in the suffering seat all the time.'

'The suffering seat?'

Nick narrowed his eyes. 'You know what I mean. She wants what's best for her mum and dad, but she thinks that if it's them who move, they'll be making a huge sacrifice, instead of moving from a city to a seaside town where they'd be close to Nish and their grandchildren, and their quality of life would be better.'

'You could suggest that she organizes the whole thing? Arranges and carries out their move single-handedly?'

Nick laughed. 'She might consider it then,' he agreed. 'Honestly, I love that woman to bits, but she is maddening sometimes.'

'Is it possible to love someone without them also maddening you?' Meredith asked, watching a fishing boat cut a path through the still water.

She felt Nick's gaze on her. 'Your Santaphilia guy?'

Meredith folded her arms. 'He does *not* have Santaphilia.'

She shuddered. 'No. He is also maddening, but of course I don't love him because we barely know each other.'

Nick nodded in an infuriatingly placatory way, and she knew Nish had told him about their kiss on the beach. 'I'd like to meet him,' he said.

Meredith grinned. 'He's harmless.'

'I'll be the judge of that,' he replied, then looked at her, aghast. 'God, sorry, Mer – I didn't mean that!'

'Don't worry.' Meredith nudged his shoulder with hers. 'You're a cutie and I love you for it.'

That sent Nick into a sulk, and they remained quiet until Andy distracted them by suggesting one of the local government councillors could hand out the treasure hunt prizes. Meredith didn't want to steal Anisha's thunder, and nothing was confirmed yet, but they were both hoping they would be able to employ the services of someone a bit more exciting than a Cornwall county councillor.

Nick's words played on Meredith's mind long after they'd finished their trawl of Port Karadow. Anisha really did take the path of most resistance, as if she was prepared to weather any challenge simply to save other people from having to face it. It was an admirable quality, even if it meant she was always working hard on something.

Meredith got her baking things out of the cupboard, and searched for a new gingerbread recipe, as if an alternative version might lead her to success. Did she take the path of least resistance? Until this year she would have said yes, especially when it came to Christmas: letting it slide past with as little fanfare as possible, not trying to make anything of it, let alone the best. This year, however, she'd been forced to give it more of her attention, and yet she still worried she wasn't doing enough.

Finn had encouraged her to be Christmassy, to sing and wear candy canes on her head, to get into the spirit of things. But through all this, her heart had remained mostly disengaged, as if she was watching herself from above. She thought of the other night, when he had showed her the festive window. She hadn't felt the intense, familiar pain at how her Christmas ten years before had ended; instead there had been a new regret, for the ones she hadn't experienced in between. She could have spent time with Tommy and Sarah, might even have convinced Mum to get involved, if she had joined forces with her brother. But she had squeezed her eyes shut and waited for it to pass. How much more could she have enjoyed, experienced, if she'd opened herself up to it?

She might not have a husband or children of her own yet, but that didn't mean she couldn't make an effort with the friends and family she did have. Could she separate her dad's death from the time of year it had happened? She had never tried before, simply accepting that it was the way things were, layering on other reasons why Christmas could be her least favourite time of year.

She could – she *should* – be doing more to change that.

Dusting the flour from her hands, Meredith went into the living room and picked up her notebook. She'd made a list of all the places where she could sell the Cornish Keepsakes hampers in person: Christmas fairs and markets were plentiful in Cornwall. She'd made half-hearted enquiries with a few, told herself that was enough, and never followed up on them.

She phoned the number and it rang several times before

someone picked up. 'Hello!' a bright, female voice said. 'This is the Cornish Cream Tea Bus. Charlie speaking, how can I help?'

'Charlie, hi,' Meredith said. 'Do you run the food markets on Porthgolow beach?'

'That's right. Are you interested in booking a space?'

'Yes, please, if you still have some left. I have Christmas hampers to sell, including a Cornish Cream Tea hamper if . . . if that wouldn't be stepping on your toes too much?'

Charlie laughed kindly. 'Of course not. The more Cornish cream teas, the merrier. That's one of my mottos. Hang on a sec while I open my booking form. We'll start with the easy ones: what's your name?'

Meredith smiled as she gave her information, the warmth spreading through her chest telling her this was the right thing to do. She could be proactive. She could lean in to Christmas, instead of away from it.

After the triumph of booking a slot at a popular food market, the disastrous gingerbread that followed sent Meredith's mood plummeting. How could baking be so difficult? She had followed the recipe to the letter, and yet the round cookies – she wasn't ready to try shapes yet – had come out as hard as concrete, and she'd almost broken a tooth trying one.

Feeling deflated, she made herself dinner and settled in front of an old episode of *Midsomer Murders*, the ultimate comfort viewing. Her phone buzzed on the arm of the chair, and it took her a few seconds to realize it wasn't a message, but a call. Her heart skipped when she saw who it was.

'Hello.'

'Meredith,' Finn said. 'What are you doing tomorrow?'

She muted the TV. 'An early swim, I've got to take some things to the post office and call my brother, but—'

'Your evening's free?'

She smiled. 'My evening is currently free. Why? What did you have in mind?'

'Dinner,' he said. 'At my aunt's house.'

Meredith nearly knocked her plate off her knees. 'I'm going to meet Laurie properly and see inside her beautiful house?'

'Yes,' Finn laughed. 'If you want to? And also, spend some time with me, if you can stand it.'

'I can stand it,' she said lightly. 'It might be something I could even look forward to.'

'Good.' She could hear the smile in his voice. 'Me too, as it goes. How about I pick you up at seven?'

'I can drive over.'

'No, that's fine. I'll get you. Crumble too.'

'That would be wonderful, thank you.'

'Good.'

'Great.'

They were smiling at each other down the phone, which had to be the sappiest thing she'd ever done.

'See you tomorrow, Finn,' she said.

'Can't wait, Meredith.'

They hung up, and she spent a few minutes enjoying the excited anticipation at the thought of seeing him again after a week. A week where their messages had slowly built the tension, neither of them saying what they were thinking, but the words implicit: *I want to kiss you again. I've missed you. You're constantly in my thoughts.*

212

'So,' she said to Smudge, who was watching her from the sofa, a look of disdainful curiosity in his feline eyes, and Crumble, who was asleep in front of the unlit fire. 'Tomorrow night.'

Neither of her pets replied, but she chose to believe they were excited for her, nonetheless.

Chapter Seventeen

Meredith took Crumble for a long walk in the after-noon. Her puppy hadn't been going on walks for long, but he loved every minute of them, sniffing the edges of pavements, stopping every time he encountered a flower or a tree, eager to meet any other people they passed. The only thing the beagle wasn't keen on was other dogs. He had an easy relationship with Smudge, even though the cat was almost as big as him, but dogs were another matter.

They encountered a mini schnauzer and two Norfolk terriers on their walk around the patchwork of country lanes, and Crumble whimpered and hid behind Meredith's legs. She picked him up. 'It's OK,' she whispered. 'They're like you. Not as handsome, but still like you.' She would talk to the trainer next time they went to class, and see what she could do to give her dog more confidence with his fellow canines.

When she reached her road, Crumble perfectly content snuggled against her chest and her arms aching, she saw

Bernie coming in the other direction. Her neighbour was dressed in a scarlet coat and purple woolly hat. She looked more approachable in cheerful colours, but Meredith was still wary.

'Hello,' she said brightly, when they were in earshot of each other.

Bernie nodded, which Meredith took as a good sign, until she said, 'I thought you were supposed to walk dogs, not coddle them.'

Meredith's cheeks heated. 'Crumble was scared of some bigger dogs,' she explained.

'Crumble. I thought I heard you calling it that, but decided I had to be mistaken.'

Anger flared in Meredith's chest. 'What's wrong with Crumble?'

'It's a bit girly, don't you think? Do you want to fulfil all the stereotypes, with your sparkly bobble hat, your freckles and your dog named after a pudding? Men like that one the other day won't stick around when they realize what you're like. I bet he hasn't come back, has he?'

Meredith was almost too shocked to reply. Bernie went to move past her, but she turned, so the other woman couldn't ignore her. 'Hang on.'

Bernie stopped and sighed loudly. 'Yes?'

'What have I done?' Meredith asked. 'How have I offended you? Why can't we just get on, or at least be amicable? We're neighbours, we could be friends. If I've hurt you somehow, then I'm very sorry.'

Bernie met her gaze. 'You really don't remember? I find that very hard to believe.' She walked away before Meredith had a chance to reply.

'I'm seeing that man later today!' Meredith called after her. 'He's invited me to his place for dinner!'

Bernie didn't acknowledge her, so she stomped the rest of the way to her house, irritation simmering in her belly. There was nothing wrong with being feminine, and Finn didn't seem to have any complaints about her being too *girly*. But it was her neighbour's last words – *You really don't remember?* – that were making her feel slightly sick. Had she offended Bernie? She honestly couldn't think what her neighbour was referring to.

She was determined to not let the confrontation ruin her day, but even so, she would aim for the least girly outfit she could manage.

Meredith was ready at quarter to seven, the process of preparing for a date much more fun than she'd remembered. She took time with her outfit, make-up and hair, which she'd attempted to tame while retaining its natural bounce. In her dark jeans and black, off-the-shoulder jumper, she looked stylish but soft, not too over the top and, she hoped, quite foxy.

The doorbell went at five to seven and, squashing down a flutter of nerves, Meredith went to answer it.

Finn stood on the doorstep, his quilted coat – now with added beagle scratches – zipped to the neck. His smile faltered when he saw her, his eyes widening.

'Hi, Finn,' she said. 'Give me two seconds to get Crumble.'

'O-OK,' he managed, then belatedly added, 'Hello.'

'You can come in if you like. It looks cold out there.'

He stepped inside and closed the door behind him, but his gaze didn't leave her for long, as if she'd turned into a mythical creature who might disappear at any moment. She couldn't help the skip of satisfaction. Bernie's words had rankled her, and it didn't hurt to make an effort with a man you really liked. And Meredith had, quite a while ago now, given up any pretence that she didn't like Finn a whole lot.

While she collected her things, Finn made a fuss of Smudge, who had homed in on him like a missile. She put Crumble's red harness on and got her bag and coat.

'Ready,' she said.

Finn stood up, his smile playful. 'What I meant to say, when you opened the door, is that you look amazing. Obviously, I have now betrayed the fact that I can't always think on my feet, especially not when faced with someone quite so beautiful.'

Meredith laughed, her cheeks bunching at the compliment. 'Don't you have to face a lot of beautiful people at the gallery? It seems like a world where appearance matters.'

Finn nodded, his smile twisting into something more guarded. 'Aesthetics are pretty much everything. I'm not used to someone whose beauty goes so much deeper than the surface layers.'

'Aren't you doing the art world a disservice, saying aesthetics are everything?' She led him to the door, giving Smudge an affectionate stroke as she went. 'Important is not the same as everything.'

Finn sighed. 'Maybe I'm looking at it with my dissatisfaction-tinted glasses.'

'What colour would those be?'

'Grey, probably. Something like flint, without any blue tones whatsoever.'

Meredith glanced at Bernie's house as they walked down the path. It would be too much to hope that she was coming outside as Meredith was there, with a gorgeous man practically drooling behind her.

She settled Crumble in the back, then got into the passenger seat and glanced at Bernie's Christmassy window. Was that her, peeping out from behind the tree?

'Is something wrong?' Finn asked.

Meredith turned away from the glass.

'What is it?' he pressed.

'Start driving and I'll tell you.'

They pulled away from the kerb and Meredith recounted her exchange with her neighbour, Finn laughing to begin with, then settling into stony silence. He held it for a few beats after Meredith had got to the end.

'Seriously?' His voice sounded tight, as if he was gritting his teeth.

'I'm not telling you to get extra compliments,' she said. 'Although the way you reacted when I answered the door did wonders for my confidence.'

'You knocked my socks off,' Finn admitted. 'You do every time I see you. I didn't expect you to go down the temptress route, and I'd like you to know that I'm in serious trouble.' He shook his head. 'Doesn't she know that freckles are catnip for men? The most discerning men, at least.'

'I have no idea what goes on in Bernie's mind,' Meredith admitted. 'But I'd like to know how I've offended her. I never meant to do that.'

'You moved in this time last year?' Finn asked.

'Yes, November.'

'Could it have been something to do with Christmas? Bernie seems like a fan, so maybe you—'

'Said something harsh about it?' Meredith finished. 'Shit. I might have done. I can't remember, but it was a stressful time, moving everything in, and . . .' She thought back, but nothing specific came to mind. 'I need to bite the bullet and ask her outright. Apologize for offending her, and try and get to the bottom of it.' She shook her head. 'Sorry to start tonight like this.'

Finn glanced at her, then swung the Audi onto the road that led to Charmed Cove and his aunt's cottage. 'Please don't apologize. No topics are off bounds with me. Laurie and Fern are fairly relaxed, too, though we might not get to practise our kissing at the dinner table – that might shock even them. Mind you, I've been trying to shock Laurie for years now, so we could give it a go.'

'Finn!' Meredith laughed. 'How long have they been together?'

'Laurie and Fern? About twenty years. I remember when I was little I thought my aunt was living with her best friend, and I hoped that, when I grew up, I'd be able to live with Charlie, who was my best mate at school. I told Mum, and she laughed and set me right about a few things. They're both great people, and I get the feeling that you and Laurie will hit it off.'

'Here's hoping,' Meredith whispered. If Laurie mattered to Finn, then she wanted to make a good impression – regardless of the fact that she was a genuine celebrity. She rubbed her sweaty palms together, and told herself it was completely understandable that she was suddenly very nervous.

* * *

The cool exterior of the white cottage on the cliffs hid a cosy and colourful interior. Finn opened the door, shouting their arrival, and Meredith was hit by the smell of pastry and the salty scent of fish, making her stomach rumble. She held on to Crumble, not wanting to put him down until she was sure it was OK, for Laurie and for her dog.

There were modern tapestries on the wall, paintings lining the open wooden staircase to the left of the hallway, and a coloured-glass chandelier creating light patterns on every surface. It was a bright, positive assault on the eyes, and Meredith thought it would be impossible to be miserable in a place like this.

'She's a bit zany,' Finn whispered in her ear, his breath tickling the tiny hairs on the back of her neck, 'but she knows what she's doing.'

Meredith nodded. Behind the colourful tapestries and paintings, the walls were snow-white, the floor and staircase pine. When she looked closer, she saw that the artworks all followed a similar colour palette: bold reds, yellows and greens. There was a harmony to everything, as if it was an over-populated gallery. Creativity definitely ran in the family.

'It's unlike anything I've seen before,' Meredith admitted.

'I'll take that as a compliment,' said a voice, and Meredith turned to see Laurie walking down the corridor. She was wearing wide-legged white trousers, a black vest top and an orange cardigan. 'It's lovely to see you again, Meredith. With less subterfuge this time.' She shot a look at Finn, but there was amusement in her eyes.

Finn rubbed his hand over the back of his neck.

'You too,' Meredith said, a blush tinging her cheeks.

'And this is Crumble?'

Meredith held the puppy out to the older woman.

Laurie held the beagle as if he was a baby, planting a kiss on his nose. 'You're the most adorable pair,' she said. 'I can see why my nephew is smitten. Come through. I'll introduce you to Fern and fix us drinks.'

She followed Laurie down the wide corridor, glancing into an open doorway on her right as they passed. She caught sight of an easel and canvases leaning up against the wall, a long, uncovered window that displayed only darkness. Her pace slowed, she wanted to linger and look at the paintings, but Finn was behind her, Laurie calling something about rhubarb gin up ahead, and she didn't want to be rude. She wondered whether it was Laurie, or Fern, who was the artist.

The corridor opened up into an open-plan lounge and kitchen, the wall at the back entirely glass, the veranda with its strings of lights visible through it. Meredith cursed the winter darkness, because she knew that beyond those strung-up lights was the drop down to Charmed Cove and the sea. She wanted to know what her favourite beach looked like from this vantage point; she wanted to see it on sunny days and stormy days, windy days and when the mist rolled in from the sea. She felt bad that she already wanted to come back here, because she didn't want to muddy the waters of her feelings for Finn.

'Meredith, this is Fern. Fern, Meredith.'

Fern was shorter than Laurie, her grey hair styled in a pixie-cut, her loose dress a swirling pattern of greens and blues.

'Lovely to meet you,' Meredith said.

'Likewise.' Fern shook her hand, then pulled her into a brief hug.

'Rhubarb or strawberry gin?' Laurie called from the kitchen. She still had Crumble hooked under one arm, but the puppy seemed thoroughly content. 'Or a vodka tonic? We also have wine or cava. Choose your poison. I'll drive you home later, Meredith, so you and Finn can relax. Rhubarb gin goes especially well with the Stargazy pie, which I thought we'd have out on the veranda.'

'Um . . . rhubarb gin sounds lovely,' she said, exchanging a glance with Finn.

'For me too, please, Laur.'

'And me,' Fern said. 'I'll slice some lime.'

Meredith turned to Finn. 'I see Laurie doesn't escape the nickname treatment, even though her name is already short.'

He shrugged. 'It's a habit, what can I say? And don't worry, I don't mind.'

'Mind what?' Meredith watched as Laurie put Crumble on the floor and he set about exploring the room, letting out a tiny yelp whenever he found something particularly exciting, his little feet pattering on the floorboards.

'Mind that you're working out how long you can keep our relationship going so that you get to come back here.' Her eyes widened and he grinned.

'Finnegan Becker, stop reading my mind!'

'I love it when you get bossy,' he said, moving closer. He'd taken off his coat and was wearing a thin grey jumper that hugged his torso. It suggested that he kept himself in good, if not gym-bunny, condition. 'Especially when you have that cat-eye eyeliner on.'

'Stop seducing me in front of your family.' Meredith put

a hand on his chest, which turned out to be a mistake, because she could feel the shape of him; how firm he was. His breath caught at the same time as hers.

'Don't mind us!' Laurie called. 'We're going to thrust you out into the night air soon enough; get as warmed up as you like before then.'

Meredith's embarrassment made her want to run and hide, but Finn squeezed her hand. 'You'll get used to her soon,' he promised. 'Then you'll love her, just like I do. Laurie, and this place, are hard to resist once you've got a taste of them. I wouldn't mind if you used our relationship to get to know my aunt better.'

'Why wouldn't you mind?' Meredith asked, recovering a smidgen of composure.

'Because I'm banking on the fact that if you want to spend more time with her, then that means you also want to spend more time with me.'

'Is this the Becker dynasty arrogance I'm hearing?'

'At least in my case,' he said, his eyes flashing with humour, 'the arrogance is justified.'

Finn led Meredith to a huge corner sofa covered in sunshine-yellow cushions. The coffee table was made out of a single plank of wood, shaped and varnished so the grain showed through. There was a selection of art and photography books laid out on it, and an orchid, resplendent in a tall glass jar, in the middle. It was stylish and colourful, and she already felt at home.

They sat down, angling their bodies towards each other, sinking into the cushions. They clinked glasses, and Meredith sipped her rhubarb gin and tonic.

'I'm not sure you could ever be miserable in a house like this,' she said. Crumble seemed equally content, sniffing a basket of firewood next to a cast-iron log burner in the corner.

Finn's silence was its own answer, and she gave him her full attention. 'Were you really down when you came here?'

He rested his arm along the back of the sofa. 'I don't want to ruin tonight with my self-absorbed nonsense.'

Meredith laughed gently. 'But I'm asking. I want to know about you. About London and your life here, what your plans are, and what – if you don't like how things are right now – you would rather be doing. Tell me all your hopes and dreams!'

It was Finn's turn to laugh. 'Starting with the easy ones, I see.'

His words reminded her of her chat with Charlie, and she wanted to tell him she had booked the slot at the Porthgolow food fair. She actually wanted to ask him if he'd go with her, but he was potentially about to reveal more about himself, and she didn't want to interrupt. So she nodded and watched as Finn seemed to unfurl in front of her, his shoulders dropping and his jaw loosening, which made her realize how tightly he usually held himself.

'I want to be in charge of my own life,' he said. 'It seems a bit late to realize that, at the age of twenty-eight, but Mum and Dad always planned for me to be part of the gallery. I did enjoy it, and it was easy, I guess, to do what they asked; to slip into this predetermined role. I enjoy talking to people, and I can talk about art for days, so it didn't feel like a compromise.'

'But now?'

Finn dropped his gaze, picking at a loose thread on his jeans. 'There are other things I want to do – or at least explore. One thing, specifically. But I would have to take a leap of faith. Believe in myself, trust other people, too. I don't know if I'm ready.'

'What is it?'

'Well . . .' He chewed his bottom lip. It was such a boyish gesture, somehow. 'Here's the thing—'

'Dinner's done!' Laurie called from the kitchen.

Meredith waited for Finn to finish his sentence. Instead, he stood up and held out his hand for her to take. She put her hand in his, let him pull her to her feet, and accepted that he would tell her when he was ready.

Chapter Eighteen

The evening chill wrapped itself around Meredith the moment she stepped outside, and all her focus went to the small of her back, where Finn's warm hand rested as he followed her onto the veranda.

The lights she had seen from inside were a string of large, old-fashioned bulbs that were draped around the wooden structure. They glowed a gentle orange, swaying in the breeze and making the shadows dance. Meredith could hear the shushing of the waves below them, could make out the ghost of the sea, shimmering faintly in moonlight broken by cloud, could smell the salt and the blistering freshness of the December night.

She sat on a bench covered with a thin cushion, Finn taking the pew opposite her, and pressed her hands into the rough wood of the table. She felt alive – alight, almost – as her senses soaked it all in. It no longer mattered that she was at the white house, looking out where for so long she had looked in. It had been a huge thing ever since she found out it belonged to Finn's aunt, but now she was here, all that mattered was drinking in the company of the man she had, quite suddenly, come to care about, and his aunt and her partner.

'I dished it up inside because I didn't want it to go cold straight away,' Laurie said, 'but I hope it's not lost any of its impact.' She set the bowls down with a flourish. They were white, with a mosaic pattern around the wide rims, but no amount of decoration could disguise what was sitting in them: pieces of pie, the pastry glazed and glossy, a fish's head – complete with eyes – sticking out of a hole in the top. A delicious smelling sauce coated the bottom of the dish, a generous portion of broccoli and green beans adding colour.

'Don't worry,' Laurie said, as Fern joined them, carrying glasses and a bottle of red wine. 'I know his beady eye is staring at you, but once you taste it, you'll forgive him the scrutiny.'

'Right,' Meredith said faintly.

'You've never had Stargazy pie?' Finn asked.

'Never,' she murmured. 'It smells amazing, though. Thank you.'

Laurie waved it away. 'No thanks until you've tried it. I've got some potato salad and smoked salmon in the fridge if this is too traumatic.'

Meredith laughed. 'I've never thought of food as being traumatic. And he *is* gazing up at the stars.'

Laurie glanced up. 'Not too many on show tonight, but the clouds are doing us a favour, along with the heaters.' She patted the upright of the glowing heater as if it was a beloved pet.

227

'Crumble,' Meredith said suddenly.

'Asleep on the sofa.' Fern pointed, and Meredith saw her puppy was almost lost in a sea of yellow cushions, his tail giving a familiar twitch.

'Phew. Thank you.'

'You can relax here, you know that, don't you?' Laurie said, then gave Meredith a sheepish grin. 'Sorry, it's what I'm always telling Finn. Sometimes I wonder if I should open this place up as some sort of retreat. The colourful home for the perpetually on edge.'

'I'm usually relaxed,' Meredith said, then wondered if that was true, if she ever really let go of all the things she held in her head: work and the pageant; worries about Anisha moving away; looking after Crumble; the constant churn of Christmas and how to deal with her feelings around it.

'Not easy to relax when your dinner is ogling you, though.' Finn scooped a healthy forkful of pie into his mouth, and Meredith, not wanting to be rude, did the same.

'Oh,' she said, once she'd finished her mouthful. 'Oh, wow! This is so delicious.'

Laurie preened. 'See? Unsettling to look at, but once you get inside you realize that it's nothing but joy.'

'You've converted me,' Meredith said, her stomach insisting that she get more creamy, salty goodness – the fish and pastry and veg and sauce – inside her.

Laurie asked Meredith about the Christmas hampers and Cornish Keepsakes, and Meredith told her and Fern about them while they ate. When she mentioned the pageant, Fern asked about that too.

'It's going to be lots of fun, probably chaotic, very festive,'

Meredith said. 'But the chaos will be completely safe. There are risk assessments!'

Fern laughed. 'The risk assessments are a highlight, are they?'

'It sounds like a lot of work,' Laurie said. 'A lot of balls that you're juggling all at once.'

'Maybe I should come and stay at your sanctuary instead.'

Laurie's eyes gleamed. 'You're very welcome to, but I think you'd be happier if you achieved all the things you've set out to do. Finn told me about your dad, about why this time of year is particularly difficult, and I wanted to say how sorry I am.'

'Oh.' Meredith sipped her wine. 'Thank you.'

'I hope you don't mind,' Finn said.

'He tells us everything,' Laurie explained. 'But that's where it stays.'

'Brownie promise,' Fern added.

That made Meredith smile. 'I don't mind. I don't consciously keep it a secret, but I don't love talking about it. My green, whiskered face at Christmas parties usually gives me away.'

Laurie's laughter was loud. 'You're not the Grinch!'

'You're so far from the Grinch,' Finn added, his voice soft.

Meredith took her time eating another forkful of pie. 'I've always had jobs where Christmas has been a thing. Even when I was a Saturday girl at the local farm shop, there were orders of turkey and goose, special cheeses with cranberry in, mince pies and festive chutneys. But then, name me a job where Christmas doesn't have an impact.' She shrugged. 'There isn't one.'

The others were quiet, and then Fern said, 'No, I can't think of one.'

229

'Christmas is all around,' Finn said quietly, and gave her a look that told her he truly, at that moment, understood how hard it had been for her. Meredith, for her own part, was beginning to think that it was a hang-up she'd had for far too long. It wasn't doing anyone any favours, least of all herself.

'You know what I do on rubbish anniversaries?' Laurie said, scooping up the last of her sauce with a spoon.

'What do you do?' Meredith asked.

'What rubbish anniversaries do you have?' Finn sounded intrigued.

'Mum,' Laurie said. 'Your grandmother.'

'She died when I was ten,' Finn told Meredith. 'Granny Ruby.'

'She was wonderful,' Laurie said. 'Eccentric, which I inherited from her, while Walter seemed to sidestep it. She said being artistic was much more important than being academic, and that's served me well. We were very close.' She sighed. 'Anyway, on horrible anniversaries, when I'm in danger of being consumed by sadness, I do something that I really want to do – some challenge or indulgence. I know Mum would be proud of me doing my own thing, so it always feels like it's for her, too, but without focusing on the fact that she's not here.'

'That's a wonderful idea,' Meredith said.

'What things?' Finn asked.

'Well,' Laurie said, 'last year, on the anniversary of her death, Fern and I hiked along the coast path.'

Fern laughed. 'We managed about ten miles before we found a pub, shared a couple of bottles of wine, then got a taxi back.'

'It's in early April,' Laurie continued, 'so the path wasn't teeming, but it was hard work and exhilarating and wonderful. The year before we booked a spa weekend, all the treatments we could fit in, hours in the hot tub. It was pure indulgence, I felt poked and prodded in all the right ways. When did your dad die?'

'Christmas Eve, ten years ago,' Meredith confessed. 'Ten whole years, and I still can't enjoy it.'

'Everyone is different,' Laurie said. 'How does your mum deal with it?'

Meredith laughed sadly. 'She's worse than me. I don't see her much; she moved to Somerset after she sold the farm, and she doesn't do anything Christmassy at all. For her, it's as if it doesn't exist.'

Laurie frowned. 'I'm sorry to hear that.'

'My brother, Tommy, is the most normal of the three of us.'

'It's nothing to do with normality,' Laurie said.

'What even is normal, anyway?' Finn put his hand on top of hers, and Meredith drew in a breath at the contact.

'Anyway,' she said, beginning to fidget under their scrutiny, 'I think your idea is wonderful, and I'm going to come up with something I can do on Christmas Eve. Your spa trip sounds tempting.' She rolled her shoulders. 'I could do with a good massage after hauling hampers about and carrying Crumble.'

'I'm great at giving massages,' Finn offered.

'On that note,' Laurie said, 'I'm going to get dessert. Sticky toffee pudding and custard. I hope you approve.'

Meredith approved wholeheartedly and, with the temperature dropping, they decided to move inside. They settled

231

at a table positioned close to the glass, almost a mirror image of the one outside, and Fern went to help Laurie serve. Crumble was lying prone on the sofa, his legs stretched in the air.

Meredith turned to Finn, the warmth slowly returning to her cheeks. 'If you love art but aren't happy at your parents' gallery, what do you want to do? Open your own gallery down here?'

'I hadn't thought about opening a gallery in Cornwall,' Finn said, moving his wine glass aside. 'When I got here, I just wanted to empty my head, sleep a lot, go for long walks. Obviously, I hadn't banked on meeting a siren.'

'I thought you said she was a mermaid,' Laurie called from the kitchen.

'I thought *you* thought I was a dolphin,' Meredith added.

Finn grinned. 'I was wrong. Now I've heard you sing, I've decided you're a siren. How many sailors have you lured to their deaths?'

Meredith narrowed her eyes. 'I think you've had too much wine.'

After a huge portion of delicious, indulgent sticky toffee pudding, Meredith decided she didn't want to move. She and Finn were back on the corner sofa, the window behind them open a crack and trailing a whisper of cool air over her neck. Laurie and Fern had refused to let them wash up, and she thought they were tactfully giving them time to themselves.

'I've had the best evening,' she admitted.

'Me too,' he said. 'Laurie and Fern love you.'

'They seem like the kind of people who love everyone, though.'

'They both have a glass-half-full attitude,' Finn said. 'I remember Laurie telling me that not everyone can be compatible, so you have to find the people you enjoy spending time with and hold on to them.'

Meredith nodded, trying to hide her pleasure at his words. She almost told him she wanted to hold on to him, too. Instead, she said, 'My mum used to say that if you always did your best, you were bound to find like-minded souls along the way. I think she was telling me and Tommy to be ambitious; to carve out good lives for ourselves, and that would somehow lead us to the right people. The farm was hard for Mum and Dad. Mum's convinced that the stress of it contributed to Dad's heart attack, and I don't think she was just trying to find some meaning, some reason, for his death.'

'You never had any desire to take over from them?'

'Never,' Meredith said. 'Even before Dad died and Mum decided to sell, it wasn't something I saw myself doing. I chose a marketing degree partly because of my summer job at a local farm shop – we weren't big enough to open our own shop – then I ended up at the Lagowan estate. But there is a world of difference between working in a fancy farm shop in the countryside, with its overpriced crackers, organic veg and cosy tea room, and actually working the farm. At least you've supported your family's business, rather than taking the easy option.'

Finn trailed his finger down the side of her face. Did he have any idea how his touch affected her? 'I don't think you've taken the easy option.'

Meredith knew he meant with Christmas, but she was grateful he hadn't said it. She felt like she'd been over it hundreds of times – mostly in her own head – and it was, frankly, exhausting. Was this a sign that she was ready to move on?

'Finn?' she asked, as he moved closer to her.

'Yes, Meredith?'

She didn't know what she was asking, and then it didn't matter, because his lips found hers, and this seemed like the right answer regardless of the question. She had time to realize that this kiss might be the best of her life before Finn's phone started ringing, the noise loud enough to jolt Meredith out of her bliss.

Frowning, he dug in his pocket and pulled out his iPhone. 'I'd better take this,' he murmured. With an apologetic smile, he got up and walked into the hallway.

Meredith stroked Crumble's warm fur. She was wondering if it was time to go home, and where her coat had gone, when Laurie sat next to her.

'OK?' She patted Meredith's knee.

'Great, thanks. Thank you for a lovely evening, and for all that wonderful food.'

Laurie waved her gratitude away. 'It was a pleasure.'

'Are you doing any theatre work in the run-up to Christmas?' she asked, hoping she didn't sound too starry-eyed.

'I'm having a quiet one this year,' Laurie said. 'There are a couple of opportunities I'm looking into for the new year. Besides, I don't think I'm cut out to play Buttons, and I don't get the Cinderella roles any more – though I have been offered one or two ugly sisters.'

Meredith gasped. 'I wouldn't take them!'

Laurie's grin was mischievous. 'I choose to believe I get those offers because everyone knows what a wonderful actor I am.'

'I bet that's it,' Meredith said. 'And you paint, too! You were certainly hit with the creativity stick when you were little – unless that's Fern with the studio?'

Laurie studied her for a moment, a gentle smile on her lips. 'I'd offer to show it to you – you caught a glimpse on the way in?'

'Just a quick one,' Meredith said, suddenly self-conscious. 'The door was open.'

Laurie nodded. 'It would be much better to see it in the daylight. That way you can appreciate the paintings in their full glory. Finn tells me you swim at the cove most mornings. Will you be going there tomorrow?'

'Definitely,' Meredith said. 'After all this wonderful food and wine, I'll need it more than ever.'

'Excellent! Come up here afterwards. I can make some breakfast and give you a proper tour. I'm confident you'll be wowed by it,' she added, her eyes wide, and Meredith smiled, trying to hide her delight at being asked back so soon. She assumed Finn would be here too, and she was already eager to spend more time with him. Getting to see the house again, as well as Laurie's art, was a rather large bonus.

Chapter Nineteen

The next day Meredith got up before dawn, even though it was Sunday and she could have gone for her swim later. Laurie's offer of breakfast and a tour of her studio acted as the world's best alarm clock. When she had explained that she couldn't stay long because of Crumble, Laurie had suggested she drop the puppy off first, which was how Meredith found herself driving her C1 down the track that led to the beautiful white house.

The sun was beginning to emerge, painting the countryside in a soft, golden light, and Meredith drank it in as she got Crumble out of the car. She was about to knock when the door opened. Laurie was wearing a patchwork dressing gown, her attractive face free of make-up.

She put her fingers to her lips. 'The others are still asleep. They'll be up by the time you've finished your swim.'

Meredith nodded and handed over her dog, then made her way to the cove, taking the track she and Finn had used the night when they'd eaten fish and chips on the beach.

It was much easier with the sun to guide her, and she found herself almost jogging, despite last night's red wine making its presence known as a beat behind her eyes.

Did Finn know she was coming back again so soon? Did he mind?

When he'd reappeared after his phone call the previous night, Meredith had called time on her visit, conscious that Laurie was driving her home. She'd sat in the passenger seat, Finn in the back of the Audi, and Laurie had spent the journey telling them about a job she'd taken in a tiny theatre in St Austell, in a play that one of her drama school peers had written about a woman who turned into a goat.

'I thought it would be good to do something so different, especially after spending time in America,' she'd said. Meredith had been desperate to ask more about Hollywood, but hadn't wanted to interrupt. 'I wasn't challenged as much as I'd hoped with the script,' Laurie continued, 'but by the end of the run, my back was killing me. No more goat women for me, but I wouldn't be against a ghost.'

'A ghost?' Finn had asked with a laugh.

'I'm auditioning for a role in series three of *Estelle*. You know the one: big budget historical drama set in Cornwall. It's been so successful that they're filming a third series next summer, and my agent thinks I've got a good chance.'

They discussed the series, which all of them had seen, and Meredith teased Finn by saying how dreamy the lead actor, Sam Magee, was. She'd glanced behind her, and he'd given her his best pretending-to-be-cross impression, which was also incredibly sexy, and had made her wonder when they'd get a chance to be alone together. Then they'd reached her house, and she'd said goodnight and a hundred thank-yous to them both for a wonderful evening.

Which meant, she realized, as she dipped her toe in the icy sea, then plunged in, that she hadn't mentioned coming back this morning. Had Laurie told Finn, or was she going to get to the house and find him all sleep-tousled and grumpy? The thought made her swim her usual route in record time.

Fully invigorated and with her stomach rumbling, Meredith got out of the water and dried herself off. She had a change of clothes with her but, she realized, no make-up or hairbrush. She glanced around her, as if the beach might hold some inspiration, then conceded that she would have to go as she was.

Her legs propelled her up the craggy walk to the house, and she took a moment to marvel at the fact that, after spending so many years idolizing it, she had been invited inside. She wondered how long her visits to it, her relationship with the people inside it, would last.

She put her swim bag in her boot and was about to knock on the door when she noticed a scribbled Post-it stuck below the handle: *It's open. Come in!*

Keeping an eye out for Crumble, she pushed the door open and stepped inside, then closed it quietly behind her. She tiptoed up the corridor, heading for the living room, but a noise on her right made her pause. It was coming from the studio. Laurie must be in there, making the best of the morning light. Meredith stepped into the room, moving past the door until she could see fully into the space. Her steps faltered and the air rushed out of her in a breath as she tried to make sense of what she was seeing.

238

The canvases – some on the walls, a couple leaning against them, another on an easel in the corner – were beautiful. They were brightly coloured, the style broad brush; the bold, atmospheric strokes capturing scenes and moods perfectly. The deep red of a sunset stood out behind a quaint market square, a few white flashes creating the parasols of an outdoor café; a patchwork of blues and greens made up a sunny, summer landscape, the dashes of ochre and cream unmistakably a herd of cows.

She loved them instantly, the sight of them all together firing something in her synapses that she didn't have time to examine because the paintings, despite their beauty, were not her immediate focus.

No, that honour was reserved for Finn.

He was dressed in jeans and a white T-shirt that pulled snug over his shoulders. He had his back to her – she could see the tight curls at the nape of his neck – and his movements were fluid as he added orange strokes to a large canvas. These were *his* paintings; this was *his* studio. Laurie had tricked them both – unless Finn was expecting her to turn up and watch him work; watch him engaged in something he obviously loved and was very good at, but which she had known nothing about.

He clearly hadn't heard her come into the room, and it gave her time to settle her pulse. She thought back to his words the previous night: *There are other things I want to do – or at least explore. One thing, specifically.*

Finn was a painter. A talented painter, who for some reason – perhaps because his parents had asked so much of him – kept it hidden away, at least from her. Was this what he was so torn about? Staying in a stable, familiar job at the gallery where he knew he could shine, or risking it all to take a chance on his passion?

She must have made a sound because Finn whipped round, paintbrush in hand, and his expression turned from slightly dreamy to fully shocked in less than three seconds.

'Laurie invited me here,' Meredith blurted. 'Last night. I said I wanted to see her art, and she told me to come after my swim. This is . . .' she gestured to the room. 'These are wonderful, Finn.'

He ran a paint-splattered hand through his hair. 'Wonderful might be pushing it.'

'You seem embarrassed. Why on earth are you embarrassed?' She stepped further into the room. 'You're so talented. I love this one. It's the cove, isn't it?' It was a haze of sunset colours above a sea shadowed with twilight hues, cliffs dark on either side, framing the beach.

'I did that when I arrived a few weeks ago. I was happy to be back, I guess.'

'Laurie keeps the studio for you?'

'Yeah. I know I'm lucky to have it – and her.'

'Don't your parents encourage this? They do know about it, don't they?'

A muscle flickered in Finn's jaw. 'They do, but there are other priorities. The gallery's full on.'

'Do you have somewhere to paint in London?'

'My flat. But I don't . . .' He shook his head. 'There's no time. There's always something else to do. An opening to go to, exhibitions to manage, clients to meet.'

'So Cornwall is where you can breathe, and paint, and—'

'And it has you,' Finn added, putting his brush down and walking towards her.

Meredith wrinkled her nose. 'We're not talking about that, though.'

'It's all part of the same thing. My inspiration.'

'You didn't have me to inspire you a few weeks ago,' Meredith pointed out. 'This is all you, Finn. This is what you were talking about, isn't it? What you want to do instead of managing the gallery.'

'This is it,' he confirmed. 'But I don't know if I'm good enough.'

Meredith exhaled, trying to settle the whirlwind of her thoughts. Finn was an artist, and he hadn't told her. He was standing in front of her, in a T-shirt smudged with paint stains, looking far too handsome, and also unsure of himself, now she'd discovered who he really was, and he was telling her she inspired him. Nobody would stand a chance, surely?

'You're good enough,' she said, quiet but firm. 'These paintings – they have so much character. They make me feel. . .' She stopped, pressing a hand to her chest.

'What?' Finn asked.

Her gaze skittered over everything, the paintings and easel, Finn's palette and jar of brushes. She found it leaning up against the wall, partly hidden by a canvas of a stormy seascape, blues and greys and a hint of purple suggesting a thunderous sky.

'Of course,' she said, though it was hard to speak past the emotion clogging her throat.

'Meredith?' Finn whispered, running a hand down her arm.

'The slate painting.' When she'd stepped into the studio, she'd been overwhelmed by the knowledge that Finn was the artist, not Laurie. She hadn't registered how familiar the painting style was, or that they were so close to the beach where she'd discovered them.

'Ah.' Finn followed her gaze to where the miniature painting rested. 'Yes.'

'You knew I'd taken them?'

'I saw them on your mantelpiece the first time I came to your house. I was flattered.'

'You didn't mind that I hadn't left them on the beach?'

'I wanted someone to find them,' he said. 'When I first tried painting on slate, I was young, and I didn't know how to get my work out there. It felt like a good way of trying something without putting any pressure on myself. I wouldn't know who had taken them, or what they thought. I was just pleased when I went back to the beach and they were gone. I was shocked when I saw them in your house; discovered that it was you who had wanted them.' He lifted his hand to her temple, stroked his fingers gently down the side of her face.

'Finn, I . . .' She swallowed, the waves of emotion threatening to overwhelm her.

'What is it?' He kissed her nose. 'Are you angry that I didn't come clean when I saw them? I hardly knew you then, and I wasn't ready to share this part of myself. But if you think I was fooling you somehow—'

'No, no. It's not that.' She stepped closer to him, into his warmth. 'I found the first one right after my dad died. It was a painting of the sea, and it was the only bright spot, when everything seemed so sad and hopeless. You have no idea how much that painting meant to me; how I went back to the cove hoping to find more. Over the years, whenever I found another one, it was like I'd discovered treasure.'

Finn's smile was soft, but his eyes were sharp with under-standing. 'My painting comforted you after your dad died?'

She nodded, and he exhaled.

'I'm glad,' he said. 'I hate thinking of you upset. Alone.'

'You've been here, coming back to this house, and I've been down there.' She pointed in the direction of the beach. 'For ten years. For a whole decade I've been looking for signs of you, except I didn't realize it was you.' Her voice had become a whisper. She couldn't tear her gaze from his.

He shook his head, his lips parted. He felt the same as she did; could sense the wonder in it. Meredith hadn't ever really thought about fate or destiny, had never believed that there was anything weaving spells over her life, making her turn in the right direction. She had always felt in charge of her reactions and decisions. But this – Finn being here, the paintings; them meeting on the beach – it was strange, in a wonderful way.

'Is that why you wanted to help me?' she asked. 'Because I had your paintings?'

Finn huffed out a laugh. 'No. I wanted to help you because I wanted to get to know you.'

'And when you saw I'd collected them?'

'Then I thought I had to hold on to you. I would have to tell you, of course, but right then I didn't want to ruin the mystery. And I was apprehensive, too: about how you'd react.'

'Why?'

'In case you thought I'd planned it all.'

'For ten whole years? That would be the longest con of all time. I trust you, Finn. I understand why you kept this to yourself. But don't you think . . . me finding the paintings, you finding me on the beach. It's almost like . . .'

'Christmas magic?' He raised an eyebrow, and Meredith laughed.

'Maybe,' she said. 'Maybe it's the universe trying to tell me something.'

'Oh?' He leaned in. 'What's that?'

'That it's time for me to embrace Christmas, instead of pushing it away.'

'You know I'm not Santa, don't you? I'm helping you with your hampers, but I'm just plain old Finn.'

'Right,' she said, trying to keep her breathing steady as his warmth and his low, teasing voice sent her senses into overdrive. 'Plain old Finn, are you? That's funny, because I don't think there's anything plain about you.'

'The feeling is entirely mutual.'

Meredith laughed. She felt giddy after all her discoveries. 'I'm so glad Laurie did this. You're an artist, Finn. You . . .' She pointed a finger at him, her fingertip hovering millimetres from his body. 'Are . . .' She did it again, this time grazing the warm cotton of his T-shirt. 'A . . .' She skimmed her fingertips over him, finding a smudge of red paint in the vicinity of his heart. 'Brilliant . . .' She placed her palm against his chest, could hear his breathing speed up. 'Painter.' The last word came out as a whisper, and she looked up just as Finn bent his head and kissed her.

Meredith pressed herself into him as his arms came around her waist. She let herself feel everything there was to feel, taking Finn's kiss and giving hers to him.

When they eventually broke apart, Meredith could feel the momentum, the spark, building between them, and she didn't want to stop. She sensed that Finn didn't either, and he confirmed it when he clutched her hem and lifted her hoody over her head, goose-pimples whispering over her skin as Finn looked at her with heat and desire.

'Laurie invited me for breakfast,' she murmured, and then, not wanting to be at a disadvantage, grabbed hold of his T-shirt and pulled it off, revealing his strong chest and flat stomach, sculpted arms that she wanted back around her.

'Laurie and Fern have gone to a car-boot sale,' he said, pulling her close again, leaning down for another kiss. 'I'll make pancakes. I don't want you to be disappointed now that you've come all the way here.' He trailed his lips down her neck.

'Very considerate of you,' she managed, as his kisses reached her collarbone. 'Maybe we could have them in a little while?'

'What do you want to do in the meantime?'

'Oh, I don't know.' Meredith wrapped her arms around his neck and manoeuvred them so that Finn was up against the one, bare patch of wall without any paintings against it. 'How about this?' She kissed the patch of skin just below his ear, then drifted lower, down his neck to his shoulder, smiling against his chest as he made a low rumble in his throat.

'This might work,' he said, and soon Meredith forgot all about his promise of pancakes.

'Have you ever looked at your paintings from this angle?'

They were lying on the studio floor, the winter sun filtering through the window, the smells of paint and sea salt surrounding them. She had her head on Finn's chest, and he had his arm wrapped around her, stroking lazily up and down her arm. He'd found a sheet from somewhere and covered them with it.

'No,' he admitted. 'They look strange.'

'They're still beautiful. The colours are so vivid. I've always wondered,' she went on, 'how do artists find their style? How do you know how you want to paint? Do you experiment with different mediums and techniques until you find one you like?'

'Sort of,' Finn said. 'It's about that, and also what feels right. I've done drawings and paintings much more technically accurate than this and felt nothing: no pride or satisfaction. I enjoy the big brushstrokes, creating the feel of a landscape or scene with suggestion, rather than detail. It just feels right to me.'

'It looks right too,' Meredith said. 'You need to do something with them. I get that it's hard, that you fit in at the gallery and you're part of a team, but I don't want you to waste this.' She shook her head. 'It's not up to me. But I think I can still, just about, look at them objectively, and I really think you need to get them out there.'

She had seen his tattoo now: a paint palette, a swirl of different colours merging in the middle, on his right shoulder blade. She understood why he hadn't confessed his secret, but surely the fact that he'd had it inked permanently on his skin was testament to how passionate he was.

He was silent for a moment, then said, 'It's a big step.'

'It is,' she agreed. 'But isn't it often the biggest, hardest steps that are the most worthwhile?'

'I've heard that somewhere too.' He kissed the top of her head, then shifted her slightly so she was lying on her back, his body partly covering hers.

'So you need to think seriously about it,' Meredith said, trying to sound stern. 'About what you're going to do. That's why you came here, isn't it? To give yourself the space to decide what you want your future to look like?'

'It is.' He kissed her neck. 'And I will.'

Meredith sighed, but she couldn't help smiling. 'And despite your incredible diversionary tactics, I'm not giving up on this. I know you can do it. You have the talent, now you just need the courage to step out of your comfort zone. *Finn?*'

He stopped what he was doing and met her gaze. 'Yes?'

'You are listening, aren't you? If you're not happy at the gallery any more, if this is what you want to do, then you have to try. You are more than capable, and I believe in you.' The last words came out slightly choked, and Finn looked shocked, as if nobody had ever said that to him before.

'Thank you,' he whispered, and pressed his forehead against hers.

They stayed like that for a moment, just breathing together, then he kissed her neck, her shoulder. He tugged the sheet down, exposing more of her. 'I'm not sure I've ever had so many compliments in such a short space of time,' he murmured.

'I think you've earned one or two,' she said, realizing this was not the time to try and have a serious discussion, instead giving into every sensation he was offering her.

'I'm going to try for three at the very minimum,' he announced, his kisses trailing lower.

Meredith smiled and closed her eyes, and wondered if Christmas magic might exist outside schmaltzy Hallmark

247

films after all. She had found the paintings and Finn had found her, and that had to mean something. She would work out what exactly it was just as soon as she could think coherent thoughts again.

Chapter Twenty

For the next week, Meredith felt as if she was living in an alternative reality. She thought back to her life a couple of months ago and almost didn't recognize it. Except that was normal for her, and this was . . . well, it was entirely bonkers.

Port Karadow was edging towards full-on Christmas madness, and Meredith had had a hand in getting it there. The Cornish Keepsakes shop was tastefully Christmassy, but with a kitsch element that Enzo had insisted on, white, pink and blue fibre-optic Christmas trees decorating the shelves. Made locally, they were available for sale but also matched the ribbons on the hampers, making everything look pleasingly coordinated. The hampers were selling well, and several of their customers had mentioned knowing the Keegans, or seeing Cecily Talbot raving about hers on Instagram. Adrian's VIP campaign was paying off, as was Meredith and Enzo's hard work.

Anisha was focused on the pageant, and Emma had taken

on a larger role, coordinating with Port Karadow businesses to ensure they were as involved as they wanted to be. The stalls were booked, the procession was finalized, and most of the Christmas lights had arrived, which made Meredith's walks to work much more interesting. On her route she passed a flamingo in a Santa hat overlooking the harbour; a small herd of reindeer with flashing, rainbow-coloured antlers, and a light tunnel at the bottom of Main Street that was drawing the crowds from dawn until dusk.

She particularly loved the little touches: the snowflakes hanging from streetlights, white and twinkling, and the real Christmas tree by the harbour, adorned with locally made baubles, brightly coloured stick figures, and tiny books with readable titles. She was in charge of marketing, and had been running the pageant promotions alongside the Cornish Keepsakes advertising, until everything blurred together into a big, festive mishmash.

She heard Christmas music everywhere she went. Drifting out of shops and through swinging pub doors, from the mouths of children on their way to and from school, and through the occasional open car window. Somehow, this made her less anxious about her solo. She had been practising at home, between rehearsals, with Smudge and Crumble her unwilling audience. The nerves were still there, they sometimes threatened to submerge her, but she was pushing through because, for the first time in years, she wanted to be part of the Christmas that everyone else was excited about.

On top of all that, Meredith had Finn.

They had seen each other every evening since Sunday. It felt fast and giddy and full on, but she loved spending time with him, and had accepted that it was one occasion where she should throw caution to the wind. He didn't live in Cornwall, but he might be spending more time here from now on, and London wasn't that far away. She couldn't seem to stop smiling, and now, whenever a Christmas song played on the radio in the Cornish Keepsakes office, she found herself singing along instead of rolling her eyes and shutting it out to focus on her emails.

Anisha, too, was visibly less fraught now that everything was coming together, and that, in turn, was having an effect on Nick.

Anisha had put him in charge of the pageant gift bags – totes full of samples and treats from the local companies involved. He had several hundred to make up, and when Meredith arrived at their house, the kitchen had been transformed into the Port Karadow version of a Christmas elf workshop. The island was covered in hemp bags and decorations made out of recycled plastic, leaflets from food companies and miniature light strings from the ironmongers. It was a tedious task, but Nick was swaying along to 'Last Christmas' while he worked.

'You're particularly cheery,' Meredith said, putting her bag on the floor and unclipping Crumble from his harness.

'It's nearly Christmas,' Nick said, pecking her on the cheek. 'The end of all this madness is in sight, and it doesn't look like it's going to be a disaster. What's not to be cheery about?'

'I heard that, Nicholas,' Anisha said, appearing in the doorway. 'Did you ever, at any point, think it was going to be a disaster?' She folded her arms.

Meredith glanced at Nick. *She* knew what the right

answer was, but he was honest to a fault. 'I did wonder,' he started, 'whether it was just a bit too much, given the timescale involved. I always knew you'd get it done, but there was a time when I didn't really know what *it* was going to be.'

'But now you know *it* is going to be a huge success?' Anisha took a step forward, and Meredith wondered if Nick was sweating yet.

He nodded enthusiastically. 'The lights look incredible, there's a procession, food and drink on offer, dancing and guising, and a carol concert everyone can sing along to after they've spent tonnes of money at the stalls and in the shops. And,' he added, lifting up the bag he was in the process of filling, 'nobody walks away disappointed if they've got a goody bag.'

'I've secured an order of candy canes from Sweet Treats,' Meredith said, and watched Nick's smile falter for the first time.

'You mean this isn't all of it?' He swept his arm wide. 'We're going to have to go back and add the candy canes to all the finished bags?'

'Yes,' Meredith said brightly. 'But they're arriving tomorrow, and Finn said he'll come and help, because I know how hard you've worked on these. If you'll have him here, that is.' She clasped her hands together, not because she was worried about the candy cane addition, but because it mattered to her what Nish and Nick thought of Finn.

'Are you kidding?' Anisha said. 'I've already had to wait far too long to meet him. How many days has it been since you had sex?'

'Anisha!' A flame ignited in her cheeks.

'I haven't even OK'd him,' Nick said.

'And I have some questions for him.' Anisha waved a piece of paper, which Meredith knew wasn't a list of questions, but still.

'I'll come and add the candy canes by myself,' she said. 'It will take longer, but at least it won't be torture.' Nick and Anisha both laughed, and Meredith found it impossible to stay indignant. 'He's really lovely, and I want you to like him.'

'Is he hanging around?' Nick asked.

'I don't know,' Meredith admitted. 'But that doesn't mean you can be annoyed with him. He hasn't tricked me.'

'But he's your secret slate painter,' Anisha said, as if Meredith needed reminding. 'I'm still trying to get my head around that.'

'Me too,' Meredith agreed. 'So much has happened, and I'm just . . . trying not to read too much into anything. I'm just enjoying spending time with him. We'll see where it goes.' She shrugged, hoping it wasn't obvious that she had already fallen hard for Finn. Just thinking about him sent her heart into unhelpful flutters, but she knew how fleeting good things could be, and she'd spent so long trying to keep her emotions subdued. This time she was embracing it all, allowing herself to be a little bit distracted, not berating herself for Finn-related daydreams. However long it lasted, Meredith was determined not to let a moment of it pass her by.

'We're happy for you,' Anisha said, 'truly. We want to meet him, but whenever you're ready. I'll make sure Nick doesn't give him the third degree.'

Nick scoffed. 'You're the one with a list of questions for him.'

Anisha gave him a wicked grin. 'True. Right then, let's see where we're up to. Cookies on the counter over there; I almost lost them to Nick's goody bags, even though they'd be stale by pageant day.'

Meredith took a vanilla and chocolate-chip cookie, enjoying the familiar banter between two of her favourite people, and wondered if she and Finn would ever be like that, with their own in-jokes and affectionate ribbing. And, because she was going with the flow, she didn't allow herself to examine how much of a premature thought that might be.

Meredith didn't know the village of Pothgolow well, so when she drove into it on Saturday morning, a week before Christmas, she was charmed by the quaint feel and the picture-perfect seafront, the elegant decorations that had turned it beautifully festive. But it was the beach that drew her attention because, even though she'd tried to be early, it was already full of food trucks. She slowed the van at the bottom of the hill, then indicated. She'd regularly driven a van working for the Lagowan estate, picking up stock or running deliveries, and she hadn't felt too rusty getting behind the wheel yesterday afternoon.

She'd hired the small exhibition truck from a company in Truro, and while it didn't have the Cornish Keepsakes logo on it, she had created a banner that they could hang up once they'd set up the hamper display.

'Where's our space?' Finn asked from the passenger seat.

He'd swapped his reindeer antlers for a Christmas hat with a colour-changing bauble, and was wearing a jumper designed like an elf costume, complete with yellow pompom

254

buttons and a row of tiny bells that jingled whenever he moved. Meredith had laughed when she'd seen him, and then had to admit that he looked great in it. He'd kissed her and given her her own flashing-bauble Santa hat, this one green rather than red. She wasn't, however, wearing a Christmas jumper.

'It's up here on the right,' she said, driving the van slowly over the bumpy sand. 'Ooh look, there's the Cornish Cream Tea Bus!' It was red and shiny, with gold edging round the windows and door. It had Christmassy bunting draped from the upper deck to the wing mirrors, and the chairs and tables outside were busy with people clutching takeaway coffee cups and eating sausage rolls, despite the brisk wind that had sent the clouds racing and turned the sea choppy.

'It's very eye-catching,' Finn said. 'Bet their cream teas aren't as good as ours, though.'

'I expect they're almost as good, because their scones will be freshly baked and warm, and ours need to last a bit longer due to being in a hamper.'

'I hope Adrian never hears you being so disloyal.' Finn squeezed her knee then slid his hand slowly up her leg, and she felt a familiar, low flutter. She glanced at him and he grinned. He knew how he affected her, but she had the same effect on him, and she started thinking up ways to get back at him once she was no longer driving a large vehicle.

'I'm a realist,' she said. 'Charlie's cream teas are perfect for right now; ours are perfect as gifts. This is us, look, right on the edge. Anyone who comes down to the sea will have to pass our hampers.'

'And with you selling them, they won't be able to resist.'

'You're quite sweet sometimes, did you know that?'

255

'I'm only just starting to realize it,' he said, unclipping his seatbelt. 'I've never behaved like this before.'

Meredith laughed, but his admission hit her in the chest. Had he never felt this way about anyone, or was it their relationship, specifically, that brought out this side of him? Was this a fun, Christmas romance where you could say anything you wanted, be flippant or over the top and get away with it because, in a few weeks' time, it would be over? She didn't want to think about that.

'Meredith?' Finn was standing next to his open door. 'You coming?'

'Of course!' She hopped down, and together they set about opening up the van so they could display the Cornish Keepsakes hampers in the most tempting way possible.

This year, Meredith had added to the variety of hampers they were selling. There was their Cornish Cream Tea Christmas hamper and a Savoury Treats hamper. One called Chocolate and Champagne, a Gin Lovers' hamper and a Santa's Saviours option. They set their van up so each one was on full display, and waited for customers. The market wasn't officially open yet, but its beach location meant it was impossible to stop people browsing. They were opposite a butcher's stand selling sausage and bacon baps, and the smell of frying onions was making Meredith's stomach rumble.

'Here,' Finn said. 'Your hat's wonky.'

'I don't think it needs to be perfectly straight,' Meredith replied, but she turned towards him, their faces close while he took a very long time to rearrange her hat and hair, which she felt as a series of tugs and tickles against her scalp. She watched his handsome face, set in concentration, and his eyes that were bluer than the sea, his full lips that were so good at kissing her. She shuddered, and his gaze sharpened.

'You should have put your scarf on,' he said gently.

'I'm not cold,' she replied, and saw him swallow.

'Thank you for asking me today,' he said, after a moment. 'I know it should be Enzo, but I'm glad it's me.'

'There's nobody else I'd rather sell hampers with, or spend my Saturday with. And you didn't need to come, because this is work, and you're not getting paid.'

'It doesn't feel like work,' he said, and leaned in to kiss her just as a tall woman with red hair and an open, friendly face stopped in front of them.

'Hello!' she said brightly. 'I'm Charlie.'

Meredith and Finn sprung apart as if they'd been blasted with water.

'Hi, Charlie,' Meredith said. 'I'm Meredith, and this is Finn. Thank you so much for having us.'

'You're very welcome.' Charlie's smile suggested she knew she'd interrupted something. 'Your hampers look really good. Ooh, Gin Lovers! And what's this? Santa's Saviours?'

'It's for all the people who have to . . . uhm . . . support Santa's visits on Christmas Eve. A treat for all their hard work, on top of the usual glass of milk, mince pie and carrot for the reindeer.'

Charlie laughed. 'That's a wonderful idea! There are a lot of people who deserve this hamper; Santa must be getting on a bit, after all. I hope you're giving him adequate support,' she added, her brows creasing as she looked at Finn.

'Of course,' Finn said smoothly. 'I'm head elf, so I'm in charge of toy design, rather than actually assembling anything.'

'Of *course* you are,' Meredith said, rolling her eyes.

Charlie grinned. 'Head elf! I should have guessed.' She turned back to the hampers. 'And what's this? Oh my goodness, look at this one! So much sparkle!'

Meredith nudged Finn in the ribs. This was the hamper she was most proud of, the one she felt most attached to. It was called Scrooge's Delight, and it was a Christmassy, twinkly explosion of a gift box that included a candle that had glitter built into the glass jar, so that it shimmered when it was alight; a box of Christmas-flavoured chocolate seashells; a brandy-rich Christmas pudding for two (or one, if you were particularly hungry) and a pair of red-and-white-striped socks that said *Ex-Scrooge* on them. There was a copper bottle-opener, a string of bauble-shaped battery-operated fairy lights, and a garland to hang over your front door. She had lined the hampers with iridescent tissue paper, something she hadn't known existed until she'd fallen down a wrapping-paper rabbit hole online.

'It's the ultimate festive hamper,' she explained. 'For people who don't love Christmas, but might be able to warm to it with a bit of careful persuading and a big dose of glitter.'

'Are there a lot of people who don't love Christmas?' Charlie took out the garland. 'Can I?'

'Go ahead,' Meredith said.

Charlie started to unravel it, and Finn took one end so she could unfurl it fully. It read: *Have a very sparkly Christmas*. 'I love this,' Charlie said. 'I know someone who isn't exactly against Christmas, but who occasionally needs reminding that all the excess should be enjoyed, rather than feared.'

'Who's that?' Meredith asked, feeling the draw of a kindred spirit.

'My husband,' Charlie admitted. She said it gleefully, proudly, and Meredith wondered how long they'd been married. 'He should hang this above his reception desk for the next week.'

'Where does he work?' Finn asked, helping Charlie wrap the garland back up.

'Crystal Waters,' she said, pointing behind them. Meredith looked up at the building sitting on top of the cliff, all gleaming glass and sharp, modern angles.

Finn laughed. 'I think the sparkly garland would look right at home,' he said, and Meredith wondered if he'd visited the hotel. She and Anisha had gone there once for a very expensive dinner when Anisha had got a promotion at work, and she loved the idea of one of the Cornish Keepsakes garlands – especially one from her Scrooge hamper – adorning their minimalist foyer.

'Could you keep one of these for me?' Charlie asked. 'I'll pay now, but if I could pick it up later that would be great. The bus gets so hectic at these fairs.'

'Of course.' Meredith tried to hide her delight at having sold one of her prized hampers before the fair had even opened – and to the organizer, no less.

Charlie paid for it and wished them luck. 'I'd better go or I'll never be back on the bus in time for opening. Any queries or concerns, just pop over and see me. I hope you have a good day.'

'Thanks, Charlie,' Meredith said, 'you too!'

They watched her walk away, and then it was just Finn and Meredith, their hamper display and the beautiful Cornish beach, with the smells of a hundred different foody treats assaulting her senses and the waves crashing close by. She was confident that they could make some good sales. If Charlie had been enamoured enough by their hampers to reserve one, then Meredith had high hopes for the rest of the day.

She turned to Finn, and he planted a quick but purposeful kiss on her lips.

'We got interrupted before, and I really needed to do that.'

'Good,' Meredith said. 'But now we need to stop canoodling and start selling. Honestly, Finn Becker, where on earth is your Christmas spirit?'

She only just avoided being grabbed by him for what could have been a tickling assault, a raspberry against her neck or something else entirely inappropriate, because an older couple approached looking wide-eyed at their display, and Meredith shot Finn a glare that definitely said *Don't you dare* and hopefully also said *But later would be lovely*, and went to greet her customers.

Chapter Twenty-One

It was the twentieth of December and the air was like the chill from a freezer. The sun had set before Meredith left work, and it wasn't just because her finish times were creeping later as she fulfilled orders, checked in with the courier and helped Enzo in the shop.

Tomorrow was the shortest day of the year, and usually Meredith would be thrilled, because that meant Christmas would almost be over, and that in the not-too-distant future she wouldn't be leaving her house in the dark and getting home in the dark, missing the milky winter daylight.

This year, however, was different. She liked the darkness, because it showed off Anisha's amazing light displays, and when she walked through town she found herself lingering at the houses with the biggest Christmas trees in the windows, watching people gathering around them, laughing and decorating, drinking and admiring.

There were five days to go, and Meredith still didn't know what she would be doing.

Would Finn still be here, staying in Laurie's house, or did he have a London Christmas planned with his parents? She hadn't asked him, because she didn't want to burst the bubble of happiness they were living in. This meant that she could easily find herself, on Christmas morning, opening the presents she'd got Smudge and Crumble, faking their gratitude to her, then eating a turkey dinner for one and watching *Only Fools and Horses* reruns like some sad old cat lady. At the age of twenty-seven.

She locked her front door and pulled her hat lower on her head. It was extra cold tonight, but at least it was dry. Carol-singing in the wet wasn't an experience she was desperate to try. She passed Bernie's beautifully festive window, and her heart sank as she recalled how she'd reacted to her putting up her decorations in November. Had she caused the rift between them by being less than neighbourly? Had she said something unkind to her when she moved in? She was coming up with more and more reasons to regret her deficit of Christmas joy.

She passed a woman whom she regularly saw walking three mini schnauzers, tonight all wearing flashing collars, and waved. Her thoughts kept pace with her steps as she strode past the Sea Shanty, where she'd bumped into Finn that time, through the town that now resembled a giant Christmas cake, bright and enticing. Anisha had done a brilliant job.

Scrooge, Meredith thought, had been able to redeem himself, despite years of keeping his heart locked away – but that was fiction. Had a decade of turning her back on Christmas – steadfastly not allowing herself to enjoy radio jingles and supermarket mince pie towers, because every innocuous Christmassy moment took her back to the worst time of her life – done too much damage?

She pictured her dad, wondering how he would react to the way she had let the grief swallow her whole and return, like the worst sort of boomerang, every year. She could see him sitting in his ratty armchair in front of the fire, chuckling while she and Tommy knelt on the rug, pulling oranges, chocolate coins and plastic farm animals out of the stripy bedsocks that doubled as stockings. He had always tried his best, even when they had no money. He had made the most of what he had. Meredith had done the opposite: she hadn't even given it a chance.

A shouted greeting brought her out of her thoughts, and she realized she had reached the town hall. The rest of the choir were standing outside, togged up in their warmest clothes and with various festive adornments: Santa hats and sprigs of fake mistletoe. A couple of people looked as if they had skinned penguins and were wearing their faces as hats. It never made sense to Meredith that you would wear an animal's head above your own; it was disturbing.

'Meredith!' Emma said gleefully. Since being part of the pageant committee – and doing a great job, she and Anisha had both agreed – she had become even more domineering. But she was mostly friendly with it, and why shouldn't she be confident when her ideas were good? 'Are you joining us?'

'Err, yes?' Meredith hadn't meant it to come out as a question, but she thought it was obvious.

'You look like you're away with the fairies,' Emma said. She was wearing one of the penguin heads, which seemed appropriate, somehow. Except Meredith wasn't going to be grouchy about Christmas any more, so she inwardly scolded herself and tried to join in.

'Don't you mean away with the elves?' She laughed, but it fell flat.

Anisha gave her a curious look, her lips twitching. Her friend was wearing a dusky pink hat with the fluffiest bobble on it, and looked like a catalogue model.

'Where's your festive headgear?' Dennis asked, jiggling side to side to animate his holly and ivy headband.

'Ah!' Meredith reached into her bag and swapped her woolly hat for the glittery candy canes.

'Nice,' a couple of people said, and there were approving nods. She wanted to tell them that Finn had given them to her, but she knew that would make her seem unhinged. He had asked if he could come and watch her sing tonight, and she'd told him he would look like a sad, lonely puppy following a bunch of carol singers around town. She had given him the option of joining in, but he had backed away from the idea as if she was pointing a gun at him, hands held up in submission. She was seeing him later, at least.

'Goodness, Meredith!' Emma admonished. 'Whatever's on your mind, please push it far, far to the back. We're here to sing!' She threw her arms in the air, and the small group cheered and clapped. Meredith wondered if she'd been wrong about her, and their choir leader was actually a despotic ruler in training.

As they walked down the hill (their first spot was outside the Sea Shanty, which Meredith wasn't convinced would go down as well as Emma hoped it would), Anisha fell into step alongside her.

'What's got into you?' she asked, and then, before

Meredith could reply, said, 'Oh, I know. Finn.' She shot her a wicked look.

Meredith tried to look outraged and not laugh. 'Anisha Glynn, wash your mouth out!'

'Tell me it's not true.'

'We are having a very lovely time,' Meredith said primly, and almost rolled her eyes at herself.

'Is he your Christmas present to yourself?'

'I don't know,' she admitted. 'I haven't asked him what he's doing, and—'

'You *haven't?*' Anisha said, just as Emma shouted, 'Right, my Sky Mastersons and Sarah Browns! We're going to start with a rousing chorus of "We Wish You a Merry Christmas!" Get in your positions.'

'We have positions?' Meredith whispered, and she and Anisha shuffled their feet a bit as if they knew where they were meant to go.

Emma waved her hands to count them in, then they all started singing, taking a couple of seconds to match each other's pitch and pace, then falling into a tuneful, resounding chorus. Meredith raised her head, feeling her candy canes jiggle pleasingly as she gazed at the dark sky. That morning's mist had left behind a clear night, the brightest stars visible even through the streetlight haze.

The pub door swung open and a couple of men, who had clearly got into the Christmas spirit several hours ago, lurched out, arms around each other, and joined in. Their voices were enthusiastic if nothing else, and Meredith and Anisha exchanged a grin, while Emma's conducting got bolder.

'It's a sing-off,' Anisha whispered in a rush between phrases.

'Emma must have known this was going to happen,' Meredith added, speaking out of the side of her mouth and feeling like a 1940s spy-film character.

The song came to an end, and there was a smattering of applause from a few people who had stopped to listen. Their impromptu new members cheered as if they were at a football match. Emma looked furious, and Meredith prepared herself for 'Jingle Bells', the next song on their set list, when Emma said loudly, '"In the Bleak Midwinter".'

There were a couple of seconds of confusion, then they started singing.

The two men, red-faced and swaying, warbled along for a couple of stanzas before giving up. They gave the choir a round of applause, right in the middle of the second verse, and went back inside to their drinks. Soon Emma was back to her sparkling self, though Meredith thought it was a bit antisocial to have sent the men running with Christina Rossetti. Surely the whole point of carol-singing was that people could join in? It was more a community singsong than a performance.

As they walked to the next spot, Meredith realized she'd been advocating for Christmas joining in – albeit in her own head. Things were changing, and she didn't feel an ounce of discomfort about it.

They took their voices to various locations across town: next to the harbourside Christmas tree, where the light-adorned boat masts cast beautiful reflections on the water; at the top of Main Street, where three twinkling squirrels sat on the low wall that separated the loading bay from the cobbles. Town was busy because the lights looked so spectacular after dark, and the owners of a hot-dog stand and a roasted chestnuts stall were taking advantage of the increased footfall, giving Port Karadow a celebratory feel – and making Meredith's mouth water – even though the pageant was two days away.

They took a break halfway round, sipping from bottles of water and stamping their feet against the cold. Meredith took her phone out of her bag and saw that she had a couple of messages from Finn:

How's it going, Siren? xx

She felt a flush of pleasure. She wasn't sure if she preferred Siren to Red, but she secretly loved that he'd given her a nickname. It was a far cry from their first meeting, where she'd been at least sixty per cent exasperated by it. His second message read:

Message me when you're almost done and I'll come to yours. xx

She had left Smudge and Crumble alone this evening, knowing her puppy was able to cope with a couple of hours on his own, but no longer. Was it ridiculous that she knew her pets would be happy with Finn being there later? She replied:

Sure thing. It's going well, though Emma isn't a fan of joiners-in, especially if they can't sing in key. Perhaps it's a good thing you didn't come after all. ☺ xx

Then, because she was feeling reckless, she added:

I miss you though. Looking forward to later. xx

She didn't have time to wait for Finn's reply because Anisha told her it was time to stop mooning and start singing, and they made their way to the next location.

Aside from 'Carol of the Bells' – any mention of which gave Meredith palpitations, despite the hundreds of times she'd practised her solo – her favourite carol was 'Silent Night'. Tommy knew this and, when they were younger, when Christmas songs were still just about Christmas, he'd annoy her by singing a long swoop on the 'silent'. *SiiiiIIIIIlent Night.* The way he sung it, it sounded more like an alarm call than a carol.

But as the choir stood outside the youth hostel, a grey, unassuming building on the edge of town that housed a mixture of walking tourists and people down on their luck who needed a place to stay, 'Silent Night' brought another memory slamming into her, so sharp and sudden that she pressed a hand to her chest.

It had been their last Christmas as a family of four, and the farm had been doing particularly badly, so she and Tommy had already been warned that the celebrations would be meagre. Meredith had tried to be stoic, thinking that, at sixteen, she was old enough to understand that *things* weren't the important part of Christmas, even while she hid her envy as her school friends talked about putting hair straighteners and laptops on their wish lists.

She and Tommy had been sitting on the rug playing

Monopoly, the volume on the kitchen radio turned up while her mum made pigs in blankets, 'Silent Night' filling the room, when their dad had walked in. She had expected tense and weary, but instead he had looked cheerful, a lightness in his expression that had been missing for so long that the sight of it surprised her. There had been a yelp, and she'd noticed the black-and-white puppy in his arms.

It had come from a neighbouring farm, he'd told them. It was the runt of the litter and wasn't strong enough to be a working dog. It was for them, he'd said, if they could commit to looking after it, to hand-feeding it. Their own pet, a collie. They'd called her Sage, and that Christmas had been a blur of feeding and lying with her in the front room when she cried at night. Sage had grown into an affectionate, beautiful dog, and it hadn't mattered that she wasn't strong or fast enough to work the farm.

Somehow, as the memories tumbled in, Meredith kept singing, keeping up with 'Silent Night' and 'Hark the Herald Angels Sing'. When they reached the end and Emma instructed them to move to the next location, as if they were a troop of soldiers under her command, she felt a hand on her shoulder.

'Are you OK?' Anisha asked. 'That's not your usual thinking-about-Finn face.'

'It's not,' she admitted, her voice sounding strange to her own ears.

'Care to share?'

'I was thinking about Dad,' she said. 'When he brought us Sage.'

'Your family dog?'

Meredith nodded. Mum had taken Sage to Somerset, and

she was an old lady now. Tommy sent her a photo every time he visited. 'I just . . . I had completely forgotten how we got her; that Dad gave her to us on Christmas Eve, the year before he died.'

Anisha squeezed Meredith's shoulder.

'We had some great Christmases,' she added. 'I'm beginning to wonder what they would have been like since then, if I hadn't let the bad memories take over. If I'd fought a bit harder, with Tommy, to keep our family Christmases going. I feel like there's so much I've missed out on, and I've never thought that before. Look at all the time I've wasted.'

'I'm not disagreeing with you,' Anisha said, her voice light. 'But it's not as if you're a ninety-year-old granny sitting on your porch stoop, rueing all the missed opportunities in your life. You're twenty-seven.' She laughed gently. 'You've got quite a lot of time stretching ahead, all being well, for you to change direction, if that's what you want?'

She nodded vigorously. 'I'm going to call Tommy later. I don't want to rush things with Mum, but I want to be a bit more on his side. I'll visit her after Christmas, and maybe we can talk about it.'

'Great! Finn's obviously got a magic touch – and I'm not talking about in the bedroom, this time.'

Meredith didn't even pretend to be outraged. 'He has. He persevered when I was stubborn, and he's . . . I don't know. He nudged me, but once he knew about Dad, he never pushed too hard. I don't think . . .' She looked at her friend. 'You've always been there, that goes without saying, but—'

'Shush.' Anisha waved her away. 'When the learner is ready, the teacher will appear, or something. I'm so pleased for you. Honestly. Not because it matters what you think of Christmas, but because it means you're letting go of the sadness, giving yourself space for happier memories, like the one with Sage. That's a great thing.' She squeezed Meredith's arm, her eyes suspiciously bright.

'I know,' Meredith said, her voice a whisper.

'What does this mean for Christmas Day?'

Meredith shrugged. 'I'm seeing Finn tonight, and I'm going to ask him what he's doing. Even if he's going back to London, Laurie and Fern might be craving some inedible gingerbread.'

'I see that brave face,' Anisha said, 'and I want to wipe it off. Because you know there is always a place for you at ours, but I also think you really want to spend it with Finn. Don't ask him, tell him what you want. He's probably as nervous about mentioning it as you are. This is so new for both of you, and Christmas has this weight to it, because you're meant to spend it with the people you care about the most.'

'You're right,' Meredith said. 'I'm going to tell him I want to spend it with him.' Her breath rushed out in a long whoosh. 'Our relationship might just be for Christmas, but if that's the case then we should make the most of it.'

Anisha flicked one of Meredith's candy canes. 'Always with the marketing slogans. That's a goodie, too. Come on, let's catch up with the others, or Emma will make us do a hundred press-ups as penance.'

Their last spot on the carol-singing world tour, which was what Anisha had dubbed it halfway round, was where two pedestrian streets met in a wide, cobbled space. In the middle was a small fountain that, though turned off for the winter, Anisha's lights suppliers had turned into a twinkling Christmas pudding. Overlooking the space was a vegan restaurant called Alvin's, which Meredith had eaten at several times, and which served unquestionably delicious food.

Emma assembled her choir around the fountain, and Meredith found herself in the front row. She realized that just there – beyond the road that ran behind the tiny cobbled plaza – was Clotted Cream Cottage. This wasn't the angle she was used to seeing it from; it was side on, and she could only make out the upper half of the house over the brick wall that ran around it, but a bolt of shock went through her. There were lights on inside.

'Last push, my little Sally Bowleses!' Emma called. 'Let's make this a good one. We'll start with "Merry Christmas Everyone". I'll count you down.'

Meredith flung herself into the song, proud of how they all sounded together and slightly less nervous about her solo on Wednesday because, she reminded herself, they were a hodgepodge little choir but they could actually sing. Finn had called her a siren, and while the murdering-men-against-the-rocks association wasn't particularly flattering, the beautiful-voice part was.

They were near the end, halfway through 'Jingle Bells', and people had come out of the restaurant, interrupting their meals, to clap and sing along, including the head chef, Marley. Emma was a lot more enthusiastic about them than she had been about the pub-dwellers, and Meredith was pondering whether that was a little discriminatory, when she noticed a taxi pull up on the road beyond the fountain.

She watched as a tall man with dark, curly hair climbed

out. He was wearing a long woollen coat and carrying an expensive-looking briefcase. He was every inch the businessman, except for his navy cowboy boots. The effect was incongruous, and Meredith watched, captivated, as a gate in the wall of Clotted Cream Cottage opened and a woman stepped out.

She was tall, slim and very blonde, and wrapped in a grey shawl. Meredith had never seen her before, and the smart couple were nothing like the people in the stories she and Tommy had told each other growing up. The man and woman embraced, then walked through the gate and disappeared inside.

Meredith wanted to tell Tommy: Clotted Cream Cottage was going to be occupied for Christmas. Her evening spent singing carols around town had been happier, and much more surprising, than she had expected. From her memory about Sage, to the drunk serenaders outside the pub, and three small children who had bounced their way through 'Last Christmas' down by the harbour – holding hands and screaming the wrong words at the tops of their voices – to this moment, when it seemed as if one of her lifelong mysteries was about to be solved.

She tuned back into the singing as Emma brought them to a close with a rousing chorus of 'We Wish You a Merry Christmas', but she couldn't help glancing at Clotted Cream Cottage and the glow coming from the windows.

The thought that came to her, bright and blinding like the Christmas star, certain and all the more unsettling for it, was that, as well as wanting to speak to Tommy, she couldn't wait to see Finn. She was desperate to tell him all the details of her evening, speculate with him about who

273

could be inside the cottage, while he wrapped her in his strong arms and kissed her forehead. Already, she had come to depend on him for a certain chunk of her happiness, and she couldn't decide whether that was a good thing or not.

Chapter Twenty-Two

The twenty-second of December started in a rather lack-lustre fashion, with heavy clouds and damp pavements. Meredith was at the Cornish Keepsakes office while it was still dark, getting the hampers ready for their stand, while the blue lights twinkled in the darkened window and carols drifted like ghosts from the radio in the corner.

They were using the same exhibition van for their pageant stand as they had used at the Porthgolow food fair, and Meredith had added another item to her new year to-do list: convince Adrian that they should buy their own van for local fairs and festivals. They could brand it so that whoever was stuck behind them in Cornwall's famous traffic queues would have Cornish Keepsakes imprinted on their brains.

Local deliveries would no longer have to happen in a C1 or an orange Audi, but could be done professionally in a branded truck, while the national deliveries were carried out by the courier service she'd contracted. Maybe one day there would be a whole fleet of Cornish Keepsakes trucks travelling the roads.

She was preparing hampers and musing on her plans for their little business's world domination, when she heard the door open behind her. She assumed it was Enzo, who would be manning the stand for most of the day, along with Patrick from the choir. There were so many Port Karadow residents involved in the pageant that she was beginning to worry there wouldn't be anyone left to have fun and spend money.

'Morning, Meredith!' It was Adrian, sounding particularly chirpy, and she tried not to fall over in shock. He was wearing grey trousers and a Christmas jumper under an open leather jacket. The jumper was covered in polar bears wearing Santa hats, and oversized, glittering snowflakes. 'Tillie picked it out for me,' he added, and she realized she was staring.

'You're here early.'

'Yes, well. Pageant day! I'm coming to help out on the stall.'

'You're going to help sell hampers?'

He chuckled. 'No need to sound so surprised. I know I'm very much a *behind-the-desk* man.' He slid his hand down the front of his jumper, glancing down sheepishly as he realized there was no tie to smooth. 'But everyone's done such a sterling job this Christmas. The VIP hampers worked wonderfully, expertly delivered by you and Finn, and sales are up, so with all that momentum I thought it was time I got my hands dirty. You'll be flitting about like the proverbial Christmas fairy, I assume?'

Meredith nodded, taken aback by his determination to muck in. 'I'll be making sure the stall owners have what they need, and that people are finding the start of the treasure hunt OK, and generally checking that everyone's having a good time.'

Adrian grinned. 'I thought as much. There's a real fire burning under that unassuming visage of yours, isn't there? So glad I have someone with genuine Christmas spirit leading the charge this year.' Meredith stared at him, dumbfounded, until he offered her a coffee and sauntered into the kitchen to make them.

By the time Enzo had arrived, the three of them had loaded up the van and were ready to drive it roughly quarter of a mile to their stand location, the sun was gaining confidence. The damp pavements glittered, and with the Christmas lights already switched on, there was a slightly surreal glow in the town. The designs were eclectic and colourful: pink flamingos and green frogs, orange stockings and purple donkeys mingled with the more traditional snowflakes and stars, so that, in certain parts of Port Karadow, Meredith felt as if she was walking inside a rainbow.

Enzo, Adrian and Meredith joined the other people setting up stalls. There was a hot dog and burger stand, a coffee and cake bar, Emma's niece selling her greetings cards for her on a table under a candy-striped gazebo hung with metallic paper chains. A tombola run by volunteers was raising money for local homeless charity, A Bed for Everyone, the soap-maker's stand smelled of lemons and geraniums, offering a whiff of spring in amongst the winter glitter, and the vintage sweet shop was selling bags of humbugs, sugar mice and candyfloss.

While they got ready, the band Anisha had hired started playing 'Santa Claus Is Comin' To Town'. A family out early lingered in front of it, a boy of about four jumping up and down while his dad held tightly onto his hand. Meredith watched as the saxophone player wiggled and wove in front of the boy, whose delighted frenzy intensified while his mum looked on and laughed.

'Kid's got rhythm,' Enzo observed. Meredith turned to answer him just as something was shoved onto her head, capturing some of her curls that had tightened in the damp air.

'Hey!' Meredith reached up and felt soft, fleecy material.

'Carrying on the candy-cane theme,' Anisha said. Meredith spun round. Her friend was wearing a smart navy suit, a dark blue shirt with silver stars on it, and shiny boots. She had her scarlet winter coat open over the top, along with a fluffy red-and-white striped Santa hat – which Meredith assumed was the same as her own – and was carrying her iPad. 'It's looking good, isn't it?'

'It looks great!' Meredith raised her voice to be heard over the band, the jaunty music vibrating through the soles of her feet. 'This is going to be a good day, Nish.'

Anisha's stare was stern, but Meredith saw the satisfaction in it. 'It's not even ten o'clock. There's a long way to go.'

'Enough time for it to get so good that Port Karadow is named as the official Christmas town of Cornwall.'

Anisha laughed. 'Oh my god, Meredith! What has happened to you?'

'I don't know!' She shrugged and danced along to the music, feeling far less professional than her friend in her jeans, boots with fur trim, grey-and-red-striped jumper and bright blue coat. She was avoiding Anisha's eye, because she didn't really know how she felt about it all, except that she wasn't overwhelmed by sadness when she heard Michael Bublé on the radio any more, or saw a tabletop Christmas tree and had flashbacks to the one sitting on the nurse's station at the hospital where her dad was taken. The hollowness that had lived inside her for the last ten years, that always bottomed out at Christmastime, was filling itself in.

'Whatever it is, it's great,' Anisha said, but in a voice that suggested she wasn't entirely convinced. Which was fair enough, because Meredith wasn't sure she believed it either. She had asked herself countless times over the last couple of weeks if it was Finn plugging the hole, and if, should he finally make a decision about what he was doing and opt with leaving Cornwall and returning to his London life, he would pull that plug out and make the hole bigger when he went.

'It *is* great,' Meredith said, because this wasn't the time to go into it. 'What's next on your list of things to do?'

'You all sorted here?'

Meredith glanced at Enzo and Adrian, who were arranging hampers with the care of professional window dressers. 'Are you good, guys?'

'Great thanks, Meredith!' Adrian said. 'Enzo, what do you think for the top of this tower? Gin Lovers or Scrooge's Delight?'

'The Scrooge one, deffo,' Enzo said. 'Draws the most crowds in the shop, that one.'

Meredith left them to it, a triumphant grin tugging at her mouth as she followed Anisha through the streets of Port Karadow.

* * *

By lunchtime the town was full of people enjoying the entertainment, music and food, the sounds of shouting and laughter mingling with the band's music and the occasional, echoey message from Andy on the loudspeaker – Anisha had given him the role of announcer, because she knew he'd love it and said it would stop him meddling – and the hypnotic clank of the boat's halyards as they swayed on the water.

Visitors bought last-minute Christmas presents and treated themselves to chips, burgers and wraps, and Dennis had told Anisha they already had fifty-five entries for the treasure-hunt competition. Having known that children would be getting help from parents, and that couples and groups of friends would also want to tour the town and mark off the different lights on the map Anisha had created, the prize was an assortment of locally produced goodies, including one of the Cornish Keepsakes family hampers.

Anisha and Meredith stood next to the small platform by the harbour, a crowd gathering around them, a restless buzz working through them like a Mexican wave.

'She was meant to be here three minutes ago,' Anisha said quietly.

'Three minutes isn't that late,' Meredith replied, peering over the people to the routes that led down to the harbour.

'Four now,' Anisha muttered.

Meredith thought of how laid-back Laurie was, and wondered if they should have asked her to arrive fifteen minutes early. She thought about calling Finn. They'd slept apart last night, because Meredith had to be completely on her game today, which meant lots of sleep beforehand – the one thing that had been suffering since she and Finn had got together. She tried not to think about the fact that she

280

still hadn't asked him what he was doing for Christmas, and it was three days away now. Her feelings had changed, but she still felt nervous about the day itself; all the things that could go wrong, including Finn already having other plans. In this one thing, it seemed she was incapable of doing anything except burying her head in the sand. But he'd promised he'd be there for the concert, and that seemed enough for now.

'Five minutes,' Anisha said darkly.

Meredith was about to give a placatory reply when she saw the object of their anxiety striding through the crowd. The mutterings took on an excited tone as a few people recognized Laurie. She seemed oblivious, her focus on Meredith and Anisha, and when she reached them – her coat like something out of a stage musical, all loose sleeves and soft, plum fabric – she wrapped Meredith in a hug.

'So sorry I'm late,' she said. 'In all my planning I forgot that the roads would be backed up. The town has been transformed, and you look lovely, Meredith. I love your hat. Both your hats.' She turned to Anisha. 'You must be Nish. It's so good to meet you, and I'm sorry, again, that I'm a bit behind. Could I have one of these?' She pointed at the candy-cane hats, and Anisha laughed.

Meredith could see that, despite having already spoken to Laurie on the phone, her friend was slightly star-struck. She hid her amusement at Anisha's loss of composure, the way her hands fumbled as she ferreted in a box beneath the podium, then handed Laurie one of the fleecy, stripy hats.

Laurie arranged it jauntily on her head, and Meredith said, 'It really suits you,' which was true, because Laurie had the kind of face that would suit just about anything.

'You don't need to flatter me because you're going out with Finn,' she said, then winked to show she was teasing. 'In fact, you don't need to do anything except what you're already doing. I can't tell you how much you've picked him up, Meredith. He's a changed man – he's happy, which was something I was concerned he'd never get around to. Anyway,' she added, 'I suppose it's time for me to officially open the pageant.'

'If you could,' Anisha said, while Meredith struggled to set aside Laurie's words and focus on her next job, which was to get the dance troupe, complete with guising masks, into position at the head of the procession.

She hurried over to Elliot, the dance leader. He was dressed as an elegant snowman in a white suit with fluffy sleeves and leg warmers, his mask a canvas of shimmering white with a button nose. The rest of the group were other Christmas characters: Mr and Mrs Santa Claus, reindeers, elves and penguins, and a couple of gingerbread people, who reminded Meredith that she still hadn't managed to bake a successful batch.

Laurie stepped onto the podium and the microphone let out a loud whine. Once the dancers were in place, and the floats lined up behind them, Meredith gave her a thumbs up.

'Good afternoon, Port Karadow,' Laurie said, her voice smooth and warm and just the right amount of excited, 'and Happy Christmas!' The crowd cheered. 'I'm Laurie Becker, and I'm here to make sure you're all having a wonderful time. Are you?'

'Yes!' someone called from the front.

'I found a purple donkey!' a young voice added, and everyone laughed.

'A purple donkey?' Laurie's eyes went wide. 'Then you're having the very best day already! And, ladies and gentlefolks, it's about to get a whole lot better, because I can officially announce that it is time for the Port Karadow Christmas procession! We have dancers, acrobats, singers and music makers, and if you're really lucky and wish for it very hard, you might even see a little bit of snow.' She tapped the side of her nose, and Meredith watched as a few people – and not just the younger ones – looked skywards. She exchanged a happy look with Anisha: Laurie had been the right person to whip up the crowd's enthusiasm.

'Don't forget,' Laurie went on, 'the stalls are all still open, and the treasure-hunt competition won't close for another two hours, so you still have time to get your entries in. At seven o'clock, we're rounding off this wonderful day with a sublime concert from the talented Port Karadow choir. Make your way to the town hall for that; it's something you won't want to miss. And on that note, I bid you all farewell. Go, make merry, spend generously, and above all, have a truly incredible Christmas!' She flung her arms into the air and Anisha pressed a button that released confetti over the crowd.

Colourful streamers rained down, winking in the afternoon light, and there was another, louder cheer. The music resumed, Elliot and his dancers all assumed dramatic poses, froze for a moment, and then, with a flourish, started dancing. They led the procession away from the harbour, towards the heart of town. They would end up back here, hopefully having delighted and amazed everyone they passed.

'That was great,' Nish said, when Laurie climbed down from the podium. 'Anyone would think you'd done something like this before.' She grinned, and Laurie laughed. 'Seriously though, thank you for doing this. Are you sure you want to waive your fee?'

'Dear girl,' Laurie said, 'you're not supposed to ask me after the fact. There's no way I want to be paid for five minutes' work in this town. It's my home, and I love it. Besides, Meredith made sure I couldn't say no to your offer.'

Anisha laughed.

'We're almost family now, after all,' the older woman added, and Meredith felt a sharp stab of discomfort. There was something steely in her gaze, as if she was warning her off hurting Finn. Meredith wanted to tell her she had no intention of hurting him, but that they hadn't known each other very long, and it was Finn who might not be sticking around. But saying all that, in response to a look she only *thought* she'd seen, would be a bit extreme.

'Is Finn coming?' she asked instead. 'I thought he would have come into town with you.'

'He was lost in a painting when I left,' Laurie explained, her features softening. 'But he broke off long enough to tell me he would be here, and I set up Alexa to blare her loudest alarm at thirty-minute intervals from – ' she glanced at her watch – 'about ten minutes ago, so he has no excuse. Don't worry – he won't miss the chance to see you. You're like coffee to him, now: can't go a day without or his mood is seriously affected.' She pulled Meredith into another hug. 'I'm off to get a burger. Can I get you two anything?'

'No thanks,' Anisha said.

Meredith shook her head. 'We'll get some food in a bit.'

'OK then, wonderful girls. See you later on.' She swooped off into the dispersing crowd, and was collared by a man

284

holding a black-and-white photograph and a Sharpie. Laurie stopped and chatted with him, and Meredith wondered how she could have her switch set permanently to 'on' like that.

'She's a whirlwind,' Anisha said. 'Is Finn anything like her?'

Meredith couldn't help smiling. 'In some respects. I hope you'll find out for yourself today.' Anisha had been called into work on an urgent planning issue when Finn had helped with the goody bags, and they'd missed each other.

'I hope he'll get to meet Nick and the kids, too,' Anisha said. 'Though I don't know where they are – they should be here by now. One errand, he said he had to run.' She rolled her eyes and looked briefly at her phone. 'Right, no time for family dramas. Let's get going.'

The sun was dipping down over the sea as the procession made its way back to the harbour. The dancers and floats had been a success, some residents coming equipped with their own masks to join in with the guising. The crowd had danced along to the music, and had revelled in the fake snow shooting out of the machine on the last float, the white flakes adding an extra spark of Christmas magic.

'Good call on the snow,' Meredith said to Anisha as they stood side by side against the harbour wall, watching the procession advance towards them. They were both jiggling for warmth, the temperature dropping as the sun turned the horizon amber, and the Christmas lights turned their town into something special.

'Andy's still sceptical about it, even though I showed him it was biodegradable. He thinks it's going to muck up the pavements for years.'

'He's just incredulous that you've pulled off something so perfect at such short notice.'

'It has been a bit of a triumph,' Anisha said.

'I didn't realize you used such lofty words about your own achievements.'

'*Our* achievements,' Anisha corrected. 'Now there's just the concert to go.'

'Yes,' Meredith said, nerves jangling in her stomach as she thought of her solo, and who would be watching it.

'Seen Finn?' Anisha asked.

'Nope. Seen Nick and the kids?'

'Nope. Not that I would have had time to spend with them, but even so.' She shook her head. 'Right, I'm going to find Emma. You stay here and welcome the procession lot back.'

'Will do!' Meredith saluted and went to congratulate the dancers. As they took off their masks, she saw the bright eyes and red cheeks of exhilaration. She thanked them all, then went to greet the other performers.

She was thanking the team running the '*Frozen*' float, a winter landscape complete with people dressed as Elsa, Anna and Olaf, raising her voice over the band, who were playing 'Christmas (Baby Please Come Home)', when she felt a tap on her shoulder.

She excused herself and turned, and was suddenly face to face with someone wearing a beautiful, intricate mask. It was a painting rather than a face: a deep blue background behind a Christmassy scene of snowy fields and a tiny cottage, with a single, glowing window, pinprick snowflakes and a moon hanging above. A pair of blue eyes looked at her through the eyeholes.

She would have recognized Finn's eyes even if the painting style hadn't been so uniquely his own, or he hadn't been wearing his green padded jacket, or had a beagle puppy in his arms, the dog straining forward so he could lick Meredith. Her heart skipped in time to the music, and she reached out and lifted the mask.

Finn looked contrite.

'I am so, so sorry,' he said, slightly out of breath. 'I meant to be here a lot earlier. We did.' He waggled Crumble's paw, and those two words, linking him with her dog as if they were her own, perfect little family, did strange things to Meredith's inside's. 'How has it been?' he asked. 'I mean . . .' he looked around him, and she took a second to absorb what he was seeing: the twinkling lights, coming fully to life now the sun was almost gone, and the floats drawing to a halt. The smells and laughter, happy people everywhere. 'It's obviously won Christmas.'

Meredith laughed and stepped closer, and Crumble nuzzled her neck. 'I'm glad you made it.'

'I would never have missed your concert,' Finn said. 'I don't want to have the chance to miss anything about you.'

He moved towards her, sandwiching the dog between them as the band began to play 'I've got my love to keep me warm.' He dipped his head, his lips finding hers as the music got louder, and there was a gentle whoosh from somewhere nearby. Finn's kiss was tender and passionate, Meredith could feel her dog's small, warm body between them, and it seemed that even though the snow float had reached the end of the route, it still had time for one final flurry, because soft, white flakes were raining down on them.

If this was what Christmas could be like, she thought,

as she kissed Finn and felt the snow settle in her hair, felt the band's trumpet all the way to her toes, and thought she heard some new applause from somewhere nearby, she didn't know why she'd been so scared of it for all these years.

Chapter Twenty-Three

As the carol concert crept closer, the lump of apprehension worked its way further up Meredith's throat, until she felt as though she might not be able to breathe, let alone sing.

She, Finn and Crumble went to get burgers, and as they waited for them to be ready, the nerves overtook her in a sudden sweep, and she thought she might collapse onto the cold ground. She inhaled slow, deep breaths, collected her chicken burger, then focused on every bite of it; the crunchy coating and spicy sauce, zeroing her concentration in on the taste and not the fact that, in less than an hour, she would have to perform in front of the whole town, her colleagues and Finn, probably Finn's aunt, who was a natural performer and—

'Meredith, are you OK?' Finn squeezed her arm. 'Are you *choking*?' His voice was raised, and there was panic in his eyes.

She shook her head. 'No.' She took a deep breath. 'No, I-I'm not choking.'

'And yet somehow, that hasn't reassured me.' He took her hand and led her to the side of the busy path, until they were standing against the harbour wall. Meredith turned so she could feel the air coming off the water, fresher than the fug of the pageant, with its popcorn sweetness and onions and spice. 'What's going on?' he asked gently.

She waved a hand in front of her face, as if that would convey everything she was feeling.

Finn narrowed his eyes, his gaze burning into her. After a moment, he said, 'You will be incredible. You're a wonderful singer, Meredith, and you will wow everyone. You can't banish the nerves beforehand, but once you get up there, you'll open your mouth and that first note will come out, just as you intended, and you'll feel like you're flying.'

'Really?' She stepped into his personal space and he wrapped his arms around her.

'Really.' He spoke into the top of her head. 'And I will be there, cheering you on – silently, though, apart from when it's appropriate, because I don't want to put you or the rest of the choir off.'

She managed a laugh.

'And,' he went on, as Meredith felt the comforting weight of Crumble settling on her foot, 'if anything *does* go wrong, just remember that you're human, it's your first time doing a solo and nobody will think badly of you. They'll all be marvelling at your talent and your courage to get up there in the first place – and most of them don't even know how hard Christmas is for you – and then, when you sing, they won't be thinking any more, because your voice is so beautiful that they'll have no option but to just feel.'

At his words, Meredith's nerves shifted from dread to

apprehensive anticipation, and she wondered how she had ever coped without his arms around her and his reassurance, the warmth of his breath on her skin and hair, and his way of breaking things down until they were simple. 'Thank you,' she said, freeing her arms so she could return his hug. 'Thank you for being here, and for saying that. Thank you for talking to me on the beach.'

'Thank you for letting me,' he murmured.

'Finn,' she whispered into his neck.

'Mmmm?'

'Do you think—'

Her voice was cut off by the loud jingle of his phone, and he stepped back, retrieving it from his pocket. He frowned at the screen.

'Is anything wrong?'

'No, not at all.' He cancelled the call.

'Sure?' She was starting to understand his body language, the way his jaw tightened when he was tense, his cheeks bunching slightly when he was happy or relaxed. Right now he was all taut, angular planes, and Meredith wondered what had happened.

'Sure,' Finn said, and pulled her to him again. They stayed like that, next to the boats bobbing gently on the water, their masts twinkling in the darkness like the flickering flames of a hundred candles, and Meredith decided to believe him. If something was wrong, she was sure he would tell her.

By the time she met up with Anisha and Emma, Dennis and Patrick and the other choir members, she had come to accept the pounding of her pulse, the metallic taste in her mouth, and her giddiness.

291

'OK?' Anisha whispered, adjusting the curls around Meredith's face and pulling her hat more snugly onto her head. 'You're going to smash this.'

'I am,' Meredith croaked, and wondered if she'd be able to get a single note out.

At least 'Carol of the Bells' wasn't first. It was third on their set list, which was perfect. It meant she would have a couple of songs to warm up, but then it would happen and then it would be over, and she could enjoy the rest of the concert without worrying.

When Anisha had stopped fussing over her, they turned to face the front.

They were standing on the steps of the town hall, the outdoor lights on either side of the door acting like spotlights. A large crowd had gathered below them, and Meredith could see clusters of friends, children standing in front of parents, a couple of smaller kids on the shoulders of dads or uncles. The audience spilled down the hill to Meredith's right, and up to her left.

She was on the middle step, the third of five, and could just see down the alley that cut through to the harbour and, at the bottom, a slice of the water. It reminded her of Finn's earlier words, and she felt immediately calmer.

She looked for him in the crowd. He had told her he'd be there; they had parted ten minutes ago, when she said she needed to go and get ready, and he'd told her he'd find Laurie. She searched for his blond hair, usually so recognizable, but couldn't see him. She found Adrian and Tillie, standing with Enzo and a slim girl who might have been his sister. Enzo waved, and Meredith waved back.

There was Cecily Talbot, dressed in a furry cream coat,

with a man who could easily have been a male model; Daisy – who often dog-sat Crumble – gave her a warm smile, and Marge and Benedict Hevingham were near the front, Marge's eyes twinkling in anticipation.

Everyone, it seemed, was there. Everyone except for Finn, and he was the one person she wanted to see more than anyone.

Emma stood in front of them, fussing with the paper on the music stand she'd brought outside, and as they waited, Meredith watched Nick, Jasmine and Ravi join the throng. Nick's cheeks were pink and his woolly hat was on wonkily, his scarf trailing behind him. Jasmine and Ravi looked perfectly bundled up against the cold, and as Nick man-oeuvred them to the front, Anisha exchanged waves with her husband and children. Ravi's wave was the most enthusiastic, his pudgy cheeks squeezed into a smile.

'Finally,' Anisha murmured. 'Where on earth have they been all day?'

'Maybe they were here and we just didn't see them?' Meredith scanned the crowd again. Still no sign of Finn.

'Maybe,' Anisha muttered.

'Right, Jets and Sharks,' Emma said, raising her arms, and a hush fell over the choir and their audience. Their choir leader turned to face the assembled throng, and spoke in her cool, clear voice. 'I hope you've all been enjoying the festivities today, and thank you for staying for the culmina-tion of what has been a fantastic Christmas pageant.'

There were cheers and whoops, and the sound of several bells jingling rhythmically, as if Santa had appeared with his sleigh. Meredith craned her neck, looking for the source of the noise, and decided she must be going barmy with nerves.

'Our choir has been working very hard to bring you a selection of festive, atmospheric favourites,' Emma continued. 'Please sing along if you want to, but also respect the singers. There are some solos in here that I'd hate for you to miss.'

Meredith smiled. Only the Port Karadow choir concerts came with a warning to the audience. She wanted to catch Finn's eye, share the joke with him, but she still couldn't see him. Her gaze latched onto a familiar figure, and Laurie's eyes met hers. They were full of apology, and a cold, hard dread solidified in Meredith's chest.

'Right then.' Emma gave a determined nod, then turned her smile on the choir. 'Ready, my lovely Kathy Seldens?'

They all nodded, and she pressed play on the portable sound-system she'd set up with their backing tracks. The music was quiet, more of a guide than an accompaniment, as they'd rehearsed without it to get the harmonies spot on.

The first bars of 'Hark the Herald Angels Sing' drifted up to them, and Meredith took a deep breath, opened her mouth and sang the right note. It was shaky, but at least it was there. She let the breath and words fill her up before she expelled them, the voices she knew so well surrounding her as they spurred each other on. But as the carol went on, her throat seemed to tighten, and she couldn't lose herself in the music like she usually did. Finn had promised her he'd be here.

The first carol came to an end and there was a burst of applause. Anisha glanced at Meredith, frowning when she didn't return her smile, but Emma moved swiftly on to 'Santa Claus Is Comin' To Town'. 'Carol of the Bells' would slow the pace after this one. Meredith didn't think she'd be able to do it.

She flung herself into the jaunty tune, relieved when she got every word out, but her voice was scratchy. The song came to an end, the applause rang out, and Meredith swallowed hard.

Anisha squeezed her hand. 'What's wrong?'

She shook her head. 'Finn . . .' she started, but there was no time, because Emma was cuing them up for 'Carol of the Bells'.

Meredith's dread and disappointment lodged itself in her throat. Her pulse was pounding in her ears, so loudly that she could barely hear what her choir leader was saying. The crowd looked on with anticipation, Emma caught her eye and nodded, and Meredith felt a bead of sweat run down her back, beneath all her winter layers.

She wanted to run down the steps but she was frozen.

Finn wasn't here. She couldn't do it.

There was no introduction to 'Carol of the Bells'. She had to come in straight away.

She felt Anisha's hand tighten around hers. She looked into the crowd and saw Enzo's bright smile, Tillie with her hands clasped in front of her, eyes wide like a child on Christmas morning. Adrian was grinning at her. She looked at Emma, whose expression had turned questioning.

'Ready, Meredith?' she said.

Meredith wanted to say no. She wanted to run. She was about to shake her head – someone would be able to step in, surely? Then her gaze landed on Marge Hevingham, and she remembered the simple happiness of singing 'Rudolph the Red-Nosed Reindeer', the delight on Marge's face, the compliment she'd got from the boy next door.

'Ready,' she said. It came out gravelly, and she swallowed

again, trying to clear her throat. She remembered Charlie's delight at the Porthgolow food market when she'd seen the Scrooge hamper, looked at the expectant, eager faces in front of her, some clutching bags of hot chestnuts. She'd created those hampers, all by herself. She'd been a big influence on this magical winter pageant. Finn might have helped her, but he hadn't done those things: *she* had. She didn't need him. She could do this.

Emma lifted her arms for the beginning of 'Carol of the Bells', looked Meredith square in the eye, and whispered, 'OK, my Elsa?'

'OK,' Meredith said.

She closed her eyes for a second, took a deep breath, then turned her gaze on the crowd, opened her mouth and sang the first note. Her voice was strong, stronger than she felt, and the world seemed to hush around her. The audience were captivated, the words taking on extra meaning as she sang loud and clear. Then the rest of the choir joined her, the carol growing to a crescendo, filling her lungs and her head and her heart while the people she knew, in this town she had come to love, watched on.

By the last verse, Meredith was soaring. She felt ready to float away, and when they came to a neat, perfect end, the crowd's applause almost lifted her off her feet once more. Emma beamed, and Anisha flung her arms around Meredith, not caring that they were in the middle of the concert.

'Well now,' Emma said, her eyes twinkling. 'Fishermen's Friends, eat your heart out.'

Meredith grinned at Anisha, then turned back to the front, her smile slipping as she saw Laurie again. The woman nodded at her, and Meredith managed to return it. Finn hadn't slunk back halfway through her performance. He still wasn't here.

'On we go, my little Grizabellas,' Emma said. 'Ready for "I've Got My Love to Keep Me Warm"? Three, two, one.' She launched them into the upbeat song, and Meredith found she was able to join in, to sway her hips as they sang, to revel in the crowd's obvious delight. It was the perfect Christmassy conclusion they had all been hoping for – except for Meredith it hadn't quite been perfect, because she'd got her hopes up. Christmas, it seemed, was intent on dashing them against the rocks, and this year was turning out to be no different, after all.

By the time the concert was over and the choir had accepted round after round of applause, Meredith felt a strange mix of accomplishment and disappointment. Her solo had gone better than she could have imagined – despite the almost-false start – and she had enjoyed it, letting the music take her and her audience to another place. But she had believed Finn, she had been counting on him to be there, and he hadn't turned up. There was no sign of him now, as the crowd started to drift away.

Anisha turned to her and said, 'Something important must have come up.'

'Sure,' Meredith replied, though she didn't know what that could be.

'Go and find him, OK?' her friend urged. 'Wait to hear what he has to say before you draw any conclusions.'

Meredith nodded. 'He's got Crumble.'

'Well then,' Anisha said, as Nick, Jasmine and Ravi

approached. 'You've got no choice, have you?' She wrapped her in a cinnamon-scented kiss.

'We did a great thing today,' Meredith said.

'We did. I saw Maisie from the ironmonger's smiling in the crowd, and Max from Sea Brew was there too, looking pretty pleased with himself, and I wouldn't have had him as a carol concert sort of person. We might have actually done some good.'

'We've done a lot of good,' Meredith confirmed. 'Go and revel in it.' They hugged again, and Anisha went to greet her family.

Meredith walked over to Adrian and Tillie, who were standing with the Hevinghams.

'That was so wonderful,' Marge said, pressing a hand to her chest. 'It's made my Christmas – even more than Adrian's kind hamper.'

'I completely agree,' Adrian said, more serious than she had ever seen him. 'You were magnificent. I hope you'll treat us to a serenade or two in the office occasionally.'

Meredith laughed. 'I'm not sure about that, but I did enjoy it, and I'm glad you all did, too.'

They said their goodbyes, and Meredith wondered where to go. She couldn't see Laurie any more, and the little town was emptying out as people made their way home or went to look at the lights now the darkness was complete. She took her phone out of her pocket, about to call Finn, when she saw him, her beagle puppy in his arms, down by the harbour. He was walking towards her, but Meredith picked up her pace, wanting to join him by the water.

She noticed most of the food stalls had packed up and gone home, only the hot dog stand remaining. The lighting was lower, and the twinkling boat masts stood out like beacons.

Meredith took stock of her emotions. There was hurt, fondness and apprehension, something that felt too big for her chest that she didn't want to examine, and a small, tight knot of bitterness. She wanted to let it go, but she knew she had to accept it until she'd dealt with the cause and could throw it away.

As she got closer, she could see that Finn's expression held at least as many emotions as she was feeling, but mostly he looked tired.

'I am so, so sorry,' he said, approaching her. 'I am so sorry I missed your solo.'

'Where did you go?'

'I got a call from Mum. She and Dad are here, they told me there was an emergency—'

'They're at Laurie's house?' Meredith was surprised.

Finn swallowed. 'No, not Laurie's house. They have their own place, sort of a romantic bolthole, in Port Karadow. Actually . . .' He ran a hand through his hair. 'It's the cream house – the one you call Clotted Cream Cottage.'

'*What?*' It came out as a whisper. She blinked, thinking back to the carol-singing, the smart couple she'd seen there, her surprise that it was occupied after all these years. She had told Finn when she'd seen him later that night, how amazed she was to finally see people in it, but he'd seemed nonplussed and changed the subject. It was something else he'd kept from her. Did the Becker dynasty own the whole of Port Karadow?

'I didn't know they were here, until—'

'Until I told you about Clotted Cream Cottage having

people in it two nights ago? You knew then that it was your mum and dad. Why didn't you say anything? Or before, when I pointed it out, told you how much I loved the house?'

He winced. 'I didn't want to—'

'You didn't want to bring your London life into it,' she finished for him, her anger rising. 'It seems like that was always going to be pretty hard when your family own half the town.'

His eyes hardened. 'That's not how it is. But yes, when we were delivering hampers, I didn't want to think about the gallery, or the mess I'd left behind. I should have told you sooner.'

Was this going to be his eternal refrain? *I should have told you sooner.* She shook her head. 'What was the emergency?'

He huffed, and she could see that he was angry too, though she didn't think it was with her. 'Supposedly we needed to contact all our most generous customers before we close for Christmas, make sure the exhibition opening in January is a full house, rather than a washout.'

'They came all the way down here to ask you to do that?'

He shook his head. 'It wasn't true. I got to the house, and they just . . . they wanted to know what I was doing here. Why I hadn't gone back to London. I left as soon as I could—'

'But you still went to them at the first sign of trouble with the gallery,' Meredith said, some of the anger leaching out of her. 'Even when you must have known you'd miss the concert.' She sounded petty, but Finn's promise had mattered to her. He'd been so perceptive up until now, so she thought he would have known that. Perhaps she had misjudged him.

300

'I shouldn't have gone, I realize that now. But it sounded so urgent, and they're still my parents: it's still my job.'

'Did you talk to them about your painting? About what you really want to do? I thought you were on the verge of giving up the gallery anyway.'

'I haven't told them yet. I know I need to, and I would have done it today, but it's not going to be a quick conversation and I wanted to try and make it back to you in time.'

'That seems like a whole lot of excuses.'

He pressed his lips together, and she saw that his anger was burning brighter now. 'You of all people should know it's not that simple to change course.'

Meredith was stunned into silence for a second, and she saw Finn's expression turn from anger to horror.

'I'm sorry—' he started.

'I know what it's like for *me*,' she said. 'But I don't know what it's like for you, because you haven't really told me.'

'What do you mean?'

'I have to squeeze out every little piece of you, with hours of coaxing, even though, if you really cared about me, you would have opened up to me by now.'

'I've told you things. You know I'm unhappy there, but giving it all up to take a chance on my painting is a big risk.'

Meredith shook her head, the action showing her that they were alone apart from a couple at the hot dog stand who, she thought, were pretending not to listen. 'I know fractions of it. I only know you're a painter – and my slate painter – because Laurie engineered me into finding out. I only know your family owns Clotted Cream Cottage because you admitted it just now. You don't give anything

301

up readily, which makes me wonder if you want to let me in at all.'

'Meredith.' His voice was low and tight as he took a step towards her.

She felt the emotion return to her throat, tightening it as she spoke. 'You have meant so much to me, do you know that? I feel different about Christmas now. I've been thinking about the years I've missed out on, worried that it's too late to make up for all that lost time. The last few weeks I've enjoyed working on the hampers, helping Anisha with the pageant. None of it has felt hard like it used to.

'The sight of a Christmas tree used to make me feel cold, because I'd forced myself towards anger, instead of the grief and sadness that was so exhausting but I couldn't seem to escape from. Now I look in houses at the decorations, and I think about how I'd decorate my own tree. I think about you taking me to see those beautiful windows, and how you were trying to show me the parts of Christmas that meant something to you. I haven't got my own tree yet, because I still wasn't sure . . .' She swallowed and rubbed furiously at her cheeks.

'Please don't be upset,' Finn said softly. 'I didn't mean to hurt you.'

'But you're not really here. Not properly. You weren't at the concert when you told me you'd be there, and then I find out your parents are here, in that house, which must have been stressing you out since the moment I inadvertently told you the other night, but you still didn't say anything to me.'

'I know.' He dropped his gaze to the ground. Crumble scrabbled in his arms, but he held on tightly.

'I can't do this.' She had been thinking it, but hadn't expected the words to come out.

'What do you mean?' He looked up.

'This.' She waved her arm between them. 'If you can't be honest with me, then what's the point? I'm getting half of you, for however long you're here. Even after what happened at the concert, the promise you made me . . . If, after all that, you can't let me in, then I'm not doing it any more.'

'Meredith.' He sounded so unlike the Finn she knew, his voice wavering.

'I didn't know what I was getting into when we started this,' she went on. 'I knew it might not last, and that was OK. It was just . . . lovely, spending time with you.' She hated that her voice cracked a little bit. She saw him flinch, but she carried on. 'Then I thought it could be something more. But you not letting me in – it's as if you were preparing for it to end almost as soon as it started.'

'That isn't anywhere close to the truth!' Finn's shout cut through the quiet, and the harbour seemed to freeze. 'None of what I've said to you, or felt for you, has been a lie. I care about you so much.' He put a hand up to her face. 'Red . . .'

Meredith straightened her shoulders. 'You can't placate me with facts about cucumbers and cute nicknames, and keep the real parts of yourself hidden. I want to know all of you, and I want to help you achieve your dreams, like you've helped me.'

'I'm happy,' he said, running his hand down her cheek. 'With the studio at Laurie's, with the beach. I get to come down here whenever I want, as long as it's between exhibitions, so . . .'

303

His soft words were like a bucket of harbour water, drenching her. 'You mean you're going back? Despite the way you feel, how much you love painting, and that your parents manipulated you into seeing them – called you away on some false errand that was supposedly life or death – you're just going back to Imo Art? Even though you're unhappy there, away from your own work, your own passions?' Was she counting herself as one of those?

He grimaced. 'The beginning of the year is always a nightmare, but after those first few exhibitions—'

She stepped back, holding out her hands, and she saw the moment he realized what she was asking for.

'Come on, Meredith.'

'You encouraged me to embrace Christmas, to let go of the things that have been holding me back, but you won't follow your own advice. You've got Laurie and the studio. You have contacts who could help you set up an exhibition of your own, or start selling your work online. You've got this giant opportunity in front of you, a chance to do what you've dreamed of, which is so much more than so many people get, and you're not going to pursue it?'

He shook his head, his arm tightening around Crumble.

'Really?' It came out as a squeak, and tears pricked the corners of her eyes.

'Meredith, please.' His voice was rough. 'I just need a bit more time to get my head straight. Seeing Mum and Dad like that – it's not easy when they've got it all figured out, and I haven't . . .' He huffed out a breath.

'So you're going back to London?'

He stepped towards her again, holding out his hand. 'Please don't cry.'

'I knew you didn't find sharing the easiest thing,' she said quietly. 'And to start with, I was glad that I was getting anything from you. But I'm not doing it like this, with you spending so much time in London. I've only got some of you as it is, and I can't cope if I have even less.'

'So – so what?'

'You know what.' She heard the weariness in her voice, a tide of sadness rising up inside her, along with distant alarm bells blaring at her that she was making a mistake. 'I didn't want us to be just for Christmas. And after all the ways you've encouraged me to be stronger, to face my fears, I never had you down as a hypocrite or a coward.'

She saw the words hit him, his face paling. She didn't know if she meant them, she just needed to end this pointless back-and-forth. He was returning to London, going back to all the things he'd told her he didn't want.

'You can't do this,' he said. 'What we have—'

'It's over. Give me Crumble.' She held out her arms again and waited to see if he would fight; if he would refuse and try to keep hold of her. But she shouldn't have been surprised at his response, because he wasn't fighting for anything else he wanted, and it seemed she was just something else he could let go of.

His exhale was a cloud as he gave her Crumble. Her dog turned his head and licked Finn's chin. 'Don't do this. Please.'

'Talk to your parents,' Meredith said through her tears. 'Tell them what you want. Don't let your life pass you by like I've been doing, just because you're afraid of what you might find if you stop and pay attention. The last few weeks have shown me it's worth it. I wish you'd try it, too.'

'I will, I—'

'Bye, Finn.' She turned away from him, but his hand closed round her arm, and he pulled her round to face him. They were so close she could see the different shades of blue in his eyes, and she felt the tug to just forget everything, to step into his arms and trust that he'd let her in eventually.

'I don't want you to go,' he said quietly. He grazed his lips along her forehead.

She swallowed. 'I don't want you to go either, but I want all of you. All of you, or nothing at all.'

Their gazes held for a second, and she watched as regret seemed to swallow him whole; the way his eyes filled as his hand came up to her nape. He pulled her against him for a tight, desperate hug. She let him embrace her, but she knew from the way his body was still tense, his arms rigid around her, that he hadn't changed his mind.

Eventually she stepped back, pressed a kiss to his cheek, rough with end-of-day stubble, then walked away from him up the hill, her puppy refusing to settle in her arms. She didn't dare look back at the dark, glass-like water or the perfect reflections of the twinkling masts. It was only as she reached the town hall, its outside lights still glowing as if it wasn't ready for the party to be over, and turned towards home, that she caught a glimpse of him.

He was leaning against the stone wall, the Cornish town's curving harbour a shimmering panorama behind him, his head in his hands.

Chapter Twenty-Four

The next morning Meredith stared at her ceiling for far too long, before convincing herself that she would feel a hundred times better if she went for her swim. She realized as she drove to Charmed Cove – a sliver of pale gold rising above the shadowy hills, announcing that the sun was going to rise like always, despite what had happened – that she hadn't got any further with her plan to swim to the next cove. Something that had been firmly on her to-do list, that she'd just forgotten about. That, she decided, was Finn's fault. If she told herself enough bad things about their relationship, then she would eventually feel better about ending it.

The cove greeted her with its calming waves and soft sand. The air was frigid, forcing her to breathe deeply, as if she was exhaling every emotion and starting afresh. It settled her mind, but couldn't wipe the memories of the night before. Not least, she thought, as she waded into the water and bit back a curse at how cold it was, because this was where she had met him. He was probably inside the house she could see as she swam south, sleeping fitfully, or perhaps packing up his things, ready to return to London with his parents for a lavish family Christmas.

Christmas. This year, Meredith had decided it had promise; it could be a happy time, with fun and frivolities that she could embrace rather than ignore. That conclusion had been as fake as what she'd had with Finn; now he was out of the picture, she felt as wretched as she did before he'd appeared, with his blond curls and blue eyes, his calm certainty and his insistence that she could enjoy it. How could she believe him, when he was lying to himself?

She kept her swim short and perfunctory. For once, she didn't want to be here, and anyway, she had so much work to do; the day before Christmas Eve would be one of the busiest at Cornish Keepsakes.

She went through her morning routine on autopilot, ignoring the text from Anisha that said:

Come round tonight. xx

Her friend had called her the previous evening to ask how it had gone, and Meredith had told her they'd broken up, though she hadn't had the energy to explain every detail. After they'd hung up, she'd turned her phone off. She didn't want to talk about the fact that she'd ended it, or that he hadn't even tried to meet her in the middle, or that she'd called him a hypocrite and a coward. She had been angry with him, but he didn't deserve that.

She got ready for work, fed Crumble, and left a bowl of food for Smudge, who was out on one of his early morning jaunts, no doubt terrorizing birds and living the high life, then got her bag and coat and opened the front door. The sun was still low in the sky, and a glance at her clock told her she was almost an hour early. She dithered, wondering whether to stay at home, where she would doubtless replay their argument for the hundredth time, or get to work and crack on. She was still deciding when she heard Bernie's door open.

She went to shut hers, but then Bernie appeared with Smudge in her arms. Her cat was the picture of contentment, his head pressed under her neighbour's chin.

'Meredith?' Bernie said quietly.

'Hey,' Meredith replied. 'Is everything OK? I'm sorry if Smudge has been a nuisance.'

Bernie shook her head. 'He's a charmer.'

Meredith almost dropped her handbag in surprise. 'Right. OK. Good! I'd better . . .' She gestured towards the road.

'Would you like a cup of tea?' Bernie asked. 'Surely work can't demand you in this early, even just before Christmas.'

Meredith went to speak, but found she couldn't.

Bernie shuffled on her doorstep. 'I heard you crying last night.'

'Oh.' Meredith swallowed.

'Are you OK?'

The tiny glimmer of kindness from her grumpy neighbour brought Meredith's emotion flooding to the surface. 'I . . . well, I . . .'

'Is it about that lad?' Bernie went on. 'The horribly attractive, charismatic one?' Her lips lifted in a smile, and Meredith burst out laughing, which was especially embarrassing as a few tears escaped as well. 'Come on,' Bernie continued, squeezing her arm. 'Come and tell me all about it. I've made some gingerbread.'

That was the last straw. All Meredith's defences crumbled. She shut her door, stepped over the low wall between their gardens, and was ushered inside.

'Bloody hell,' she whispered, as Bernie helped her take off her coat and led her to a sofa that was covered in a white, fluffy throw, like the hide of a polar bear. If she'd been planning a grotto as part of the pageant, she would have copied this place exactly.

'Christmas is the one time you can really let go,' Bernie said. 'And I make no apologies for it, even if not everyone's as keen as I am. Get yourself comfy, I'll be back in a jiffy.'

Meredith settled herself on the plush sofa and looked around her. There was the beautiful tree decorated in red and gold that she'd seen from the road, five stockings hanging along the tiny fireplace, an Advent candle on the mantelpiece above, and a nativity scene with beautiful, hand-painted figures on a table next to the kitchen doorway. A chocolate Advent calendar was leaning against the TV stand, and swathes of tinsel covered the ceiling in loops that made the room seem smaller, but with the strategic placement of the lamps, also made it glitter. The sofa below the window, opposite where Meredith was sitting, was covered in a midnight-blue throw with silver stars dancing across it. A huge, cuddly snowman sat on one of the cushions like a toddler. It was a showcase of Christmassy excess.

She examined her feelings, waiting for cynicism followed by a desire to escape, but found she wanted to stay in this room that was like the inside of a Christmas elf's head, and soak it all up. Then Bernie returned with a tray, the smells of coffee, sugar and gingerbread a welcome assault on the senses, and she wondered if she should message Adrian and tell him she couldn't make it into work today.

'There now,' Bernie said soothingly, as she put the tray on the low coffee table. 'This should perk you right up.'

Meredith took a gingerbread man. It was actually shaped like a man, with icing in all the right places. It looked better than the ones in the shops. 'This is amazing, Bernie. Thank you.' She bit into it, and the spicy flavours exploded on her tongue. 'Oh. Oh, wow.'

Bernie sat opposite her, next to the snowman. 'Glad you approve.'

'This is delicious. And your room – I love it. It's so . . .'

'Extreme?'

'So happy,' she said, her voice cracking. She took another large bite of gingerbread to wedge in her emotions, and almost choked.

'Steady love,' Bernie said. 'Why not take it slow, tell me what's happened? If you want to, that is. I won't go gossiping about it. Just . . . you sounded so wretched last night, and I know you're not usually one for Christmas, so something must have turned things on their head.'

'You know I don't like Christmas?'

Bernie gave her a rueful smile. 'You made that fairly clear last November, just after you'd moved in and I put all my decs up.'

Meredith swallowed her gingerbread. 'I did? I . . . I don't remember.'

Bernie nodded, as if she'd expected this. 'You were pretty

hectic, running around like a dizzy bluebottle, and fired up. I don't think you meant to be cruel, but it was clear that you weren't a fan. I suppose it just came out harsher than you expected, and I took it too much to heart.'

Meredith exhaled. 'I am so sorry,' she said. 'I didn't mean to offend you. I would never have done that intentionally.'

'There, there.' Bernie reached forward and patted her knee. 'I've held on to it for far too long in any case, so I'm not innocent in all this. Let's put it behind us. You've got other things on your mind.'

'Thank you,' Meredith said. She took a sip of hot, milky coffee, composing herself before speaking. 'I broke up with Finn. He's the man – the one you met.'

'Did he turn out to be too good to be true?' Bernie asked softly.

Meredith thought about it. 'No,' she said eventually. 'He was as good as I thought he was. He's generous and kind. He makes me laugh and . . . and believe in myself, just a little bit more.'

'Hard to find, that sort of thing,' Bernie replied. 'Go on, then.'

'Something happened,' Meredith said lamely. 'And I . . . he's dealing with some things. Except that he *won't* deal with them, for whatever reason, and he won't talk to me about it. He knows what he needs to do to be happy, but there's something stopping him, and I—'

'You lost your patience?' Smudge had come back inside with them, and he hopped onto Meredith's lap and settled down; a comforting, purring weight.

'I said some horrible things to him,' she admitted. 'He's helped me see things so differently, and I wanted the same for him. But where he's been kind and gentle with me, I – I sort of . . . I lost it at him. He said he was going back to London, and so I just . . . even though we could probably . . . and now it's all ruined—'

'It was too many feelings,' Bernie said. 'I understand. Whatever you said, you shouldn't be too hard on yourself. If you care about each other, those bonds will hold tight, even if you've chipped away at them. Even if you called him a fuckwit,' she added, and Meredith laughed, startling her cat.

'I didn't,' she said. Then, her heart sinking, she added, 'But I did call him a hypocrite. And a coward. I think I . . . I'm worried I was just like his parents. They put so many expectations on him, and I was exactly the same. I tried to force him to do something he wasn't ready for.'

'But you've got hope.'

'I have?'

The older woman nodded, shifting on the sofa. The snowman wobbled beside her. 'I think so. If you want to make it up to him, if you regret what you said already, you should try. I had a beau,' she went on, her eyes avoiding Meredith's. 'Last year. We were inseparable for a time, and then it went wrong; misunderstandings and voices raised, things said in the heat of the moment, just like you and your Finn. I let the anger simmer, and I didn't go to him. He was the same, and with that festering, it grew too difficult. By the time I decided he mattered too much for me to let him go, it was too late.'

'Too late?' Meredith asked.

'He'd left Port Karadow. Changed his number, blocked me on Facebook. I have been rueing that decision, those words I said, ever since. I have not been the nicest person, to anyone. To you especially, Meredith. What you said about my Christmas decorations, I took it too personally, let it slice into an already open wound that was about something entirely different. I'm sorry for that.'

'Please don't apologize,' Meredith replied. 'I should never have said anything. And I'm so sorry about you and your . . . beau.'

Bernie nodded. 'It is what it is. I let my pride get the better of me, and it has ruined my life. Now now,' she continued, when Meredith went to protest, 'not for ever. But I loved him dearly, and when I heard you last night . . . I recognized that wretchedness.' She gave her a sad, soft smile. 'Do you think there's hope, then, for you two to patch things up? For you to apologize, and for him to forgive you?'

Meredith had been thinking of nothing else almost since the moment she walked away from Finn at the harbour. But she had accused him of some awful things. 'I don't know,' she admitted, then picked up another gingerbread man because she didn't like that truth. 'But,' she added before she took a bite, 'I'd really like to try.'

Meredith left her neighbour's feeling warm and hopeful, and not just because of the coffee and delicious gingerbread.

She tried calling Finn, but his number rang and rang and then went to voicemail. She didn't feel composed enough to leave a message, knowing she'd ramble, so the next thing she did, once she'd got to work and had settled at her desk, still the only one there, was send him a message. She sat there for ten minutes, waiting for the ticks to turn blue. They didn't. He'd received it, but hadn't read it yet.

When that didn't work, and after a long day of packing up hampers and being sparkly with customers in the shop, while also waiting for the blue ticks with growing despair and dwindling hope, she called her brother.

She waited until she'd got home, had fed her pets, and was curled up on the sofa in her red tartan pyjamas – even though it was just after six o'clock – with a hot chocolate and a bag of giant Wotsits. She wasn't ready to go to Laurie's, to face the physical rejection her ignored messages were hinting she'd receive, so instead she thought she would get a man's perspective. Because she hadn't mentioned Finn to her brother, this meant telling him the whole story, which also meant putting up with his outrage that he was only just hearing about it.

The first thing he said, when she'd got to the end of her sorry tale, was, 'For someone who has possibly ruined a good chance at happiness because you accused this bloke of keeping things from you, you've done an excellent job of hiding things yourself!' It made her feel a hundred times worse.

'It wasn't just that,' Meredith said defensively. Smudge and Crumble had curled up either side of her like furry disciples, and she thought how miserable she would be without them.

'What was it, then?' Tommy asked, much more gently.

She huffed out a breath and sprinkles of Wotsits dust landed on Smudge's head. She wiped them off. 'Most of the time, when I was with him, he made me so happy. Occasionally infuriated, often laughing, always alive. But it was like he shone this spotlight on me so he could hide in the shadows, and every time I tried to reverse it, he turned it off.'

'So he's a closed-off guy,' Tommy said. 'Not exactly an endangered species.'

'I know *that*,' Meredith said. 'But even when we argued, after his parents made him miss the carol concert, he acted like . . . like he wasn't even going to give his painting a chance. He was going to go back to the gallery and settle into his old life. He's so talented, Tommy. He has the personality and the skills to go as far as he wants to!'

'So you broke up with him because he refuses to fulfil his potential?'

'You're twisting things,' Meredith said.

'Am I? Shouldn't you be supporting his decisions? If you care about him, and want him to be happy, then shouldn't you be behind him instead of nudging him in a different direction?'

'But he *isn't* happy,' Meredith said, her frustration growing. She picked a stray, melting marshmallow off the side of her mug. Sometimes her brother drove her up the wall.

'And he needs to get where he wants to be in his own time, with people supporting him.' There was a beat of silence, and then her brother added, 'Doesn't he?'

Meredith let the marshmallow dissolve on her tongue. 'I suppose.'

'I get that he's not been honest with you about some things,' Tommy continued. 'His family stuff, them owning Clotted Cream Cottage – which is a total bummer, by the way, because I wanted it to be owned by a benevolent old lady who died in the Eighties and has been haunting it ever since. But Finn wasn't doing it to mislead you, was he? And who, in this lifetime, hasn't avoided things they're uncomfortable with? Specifically family-related things?

Specifically by pretending they didn't exist? Sound familiar, Meredith?'

She rested her head against the sofa, and her cat and dog climbed onto her lap, tussling for position. Crumble put his paw in the dregs of her hot chocolate and she sighed and put the mug on the floor. 'You're right,' she said eventually.

'I'm always right.' Tommy didn't even attempt to hide his smugness.

'Yeah, yeah.'

'So, what are you going to do, sister of mine?'

'Hide under a rock until January?'

Tommy made a sound like a quiz-show buzzer announcing she'd got it wrong. 'There is only one thing you need to answer right now.'

'What's that?' Meredith was so tired. Why was this all so complicated?

'Is what Finn's done too big to get over? Are the rules he's broken or boundaries he's crossed more important to you than knowing him, and having him in your life?'

She closed her eyes and pictured their first meeting on the beach, the light in his blue eyes as he'd looked at her; then soaked and dripping in the car after delivering hampers, wearing ridiculous Christmas headgear; sitting on the sofa with him at Laurie's house, feeling utterly content; lying in his arms in the studio. They both came with history, and he'd helped her with hers, with the potholes she still fell down, but she'd had no patience for his. It was her fault this had happened. She'd pushed him away, accused him of things when she should have been showing him the same kindness.

'No,' she said. 'No, it's not too big to get over. I've got it all wrong, Tommy. I think – I don't know if he'll forgive me.'

She heard him sigh, imagined him sitting in the airy living room of the house he shared with Sarah, a bottle of beer on the table. She wondered what their Christmas decorations looked like this year, and had a sudden urge to see them. 'There's only one way to find out, isn't there?' he said eventually.

'Yes,' Meredith replied. Once again, she had to concede that her brother was right.

Chapter Twenty-Five

It was close to nine o'clock at night, and Meredith was about to go out. Now she had decided that she needed to apologize to Finn, she wouldn't be able to rest until she had.

She looked at the biscuit tin she'd placed reverently on the sofa, and wrinkled her nose. Then she went upstairs and got dressed, pulling on jeans and a pale grey jumper woven through with silver thread that made her think of posh Christmases she'd never had; drinking champagne on balconies overlooking snowy landscapes and starry skies. She added lip gloss and mascara, and discovered, when she poked herself in the eye, that her hands weren't entirely steady.

'I won't be long,' she told Smudge and Crumble as she put on her coat. Smudge's expression was disdainful, Crumble's hopeful. She knew this was how it was with cats and dogs: they were the angels on her shoulder, one encouraging, the other cynical. Neither of them was coming with her, though. She was doing this on her own.

She put the biscuit tin on the passenger seat and waited, in the cold and dark, while the engine warmed and de-misted the windscreen. She felt like she had a bag of tiny, wriggling kittens in her stomach. What would Finn say, if he even agreed to see her? She wouldn't blame him if he refused. *I never had you down as a hypocrite or a coward.* She winced, checked she could see through the windscreen, and pulled out.

As Meredith drove towards the coast, stars peppered the dark sky like crystals. It was beautiful and romantic, and she thought that if she had considered how hard it was for Finn to break the professional ties with his parents, to step completely into the unknown with his art, then she might be enjoying this view with him. She might be spending Christmas Day with him, instead of having no plans at all.

There were lights on inside Laurie's house as Meredith crawled up the drive, and she could feel her heart pounding, as if it had grown to three times its normal size and taken over her whole chest.

'You can do this,' she whispered to herself, and got out of the car.

She knocked on the door, holding her biscuit tin against her, and didn't have to wait long for a wavy silhouette to appear in the distorted glass partition. She knew instinctively that it wasn't him.

The door swung open to reveal Fern, her expression friendly. 'Hi, Meredith.'

'Hello, Fern.' She took a breath. 'It's good to see you.'

'You too. Come in. Finn isn't here, but Laurie is.'

'Oh, OK. Thank you. I know it's late, but—'

'Tush. You're always welcome here.'

'I am?'

'Let's go and have a drink,' Fern said, leading Meredith down the corridor. She couldn't help glancing to her right, the memories making her cheeks warm, but the studio door was closed. It felt significant, somehow, and by the time they reached the cosy living room, Meredith's heart had fallen to her feet.

'Darling Meredith,' Laurie said, sweeping her into a hug. She smelled sweetly floral, a scent that reminded Meredith of summer. 'Come and have a cup of tea. I have a calming blend, which I'm sure you could do with.'

'I'll make it,' Fern said. 'You get settled.'

Meredith and Laurie sat on the sofa, and Meredith decided honesty was best. 'I don't think I deserve your kindness,' she admitted. 'I was horrible to Finn.'

Laurie's smile was soft. 'My dear girl, you are one of the good ones. You should know that.'

'Did he tell you what happened?'

'He didn't tell me much of anything last night. He flung a few things in a bag and left, with only a few terse words. I understood that you had had a fight, and that Walter and Imogen are in Cornwall. He wouldn't have been in a good place, anyway, after seeing them.'

'I made it worse.'

Laurie shook her head. 'I doubt you could make anything worse. Not for Finn.'

'Unless I told him I thought he was a coward and a hypocrite for not following his dreams, and that I didn't want to be with him any more?'

Laurie studied her for a few moments, her expression thoughtful. 'No wonder he was so closed off.'

'See?' Meredith said. 'I did make things worse! And I didn't mean any of it. I was just angry.'

'You're making him confront the reality of his situation,' Laurie replied. 'Of course he's not going to like it, but he also needs to hear it from someone who he cares about.'

'You're being too generous. And anyway, you said he packed a bag, so my words have sent him back to London. It hasn't worked out well for either of us.'

Laurie sighed. 'No great love is without its teething problems. If it all went swimmingly from the beginning, it wouldn't be a great love, would it?'

Fern handed them each a cup of tea, and Meredith inhaled the steam rising off it, fresh with mint, fennel and camomile. 'A great love,' she murmured, and wondered if that could have been true. Reality slowly sank into her bones. Finn was gone. She had to face the consequences of her actions. 'Do you have his address in London?' she asked Laurie.

'Of course, I'll give it to you. What's in here?' She pointed at Meredith's tin.

'Nothing,' she mumbled, pushing it behind her.

'Don't give me that,' Laurie chided gently. 'It's something for Finn?'

'I thought that if I could bring him some gingerbread, it would remind him of before. When things were fun.'

Laurie's eyes brightened. 'It worked this time?'

Meredith sighed. 'I don't think so. The consistency is a bit better, but the taste . . .' She opened the tin and waited for Laurie to select a biscuit. Fern took one too, and even though Meredith had tried one when they'd come out of the oven, she didn't think she could subject these two women to her baking without having another herself. They

322

bit into them simultaneously, and Meredith watched their faces as they chewed.

Laurie and Fern exchanged a glance, Fern's lips pressed together.

Laurie turned to Meredith, her eyes bright. 'At least with Finn you know it isn't cupboard love.'

Meredith's laugh was choked, but it made her feel slightly better. 'They're terrible, aren't they?'

Fern tipped her head to one side. 'Interesting, certainly.'

Meredith's sigh deflated her torso. 'Maybe it's a good thing he isn't here any more,' she said. 'He might have been prepared to forgive me until he tasted these, then realized what he was letting himself in for.'

'Oh, Meredith, come here.' Laurie held her arms out, and Meredith accepted the hug. She would take all the comfort she could get, even if she didn't think she deserved it.

When she was leaving the white house, the tea sloshing around in a stomach that, devoid of its earlier kittens, now just felt hollow, Anisha called her.

'Do you fancy coming round?' she asked without any preamble, and Meredith remembered her message, sent hours ago, that she hadn't replied to.

'Nish, I'm so sorry! I – you still want me to come? *Now?*'

'Yup.' Anisha sounded excited, and Meredith decided that the least she could do was celebrate when her friend had something positive to tell her.

'I'm on my way.'

'Really?' Anisha laughed.

'If you want me, I'm coming,' she said, and hurried back to her car.

Two days from Christmas, Anisha's road was a picture postcard of cosy, Cornish festivity. Each of the houses had their own display of elegant adornments. There were lights and wreathes, baubles hanging from outside trees as well as the ones in the windows. Each house had its own colour scheme, but none was garish or kitsch, like the penguins in the Hevinghams' front garden.

Meredith realized, because she'd had time to consider it this year, that you didn't have to follow any rules for how you celebrated Christmas. You could have it exactly as you wanted: cheesy or pared down; extravagant or achingly classy. She had chosen to have no kind of Christmas for the last ten years, and now she'd left herself with little choice, she realized it wasn't what she wanted any more.

She parked in Anisha's driveway, took a moment to drink in the golden bulbs threaded through the wisteria branches, and pressed the bell.

Anisha answered the door wearing jogging bottoms and a white shirt. She took Meredith's hand and dragged her over the threshold.

'What is it?' Meredith said, laughing.

'Come see.' Anisha pulled her through the house to the large family room at the back. There, she came to a halt all by herself. She stared, incredulous.

Anisha's dad Onir stood up and waddled towards her, his arms outstretched. 'Lovely to see you, Anisha's best friend!'

Meredith accepted the hug in a state of shock, peering at Anisha's mum over Onir's shoulder. Pari waved. 'Merry, my dear,' she said. 'Happy holidays.'

Meredith returned her greeting as Onir sat back down. 'You've come here for Christmas?' she asked.

'We've come for good,' Pari corrected, as Meredith gave her a gentle embrace, feeling how stiff the older woman's shoulders were.

It took Meredith a moment to absorb what she'd said. 'For – for *good*?' She looked at Anisha, and then Nick, who'd just walked into the room.

'It wasn't easy to get Jas and Ravi off to sleep,' he explained, laughing. 'They're a bit overexcited about having their nana and gramps here in time for Christmas.'

'The best present of all,' Onir said, chuckling.

'But what's happened?' Meredith asked, as Anisha handed her a glass of lemonade.

'These guys,' Anisha said, swivelling her finger between her parents and her husband, 'have been scheming. You know the house down the street that was for sale?'

'Number fourteen,' Meredith said. 'The one with the pampas in the garden? There was tinsel on the *For Sale* sign.'

'Right. Well, Mum and Dad bought it, and arranged to move down with Nick's help. That's why he was so late to the pageant yesterday: because they were *moving in!*'

Laughter bubbled out of Meredith. Her friend looked so happy: they all did. Ordinarily, Anisha would hate having something this monumental organized behind her back – not being in control was a state she wasn't used to. But on this occasion, the room was bursting with good cheer, and with relief. Her parents were here to stay.

'This is incredible,' Meredith said. She put her glass down and hugged Onir and Pari again, and then Anisha, who squeezed her so tightly Meredith could hardly breathe. The last hug she saved for Nick. 'You know all those times I dismissed you as being incapable of being a spy or a body-guard or . . . or anything remotely un-transparent?'

'Yeah course,' Nick said.

'I take it all back. This is a feat of astounding subterfuge, and you've fully pulled it off. I'm amazed and awed, and I don't think I will ever, ever get over it.'

'Cheers,' Nick said, laughing, 'I think.'

Meredith couldn't remember the last time she'd been in a space that radiated so much joy. It was so different to the feelings she'd been mired in for the last day, and she revelled in it. She sat on the sofa with her glass of lemonade, and Anisha produced some iced biscuits, which made her cringe in shame that she'd offered her gingerbread to Laurie and Fern.

'I'll have to take you to Sea Brew,' she told Onir and Pari. 'They do great cakes and coffee – though of course, Anisha and Jasmine's cookies are superior. Oooh, and – and when you're feeling a bit better, Pari, I'm taking you swimming in the cove.'

'Not in December, though,' Pari said, laughing.

'Don't count on it,' Nick warned. 'Meredith swims there most days, even at this time of year. She's like a fish.'

Pari looked aghast.

'I will come to the café,' Onir said, 'and my wife can do the swimming. That seems a fair division to me.'

'Not on your life, Onir,' Pari replied. 'If I do the swim-ming, *you* do the swimming. You're my carer, after all.' She wiggled her stiff shoulders experimentally. 'Yes, I think we'll enjoy this ocean swimming. Thank you for the invite, dear Meredith. It will do us both the world of good.'

The laughter that followed, from everyone except Onir,

was loud enough that Jasmine and Ravi came back downstairs, blinking sleepily in their pyjamas, and as it was the night before Christmas Eve, and their grandparents were here, living in Cornwall, and there was a lot to celebrate, neither Anisha or Nick seemed inclined to send them back to bed immediately.

The night had produced one happy, entirely unexpected outcome, and one miserable outcome, which Meredith had known, in her heart, was coming. Finn had gone. He'd told her he was going back to London, and she was sure her words had sped up the inevitable. She should count her losses and be happy that, after all her hard work, Anisha had the perfect family Christmas – the extended family life – that she deserved.

All of this was about families, in one way or another. Ties to them, whether good or bad, couldn't be easily severed. She had been living with the reality of that for ten years. Finn's circumstances were completely different, but the result was similar. He was being held back – whether by his parents' expectations of him, or his own – and he had to work through it in his own time. He should have been doing it with her at his side, ready to support him in any way he needed her to, but she'd ruined that chance.

Meredith arrived home without taking in any of the journey. She went inside her house and leaned against the front door, and then, like they did in all the films, slid down it until she was sitting on her welcome mat. Smudge and Crumble clambered onto her lap. She pulled her pets close and buried her head in their fur. Finn was gone, and all she could do was get through the next couple of days, the excitement and good cheer, the talk of family gatherings, of food and wine and gifts, then step out the other side into a brand-new year, where Christmas was behind her and she wouldn't have to think about it again for at least another nine months.

Just like she always did.

Chapter Twenty-Six

There was a small part of Meredith's heart that had been convinced, as she lay there struggling to sleep that night, that Finn would have returned to Laurie's house, heard about her visit, full of repentance and with suitably horrible gingerbread, and realized how much she cared about him. She had half been expecting a knock on the door in the middle of the night, like something out of a romcom. Perhaps it would be raining, and his blond hair would be damp and mussed, and he'd be breathless as he told her he'd missed her every moment of their time apart. He would forgive her and they would have Christmas together.

But no. There was no knock, no reply to her messages, no phone call.

When her alarm went off, Meredith wondered what her day would look like. How would this Christmas Eve unfold? What would happen to make everything she'd thought for the last ten years – that Christmas was not for her – irrefutable? Enough had happened already this year. Except, if she listened to what Finn had told her, had *taught* her, she didn't have to let things happen to her. She could control them. She thought of Laurie telling her about the ways she marked difficult anniversaries and decided she could do something similar. She could do it for herself, and for other people, too. Her dad, she knew, would have loved what she had in mind.

She leaped out of bed, the wooden floor cold beneath her feet. She showered and dressed in jeans, a warm lilac jumper, and her boots with the fur trim. She blow-dried her hair into loose waves, put on eyeliner and sparkly silver eyeshadow, a sprinkling of blusher. She fed Smudge and Crumble, made herself eggs on toast, then put her puppy in his red harness. She put on her blue coat and, instead of her cream woolly hat, she took her candy-cane headband from the hook by the door.

She wouldn't be doing this if it wasn't for Finn. He might be gone, but their time together had left a mark.

She and Crumble walked into work as the powdery December sun emerged. The houses were in shadow, curtains left open and Christmas trees twinkling, so she felt she was being cheered on by a thousand lightbulbs: blue and red and golden and white, set to shimmer and fade, to pulse and dance. Bulbous Santas climbed towards rooftops and reindeer stood proudly in front gardens. Wreaths seemed to smile at her as she passed. There was Christmas music in the air, coming from car stereos and kitchen radios, spurring her on. They told her that this was right; that she could do this, even without him.

She unlocked Cornish Keepsakes and walked through the darkened shop, switching on the lights in the window, noticing that Enzo had restocked before he'd gone home the night before, so the space looked full and enticing, hampers lining the lower shelves, gift boxes and individual items on the higher ones. The candles smelled sweet and musky and fresh, a headiness that hit her as she walked through the office to the kitchen. Beyond it, there was a small storeroom, and she knew that, in here, was the thing she needed.

It was a small trolley, the kind used in garden centres to ferry plants about. It was white and unassuming, with a long handle so it could be pulled from an upright position. Meredith had thought of it in the middle of the night, a memory coming to her of Enzo climbing into it, his long limbs trailing as she'd pushed him around the shop, on one of those mad afternoons when she'd been getting to know the company and its quirks, and her brain was full up by lunchtime. Adrian had found them, tsked for a couple of seconds, then asked to have a go.

She took the packets of kitchen towel out of the trolley and wheeled it into the kitchen. She washed the sides, turning them from murky grey to sparkling white.

When Adrian found her, she was using the staple gun to attach a trim of red and green tinsel around the edge. She had already wound red tinsel around the handle, and looped a set of jingling bells over it, so she would have a soundtrack as she walked.

'What's all this?' Adrian asked, and then added, 'Happy Christmas Eve, Meredith! Loving the festive headgear.' Crumble, who had been chewing the blanket in his bed after Meredith discouraged him from going near the tinsel, bounded forward, barking.

Adrian crouched down. 'Hello,' he said, laughing. 'He's getting more confident, isn't he?'

'He is.' She smiled. It was true that her puppy, while undoubtedly affectionate, usually waited for people to come to him. Until Finn, she realized: the beagle had gone straight up to Finn every time. She watched Adrian make a fuss of him.

'Why is my trolley getting a spruce-up?' he asked eventually.

'I thought I could sell hampers around the village today. Give it one last push. I can fit four on here easily, and I can come back and restock as often as I need to.'

Adrian looked at her, his large hands stroking Crumble's ears. Meredith held his gaze, her smile faltering when it started to become uncomfortable. 'What is it?' she asked.

Adrian's smile was warm. 'Maybe your dog isn't the only one who's gaining a bit more confidence.'

Meredith laughed. 'It's not my usual style, I know. But we've done all we can with the digital side of things – though I thought I would do some Instagram stories of my day – and if a few people see me prancing round town with candy canes and a dolled-up trolley, they might remember Cornish Keepsakes into the new year.'

'They'd be hard-pushed to forget you,' Adrian agreed. 'Well, I'm all for it. Nobody ever remembered anyone who hid under a rock, did they?'

'The parable of Adrian Flockhart,' Meredith said. 'Not a truer word has been spoken.'

Adrian stood, his knees cracking. 'I'll make you a coffee while you finish your sleigh.'

Meredith sat back on her heels. It *did* look like a sleigh. Why hadn't she noticed before now?

Enzo was equally enthusiastic about Meredith's project, but was also incredibly picky.

'Your coat's blue, though.'

'Yes.'

'It should be red, like Santa.'

'But it isn't,' she said. 'I don't own a red one.'

Enzo folded his arms, his gaze thoughtful. 'At the very least, you need to wear a Santa hat.' He took one off his desk and flung it at her.

'I can't,' she said, catching it.

'Why not?'

'I have to wear the candy canes.'

'Why?' Enzo frowned.

Meredith pressed her lips together.

'Ah,' Enzo said, before she'd worked out what to say. 'Finn.'

She looked down at her Christmassy trolley. 'He's gone back to London.'

'Oh,' Enzo said. 'Fuck.'

'Yeah.' Meredith sighed. 'Fuck. *Fucksticks*.'

'Big fucky fucksticks with a big sticky stick,' Enzo said.

Meredith laughed and gave him a grateful smile.

'Here, then.' He took the candy canes off her head, put the Santa hat on, pulling it down gently until it sat comfortably, then put the candy canes back on over the top.

'Both?'

He shrugged. 'It's Christmas Eve. Go large or go home, I say.'

'And you'd be right,' Meredith said, getting to her feet, feeling both ridiculous and proud in her overly festive getup. 'There's a lot of male wisdom floating around this place today.'

333

'You say that like it's unusual!' Adrian called from his office.

'And *you* said that like you don't know full well that it is,' Meredith replied. 'Right then, let's get this shameless selling opportunity on the road. Come on, Crumble, you're my reindeer today.' The dog looked up at her, barked his tiny, puppy bark, then jumped into the trolley, in the meagre space between two hampers. Meredith sighed. 'All right then, you can be Santa for a bit, but I hope you're going to pull me along when my legs get tired.'

Enzo helped lift the trolley, complete with its four beauti- fully ribboned hampers and additional puppy, over the steps from the office to the shop, then down the step into the street. It was just after nine, the town was beginning to come to life, the air fizzing with the excitement and panic that Christmas Eve brought with it. The door to Sea Brew was swinging almost constantly, expelling smells of coffee and bacon, along with customers carrying takeaway cups and paper bags.

'Give me a shout if you want a break,' Enzo said. 'I'll make sure there are hampers ready, so if you sell them you can restock quickly.'

'*When* I sell them,' Meredith corrected him, reaching up to feel her candy canes.

If things had been different, she would have got Enzo to take a photo of her, Crumble and the trolley and sent it to Finn, to show him how far she'd come. But she wasn't doing this for praise. She was doing it because she wanted to, and because it was right for Cornish Keepsakes. Enzo held his hand out anyway, and Meredith passed him her phone and struck a jaunty pose, one booted foot up on the tinselled rim of the trolley, while he snapped a few shots.

'For Instagram,' he said, handing her phone back. 'And also, you know it's going up in the office.'

Meredith laughed. 'Good!'

'Got all you need?'

'Definitely.'

'Good luck then, Mrs Claus.'

'Thanks, Enzo the Elf.'

He grinned. 'That's pretty good!'

She grabbed the trolley's handle, checked that Crumble was settled and not about to fall out, and set off up the hill, waving and saying hello to people, asking if they needed a last-minute hamper. Today, Meredith Verren was going to embody the spirit of Christmas.

It started slowly, because Meredith didn't have the confidence needed to push herself and her hampers in everyone's faces. Most people were hurrying with their heads down, because it was the day before Christmas and time was of the essence. And it was cold, so lots of them were wearing hats, which meant she couldn't catch their eye easily. She started with cheerful greetings which a few ignored and some returned, casting curious looks at her and her trolley. When this happened she would say, 'Want a last-minute hamper?' as they rushed on by, and she was left with no sales and the distinct feeling that she was an idiot.

When she reached the top of the hill and turned towards the fountain, a young couple holding hands gave her warm smiles and shook their heads when she mentioned her hampers. Meredith was left deflated and envious: they would be spending Christmas together, no doubt. Who would she be spending it with? She shoved the unwelcome thought aside and bounced on the balls of her feet, her hat and candy canes jiggling on her head. A little girl pointed and squealed in delight, and even though the mum barely paused, that one reaction gave her a boost of confidence. She needed to step it up a gear if she was going to sell any hampers. This was not the time to be embarrassed or glum.

'Right then, Crumble,' she said, holding out her fist to him. 'Let's do this!' To her surprise and delight, Crumble patted his front paw against her closed hand. It was solidarity. They were a team. They *could* do it.

She started quietly, testing her voice out, but quickly found that she could be loud, and that it sounded good: that the act of filling her lungs with fresh, seaside air, and then expelling it in a happy, festive song – 'Have Yourself a Merry Little Christmas', but with the word *Christmas* exchanged for *Hamper* – was cheering. Soon she was walking through the streets of Port Karadow, pulling her trolley and singing at the top of her voice.

Now everyone raised their heads, however harassed they seemed, and a few people grinned at her, some even clapping as they passed.

'These hampers for sale, love?' a bald man asked as she passed the ironmonger's.

She stopped singing abruptly. 'They are! Would you like one? They're on special offer, as it's Christmas Eve.'

She showed him the contents; the candle and shell-shaped chocolates, the Christmas pudding and crackers, the drinks swizzlers and one of her star jars filled with humbugs.

'Great. Yeah. I can have this one?'

'Yes! Please, take it.'

He gave her some crisp notes, which she put in the purse

she'd bought specially for the food markets and fairs, then she retied the ribbon and gave him the hamper.

One sale down, her confidence soared along with her voice. Without Emma to guide her in a specific playlist, she chose the songs she fancied, depending on which part of town she was in. Around by the care home she sang 'In the Bleak Midwinter' and Slade, and as she approached the Sea Shanty, even though it was too early for it to be open, she sang 'Fairytale of New York', altering her voice between the male and female parts. By ten o'clock, she was back at Cornish Keepsakes, restocking her empty trolley.

'Bravo!' Adrian said. 'You look very rosy-cheeked.'

'It's going well,' she replied, her voice rasping.

'Coffee?' Enzo asked.

'Please.'

She sipped her Nespresso while Enzo and Adrian fussed around Crumble and the trolley, loading more hampers onto it, and Adrian added some bags of sweets tied with Christmas string.

'You could give these out to any children you pass.'

'That's a great idea,' Meredith said. 'Thanks, Adrian.'

'Thank you for working so hard for this company, Meredith. You really are turning things around.' He looked at Enzo. 'You both are. The dream team!'

Meredith laughed. 'I don't know about that.'

'I do,' Adrian said, his face serious.

With her throat soothed, her trolley full and Crumble stowed safely on board, off she went again, with more songs in her arsenal and confidence buzzing through her. She sang and sold her way through town, which was much busier now, and, it seemed, not against this strange version of Santa and her sleigh full of goodies.

The water in the harbour was a pale, pearlescent blue, a few boats with their lights on even though it was sunny. The air was fresh and the view was unbeatable, and Meredith tried to banish the memories of a couple of nights before, the things she had said to Finn. She checked her phone, but she had no notifications from him. There was one from Anisha: a photo of the six of them – Nish and Nick, Jasmine and Ravi, Onir and Pari – sitting on the sofa next to their giant Christmas tree. Meredith sent back a flood of happy and festive emojis, and finished with ten hearts.

She put her phone away and sang the first lines of 'Santa Baby' as she walked along the harbour wall, drinking in the view.

'Here they are!' She turned at the voice and saw a teenage girl running towards her, long dark hair flying, her parents – Meredith presumed – hurrying to keep up. 'Wait!' The girl waved her arm, and Meredith stopped.

'Hello,' she said, as the girl approached.

'I found you!' She put her hands on her knees as she got her breath back.

'You've been looking for me?'

'There's been a rumour going round town,' the girl's dad said. 'About a singing siren selling hampers!'

'And now we've found you,' added the mum.

Meredith managed a smile. 'A singing siren?' Her heart thudded at the familiar nickname.

'I think because we're by the sea,' the girl explained, peering at the hampers. 'And your voice is so beautiful.'

'Ah,' Meredith said, trying not to let disappointment

consume her. 'Thank you. I promise if you want to buy a hamper, there are no catches. No trips into the foaming brine, except obviously that's "Oh My Darling, Clementine", and nothing to do with Christmas.'

'And no cockles and mussels in your barrow, so you're safe from fever,' the man pointed out.

'"Molly Malone"!' Meredith said. 'I love that song.'

'It's not particularly cheery, though,' the woman added.

'None of those songs seem to be.' The teenage girl was petting Crumble, who was lapping up the attention. 'Best to stick with Christmas music.' She gave Meredith a cheeky grin. 'I don't suppose your dog is for sale?'

'Afraid not. But if you buy a hamper, you can have a couple of bags of sweets as a bonus.'

'If you sing "Santa Baby" all the way through, from the beginning again, I'll buy two hampers,' the man said.

Meredith couldn't refuse an offer like that, especially as 'Santa Baby' was one of the songs she *did* like, because it didn't shy away from the commercial side of Christmas, and managed to be festive and cynical at the same time. She stood by the harbour wall, with the sea shimmering behind her and the cold air caressing her face, and sang the Eartha Kitt song, while the family stood and watched, the woman and girl swaying along, Crumble in the girl's arms because Meredith had said it was OK.

A few fishermen watched from their boats, and by the time she'd finished, a small crowd had formed, some people clapping in time to the tune. When she got to the last line, the rhythmic claps became a swell of applause.

'Can you do "Fairytale of New York"?'

'I love "Last Christmas".'

'What about carols? "Silent Night" is my favourite.'

It was a good-natured bombardment, and Meredith was astounded that she alone, with her one voice, a candy-cane headband over a Santa hat, her festive trolley and her puppy, could inspire so much interest.

'I only have two hampers left,' she said, raising her voice to be heard above the crowd. 'And a handful of bags of sweets! But there are more at Cornish Keepsakes so if, after this, you want one, you can follow me to the shop and buy any last-minute gifts you're missing. We have a great range of stock, not just the hampers but smaller items too, most of them locally produced. Now, what was the first song?'

The requests were repeated, and Meredith sang them all, a young woman getting her a milky coffee from Sea Brew halfway through, when her voice started to fail. For someone who hadn't seen the good side of Christmas for a very long time, she had a lot of festive songs stored in her head. But she had always sung, always been attuned to the music around her, and those songs were played so often at this time of year that it was hard to avoid them even if you wanted to. By the time she'd sung everything that had been requested, the sun was dipping towards the horizon, the town's twinkling lights coming on to take its place, and the temperature had dropped.

'All who've requested hampers,' she croaked, 'if you want to come with me now, you can buy them before you head home.' A small crowd stayed after the applause had died down, including the family who had started it all off.

'Here's Crumble,' the girl said, handing her puppy back. 'Thank you so much. This has been lovely.'

'Thank you for inspiring it,' Meredith replied, gesturing to the departing families. 'I hope you have a wonderful Christmas!'

'You too,' the girl said, as her parents paid for and collected their hampers.

The other hampers were sold a moment later, but there were people remaining, and as Meredith put Crumble back in the empty trolley and led the small group through Port Karadow to Cornish Keepsakes like a festive Pied Piper, she hoped there would be enough hampers left for them in the shop.

Adrian and Enzo took over when she arrived with her followers. They tied hampers with the customers' choices of ribbon, added bags of sweets, and sold candles and puddings and boxes of luxury crackers, a Christmas radio station taking over from Meredith's voice, which was completely worn out. She said goodbye to the people who had watched her perform, and went into the office, listening to an enthusiastic retelling of her impromptu concert while she took the tinsel off the trolley.

'She was just singing there, and taking requests, too. It's so long since I've heard "Blue Christmas" sung so beautifully.'

'She sang *anything?*' That was Adrian.

'Anything Christmassy,' someone else chipped in. 'It was a treat. I'm properly in the mood now!'

'Selling with a song,' someone else added. 'That doesn't happen much, and it bloody well should. As long as they can sing like her.'

'Well done, our Meredith,' Adrian said fondly.

'She's called Meredith?' Another voice piped in. 'As in

Merry? That's a serendipitous thing, if ever I heard one. Oh, what a beautiful ribbon; thank you, Adrian.'

Enzo cleared his throat. 'Uhm, actually,' he said, 'I think she likes being called Red.'

Meredith took her candy-cane antlers off and looked at them. If she'd let Finn call her Red, would they still be together? That ridiculous thought made her realize how tired she was, and that it was time to go home.

She helped Adrian and Enzo clear up the shop, which looked happily decimated after their last-minute rush.

'Well done, you wonderful people,' Adrian said, squeezing Meredith and Enzo's shoulders.

'When we come back,' Meredith rasped, 'we'll have an online shop, and a distribution site and couriers.'

Adrian winced. 'Your voice, Meredith!'

'It's OK,' she said, and was about to add that she wouldn't be doing much talking over the next few days, but then realized how many questions that would lead to, so she just said, 'Tommy can speak enough for both of us.'

'Great that you're spending the day with your brother,' Adrian replied. 'You should bring him into the shop next time he's here.'

'Will do.'

They switched off the lights and wished each other Happy Christmas on the doorstep. Meredith walked to the top of Main Street, then down to the harbour, the sea and sky merging into an inky darkness, lit by the shimmering lights that, she now realized, she would miss when they came down in the new year. They brightened everything up, made even the simplest things look special. She didn't know why they should be limited to Christmas time.

As she was walking home with Crumble, wondering if Anisha would believe she was with Tommy tomorrow, and Tommy would believe she was with Anisha, her phone rang.

She pulled it out, her heart skipping and then settling when she saw who it was.

'Hey,' she said.

'Bloody hell,' her brother replied. 'Are you ill? You sound terrible.'

'I've been singing all day,' she scratched out.

'What happened with Finn?' No preamble, which was unusual for her brother.

'He's gone back to London,' she said, her thin voice making her sound even more pathetic.

'Shit,' Tommy murmured. 'I'm so sorry. Are you with Nish and Nick tomorrow? We're still getting together before New Year's Eve, right?'

'Yup!' she said. 'All sorted.'

'Good. I'm glad. If there's one person who knows how to celebrate, it's Nish. Call me tomorrow though, yeah? If you've got any voice left.'

'Of course. But I'd better go now, unless you want a one-sided chat.'

Tommy laughed, sounding buoyant. 'Right-O! Merry Christmas, Sis.'

'Merry Christmas to you and Sarah,' she said, and after their goodbyes she hung up.

It really was that simple, she thought, as she reached her road, the happy scenes in the windows less cheering now that she was so tired, that there had been no Christmas miracle despite her successful day, and Finn hadn't materialized. Everyone thought she was spending Christmas with someone else, the person she really wanted to be with was no longer in her life, and it was all her fault. Despite all that had happened over the last few weeks, all the progress she had made – and she *had* made progress; today proved that – she would still be alone for Christmas.

Sometimes, Meredith realized, as she put her key in the lock, took off her coat and hung it on the hook, placing the candy-cane headband gently on top, things didn't change very much at all, even when you thought they had.

Chapter Twenty-Seven

It was Christmas Day and Meredith woke up alone, the whole day stretching ahead of her, full of . . . what?

There weren't even any Christmas specials on the BBC any more, unless you counted *Mrs Brown's Boys*, which she didn't. She would plan a schedule of films on Netflix, all decidedly un-Christmassy, and have pizza for dinner. That decided, she felt a tiny chink of satisfaction that sat next to the one her hamper-selling and singing had given her yesterday. She chose to ignore that they were both overwhelmed by the loneliness and heartbreak that took up a much bigger space.

She got up and, still in her pyjamas, went downstairs to feed Smudge and Crumble. She had presents for them – posh treats she'd got from an organic pet store in Truro – but gift-giving could wait. She would feel better after her swim.

She pulled back the curtains and saw the sun rising above the houses opposite, a pinkish-grey cloud forming to the south. Would it snow on Christmas Day? That would be the plastic Santa on top of a particularly ironic Christmas cake. She banished the thoughts that kept sneaking in, the ones that told her this day could have been very different if she hadn't ruined everything with Finn. Or if she hadn't chosen to wallow in her self-created misery and had accepted Tommy's offer, or swallowed her pride and asked to be a part of Anisha's family celebrations. It was too late for that.

She went upstairs, tugged on her wetsuit and pulled her hoody and joggers over the top. She put Crumble in his harness and left the house, rubbing her hands while her car engine blew cool air at her, and the windscreen cleared. She drove through Port Karadow, past houses with glowing trees in the windows, and pictured families waking up, children reaching for stockings at the ends of their beds, glossy wrapping that had taken ages to perfect being torn off presents without a care except for what was inside.

The roads were empty, her journey the most straightforward it had ever been, and as Meredith approached the cove, her heart lifted slightly. The water would hold her up: views of the Cornish coastline, stretching as far as she could see, would remind her how small her troubles were in the grand scheme of things. The new year was nearly upon her. Time for another fresh start.

Meredith turned off the main road and onto the familiar, bumpy track, frowning when she saw a car parked on the patch of gravel. She drove closer – there were two cars. This was unheard of – and on Christmas Day?

She parked and lifted Crumble from the passenger seat – she had wanted him with her today. She got out of the car and the door of one of the other cars opened. Adrian emerged, bundled up in a warm-looking coat and red and blue Alpine-style hat, tassels hanging down either side of his face. Meredith would have laughed if she hadn't been so surprised.

'Adrian!'

'Merry Christmas, Meredith! Merry Christmas, Crumble!'

'Happy Christmas!' Tillie got out of the passenger seat, looking immaculate in a fake-fur coat the colour of raspberries.

'Happy Christmas, Tillie,' Meredith said slowly. 'What . . . what are you—?'

'Happy Christmas, love!' Bernie climbed out of the back of Adrian's car. 'Do you want me to take Crumble for you? Come here, puppy, come on!' She held out her arms, her voice turning syrupy.

In a dreamlike state, Meredith handed her dog to her neighbour. 'How do you know each other?'

Adrian chuckled. 'Oh, we've been introduced.'

'And what are you doing here?' Meredith asked.

Adrian's smile widened. 'We came to see you do your Christmas Day swim.'

Meredith laughed nervously. 'But it's not a . . . a spectator sport. It's just me, exercising.'

'We know.' Tillie was beaming. She petted Crumble then took Adrian's hand. 'Shall we go?'

'OK then,' Meredith murmured.

She took her usual route over the gravel, the horizon appearing, the sea unfolding before her with each new step. Her brain was a muddle. Had she told Adrian she was doing a Christmas Day swim? Was this something she'd organized and then, in her heartbroken state, promptly forgotten about? She decided this must be the case when she walked a couple more paces and saw her brother and his girlfriend, along with Enzo, standing at the top of the cliff. There were two other people behind them, who were . . . Meredith moved slightly, and her breath caught as she saw it was Laurie and Fern.

'Happy Christmas!' they chorused. Tommy grinned at her. 'What's going on?' she asked. 'What are you all doing here?'

They all looked at her, stupid smiles on their faces, and Tommy said, 'Check out Charmed Cove, Sis.'

Meredith tore her gaze away from them, took the last few steps so she could see the entire beach below her, and felt her composure dissolve. Her whole body tingled and she blinked, trying to decide if what she was seeing could possibly be real.

Then he called up to her. 'Happy Christmas, Meredith!' His teeth were chattering – she could hear it in his voice – but even if she hadn't heard it, she would have known, because how could he not be frozen half to death?

Finn was below her on the sand, and he wasn't wearing his padded jacket or jeans, or even a wetsuit. He was standing close to the water, wearing a tiny pair of swimming shorts, gazing up at her. Laid out on the sand in front of him, he'd arranged pieces of slate so that they spelled out a message, the three words filling up the cove, big enough that an aeroplane flying overhead would have been able to read what it said:

I love you.

Finn was in their cove, declaring his love for her, but it wouldn't matter because he was going to die of hypothermia before she reached him.

'Holy shit,' she murmured, heading for the steps. She was careful, but she knew them well and she made quick work of the descent, feeling the hard stone change to sand beneath her trainers.

'What are you doing?' she called out, running towards him, through the pieces of slate. She was laughing and her cheeks were damp, but she didn't have time to process what she felt, because Finn would start going blue any moment now. 'What are you doing?' she repeated. 'Finn?' She stopped in front of him, could see the goosebumps on his skin, his breath coming out in clouds.

'You said to me,' he chattered, 'the first time we met, that only fools or the foolhardy would come swimming here naked. T-this is the closest I could get without offending anyone.'

'Finn.' She took off her hoody. It was pink and fleece-lined.

'I have been a fool, Meredith,' he said. 'I held you away from me, even when I wanted all of you. It wasn't that I didn't trust you, but that I didn't trust myself. I haven't – n-not for years. That's why I haven't been able to leave the gallery, to do what I want. But now . . . having you, and then l-loosing you—'

'Put this on,' she said, holding out her hoody.

'Meredith, I can't lose you.'

'Put it on,' she said forcefully, waggling it. He looked so cold, standing next to the icy water in the world's smallest swimming trunks. It didn't matter that he looked good in them. He was about to become the statue she had accused him of being the first time they met.

Finn stared at her, questions burning behind his blue eyes.

'On,' she said quietly, and held the hoody out, arm first.

He turned and she slid his arm into it, then the other one, and then zipped it up to his neck, stepping closer until she could have kissed him with a tilt of her head.

'This, Finn Becker,' she said, 'is the most ridiculous romantic gesture of all time.'

'It got your at-tention though,' he replied. He put his arms around her, pulling her close and looking down at her. She decided she would give him three minutes before she hauled him to Laurie's house and a hot bath.

'I am so sorry,' he said.

She shook her head. 'I'm the one who needs to apologize. The things I said to you—'

'No.' He touched her nose. 'I wanted to show you that you could do anything if you put your mind to it, and I thought, while I was helping you, while I was showing you that, I could ignore my own issues; what I wanted seemed too difficult. But everything you said was right.'

'Finn, what you do with your life is up to you. I should never have tried to force you into anything. Apart from this hoody – that was non-negotiable. How are you feeling?'

'Chilly,' he admitted with a laugh, and kissed her forehead.

Meredith felt her smile, tentative at first, and then, as Finn's arms tightened around her, growing wider, fuller. More real.

'Do you think we could give us another go?' he asked.

'What? Because you got naked on the beach and wrote *I love you* in slate, like a desperate rescue message at the end of a zombie film?'

'Was it not meaningful enough? What else would you like me to do? I might sound calm right now, but that's because I'm starting to lose feeling in some vital places. I care about your answer. A lot. I—'

'I missed you,' she rushed. 'I missed you so much. Almost as soon as I said those things and walked away, I knew I was wrong. I knew that I didn't mean them, and that you were more important to me than almost anything. I wished I could take them back.'

'So you . . . you think we can? Try again, I mean?' He rested his forehead against hers.

She felt the tears well up, tracking a course down her cheeks. 'Only if you promise me one thing.'

She felt his breath falter against her lips. 'I've left the gallery,' he said. 'I told Mum and Dad that I want to paint, that I'm going to do it down here.' He ran his thumb along her jaw, setting off tiny fireworks inside her. 'Laurie says I can stay with her until I find my own place, so . . .'

She saw the hope, the anticipation, in his eyes. There was vulnerability there too, that he'd taken the leap before he knew whether she would be a part of his new life. Except, how could he not know?

'Finn Becker.' She pressed her warm palms to his cold cheeks, and stood on her tiptoes so she could kiss him. Before she did, she whispered, 'I love you,' and then sealed it with her lips. She kissed her warmth and her love into him, and he kissed her back. She heard the applause, the whistle that was definitely her brother's, the tiny yelps from Crumble.

She pulled away, laughing.

'You really want this?' Finn asked. 'You're not just saying that?'

'I want *you*, Finn, and everything that comes with you. Did you get everyone to come here?'

His smile turned mischievous. 'It's Christmas Day,' he said. 'Also, I wanted you to know that I mean it, how I feel about you, and about my painting. I wanted witnesses.'

'You wanted everyone to see how much like a Michelangelo you really are,' she said, tugging the hem of her hoody down. 'But it's backfired a bit.'

'How so?' She loved the way he raised a single eyebrow, the way she felt it all the way to her toes. If their friends and family hadn't been watching – and presumably waiting for them – she would have dragged him to Laurie's and warmed him up in the best way she could think of.

'This is not the smartest thing you've ever done,' she said. 'A lovely thing, but not a smart thing. What if I had decided not to come for my swim? How long would you have waited? You could have got hypothermia. You still could,' she added, when he shivered. 'We need to get off the beach. You need some clothes.'

'I told you,' he said, 'I was a fool. I was wrong to keep things from you, and I—'

'No.' She pressed a finger to his lips. 'The only foolish thing you did was stand here in your tiny swimming trunks. Those shorts aren't appropriate even in the height of summer. The rest of it – being apprehensive about leaving the gallery, not sharing everything with me, I get it. I was wrong to push you. We can talk about it whenever you want to, whenever you're ready, but right now, we need to get you warmed up. What are we—' She glanced behind her and saw that, along with everyone else, Anisha and Nick were there, with her parents and Jasmine and Ravi. She waved at her friend and turned back to Finn. 'You brought everyone!'

'I thought we could all have Christmas together,' he said. 'I spent yesterday helping Laurie and Fern. We've prepared a feast. Will you join us up at the house?'

Emotion clogged her throat. 'Everyone? Adrian and Tillie, Bernie and Enzo?'

'Your brother and Sarah too,' Finn said. 'I didn't think it would make sense without them. Tommy tried to get your mum to come as well, but he said she wasn't ready. That maybe next year—'

Meredith flung herself at him, kissing him and wrapping her arms around him. Finn lifted her, and she wrapped her legs around him, too. As they kissed on the beach, the eerie cloud she had seen out of her window that morning reached Charmed Cove and it began to sleet. Thick, wet drops that weren't quite snow landed on Meredith's cheeks, cold and soft and almost, *almost* romantic. But practicality won out, and she pulled out of Finn's grip, letting her feet find the sand.

'Inside,' she said. 'You need the biggest, woolliest socks imaginable.'

'Understood.'

She held out her hand and he took it, and they walked across the sand together. Laurie shouted and waved, pointing in the direction of her house, and Finn gave her a thumbs up as everyone got back in their cars, presumably to drive the short distance to Laurie's rather than take the precarious, clifftop route.

Meredith and Finn were left alone on the beach.

She glanced at him, walking alongside her, wearing her pink hoody and with his legs bare, sleet landing in his hair, and felt such a rush of love for him – for this beautiful, funny, ridiculous man – that she had to resist the urge to stop and kiss him again. There would be time for that, she realized with a smile.

They reached the path that led to Laurie's cottage, the lights on the veranda glowing above them in the murky gloom, the sleet falling on the path ahead. There was a pile of clothes at the edge of the beach, and Finn stopped to put on his jeans and shoes. He didn't take off the pink hoody, instead holding his navy woollen jumper out to her. She raised her arms and he tugged it on over her wetsuit. He lifted her hair out of the collar, then bent to kiss her.

'Warmer?' she asked.

He nodded. 'My jumper suits you.'

She laughed. 'Mine doesn't suit you.'

'Oh, I don't know.' He grinned. 'I can pull off pink in certain circumstances. Amaranth, anyway. Maybe not cerise.' They started the ascent up the rocky path. 'How are you feeling about Christmas?' he asked, pointing to their destination, where Meredith could already see lights on inside, figures moving about. 'This won't be too much, will it?'

'I'm looking forward to it,' she said. 'I can't believe you've arranged all of this. I thought you'd gone back to London.'

He squeezed her hand. 'I'm sorry I wasn't in touch. I just – I knew I had to sort this thing out with my parents before I saw you again. I've been trying to get up the courage for ages, and I wanted to show you that I could do it. I wanted us to be together without that shadow hanging over me. But I should have let you know I was still in Cornwall. Except then . . .'

She glanced at him. 'What?'

'Would you still have gone around town yesterday, singing and selling hampers?'

'You heard about that?'

'When I called Adrian to invite him and Tillie for Christmas. I wish I'd seen you. I know you were amazing.'

'You don't know that.'

'Yes, I do.' He stopped on a wide section of the path and tugged her round to face him. The sleet was still falling – they really needed to get inside – but she knew that, once they reached Laurie's house, with the fire crackling and carols playing in the background, there would be people to talk to and laugh with, and Finn's antics to relive, and they wouldn't get any time again, just the two of them, until much later.

'I know you were amazing,' Finn continued, 'because you *are* amazing. Every bit of you, from the tip of your big toe to this bit of hair.' He gently lifted a strand, holding it in front of her face so she could see it. 'I have never felt this way about anyone, and I don't ever want to let you go. I will lay myself bare in front of you: you can have all of me, if you want.'

'I do,' she said, taking both of his hands. 'I want all of you, to talk to and to hold, to go to that weird, shady pub with. I want us to take Crumble for walks and swim in the cove together.'

'Swim? I—'

'I am buying you a wetsuit, though. None of this tiny-shorts nonsense.'

His lips twitched. 'OK.'

'I want to be there when you sell your first painting,' she continued, 'and your hundredth. And when you have your first exhibition, I'm going to make a speech and toast you with champagne, and then take you to bed when we're both a bit drunk and high on the wonder of it all. And mostly,' she said, 'I want to have every Christmas with you. This one, here, is going to be the first of many.'

'It is.' He nodded decisively, and she could see, even through the sleet, that his eyes were bright. 'Meredith—'

'Red,' she said.

'What?'

'You can call me Red, if you want to. Only you, though.'

This, more than anything else that had happened that morning, seemed to affect him. His blue eyes brimming, he tipped her head up so he could kiss her again, folding her into his arms while the sleet fell on them, thickening and softening, until some people might have said it was snowing. On Christmas Day. In Cornwall.

Above them a door clicked open, and the sound of laughter and talking, and Andy Williams singing that it was 'The Most Wonderful Time of the Year', spilled out to join them.

'Finn! Meredith!' It was Laurie. 'Where are you? It's horrible out here, and there's champagne and coffee inside. There's gingerbread, too, Meredith! I'll show you how to make it sometime, if you ever get back here!'

Finn grinned and shouted, 'We're on our way!'

'Don't, after all this, die in a bloody snowstorm, for God's sake!'

Meredith and Finn laughed, their breaths mingling, and just before they went inside, they turned to look at the sea; the sullen, churning waves were just visible through the haze of sleet, the horizon dissolving into the wintry sky, a pallet of greys and whites, with the occasional hint of blue. Finn would paint this, Meredith thought, as she squeezed his hand and realized that Charmed Cove was every bit as magical as she had believed it to be.

She had found Finn's paintings here, had met him here, and had begun to see that she could move forward, finally, and remember her dad with happiness instead of regret. She could release Christmas from the unhappy past she had tied it to, and let it into her present, and her future, instead.

'Merry Christmas, Red,' Finn said.

'Happy Christmas, Finn.'

They turned and walked the last few steps to the white house; to friends and family, food and champagne, laughter and merriment.

Meredith realized then that it wasn't just Charmed Cove that was magical. She knew now that Christmas was as well. It was finally here, and this time round she was ready to embrace every single sparkling moment of it.

Epilogue

It was March, but it could have been December for the icy chill that was coming off the water. Charmed Cove looked particularly beautiful, the sun high in the sky while the sea was a deep navy, shot through with green and turquoise, the waves arriving on the sand frilled with white. The sky was a watercolour blue, Meredith thought, and smiled, wondering whether Finn would want to immortalize this day on canvas.

'Are we really doing this?' the man in question asked. He looked handsome in his black and grey wetsuit, his lean, strong frame and blond curls making him look like a born surfer.

'We're really doing this,' Meredith confirmed. 'You're a good swimmer, Finn. And you've been in the water every morning.'

Finn huffed out a breath and waggled his hands at his sides like he was some kind of Olympic athlete, and Meredith tried not to laugh. She loved that her boyfriend could be thoughtful and tender one minute, and ridiculous the next. There were so many things she loved about him already, and they were only a few months in.

They were the only two people at Charmed Cove this morning, unlike Christmas morning when Meredith had *thought* she was about to have an audience for her usual, unremarkable swim. That was because today, when she and Finn were swimming to the next beach along the coast, everyone had wanted to wait for them there. That included Anisha and her brood – including Onir and Pari, who had settled very quickly into their new, Cornish lifestyle – Adrian and Tillie, Laurie and Fern. Tommy and Sarah had made the journey from Somerset, Bernie had Crumble with her, and even Emma was coming, though Meredith had drawn the line at them being serenaded by the Port Karadow choir on their arrival.

She would have been even more nervous doing it on her own, but Finn had – in what she thought was probably a moment of overenthusiastic encouragement – offered to do the swim with her, and she hadn't let him forget it. They had been training at Charmed Cove together, though Finn's tiny swimming trunks had been consigned to the back of the chest of drawers.

Meredith took his hand and they walked towards the water, the breakers lapping at their feet. It was cool and calm, the horizon stretching out before them, and she felt serene and exhilarated, all at once. She was here, in her favourite place, and she didn't have to face anything alone if she didn't want to.

'What are you thinking?' Finn asked. 'That we should go to Sea Brew and get a bacon sandwich instead?'

She laughed. 'No, I'm not thinking that. I'm thinking how different this is from how I imagined it would be.' She turned to look at him. 'There are more people waiting at the next beach than I thought was possible. And they're waiting for *us*, not just for me.'

'They might only get you, though,' Finn said, shooting a nervous glance towards the open water.

'They will not,' she said firmly. 'We're in this together, and I wouldn't have let you come if I didn't think you were strong enough. I don't ever want to lose you.'

His smile was soft and warm, and Meredith's heart skipped at that simple gesture, at the knowledge that he was hers, and he was here, in Cornwall, for good: staying at Laurie's – though he was mostly only there to use the studio, and spent the rest of his time at Meredith's house, with her, Smudge and Crumble – and working on his paintings.

He had sold one already, and two others were on display in a gallery in Charlestown. They had gone up last week, and Meredith didn't think they'd be there for long before someone bought them.

Late on Christmas Day, when the revelries at Laurie's house had died down and they had some time on their own, Finn had told her that when he'd spoken to his parents about what he wanted to do, that he was going to leave the gallery, they were pleased for him. They were sorry to lose him, both from Imo Art and London, but were glad he was ready to use his talent. Finn had put the expectations on himself, and it had taken someone new in his life, someone who cared, to give him the final nudge he needed. In some ways, it was exactly like her and Christmas: unable to see past the weight of grief she'd been carrying, until someone showed her that things could be different.

Since leaving the gallery and moving to Cornwall permanently, Finn had found an ease in himself that Meredith hadn't realized was missing until it suddenly appeared. He was still charming and confident, still endlessly playful, but it was as if someone had added an extra battery pack. He shone more brightly, laughed more freely, and loved her openly and completely now that he had decided to trust himself.

'Are you ready?' she asked, returning his smile.

He pursed his lips and then, instead of replying, cupped her jaw and kissed her. It took her breath away, as it always did, which wasn't ideal when she was going to need her entire lung capacity – and he would need his – for the task ahead.

'I had to do that before we set off,' he said.

'In case we don't make it?' Meredith asked.

'No,' he replied. 'I know we're going to make it, really. It's just that when we get to the end, there will be so many people demanding your attention, and I'm not sure when I'll get to do that again. It felt essential that I got a kiss in now, while I could.'

'Excellent foresight,' she said, as she dragged him further into the water. 'But if we don't go now, they'll think we *have* drowned, and they'll call in the emergency services and we'll have to have a very embarrassing conversation with the Cornish coastguards about why we're still standing on the beach. We told them we'd be setting off ten minutes ago.'

'Come on then,' Finn said, 'let's stop dallying.' He gave her a blistering smile and they waded further out. The currents swirled around them, the cold exhilarating, the cove receding behind them until there was just sea and sky and the two of them, bobbing in the water.

Meredith swam closer to Finn and planted a wet, salty kiss on his lips. 'Ready to do this, Finn Becker?' she asked.

'Ready as I'll ever be, Red.'

They turned away from Charmed Cove and the white house on the cliffs, and began swimming, safe in the knowledge that there was a whole gaggle of people waiting for them at the next beach. And although last year's festivities were firmly behind them, and the year ahead looked bright and promising, full of so much before they even had to start thinking about Christmas again, Meredith's thoughts often returned to that time.

Last Christmas had brought Onir and Pari to Anisha, and it had given Meredith Bernie's friendship, and Laurie and Fern, and a new appreciation for the simple joy of celebrating with people you cared about. And, of course, it had given her Finn.

He was her funny, compassionate Michelangelo, and it turned out that, although he hadn't found her, like he'd claimed when they first met at Charmed Cove, he had helped her find a part of herself that had been missing; a part that was warmer, happier and more fulfilled, and that was something she wanted to celebrate every day, not just at Christmastime.

Acknowledgements

This is my tenth published novel. How did that happen? A lot of the people who were instrumental in getting my first book published are still here, seven years and ten books later, and still deserve a huge thank you.

Kate Bradley, my wonderful editor and friend, is still championing me as much, if not more, than she did at the very beginning. She always knows which direction my stories need steering in; my books are so much better because of her guidance and enthusiasm, and she makes the job of being an author so much fun.

Hannah Ferguson, my agent, is always there for me and knows exactly the right thing to say or do. She has helped me build my career, and I'm so grateful for all the ways – big and small – she looks after me. The whole Hardman and Swainson team are brilliantly supportive, and I'm lucky to have them.

A book needs the work, inspiration and input of so many more people than just the author, and I am so grateful to the whole HarperFiction team for being behind mine. Thank you especially to Chere Tricot, for always being so helpful and positive. Thank you to Penny Isaac for wonderful copy-editing skills, for knocking my book into shape when it's still a bit lumpy. I adore all my covers, they're so dreamy and escapist and the perfect advert for my books, but this one – THIS ONE – is a cut above. It's utterly magical, and so a huge thank you goes to Holly MacDonald, Caroline Young and May Van Millingen for creating it.

Thank you to my writer friends for encouraging me and spurring me on when I needed it most, for understanding all the weird ways this job can be hard. There are a lot of you, but special thanks to the Book Campers, Sheila Crighton and Kirsty Greenwood.

Huge thanks to my Mum and Dad for always being there, for being endlessly enthusiastic and proud of me, and for being a sounding board for all the writing related nonsense I spout at them. Their patience knows no limits. Thank you to Lee, to Katy C, Kate and Tim, Kate G and Kelly. It has been so good to actually SEE some of them while I was writing this book, as opposed to just 'drinks via Zoom' which was fun and needed, but a poor substitute for the real thing.

A special thanks to Michael Bublé, Eartha Kitt, Mariah Carey and St Paul's Cathedral Choir for the Christmas playlist that helped get me in a festive mood when we were experiencing our very brief summer. My imagination sometimes needed a boost to fully transport me to Christmassy Cornwall, and they were there to give it to me.

David is the most supportive, optimistic and encouraging husband; sharer of lockdown and life, best coffee-bringer.

He is a happy co-watcher of endless *Criminal Minds* episodes when I need to get my head away from my book so I can reset, and even put up with many awful renditions of 'All I Want for Christmas is You' in June, when it got stuck in my head. Sometimes I can't believe I'm with someone so wonderfully reassuring, endlessly funny, patient and kind. It's like something out of a romcom!

A huge thank-you to everyone who has picked up one of my books and read it, who has got in touch with me, or told a friend or family member, or shouted about it online. I appreciate every single nice comment and message, because they remind me that the characters I've created, the novel I've sweated over, has provided joy or comfort or escape. I love writing happy-ever-afters, and knowing they've meant something to someone. Please keep chatting to me – especially on Instagram. I really hope I'll still be doing this in another ten books' time, and that you will still be here, reading my stories.

EXCLUSIVE ADDITIONAL CONTENT
Includes an exclusive piece from Cressida
and details of how to get involved in *Fern's Picks*

20 things that make a perfect Christmas

By Cressida McLaughlin

1. People you care about. Whether it's your birth family, inherited family, or friends, Christmas is about spending time with the people you love. Sometimes, inevitably, you end up seeing people you'd rather avoid, but I hope you also get to hug and pull crackers with the people in your life who really matter.

2. Lights! This is, of course, non-negotiable. Christmas lights, whether a rainbow string looped around your tree, shimmering gold stars draped along your roof or flashing lights round the fireplace, are a very important part of Christmas. Brighten up those dark winter days and turn your sparkle to high beam.

3. Roast potatoes. There are so many variations of the ideal Christmas lunch, but a great roast potato is on most people's list. Even if you're veggie and turkey is definitely not your thing, a Christmas Day meal would be incomplete without a fluffy-on-the-inside, crispy-on-the-outside roast potato, and a bit of gravy to dip it in.

4. Pigs in blankets. These aren't for everyone, but for my perfect Christmas, pigs in blankets are a must. Juicy little sausages wrapped in crispy bacon, small enough that you can nab a couple every time you go to the kitchen, but with a big flavour payoff. Even when we had salmon one year, I insisted we still had pigs in blankets.

5. Small gifts. Some of my friends used to get pillowcases full
    of gifts instead of stockings! We had my Dad's very old, dark
    green bed socks. They were long and thin, so you could try
    and guess the gifts from the shapes they made through the
    cotton. One of my very favourite parts of Christmas Day was
    waking up early and feeling that sock, heavy and lumpy, at
    the foot of my bed. Now we're grown up, Mum puts gift bags
    under the tree. I love the tradition of exchanging small, silly
    gifts, it's one of the most magical things about Christmas.

6. A power cut. One Christmas when I was growing up, we had
    a power cut that lasted several hours. Luckily our cooker was
    gas, and it didn't ruin Christmas dinner. We had our roast
    Turkey by candlelight, and although serving was a bit of a
    challenge, having our meal like that felt really special. The
    power came back on later that evening, so we didn't miss out
    on the next item on my list.

7. Telly specials. I was outraged when (spoiler!) Matthew
    Crawley was killed off in the Downton Abbey Christmas
    special. Honestly, Dan Stevens was the only reason I watched
    it. The rage! Anyway, Christmas specials are such a good part
    of Christmas Day, though they seem to have got less exciting
    over the years. I remember getting home from a Christmas
    Day spent with extended family and watching the *Birds
    of a Feather* Christmas special while I played with my new
    Spirograph.

8. Connected to this, and a ritual in so many families, is
    getting the bumper issue of the *TV* or *Radio Times* and going
    through it with a highlighter, marking all the programmes
    you're planning to watch. This is one of those moments when
    you know the festive season is really upon us. Time to get
    excited!

9. A Christmas walk. These are especially good if you've been
    given a new scarf or hat for Christmas, and ideal for walking

off Christmas lunch or working up an appetite for the next, imminent round of food. Fresh air can easily be forgotten at Christmastime, so it's always a good idea to clear away the tinselly cobwebs.

10. A tipple. Not for everyone of course, but for a lot of people, Christmas booze is special booze. My gran used to bring out her dusty bottle of cherry brandy for our present opening session on Christmas morning, and I remember the joy of being allowed a glass and feeling like a grown up. Now it's champagne when people arrive, a good bottle of red wine with dinner, or a whisky or flavoured Baileys in the evening. If they came without the Boxing Day hangover, they'd be even better.

11. Special foody editions. Whether it's giant buckets of Roses, limited edition Chocolate Oranges or cheesy footballs in tubs, the stressful Christmas food shop can be made slightly happier if you fill your trolley with these treats, in anticipation of the rare moments you will have to survive between meals. I wish they would bring back the popping candy Chocolate Orange, but I might be the only one.

12. Carol singing. Does this happen anymore? I can't remember the last time a group of carol singers showed up on my doorstep and sang 'Away in a Manger' in their bobble hats. I've put it in my book, because I think there is something so special and so unashamedly festive about it, but apart from organised concerts and busking, it feels like a lost tradition. If it does still happen in some places, then I'd love to know.

13. Christmas tree/lights hunting. This is a bit of a cheat, because I've already mentioned lights and walks, but I think it deserves an item of its own. I really love going for walks around our neighbourhood, spotting lights and trees and decorations. I remember once when I was quite young, being incredibly sad about something now long-forgotten, and

Mum taking me for a walk round our local London streets to count Christmas trees in windows. It cheered me up so much, and it's something I still love doing now.

14. Christmas trees in the dark. The shadowy sight of a Christmas tree when you walk past the doorway of a darkened room, only its twinkly lights providing illumination, the bulky shapes of presents just visible beneath. It's an image that always sends a thrill of excitement through me, even though, by the time you read this, I will be forty.

15. A list of Christmas lunch timings that has one major mistake on it. You work out all your timings, for the turkey or beef, the roast potatoes and sprouts and pigs in blankets, backwards from the point of serving. If you get this completely right then you are incredibly smug, possibly magical, and also, it's not really Christmas.

16. Cheerful people in the street. Most people just seem happier at Christmas. Or maybe it's that *you're* happier, and you project your happiness onto them. I love seeing people out in public wearing stupid outfits (see next item), or dogs with flashing collars: all the things that break down boundaries, remind us that we're all just crazy humans trying to navigate this weird world together. I wish it would happen all year round.

17. Ridiculous costumes/jumpers/headwear. I once travelled across London to see family, on trains and tubes, wearing a pair of fluffy, sparkly reindeer antlers. My husband, David, had tinsel woven round his hat, and on the way back we went to a pub near Trafalgar Square. We talked to so many people, met Santa Claus, and felt more festive than we had done for years. You can't have a perfect Christmas without some sort of silly outfit or accessory. Them's the rules.

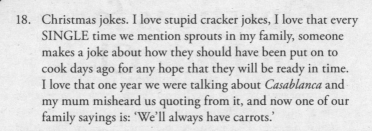

18. Christmas jokes. I love stupid cracker jokes, I love that every SINGLE time we mention sprouts in my family, someone makes a joke about how they should have been put on to cook days ago for any hope that they will be ready in time. I love that one year we were talking about *Casablanca* and my mum misheard us quoting from it, and now one of our family sayings is: 'We'll always have carrots.'

19. Books. Books are key at every time of year, but Christmas Books (ho ho ho) are magical. If you're missing Christmas when it's too hot in July, then dive into a romantic, wintry tale with snow, kindness and an overdose of twinkly lights. I also know lots of people who reread their favourites at Christmas – *A Christmas Carol* or *The Woman in White*. Christmas isn't Christmas without a festive read.

20. Narrowing down the books theme, and a good one to end on because it's one of my favourite things, is ghost stories. Gather round a crackling fire (or a TV set with one of those YouTube fireplace videos playing) with your friends or family, turn all the lights off except the Christmas tree lights, equip yourself with a Baileys or a hot chocolate, and tell each other spooky tales. I love a good ghost story, and they always seem more atmospheric if you tell them at Christmastime. Some people think that ghosts don't exist, but everyone knows that Santa Claus is real.

Happy Christmas everyone!

Questions for your Book Club

Warning: contains spoilers

- Are you more of a Scrooge or an Elf when it comes to the holiday season?

- What is your favourite thing about Christmas? Do you have any special traditions?

- There is a fabulous cast of characters in this story, who was your favourite?

- Finn initially hid his true identity from Meredith. He did this so he could be himself without any familial pressure. In his shoes, would you have done the same?

- Meredith asks Finn to stand up to his family, quit his job, and become an artist full-time. Do you think she was right to do so?

- What was your favourite moment in this book?

- Have you ever visited Cornwall? And if you haven't, has this book made you want to?

- Have you read the rest of the author's Cornish Cream Tea series? If yes, which is your favourite, and why?

An Exclusive Extract from Fern's New Novel

Daughters of Cornwall

Callyzion, Cornwall. December 1918.

I leant my head on the cold glass of the train window, drinking in the outside scenery. Bertie had described all this to me time and time again. He had insisted on reciting all the romantic names of the Cornish station stops.

'As soon as you are over the bridge, you come to Saltash. The Gateway to Cornwall.'

'Why is it called Saltash?' I had asked.

'No idea. Then after Saltash it's St Germans, Menheniot, Liskeard—'

I interrupted him. 'I'll never remember all those names. Just tell me where I need to get off?'

'I'm getting to that, Miss Impatience.' He inhaled comically and continued. 'Saltash, St Germans, Menheniot, Liskeard and then Bodmin. I shall be waiting for you at Bodmin.'

'Will you really?' We had been lying in the tiny bed of our Ealing home. 'I'm not sure I have had anyone wait for me anywhere before.'

'What sort of blighter would I be if I didn't pick up my beloved fiancée after she's travelled all that way to see me?'

'You'd be a very bad blighter indeed.' I smiled.

He held me closer, dropping a kiss onto my head. 'I can't wait for you to meet my family. Father will adore you. Mother too, though she may not show it at first, she's always cautious of new people. But Amy and you will be great friends. She's always wanted a sister. Brother Ernest can be a pompous ass but he's not a bad egg.'

'It'll be wonderful to feel part of a family again.'

'You are the bravest person I have ever met.' He squeezed me tightly, his arms encircling me. 'My stoic little squirrel.'

At this point, I am sorry to say I had already told a few lies to Bertie about my upbringing. Needs must sometimes.

'My parents were wonderful,' I fibbed, 'and I miss them every day, but I feel they would be very happy for me now.' Shameless, I know.

'Do you think they'd approve of me?' he asked.

'Oh Bertie,' I smiled. 'They would adore you.'

In the peace of my carriage, I searched my little bag for my handkerchief, angrily wiping away hot tears as, with a jolt, the mighty train wheels, powered by coal and steam, started to slow down.

The train guard was walking the corridors as he did before arriving at each station.

'Bodmin Road. Next stop Bodmin Road.' I readied myself to disembark.

Standing on the platform, I watched as the train chuffed its way down the line and out of sight on its journey towards Penzance. The Cornish winter air blew gently on my skin, and I took in lungfuls of the scent of damp earth.

Bertie had told me that it was warm enough down here to grow palm trees.

'You are pulling my leg.' I had laughed.

'No, I'm telling the truth. We have one in our garden. I will show it to you.'

I picked up my bag and walked past the signal box painted smartly in black and white, towards the ticket office where a sign with the word TAXI pointed. Even now, the half-expected hope that Bertie would be waiting for me made me breathless with longing. I imagined him running towards me, his long legs carrying him effortlessly. His strong arms collecting me up easily, lifting me from the ground so that my face was above his. The look of love shining between us.

'Excuse me, Miss.' A man with a peaked hat was walking towards me. 'Would you be Miss Carter?'

'Yes.'

'I thought so. You looked a bit lost on your own.' He had a kind face, but not too many teeth. 'Welcome to Cornwall.'

Available now!

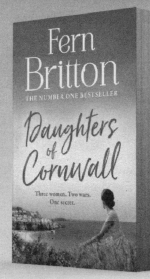